J. M. M. BUTTERFIELD

BASTION: HOLY CITY

CHRONICLES OF A STAR-BORN KING
BOOK ONE

First published in Australia in 2019 by J. M. M. Butterfield
Copyright © 2019 by J. M. M. Butterfield
Second print 2023

A catalogue record for this book is available from the National
Library of Australia.
ISBN 978 0 6483943 0 3 (paperback)
ISBN 978 0 6483943 1 0 (ebook)

Printed in Australia, United States or United Kingdom by
Ingramspark, Lightning Source Inc

Cover by Lara Hardy from Billie Hardy Creative
Images on license from Shutterstock

ACKNOWLEDGEMENTS

My thanks go to several people, all of whom helped in their own way, even if it was merely reading an early draft and telling me I was on the right path. So, to my test readers: Carol and Greg Butterfield, Jemima and Steve Hoult, Marisa and Rod Harper, Lisa Walker-Speers, Emma Elphinstone, Karen Pennington-Smith, Kelly Butterfield and Damien Dwyer, a resounding thank you. To my editors, Sarah Buist and Lynette Ireland, this book would not be as polished as it is without your time and perseverance. Thank you also to Jane Shepherd for her meticulous proof reading, and to Argy Kalogiannopoulos for his help in guiding the story. You said exactly what I needed to hear. Thanks mate.

I would also like to thank every kind soul who asked how the book was travelling over the years, encouraging me to continue and generally excited to read the story I'd been writing for so long. I've lost count how many conversations I've had over the coffee machine, but I'm sure there will be more to follow. Thank you.

Bastion: Holy City, is dedicated with love to my wife, Kelly, and our two children, Keira and Angus. I could not have completed this novel without your unwavering support. It has been one very long journey.
But it was worth it.

BASTION: HOLY CITY

PROLOGUE

The chalk in her hand crumbled to dust.

Avra Creswick was a bundle of inky darkness as she knelt upon the floor, her scrawny hand marking blackened flagstones about a slab of granite eight-foot long. A cloak of sable blanketed her wiry form; an equally black hood shadowed her face. With a noticeable tremble, she flicked hoary hair from her brow, to better see the lines of power she'd drawn on cold flagstones. A dozen whorls and symbols stared back at her, a means of protection as well as focus. Satisfied, she rose from bony knees and shuffled back a pace, her eyes squinting in the dim candle light as she sought abnormalities. There were none. For two decades, she'd performed this ritual as often as possible. She didn't make mistakes.

At least not anymore.

'Vantos,' she cursed the name with teeth clenched, the sound a hiss to break the silence. She'd made a mistake once, long ago, a mistake in trust and loyalty. It cost the life of her only daughter. Since that day she'd vowed to see the perpetrator dead . . . as well as every child he cared to sire. Years in the making, she was terribly close to fulfilling her wildest, tormented dreams.

She felt the pull of aged skin tighten as her smile widened, before she hobbled towards a wooden bench lined with a dozen candles the colour of a deep bruise. Their paltry light was barely enough to illuminate the vast underground chamber, but it would suffice for now. Avra barely noticed, for down here, deep below the surface of her ancient keep, was her shadowed world. It was here she most belonged; it was here she felt safe. It was her summoning chamber, her sanctuary. It gave her life purpose, taught her the true meaning of perseverance.

It also gave her means to exact revenge.

With deliberate steps, she reached a stone wall lined with arched alcoves, their contents many and varied. A gnarled finger traced a line through dusty cobwebs as she walked past polished skulls, vials of tapered bark and dried herbs hanging in clusters. Below sat an ivory horn edged in copper, its ashen flanks blood-stained, but it was an ebony candle as thick as her wrist she reached for. This she held reverently before moving to place it at altar's end, standing it upright within a brass bowl. As she stepped back to admire the room, a gentle knock came from the only door. It was her servant, Rolon, returning from the Veiled Room with his trophy.

'Come, Rolon,' she croaked as the door swung inward on silent hinges. He stood there, a concealed mirror under one heavy arm, a vacant look on his round face. 'Place the mirror in its frame before the altar,' she said with a gesture towards the granite slab.

A crooked smile crept across her face as he obeyed. He was her creature, had been since the day she found him wandering alone in the forest. A large man with simple needs, he was often ridiculed due to his abnormal size and lack of wit. He stood well over six feet in height, was broad and thick of arm. Yet he was a gentle giant for all his bulk, a giant with the mind of an innocent child.

She watched as he stepped carefully over her chalk symbols, the large mirror under his arm draped in black velvet. With meaty hands, he placed the mirror into a steel frame strong enough to hold its weight, before screwing several bolts to lock it in place. A long stride followed as he took his position behind the altar, next to a metallic gong, his hand grasping a bronze mace resembling a demon's snarling head. Satisfied, Avra flicked her fingers towards the ebony candle and smiled as verdant flame sprang to life.

'Good,' Avra whispered as she made for the mirror. With a clawed hand, she reached high to pull the black velvet. It fell to the floor, a jumble of darkness in a darkened room.

With purpose, she returned to stand before the altar, spinning to peer into the revealed mirror. Her eyes narrowed, a thousand lines creasing her face as her mouth opened wide to reveal speckled brown teeth rotten with age.

'Where are you, bitch?' her voice rasped as she sought movement. 'Where are you hiding?'

The silver surface shimmered before revealing a reflection of her chamber. Then slowly, ever so slowly, a young raven-haired girl began to appear within. As the image clarified, Avra lifted a finger, a signal for Rolon to begin his appointed task.

A gentle strike of the gong provided a slight resonance throughout the chamber. A ripple of energy floated across the mirror's surface, like a stone dropped into a still pool. As it dissipated, she raised her finger once more. This time Rolon raised the bronze mace with its savage countenance high, and with all his strength struck the gong to release a clarion call. Avra smiled as her servant fled the room, closing the wooden door behind him, his task complete. Her gaze returned to the mirror.

The ripple of energy intensified, and Avra spied a bulge warp the mirror's centre, like a bubble about to burst. With a foul word, she enticed the silver swelling outward, her fingers moving hypnotically, like some crazed puppet master pulling invisible strings. The bubble grew larger, straining, before an almighty heave saw the mirror disgorge its contents onto the altar with a wet slap. The young girl, wearing a stained blue dress, flopped onto the hard granite. She was barely conscious; her eyes narrow slits, her pallid skin pulled tight across a bony frame. Avra quickly placed the girl's wrists and ankles in shackles bolted to the floor. The girl was now spread-eagled across the altar, held firm in an iron grip.

Obscene words flew from Avra's mouth with customary ease as she sprinkled quartz dust across the girl's body. She then spun towards the wooden bench to gather her most prized possessions. The first was a knife fashioned by the darkest of craft. It was the length of her forearm, curved and sharp, and made from some hideous black steel speckled violet. The second item was a relic from another age, to the naked eye no more than a lantern, old and stained. The *Sawolegere*, it was called, the "soul gatherer".

With utmost care, she placed the lantern beside the girl's head, whilst the knife she held in one white-knuckled grip. For several moments she chanted arcane words, her free hand directing pungent smoke from bruised candles, green flames dancing high. She could feel raw power swimming through her veins as she continued her chants, could feel the tingle and crackle as her scraggly white hair sought to stand on end. With frenetic rhythm she swayed and bobbed, twisted words slipping between her teeth, before an impulse saw her raise the arcane knife high. Its purple-black blade was now emerald-tinged, gleaming unnaturally as it hung above the young girl's breast.

Then it swung down, swift as an eagle, plunging deep. Avra continued to chant sinister words as the knife sliced through flesh and bone. Then with a hop she scrambled atop the altar itself. With mystic strength, she thrust a clawed hand into the cavity to grasp the girl's steaming heart, thick strands of blood streaming down her scrawny arm as she held it high. A cry of triumph escaped her lips as she reached for the lantern. Trembling, gory fingers clutched at the handle, lifting it to hover above blood and bone. A final word was spoken, its meaning lost to the world of men, before a sound like grinding teeth echoed within the chamber. A tar-like substance began to seep from the lantern, pooling into the shape of a hand, fingers clawing for sustenance tantalizingly out of reach.

Avra's black robes flapped, touched by an insidious zephyr as she placed the victim's heart atop the lantern with a hiss. As if on cue a single mote of light sailed into view from the corpse beneath her, a golden bauble drifting high. A second later the shadowed hand grasped the light within a tightly clenched fist.

Avra swooned. She was close to realising her dreams, suffocatingly close. She could almost feel His presence, the one she dared to summon. She opened her eyes to see candles dancing to an unseen breeze, hissing like words rarely spoken. Now was her moment, she could do this.

'It is time, Rolon,' she called, blood dripping from her clawed fingers as she gestured towards the door. It swung open, dropping a startled, eavesdropping Rolon onto cold flagstones. Avra took deliberate steps to where he'd fallen, her arms bloodied, her eyes burning with an unnatural light. 'Nine hundred and ninety-nine souls I have gathered, Rolon,' she spoke with a feral grin. 'I need only one more.' She trailed a bloody finger across his forehead as she reached him. 'One thousand souls to summon the Dark Lord's shade,' she continued, 'and the soul of a king to grant him flesh.'

She cackled as Rolon quivered. 'Be still, my pet, tonight is an auspicious night, a night of celestial . . . arrangement, if you will.'

'Would you like me to gather another trophy?' Rolon asked with his slow, deep voice.

Avra considered his question as she walked back to the altar. After unclasping the girl from her manacles, she spun to face the cowering giant on the floor. 'No, Rolon, you shall be my last sacrifice. I saved that position for you.'

'Me?' a large hand slid to rest on his chest.

'Yes, Rolon,' she purred, catching the look of terror now radiating from his eyes. It was intoxicating, served to remind her of the power she possessed in this chamber of dark secrets.

'No!' he screamed in return, rising to his feet. He stood there, eyes flickering between her and the open door.

'You cannot run from me, Rolon,' with a gesture the wooden door behind him slammed shut. 'I will not allow it.'

He spun regardless, and Avra thought for a moment he might attempt to smash through the door. A single step in retreat was all he managed before an enormous mirror floated down from shadowed heights to rest softly before him. It caught his gaze in an instant, trapping him with its magical enticement. Being a weak-willed man, his fight was all too brief. Several minutes after catching his glare, Rolon, servant to Avra for fifteen years, no longer stood in the chamber.

Instead, he watched Avra from within the mirror, his face a mask of horror.

*

Avra crouched in the shadows, the *Sawolegere* cradled in her lap.

It was late. Before her lay Rolon's corpse, his blood-stained body draping hard granite, his chest ripped open. Beside the body hovered darkness, a roiling cloud slowly coalescing into the outline of a man. Avra watched it settle and then drift towards her. With fear gripping her heart she bowed her head in reverence, too afraid to meet her Dark Lord's ember eyes. Then she spoke whilst caressing the lantern, her gnarled hands stained with viscid gore. 'Welcome, Ahriman, my lord,' she began. 'Welcome to the real world.'

Ahriman swirled before her, his form now ash and smoke and flame. Then with a sound like distant thunder he replied, 'You have accomplished much, Stealer of Souls. I am most pleased.'

'I did as you bid, my lord, nothing more.'

'And the king?' His voice encompassed her entire being, penetrating to her core and shaking her foundations: those same foundations she'd built on revenge and hate and anger. 'Where is he? Without a king's soul, the ritual is incomplete. If I am to become flesh . . . if I am to feel and breathe of this world, I need his soul.'

Avra cringed at his words, yet despite the terror, she knew her dream to see the king of Dervae dead was about to be realised. She timidly spoke. 'There were complications, my lord, and unforseen distractions.' The chamber's candles wavered as Ahriman flared in agitation. She risked a glance, only to see his eyes ablaze. 'Fear not, my lord,' her voice sounded weak, 'for I have allies in Bastion. Once we reach the city, King Arkos will be delivered to us. It has been arranged.'

A shadowed fist hovered close before an ebony tendril snaked forward to caress her chin, lifting her wrinkled face high and forcing her to consider his eyes. Their depths were endless and full of torment. She shuddered, then wrenched her head to the side lest she scream in terror, only to see rivulets of molten flame twinning across her chamber floor. The heat was intensifying, and soot-black smoke smouldered from her wooden bench. 'Fail me again and the punishment I mete out will be catastrophic,' he cautioned. 'Now where is this city you speak of? Where is Bastion?'

'South, my lord, by the sea,' Avra's voice was no more than a whisper.

'Then let us be on our way.'

Avra saw his shadow reduce in size and seep back into the *Sawolegere*. As he departed, so too did the flames about her chamber; along with her immediate fear. She was fortunate to be alive, yet few could have orchestrated a feat of such magnificence. One thousand souls she had stolen for her Dark Lord, a task spanning two decades. *I need only one more*, she thought, as she crossed to the smouldering bench to retrieve her possessions. Long had she held a torch of hatred for the king, Arkos Vantos. Their family's feud could be traced back generations. She knew her time for revenge was now. Once they reached Bastion, Arkos Vantos would die, for it was written in blood.

Ahriman, her Dark Lord, would then cease to be a shadow. He would become flesh, fully realised, his fury boundless.

He would become Chaos incarnate.

CHAPTER ONE

Arkos Vantos, king of Dervae, was an aging man.

It showed as he paced his throne room, for there was a sense of frailty to his once broad shoulders, a slight hesitation to his long, commanding strides. Even his heavy fists, rising with every curse to roll off his tongue, were barely clenched. His white hair sparsely covered his pate, his beard, normally groomed and well kept, was dishevelled to match his creased, cerulean robes. Then there were his eyes, for so long a set of icy blue that could turn a man speechless, only now they were clouded with doubt.

'Are you certain?' he practically yelled across the large hall.

A tall man cloaked in black returned his gaze from the shadows, his features even older than his kings. 'I am certain, my lord,' was the gravelly reply.

Arkos shook what was left of his once prodigious mane and looked to the high ceiling. There were no answers to be found in its vaulted height, nor would he find peace from behind the fluted columns that ran the length of his hall. Still, his gaze remained elevated in any case, searching for answers as muted hues from stained-glass windows splashed colour above his blackwood throne. For more years than he cared to remember he'd played a dangerous game with those once aligned to the Creswick family, a bloody vendetta fashioned by his ancestors. *The wyverns of House Creswick will always seek battle with the jaguars of House Vantos.* So it had been said in the past, so he knew it to be true. Now only one Creswick remained: the witch known as Avra. Yet no matter how unyielding his desire to see her vanquished, he'd failed to seal the bargain once promised to his father.

He touched a silver chain about his neck, his broad fingers caressing its length until they found the amulet at his throat, a silver sprig of rue to ward off witchcraft. 'She is coming here, to Bastion?'

'She is, my lord,' the old man in black stepped closer to his king. His name was Cappitus, an elder of the Brotherhood of One.

'And how long do we have before she arrives with her summoned god?'

'If I know the witch, and I do, she'll aim to be here in three months time. It will coincide with a particular conjunction of celestial bodies.' Cappitus scratched at his long, wispy beard. 'All we know for certain is that Benwith has been vacated. The whereabouts of Avra and her summoned god remain a mystery, though.'

'I'll see a thousand men patrol the road between here and Benwith!' he shouted back. 'I'll not have that craven witch bring her scurrilous designs to Bastion!'

'If she does not wish to be found, my lord, you will not find her.'

Arkos cursed once more and walked to his carved throne. As he reached the seven steps leading to his chair of office he paused, then after a moment of silent contemplation he lifted heavy feet to ascend the dais and take his seat. His long blue robes remained creased as he placed curled fists on his knees. 'What else do have to tell me, old man? I can see your eyes are not yet dimmed.'

Arkos watched the elder offer a slight bow before stepping closer, not because he feared others would hear his words, for they were alone in the throne room at this hour, but most likely due to the nature of what he had to say.

'There are whispers coming out of Al-Za'im, whispers suggesting war is no longer a possibility, but a reality.'

Arkos felt a cruel smile touch his lips. The elder's words were music to his failing ears. War was something he could handle, as those close to him well knew. He wasn't called the Battle-King for nought. As a youth, he'd spent eight years fighting the Herkosians to the north, before his father died and he claimed the throne. Then he'd endured another three years at war with the Corphites on land and sea. All felt the cold, hard steel of his forces in that time; and all bent the knee in the end. Now, after almost three decades of relative peace, the desert riders of the south were stirring into action.

'Prince Rahesh must have bigger balls than I give him credit for if he thinks he can strike into Dervae unopposed?'

Cappitus stifled a cough. 'His demands are questionable, my lord, and mostly without merit. I fear there is more to his beating drums and braying horns than first appears, though.'

'Aye, they breed like rats down there. Al-Za'im is home to more than half a million of the bastards if I'm not mistaken.' Arkos thought of the demands placed before him several months ago, taking a moment to muse over the negotiations already discussed. 'He still has no ground for war, though, considering his gripe over coin in the first place.'

'No, none of his demands appear practical. If he isn't after something specific, then someone else is.'

Arkos gritted his teeth. 'He lives in a city surrounded by the shifting sands of the Great Desert. Nothing they do down there makes any sense. I've half-a-mind to ride into Al-Za'im and torch the place. Then we'll see what irks the rapacious fool.'

'Perhaps you shouldn't treat them like vassals.'

'Perhaps they shouldn't be so conniving!' Arkos spat to the side in anger. His kingdom, the kingdom of Dervae, was wonderfully abundant. Rich, volcanic soils blanketed the land, producing crops of quality. Whilst to the north-west, behind the mountain range known as "Gods Serpent", spread an untamed forest of emerald green for as far as the eye could see. Timber was thus plentiful and, for a seafaring kingdom, greatly prized. It was only a month past since he commissioned the construction of three new war ships, a task requiring the felling of over seven thousand trees, and those mostly oak. Few neighbouring kingdoms could match such a grandiose act. A fact he knew all too well. Yet on more than one occasion he felt ruling a wealthy kingdom was more curse than good fortune, especially when such abundance was expected.

'Do you remember the end of the Corphite conflict?' Cappitus asked as he moved closer, stepping silently past the coloured shafts of light beaming through the high windows.

'Aye, I remember the day well,' Arkos narrowed his eyes, recalling the clash of steel blades and the dying screams of the vanquished. He and his men had fought until the island nation's forces were spent, their leaders disillusioned. What at first had been a tactical thrust by the Corphites seeking the acquisition of vacant land, had eventually become a pragmatic retreat ending in defeat. In the end their ruler, King Fergus Lambreek, bent his knee and offered his daughter, the princess Chrissa, as a peace offering.

'As one does when they meet their queen,' nodded the elder, his hands coming together.

'So you say,' Arkos replied, 'but I swore I'd refuse the offering when I stepped ashore. I'd sooner marry a desert bitch from the south than some pirate's daughter masquerading as a princess.'

'But you did not refuse.'

'How could I? She was the most beautiful woman I'd ever laid eyes on.'

Elder Cappitus shared a knowing look. 'Mayhaps Prince Rahesh has a daughter he wishes to offer. Maybe all his gnashing of teeth and beating of drums is mere theatre and jest.'

'Does he have a daughter?'

'Fifteen, I believe, at last count. Although his harem is considerable. It is quite possible he may have sired another without us being aware.'

The king shook his head. 'I told you they breed like rats. In any case, I've no desire to wed again. I'm too old.'

'Perhaps it is your sons who will be made the offer, my lord, and not you.'

Arkos took a moment to mull over the suggestion. It was conceivable. Both his sons were now of age, Prince Theos twenty-three in years, Prince Atillus twenty-one. Neither had been promised a bride yet, but such an eventuality was fast approaching. Not for the first time he wished their mother, Queen

Chrissa, was still alive. It was a situation best dealt with by a woman's touch.

'I'm too old for such mind-games,' Arkos fumed. 'If Prince Rahesh wishes to wed one of his daughters to my sons, he should seek dialogue, not play at war. It is a costly game he's playing otherwise. One I doubt he can afford.'

Elder Cappitus concurred with a smile, his head bobbing in recognition. 'In any case, my lord, I suggest you speak to your councillors concerning Al-Za'im. Regarding the other, I'll be in touch. If I, or any of the Brotherhood, discern the whereabouts of Avra the witch, we'll let you know.'

Arkos waved the old man away and stood to his feet. He'd dealt with enough drama this day, and he was still required to speak with his aides before the evening feast. With a frown creasing his brow he walked to the right of his throne room and slipped past a set of bronze doors, heading along the Hall of Kings with their towering statues casting silent judgement, before continuing towards his private study. There was much to ponder as his feet clicked against marble flagstones, more than he cared for. Still, whatever trickery Avra planned for him, he vowed to be ready. Events were already set in motion by his own hand, with more to come. He reached his study and pushed the solid oak door inwards. Three lit torches offered their subtle orange glow to the room, highlighting flashes of silver and bronze, reflections from an assortment of weapons and armour. His desk was cluttered with beads and silver chains, a dozen minute trinkets dangling from gossamer threads, whilst a handful of priceless gems were arranged in a neat row atop a shelf; garnet, jade, sapphire, and an exquisite pearl. Behind rested his twin swords: the jaguar blades. Even now he could feel their call as they sat upon the mantle, sense the tingling in his hands as they flexed in anticipation. He staved off his desire to grasp their leather hilts and instead shared a respectful glance. A fraction longer than a typical short sword, they were marginally curved with a single edge honed to perfection. Silver pommels resembling the snarling jaguar, his family crest, lent an air of invincibility; the only other adornment their beautifully cut emerald eyes. They were the greatest blades in the kingdom, with only one other their equal.

He spun to peer across his desk, looking to his right, towards the far corner. Grabbing a torch from a brass sconce he made his way to stand before a chainmail hauberk resting atop a wooden frame, an elaborately carved breast plate and spaulders finishing the ensemble. It was an exquisite piece of workmanship, a suit of blue-steel chain links fashioned from the same metal as his twin swords, incredibly thin but impossibly strong. The flicker of orange light played across its surface, dancing in endless pools, its passage hypnotic. Priceless, it was the only one of its kind. Yet it was not for him, nor was it for either of his two sons.

His hand reached for the chainmail, marvelling at how smooth it felt, almost like a second skin. 'You are the final thread,' he whispered, his admiration for the suit of mail undimmed even after all these years. A great sigh escaped his lips as he stood there, contemplating. There was still so much to accomplish in the days ahead, so many pieces to be placed. This suit of armour, a piece never worn, would be his final gift.

As he stood there he wondered, and not for the first time, whether the recipient was worthy. For countless nights, he'd prayed for an answer, but he'd been offered nothing in return. He took that as a sign, found solace in the silence. The gods alone knew how desperate he felt right now.

The man he'd chosen had to be the one. There was no other with his experience, no other with such poise. Nor could anyone wield a blade as fast. Convinced he'd made the right choice he let the chainmail fall from between his fingers and walked back to his desk. As he took his seat, though, he continued to ask the question that had vexed him for so long. If the man he'd chosen was the one . . . then why in Aston's name was he not in Bastion?

*

A warm evening breeze offered scant relief as Arkos Vantos stood upon the balcony attached to the Banquet Hall: a vast dining room situated on the third floor of Highcastle. He cut a respectable figure in his black silk shirt and pants, their edges trimmed in gold to match the crown atop his head. The Jaguar's Eye: a polished jade piece, sat at the crown's centre, a direct contrast to the king's brooding eyes of blue. Behind him, past the glass framed doors, countless voices rose in an endless stream of idle chatter as dignitaries from Bastion and abroad sought to regale each other with perceived wisdom. He'd endured enough of their petty talk; his mind was elsewhere. Now he craved fresh air for his soul, a place to breathe deeply. Standing here, sixty feet above Highcastle's courtyard, he could savour the peacefulness whilst enjoying the vista.

He sighed deeply as he cast his gaze towards the paved streets, admiring the corner lanterns as they highlighted an ordered city. Half-a-dozen broad thoroughfares, meticulously planned, stretched outwards like the spokes of a wagon wheel to connect the city. At her centre sat the pyramid, Aston's Tear, her granite flanks caressed by shadow, her capstone shining silver-blue despite the sun's imminent descent. She was a marvel, too be sure. Five hundred feet high she soared, solid and immovable, a relic from another time. Few knew who built her, and those who claimed to know spoke infrequently about such a time. "A thousand mysteries for a pyramid thousands of years old", it was often said, and not a single mystery realised. It had taken all his willpower as king not to order men the task of demolishing such a beauty. Whatever secrets she held would remain hers to divulge, when, and if, she was ready. He smiled at the thought, wondering if her inner halls, if she had any, were swamped with gold and jewels from floor to ceiling. It was a fancy many shared throughout the kingdom.

With a shake of his head he looked to his right where the sprawling gardens of The Domain resided. It was a vast tract of forested land large enough to conduct small hunts with his most trusted companions, yet with regretful fondness he looked beyond the thirty-foot walls, towards the Royal Docks. It was a hub of activity even at day's end, his shipwrights working tirelessly building craft for their king, whilst soldiers patrolled to the sound of sergeant's curses. Separating the Royal Docks from the rest of the city was the river Atvia, two hundred feet wide at her mouth, flowing with small craft both night and day, her opposite flank the beginning of the equally busy Southern Docks, now basking in twilight glory. He could already picture the swagger of sailors disembarking after a long journey, coins rattling in their pockets, hunger in their eyes. The taverns and drink halls lining the Bay of Pennants would be crowded this evening; much like any other. He briefly wondered how many would see night's end, curled in the warm embrace of a Lady of the Night. From the sailors he knew during his youth, he doubted many would last the distance.

He shifted his sight back towards the darkening city, noting the shadows creeping further east. The sun was about to sink into the west, its last feeble rays of gold and violet already lost from view by the towering mountain range behind Highcastle. Looking over his shoulder he searched for the highest peak, barely visible in the fading light above the blue-grey tiled roof. It stood there, resolute, awe-inspiring. Mount Oros, she was called, the highest peak above Bastion. He knew her foundation began behind Highcastle, where sheer granite walls rose six hundred feet into the sky. After a brief plateau, another cliff soared higher still, merging with another, until three thousand feet later her jagged peak was formed. Some suggested they were giant steps carved into the earth, a means for the gods to ascend to their rightful abode in the heavens. Arkos knew they were simply nature's grand design; colossal, and thankfully somewhat protective. In winter, her peak was cloaked in snow and ice, her nature incredibly treacherous as she sparkled with opalescent light, but tonight she was naked, her sheer flanks as bare as those of a new-born babe.

A shuffle of feet sounded behind him.

'Your majesty,' the inevitable interruption reached his ears.

He caught sight of one of his councillors, Kerros Gavony, standing nervously before him. The man was small and rotund, with slicked hair and a pudgy face. He was best known for his fidgeting and less than masculine voice. Yet his mind was sharp and his knowledge vast. He wasn't high on Arkos' list of favourite people, but he did have his uses.

'What is it, councillor?' Arkos asked, noting his silk shirt of mauve and his gaudy, olive-green pantaloons.

The man twiddled his thumbs together. 'My lord, I was contemplating your earlier suggestion concerning Prince Rahesh and his press for war.'

'Yes.'

'I thought it may be an opportunity for your sons to test their mettle, as they say, and lead a campaign to the south as a show of strength from Bastion. In fact, I deem it prudent that you do so. A sizeable contingent of knights and men-at-arms sweeping into Sovarto may deter Prince Rahesh from any foolish ideals he has concerning the coming confrontation.'

Arkos nodded in acknowledgement, his mind already organising the necessary personnel to accompany his sons on such a campaign. The logistics he could delegate to one of his generals. It was a sound idea. Not only would his sons learn firsthand about the mustering of an army and the art of warfare, they would also be far from Bastion when the real enemy revealed itself.

'I'll think upon it,' he replied after giving it some thought.

Kerros Gavony bowed, muttered a quick 'Thank you, my lord', and shuffled back into the Banquet Hall and its enveloping throng.

The idea had merit, he mused. For too long his sons had merely practised at war, their hardships fabricated, their true fears unrealised. They were both strong, intelligent men, yet they'd never truly been tested. It was certainly a chance for the princes of the kingdom to prove their worth.

He was about to return to the interminable banquet when a blaring trumpet sounded from below. He moved to the balconies edge, peering between the battlements as he traced an eye towards the courtyard. A line of men, in full regale, strode with purpose towards Highcastle, their backs straight and their armour expertly polished. Deep blue pennants, barely seen in the fading light, flapped from spears held aloft.

'What in Hell's name is that all about?'

Arkos smiled at the sound of Lloyd Henrickson's voice. He looked to his left as the old soldier walked to stand beside him, his back as straight as the men below. Almost sixty years of age, with hair whiter than grey, the old sword master was one of few men he could truly call friend.

'Well?'

Arkos' smile widened as he watched Henrickson's swooping white moustache bristle. 'That will be Lord Beaumont of Rochdale.'

'Why all the fanfare?' Henrickson's voice was as gruff as his demeanour. 'Is he so enamoured with the spectacle he needs to alert everyone to his presence?'

The king stifled a laugh. 'No, my friend, rather he is a stout old warhorse, much like yourself, who feels it necessary to remind everyone that he is still alive when he presents himself.'

'Lord Beaumont, did you say?'

'Aye, from Rochdale. You'll remember when you see him. It's been several years since he graced our halls.'

The two men watched the procession pass beneath them before Henrickson spun to face his king. It took only a second for Arkos to recognise the look in his eyes. The man had been drinking; in fact, he still held a horn of ale in his left hand. It wasn't a sign of excessive consumption, for he rarely drank. Rather it was a prelude to a discussion of importance.

'What is it, Lloyd,' he asked, aware they were alone on the balcony.

'This business in Al-Za'im,' he waved a hand to the south, even though the city was thousands of leagues away. 'It stinks of subterfuge.'

Arkos nodded in return. He knew Llyod Henrickson better than any other man in the kingdom. There was less than a year between them in age, and they'd trained together and fought together since their late teens. Since their first introduction they'd remained close friends. If there was one man he could trust throughout the kingdom of Dervae, it was he.

'You're not telling me anything I don't already know,' Arkos replied.

'Good,' Henrickson slapped him on the back, 'it's nice to know your faculties remain. You're not as young as you once were, and I know the burden you carry must be tearing you apart.'

Arkos grimaced at his friend's words. The burden he carried; the one he shared with so very few. 'Despite my stoicism,' he explained, 'I feel tired. I'm tired of listening, I'm tired of talking. I rule the greatest kingdom in the known world and yet here I sit, weaving a tapestry, whilst the shadow creeps ever closer.'

'Is your tapestry complete?'

'Almost,' Arkos raised his face to the night sky. 'There is a final thread still to be found. Without it our plans are forfeit. Don't ask me how I know, just believe me when I say it is so.'

Henrickson placed his empty horn on the battlement. 'This thread you speak of, is it the same as the one you lost?'

'Aye, it is. Three years ago, and you were there. We need him still. Without him we are nothing.'

'And, where is he?'

Arkos sucked in a lungful of air before breathing out slowly. 'I wish I knew.'

The two remained silent for some time, both wearing frowns, their minds heavy. Every contingency plan they'd devised was already in place, ready to take effect. Deep down, though, they knew there was little they could fashion to deter a hungering god. Arkos and the Brotherhood of One had known of Avra's intentions for years. The sheer audacity of the witch, or was it blind stupidity, was staggering. Never did he believe she would sink so low. For a time, he hoped and prayed her agenda would fail, did everything in his power to thwart her. Only she did not falter. Elder Cappitus had confirmed her success. His order became aware of a tremor within the arcane realms, a warping of the fey lines, the minute she released his shadow.

Now they were heading for Bastion with vengeance in mind.

So much of what he and his aides had planned was about to erupt in a riot of colour and hysteria. The world they knew, the world they loved, was teetering on the edge.

'You have told me on occasion about the visions you see at night,' began Henrickson, his deep voice cutting through the warm air. 'If the man you seek does return, how will you receive him? He practically threatened to kill you should you meet again.'

Arkos winced as he recalled the events of three years past. They were not to his liking. Still, there were more pressing matters to attend than the damaged ego of a king.

He looked out across the city, seeing once more the dark smudge of the river Atvia. She kept the city alive, an arterial route pumping life into the canals and waterways, providing a means for transport. Without her the city could never have been so vast and prosperous. Not only did Bastion rely on her benevolence, so too did the kingdom of Dervae. Like the forests to the north-west, the river Atvia played an integral role to the success and well-being of the Dervani people. Yet like the city, she was already beginning to suffer due to a winter devoid of customary rains. He could feel the difference in the air as he stood with his hands on the battlements. Henrickson had already commented on the warmth days earlier. Spring had arrived, but truth be told, it felt more like summer. He'd lost count how many times he'd heard a sage comment on Mt Oros and her lack of a snow-covered peak. It bode ill for the coming months, in more ways than one, but then Arkos knew what was to come. He'd seen it before. It was what he dreamt about each night when he closed his eyes.

The destruction of all he knew and loved.

'I will not meet him again,' Arkos finally said, and even he could hear the fear in his voice.

Henrickson spun to look him in the eye. 'Whatever do you mean?' he asked, concern etched deeply upon his weathered skin. 'If we find him, we can bring him before you. We've men searching for him now . . .' His voice trailed off as a glint appeared in his eyes. 'It's those cursed visions of yours, isn't it?'

Arkos waved a hand, a subtle suggestion to cease his line of thinking.

'It is, damn it!' Henrickson would not be deterred. 'What have you seen, Arkos? What do you know?'

A deep sigh eased from his lungs, and with it escaped a portion of the burden he carried. 'I will not see the coming confrontation,' he began, 'nor will I see the man destined to save our city.'

'Is such an outcome through your own design?'

'I do not know, my friend, for the visions are sporadic, inconclusive, and entirely open to speculation. But they *are* prophetic. I will not see him in the flesh, and that decision has been etched in stone.'

'So, who will tell him what he needs to hear?'

'You will have that responsibility, Llyod Henrickson, for you and no other knows of Tarsin Va's history. We've kept his past hidden. It was all we were ever meant to do.'

'And the armour?'

'It is his. It was fashioned for him alone. When you find him, you must show him.'

Arkos could see clouds of confusion sweeping across Henrickson's face. Only now was he beginning to grasp the enormity of the task ahead. Only now was he beginning to realise his king would rule for but a short while longer. With a deep breath to infuse his old lungs with perceived vigour, Henrickson straightened his shoulders and puffed out his chest. 'It will be as you command, my friend and king.' A glint of moisture seeped from one eye. 'I will find him for you. Then I'll pray he can save the city you love.'

Arkos grasped Henrickson's elbow with a strong hand and squeezed tight. 'Aye, my brother-in-arms, find the swordsman we so desperately seek.

'Find me Tarsin Va.'

CHAPTER TWO

Dawn's gentle glow kissed the sandstone buildings of Al-Za'im, a southern city surrounded by desert sands, palm trees and the warm waters of the Boundless Sea. Tarsin Va, swordsman and mercenary, watched the sunrise as he stood atop the flat roof of his current abode. He was a tall man, broad of shoulder, muscular, his eyes a fathomless blue that spoke of years beyond his three decades. That he was a fighter there was little doubt, and a single glance into those deep blue eyes was all it took to realise he was deadly. This morning his usually calm demeanour was absent, though. His fingers tapped against each other and his mouth was a narrow line. He was troubled and concerned, despite the pleasant scent of pungent spices drifting on the morning air.

'Your pardon, master,' came a soft voice from behind.

Tarsin spun on a heel as he ran a hand through his close-cropped dark hair, spying young Salim with head bowed, his hands clasped before him as he stood at the top of the stairs. He was a dark-skinned slip-of-a-lad dressed in a white gown with leather sandals for his feet. 'I take it Ruvin Ciricello has returned?' Tarsin's voice was deep and commanding.

'Yes, master,' Salim kept his eyes downcast.

'And . . .?'

Tarsin watched the young lad compose himself and straighten his back. 'Although he underdstood your desire to see him board the *Lioness* immediately upon his return, he insisted on gathering a number of curios before departing by ship; objects he claims too valuable to leave behind.'

Tarsin cursed and returned his brooding eyes to the rising sun.

'Will there be trouble, master?'

Tarsin shrugged his shoulders and thought of his past two days in Al-Za'im, knew it was only chance he'd left Ruvin and returned early from the ruins of Bel-Afii. Time enough to discover Al-Za'im's ruler, Prince Rahesh, harboured a fervent desire to declare war with the north. He wasn't the least surprised by such talk, but the timing was a concern.

'It's highly likely,' he said, 'although I'll do my best to avoid trouble if I can.' He noticed a quizzical look on the young boy's face; realized Salim couldn't have possibly heard the latest gossip. 'It's rumoured Prince Rahesh will declare war with Dervae; talk on the streets suggests as early as today.'

Salim shuffled his feet, then looked skyward to watch a hawk as it circled on thermals overhead. 'Master, if war is declared, you'll not be able to leave the city. If you wish to return to your homeland, you must leave now . . . immediately.'

Tarsin nodded, still amazed at how discerning Salim could be for one so young. 'Even more reason for Ruvin to seek the *Lioness* upon his return,' he growled. 'Al-Za'im is a dangerous city, more so now. Any man with kingdom blood will be sought. If we're to escape the city and avoid a blockade of the Princes' war galleys, we need to act fast.'

'What can I do to help?' Salim offered.

Tarsin's lips tightened back into a thin line. 'Go downstairs and seek Bevan, tell him to gather the men and make for the foyer.'

Salim made to leave. 'Is there anything else, master?'

'No, that is all,' Tarsin returned his gaze to the east, watched as a sliver of golden light crested jagged mountains to fall upon yellow sands. He heard Salim's hurried footsteps retreat down the stairs, then closed his eyes and let out a sigh, feeling the sun's first caress wash over his tense body. *Three years,* he mused. *Three years in this hell-hole and now I can leave.* Still, if they were to flee as planned and reach the open sea, their next destination would be Bastion, capital of Dervae. It was home for Ruvin Ciricello, it was home for his men. Unfortunately for Tarsin, it remained the one place he'd rather avoid. Too many memories from a time best forgotten surfaced at mention of the capital, memories he'd tried hard to forget.

'Ruvin, you old fool,' Tarsin muttered as he swept his gaze over the sprawling city with its myriad temple spires and heaven-reaching minarets. Half-a-million people crammed into the sandstone conglomeration that was Al-Za'im, and now he would have to extricate his men from this nest of vipers. Already the first bells and chimes were beginning to peel as the sun lit their white-washed walls, and he could hear the faint ululations of the truly devout singing prayers with a zeal rarely witnessed in the north. Here they prayed to more than a hundred gods, each providing numerous places of worship. On more than one occasion he'd witnessed locals invoke a dozen gods for good fortune simply to cross the street. Such fervour was lost to outsiders, especially those who deigned to pray at all.

Yet Tarsin offered a silent prayer now. He was a foreign man in a foreign land, and now, if rumours were true, he and his men were soon to be marked as enemies of the state.

Without a second thought Tarsin made for the staircase and descended, his mind racing with dire scenarios, the thought of not reaching their ship at all a distinct possibility. As he reached ground level he rushed to the rear of the establishment and Ruvin's private study.

'Ruvin!' Tarsin barked the name as he reached the door. It was unlocked and opened with a gentle push. Inside the room was dark, the curtains drawn.

'I am here.'

Tarsin spun to see Ruvin walk from behind a wooden screen. He was an older man, in his fifties; short with a wiry frame. He was dressed in loose fitting pants of black wool, calf-high boots and a leather vest over a white shirt. Shoulder-length grey hair had been tied at the nape of his neck with a strip of scarlet.

'We need to leave,' Tarsin spoke in a rush.

'I know. I heard the news.' Ruvin walked to his desk where a satchel rested and began to place parchment inside. Once completed, he faced Tarsin, his eyes momentarily downcast. 'It appears I owe you an apology, my friend.'

'Why?'

'Because I fear greed got the better of me, young man, and it is only now that the wisdom of your words becomes apparent. We should have departed for the *Lioness,* as you suggested.'

Tarsin nodded, then watched as Ruvin slung the satchel over his shoulder before scanning the room one last time. He was an intriguing man, Ruvin Ciricello. Inquisitive to the point of recklessness, some would say, but the man professed a passion for unlocking the secrets of the past. Tarsin had been swept along on his quest, appointed Master of Swords for Ruvin's mercenary company and tasked with watching over his operations. 'Forget the apology,' Tarsin moved towards the door, motioning Ruvin to follow. 'We need to make haste. The streets will most likely be watched, and it is no secret that you are here. As I said earlier to Salim, any man of kingdom blood is now a potential enemy.'

'We'll move quickly, then,' Ruvin nodded.

'Where are the rest of your men?' Tarsin asked, knowing more than a score accompanied Ruvin into the city.

'I sent them onwards to the *Lioness*, as you requested.'

'And the relic you found,' Tarsin caught the old man's eye, 'where is it?'

Ruvin patted the satchel he'd slung over his shoulder. 'Here, where I know it is safe. I haven't spent three years from home, scouring this god-forsaken desert to pass it on now. It stays with me until we return to Bastion.'

Tarsin could see the old man's grim determination as he ushered him into the foyer. Without hesitation, he belted a scimitar to his waist before donning a white robe. Completing his preparations, he heard the approach of young Salim, Bevan and seven mercenaries bustling behind him as they filed down the stairs.

'The men are ready, as you requested,' Salim's olive eyes were wide as he stepped to his side.

'Thank you,' he affectionately patted the boy's head as he sought Bevan's face. The man was his second, a swordsman of experience, evident in the older man's lined face and greying hair. 'You ready?' Tarsin asked, chancing a glance over his remaining men. All were dressed accordingly; white robes over leather, scimitars at their waist.

'As you command,' Bevan returned, the hint of a smile playing across his lips.

Tarsin looked down at Salim, 'Listen to me, lad,' he knelt so that he could peer into the boy's olive eyes. 'Once we open the door and head into the street, you need to leave here as quickly as able. Hide yourself and stay hidden for several days. Do you understand what I'm saying?'

Salim nodded his head. 'If the Prince's men find me, they will kill me, yes?'

'It's possible.'

'Then take me with you,' came the quick reply. 'I can help you; I have always helped.'

Tarsin shook his head. 'Not this time, lad. We need to reach the docks and the *Lioness* with haste. We cannot be delayed. I have a feeling blood will be spilt, and I would rather it not be yours.' He placed his hands on the boy's shoulders, 'Besides, this is your home. You belong here, Salim.'

The young boy nodded his head, saddened. 'Here,' Tarsin fished a coin out of his pocket and placed it in Salim's hand. The boy's eyes widened as he gazed upon the gold piece. 'In recognition of your help, friend Salim,' he said. 'May your many gods watch over you.'

Salim clutched his coin and moved behind the mercenaries as Tarsin offered a final word and opened the door. The street was more shadow than light this early in the morning, and thankfully empty. 'Goodbye, Salim,' he nodded his head and watched the boy do likewise. Then he was out the door and walking briskly down the street.

*

Tarsin exited a side street and slowed his pace so Ruvin could walk alongside.

'We're being followed,' he said quietly.

Ruvin peered at his taller comrade. 'Are you certain?' he whispered.

'Aye, my friend,' Tarsin replied, running a hand across his unshaven chin. The two men subconsciously quickened their pace. After leaving their quarters, Bevan and his seven mercenaries had separated, four taking a street to the right, the others turning left. Tarsin and Ruvin had walked ahead, keeping their path as straight as possible towards the docks lining Sickle Bay.

'Are they friend, or foe?'

Tarsin walked through a narrow section between sunbaked buildings where food vendors prepared their morning wares. He flicked a hand under his robe to produce a bronze coin, exchanging it for two skewers of leathery meat. They smelt of charred wood. He handed one to Ruvin and chanced a glance behind him, saw a black cloak swish out of sight behind a pillar of stone.

'I would hazard a guess as to foe,' he said around a mouthful of meat. He peered ahead, noting the morning crowds thickening as Al-Za'im's residents rose to participate in early trade. 'Come, we'll head to the bazaar and seek to lose him there.'

He moved forward, the older man behind him. Even with the sun barely cresting the mountains to the east the bazaar would be congested. Fishermen, bakers and countless hawkers of fruit and vegetables would be shouting in unison, each calling forth the names of countless gods to bless their produce. In fact, he could hear their shrill cries even now, cascading through narrow streets like some beckoning call. Within minutes they rounded a corner to find the entrance to the sprawling marketplace, a cacophony of noise rising in half-a-dozen languages as bartering and bickering reached a crescendo.

'This place reeks of filth,' Ruvin spat as he threw what remained of his skewered meat to the ground. Several dogs appeared from nowhere to snarl and fight over the morsel, but the sound faded into obscurity as the men jostled their way into the crowd.

Tarsin barely heard the man, his eyes peeled as he moved past the carved stone entrance and into the shadowed bazaar. To either side of the narrow walkway hung canvas sheets protecting wares from the heat of the sun. Hessian bags of nuts and seeds, nutmeg, mace, cinnamon and delicately picked saffron lay to either side, whilst overhead dangled skewered scorpions from hand-woven vines. Further along simmered lizard skins in hot oil, exotic fruits atop wooden tables and the relentless sound of chickens pecking grain strewn across the hard-packed clay. The noise was tremendous, even at this early hour, and Tarsin was aware Ruvin Ciricello, a man of etiquette and social standing when not digging amongst the ruins of antiquity, was a touch flustered.

And in his satchel rested an artefact from the past: a priceless piece greatly desired by men of importance back home.

With haste, the two men bustled their way into the heart of the bazaar, seeking the eastern quarter where it was but a short stroll to the docks lining Sickle Bay.

'Are we still being followed?' Ruvin asked.

Tarsin tilted his head and risked a furtive glance over his shoulder. He couldn't see the black robed man, but to believe they'd slipped his vision would be folly. He pushed Ruvin ahead, then stepped past a stall of hand-woven rugs before yanking the old man to the side.

'What are you doing?' Ruvin said as his eyes darted from beneath his hood.

'Slipping our tail,' Tarsin grabbed a fistful of Ruvin's robe and pulled him onto an adjacent street. 'If someone follows, then it's highly probable your transgressions concerning the ruins of Bel-Afii are known,' he said.

'Surely they're ignorant concerning the relic? It's been lost to mankind for centuries.'

Tarsin shrugged. 'Whatever their goal, their presence is a problem. Nearly all your men await you aboard the *Lioness,* ready to sail at a moment's notice. If we're caught, they'll not wait for long. Your orders, remember.'

The heavy thud of a man's cleaver cutting through meat and bone sounded to Tarsin's left. He chanced a glance to see the carcass of a lamb being expertly butchered by a black-bearded man with a blood splattered apron before looking over his shoulder, but the press of bodies was growing. It was almost impossible to determine which black cloak, if any, sought to follow. With a wary eye, he moved with the crowd until they reached a series of wooden pens, the enclosure harbouring an assortment of thin-haired grey goats. The air was ripe as he slunk behind a collection of men bartering over the filthy specimens, Ruvin beside him.

'See this road,' Tarsin pointed to the side, 'it leads to an intersection with the old fountain of Inam at its centre. Follow it until you reach the ornament and wait for me.'

The older man nodded consent and shifted, tucking his leather satchel under his arm. 'What if I'm followed?'

'Then whoever does so will find a knife at his throat before he reaches you. Trust me; I'll keep my eyes peeled.' Tarsin gave Ruvin a comforting nod. He could see the hard lines, the burden of long years sweltering in the sun and digging in the sand, creasing his face. He was weary, looked like a man who wished to be home.

'After we reach the fountain,' Ruvin asked, 'where to then?'

'We'll head to the docks. I've an acquaintance, Omar, a fisherman who likes the weight of silver who has provided his little hut by the bay. Once there we'll commandeer his fishing boat and row to the *Lioness*. Hopefully the rest of our men have made a similar journey.' Tarsin shifted his position to scan the market crowd. 'Go now, Ruvin, and keep your wits about you.'

The older man left, his head bowed as he shuffled into the morning crowd.

Tarsin watched as his employer walked to the right and headed towards the fountain of Inam: an ancient and often ridiculed depiction of a sea god now standing cracked and broken in a bed of dust. The walk would be brief.

Several minutes passed before Tarsin moved away from the pens, his eyes alighting on a shadowed doorway across the street. He moved with caution, keeping his movements slow, his face concealed by the cowl of his robe. Once within its dark confines he spun to watch those who passed. Now the time had come to take matters into *his* hands. It was what he was trained to do. It was what he did best.

As the cautionary movements of a black robed man swept past his place of concealment, Tarsin blended into the crowd and began to follow. As he did so, his hand reached for the dagger sheathed at the top of his boot. His finger pressed against the tip of the blade as he drew it forth. It was deadly sharp, and it was about to taste blood.

*

Ruvin kicked at a stone lying amongst the dirt, frustrated at the delay. He had sat, the white cowl of his hood low over his face, waiting patiently for Tarsin to arrive. Now he paced the ridiculous statue of Inam, his eyes seeking any sign of his Master of Swords.

Another circuit of the fountain had him peering back down Trader's Way, a straight but cluttered road that led directly to the bazaar. It was a short walk, but there had been no sign of Tarsin. With so much at stake he feared he would have to decide on his own before long. The *Lioness* was his ship, laden with curios and artefacts from another age, acquired at cost in harsh conditions and frequent danger. No matter what occurred, he planned to be aboard. Not even the galleys of Prince Rahesh would stop him returning to Bastion.

With such angst coursing through his veins, he almost missed the waving hands of a black robed man running towards him, his voice rising above the din of the everyday crowd.

'Run!' shouted the man in the kingdom tongue, and Ruvin tilted his head to the side, wondering if he yelled at him.

'Run!' the man pushed past a group of long-haired men, the cowl of his hood slipping back to reveal the close-cropped hair of Tarsin Va.

Ruvin gasped, for although he recognized his Master of Swords, he could see a dozen men giving chase, black hoods masking all except their eyes. The street behind Tarsin was literally awash with men clamouring through the crowd, their guttural yells seeking to clear the way. Steel glistened in the morning sun, reflecting from curved blades and daggers alike. A moment later Tarsin was by his side, whipping out a hand to grasp a fistful of his white robe. He quickly found his feet and sought to keep pace. For several minutes, they raced towards the docks, weaving between passersby, leaping laden baskets of nearby stalls.

'This way!' shouted Tarsin as he veered to the right, entering a cluttered side street almost obscured by piled refuse.

A sudden whine sounded behind them, escalating until he felt Tarsin grab his shirt and yank him to the side. A resounding crack followed and Ruvin grimaced as a score of stone shards flecked his face. 'Hell's Fury!' he spat. 'What was that?'

Tarsin quickly pointed before dashing away. Ruvin's brief glance showed him a five-pointed steel star embedded in the sandstone wall where his head had momentarily been.

'Run hard, old man!' Ruvin heard Tarsin's order and lifted his aging knees higher, his hands clutching his leather satchel. The street they traversed became more cluttered, if that were possible, until they stumbled upon several women, their tattooed skin sagging from bony arms as they sought to hang wet sheets from cord stretched across their path. Tarsin ducked under the washing, saw an open door to his left and hastily ushered him inside.

'Where did your black robe come from?' Ruvin panted as Tarsin passed through one wash room after the next. 'And by Aston himself, who tails us with such fervour?'

Tarsin declined to answer, intent on seeking an exit from the wash house. They passed through three rooms before entering one with a square pool of water, a large rectangular mirror placed on the far wall. Ruvin kept running, already moving towards an arch on the other side, but as he reached the egress, he realised Tarsin was no longer with him.

'Tarsin!' Ruvin yelled as he spun back towards the swordsman. He stood there peering into the mirror, his face an expressionless mask. 'Tarsin, let's go!'

The swordsman didn't move, in fact Ruvin wondered if he'd even heard his words. He just stood there, still as a statue, fixated with his reflection on the other side of the pool.

A second later a black robed assailant came hurtling into the washroom.

Ruvin yelled, realized he didn't have the time or speed to aid his Master of Swords. A wicked knife was raised as the unknown man rushed in for the kill. Ruvin drew his scimitar from its sheath, prepared to avenge his friend or die trying.

The flicker of black robes across the mirror's surface must have alerted Tarsin to the danger. At the last instant, he swerved to his left and ducked, then his right foot snaked out to smash against his assailant's knee. A loud crack sounded, accompanied by a muffled grunt of pain, then Tarsin, quicker than lightning, struck the man with rigid fingers in the throat before flipping him into the pool with a splash. Ruvin put his scimitar away. 'Are you alright?' he looked towards the door, hoping the man was alone.

Tarsin shook his head and made for the archway. 'Sorry,' was his reply, his eyes glazed. Then he was gone. Ruvin raced after him. After several turns they found an empty hallway with an unlocked door at its end. As Tarsin opened the door Ruvin saw a wide street bustling with activity. He then reached for Tarsin's shoulder and spun him round. 'So,' his eyes bore into the swordsman's, 'your robe, where did it come from?'

'This,' Tarsin said as he squirmed out of the garment and threw it to the floor, 'once belonged to our tail. As to who follows in our stead, I fear it's the *Vepollah.*'

Ruvin hissed as he wriggled out of his white robe. 'The *Vepollah!*' he whispered back, also throwing his garment to the ground. 'Are they not the Prince's personal assassins?'

'They are indeed, my friend.'

'What in Hell's name do they want with us?'

Tarsin moved quickly into the throng and Ruvin followed. For several minutes they kept pace with the crowd before ducking into a small eating hall to their left. Ruvin risked a glance behind him as they stepped inside; saw nothing to suggest they'd been seen. 'With us,' he heard Tarsin whisper into his ear, 'nothing. It is *you* they want.'

Ruvin felt the colour in his skin drain away. 'Me?'

'Aye, you my friend,' Tarsin said as he moved through the hall and out a side door. 'Somehow, someone has taken an interest in your dealings and discoveries. With the Prince certain to declare war with the north, you suddenly become an important pawn in the scheme of things.'

'I am nobody's pawn!'

Tarsin began to move once more, and Ruvin scuttled forward, wondering how long they'd continue to skulk through narrow streets before they could head towards the docks. He could smell salt on the air, knew they were close to Sickle Bay. 'You are no-one's pawn yet, my friend,' Tarsin said as he scanned the crowd, 'but the Prince is a canny man and he knows of your wealth. Holding you for ransom is a viable option.'

'He has to catch me first.'

'True, and I guess that's where I come in.'

Ruvin snorted, felt half a smile crease his face. 'You do have your charms, Tarsin Va. I knew when you walked off the street all those years past I'd be a fool to let you go. Now your true test has come, methinks,' he clapped a hand to the swordsman's shoulder, his eyes darting nervously. 'Show me how good you really are and get me aboard my ship.'

Tarsin side-stepped a cart bearing crates of silver-scaled fish, his hand resting on the pommel of his scimitar. Ruvin chanced a brief look behind; saw no sign of their pursuers. 'I'll do better than that, Ruvin Ciricello,' he heard Tarsin whisper back; 'I'll get you home.'

*

The hut was quiet. Ruvin sat with his back against a small row boat, his satchel and two oars nestled within. Ahead of him stood Tarsin, his hands upon the double doors as one eye peered between warped panes. It was almost midmorning.

'Surely we're clear to move?' Ruvin had grown increasingly impatient, his nerves highly strung and close to snapping.

Tarsin lifted a hand, suggesting caution. He'd spent an immeasurable amount of time with his eye pressed to the door. Ruvin had waited, patiently to begin with, although he now rose so he could stretch, unable to sit any longer. As he walked the few steps to where Tarsin stood the heavy staccato of spring rain began to pound the roof.

'Can we leave? My ship is waiting.'

Tarsin gave a nod of consent, moving from the door to where the row boat sat, propped atop a wooden frame. 'We'll make this quick,' Tarsin said. 'The weather has turned for the worse, but these storms are generally brief.'

Ruvin cracked his knuckles in reply, eager to be on their way. He watched Tarsin walk back to open the double doors, then turned for the rear of the boat in preparation to push. A moment passed before the doors clanked open with a bang and Ruvin spun to see if Tarsin was clear. Instead he saw a man dressed in black, his face masked. He froze; his blood icy cold. There was no sign of Tarsin. Ruvin gulped, seeking a breath to fire his blood as he watched an inky hand snake forth brandishing a knife. It was long and slender, shaped like the horn of an animal, re-curved and as sinister as any he'd seen. The dark man crept closer, inexorably making his way to where he stood. He'd heard tale of such a knife before. It belonged to the *Vepollah*. It was their *raikin*. He wondered briefly what chance he stood against the assassin. Wondered if he should call for help.

A loud crash broke the spell. Splintered timber flew in all directions as a shape hurtled across the room, the side wall of the hut now broken and open to the elements. There stood Tarsin, his scimitar slick with blood and rain. A sudden gust of wind tore through the room, mingling with the screams of a dying man. Ruvin winced at the noise; startled to find he was still alive, felt like he was in the middle of some freak tempest. Heavy rain continued to fall as a blade reached for him in the confusion, snapping him out of his panic. He stepped back quickly and drew his scimitar in preparation for a fight to the death.

A leaping Tarsin entered the fray, bounding over the row boat and clearing the dead man thrown through the wall. He moved with frightening pace, snarling like some wild beast. Steel grated against steel as the *Vepollah* confronted his new foe. Ruvin stepped away until he felt the rear of the hut against his back, then watched as the combatants traded blows, smarting at the furious sound of clashing blades. Mere seconds passed before a sickening thud was followed by a weakened grunt. He blinked and saw a man fall, heard the clatter of a knife as it slid from nerveless fingers. The rain stopped.

'Come.'

Ruvin lifted his eyes. 'Pardon?'

'Come, Ruvin. Come quickly.'

The old man shook his head, clearing the icy tendrils that gripped his soul.

Tarsin dragged a body across the floor, allowing space for the boat to be tipped into the bay. Within seconds they'd pushed off, the boat slapping hard against the water, both men firmly grasping an oar and leaning into their strokes.

'That was close, my friend,' Ruvin finally broke the silence after what seemed an eternity, wiping sea water from his eyes.

A familiar screeching whine was halted by a loud whack to the rear of the boat. Both men ducked before peering over the rail. A five-pointed steel star quivered in the wooden panel. Seconds later three more thudded into the hull.

'Hell's Fury!' Ruvin's voice shrieked as he and Tarsin looked back towards shore. Half-a-dozen black robed men jostled near the battered hut. A large man, a head taller than the rest, pushed himself to the front.

'No!' Ruvin heard Tarsin scream and stand to his feet, causing the boat to rock alarmingly from side-to-side. He peered towards the docks and saw a large man holding a squirming Salim in his meaty grip, the boy's legs kicking futilely a foot above the ground. Even from here they could see his pleading eyes.

Then it was over. There were no demands shouted across the water, no effort to barter or reconcile. There was simply a flash of silver as cold steel traced a crimson line across Salim's throat before he was unceremoniously dumped into the sea. A scattering of bubbles surfaced, the froth tinged pink. Then he was gone.

Ruvin gasped as Tarsin drew his sword, his knuckles white.

'Tarsin!' Ruvin shouted, seeking to reach the swordsman, fearing the small boat would capsize, 'Tarsin, we need to reach the ship.'

This time the swordsman heard his shouted words, even though anger flared clearly upon his face. Ruvin winced as the boat rocked wildly, then watched as Tarsin knelt forward to pry a silver throwing star from the hull.

'Killing them will not ease the pain,' Ruvin offered as he reached for his oar, 'and we need to reach the *Lioness*.'

Tarsin nodded and stood to his feet once more.

'What are you doing?' Ruvin cast pleading eyes heavenward.

Tarsin declined to answer. Instead he peered across the expanse of water, seeking out the black robed man. Ruvin, one hand holding firmly to the side, watched as Tarsin drew his arm back and let fly with the star-shaped steel. It screeched towards the assassin, a flash of sparkling silver as it sliced through humid air. The assassin never saw it coming, heard its whine all too late. One moment he was barking orders to his men to commandeer vessels for the chase, the next he was down on his knees, weak hands reaching for his throat.

Seconds later he fell into the water, as dead as young Salim.

Tarsin sat back down and grabbed his oar. 'Now we can leave,' his face was grim.

Ruvin slapped his oar into the water, began the arduous task of rowing towards the *Lioness*. He could see black shapes scouting the docks for craft. It would be to no avail. Once they reached his ship they'd be safe. Eighty crew, sailors and mercenaries alike, were aboard, armed to the teeth and itching for a fight. Silently he hoped they would try and take the vessel.

'We're almost there,' Tarsin broke the silence as he looked over his shoulder.

'Are you alright?' Ruvin didn't know what else to say.

Tarsin offered a grunt, his eyes simmering with suppressed anger. 'Three years for it to end like this,' he said. 'Salim's blood is on my hands, I can't deny it. I should have agreed to bring him along, to allow him safe passage.'

'Tarsin,' Ruvin's voice cut through his dark thoughts, 'you could not have known. And it may have changed nothing in the long run. You are still a man of your word.'

The swordsman nodded, but Ruvin knew Salim's tortured eyes would haunt him still. 'I said I would see you safely home, Ruvin Ciricello,' Tarsin offered, his voice rough, deep. 'It's a pity I couldn't offer young Salim the same.'

Ruvin didn't respond, he simply grabbed his oar and lent into his strokes until a familiar shout was heard from behind. He chanced a glance over his shoulder to see the glistening flank of the *Lioness*, her timbers still wet from the brief storm. A dozen men lined the rail, and he could see preparations underway aboard the three-mastered carrack, her sails already unfurled as sailors fastened lines at the behest of their captain.

Ruvin felt a twitch at the corner of his mouth. His quest was almost over, his time in Al-Za'im at an end. Still, the surge of relief he expected was disturbingly absent. Salim was dead, a victim of their nefarious trade, an unnecessary sacrifice.

He clutched the satchel he'd slung about his shoulder, felt the hard edge of the relic he'd salvaged from the ruins. It was priceless, he knew, and greatly coveted back home in Bastion. He wondered, and not for the first time, whether it was worth it.

Somehow, he knew Tarsin asked the same question.

CHAPTER THREE

Calm waters and a gentle breeze marked the day as the *Lioness* glided seamlessly through the blue. It was early morning, and Ruvin Ciricello stood at the helm alongside Captain Jarvis Vasco, a tall, barrel-chested man with a curly black beard and hammer fists. Two days sailing saw the *Lioness* safely away from Al-Za'im and her war galleys, a tribute to the fine skills of the Captain and his crew. Now they were headed south-west, following the coast lying to starboard before rounding Cape Grim. From there they would come about and head almost due north towards Bastion, a journey of six weeks if the weather was favourable. Yet Ruvin kept an eye to their stern, fearful of pursuit and still unable to relax. The flight from Al-Za'im had been harrowing, and Ruvin, no longer a sprightly young man, felt unnerved even now.

'Tarsin is still a quiet one,' Vasco broke the silence.

Ruvin nodded, looking towards the foredeck where Tarsin sat cross-legged, his hands on his knees, his back straight. He'd been sitting in the same position for some time now, gently rocking from side-to-side with the motion of the ship.

'Is he alright?' asked Vasco, concern in his voice.

Ruvin looked out to sea. 'I believe so. He feels responsible for Salim's death; believes he should have brought the child along.'

Captain Vasco nodded sagely, and Ruvin caught a look in his eye that he'd seen before. Both had experienced first-hand the loss of men under their command: Ruvin as leader of a mercenary company, Vasco as Captain of a ship. He knew every time a large storm struck the *Lioness* the risk was high. It was the nature of the wide-open sea. You couldn't tame her, and no man could restrain her. When the time came, all you could do was ride her out and pray the gods required only a small sacrifice as means of appeasement.

'Remind me, Vasco, to never bring Tarsin back to Al-Za'im,' Ruvin watched Vasco's eyebrows arch as a quizzical look appeared on his face.

'Do you fear for his safety . . . or for the city itself?'

'Both, my friend,' Ruvin replied, his gaze swinging back to the seated swordsman. He looked a lost soul, almost distraught, a man in desperate need of comfort. Yet how did you broach a subject of compassion to man who was bred to kill? Ruvin still couldn't believe the skills he'd witnessed during their flight through Al-Za'im. The man was so controlled, his anger superbly balanced. It was only now, days after the encounter that a semblance of emotion had seeped back into his face. Prior to today, his visage had remained flat and unreadable, as likely chiselled from stone as from flesh.

'He is troubled, I grant you that, Ruvin, but it will pass.'

Ruvin nodded. 'You're right, I know, but I cannot help thinking how efficient he was, how deadly.' He looked his friend in the eyes. 'We know very little about him, Vasco. Three years he has been with us, but his past remains a mystery. In truth, the only facts I'm certain of concern his temperament and killer instinct.'

'And his loyalty,' Vasco clapped a hand onto his shoulder, 'To be honest, my friend, I'm just glad he fights for us. And you should be doubly glad, for he saved your life by all accounts.'

'He did, Vasco, and more than once.' Ruvin returned his gaze to where Tarsin still sat cross-legged on the deck. 'I owe him my life, Vasco, but the death of Salim haunts him. I can see it in his eyes.'

'Give him a week and he'll be fine.'

'Aye, I know, there is truth in what you say.'

'What of Jarred? How does the lad feel?'

Ruvin sighed as he thought of the youngster. Jarred had been under his care for several years now, a stowaway initially, now a "Gatherer of Information". He earned his keep doing menial tasks, both on land and aboard the *Lioness*, forever learning, always complaining. Still, he was a good lad; bright, skilful and full of energy. He was of an age like Salim, and the two had become fast friends.

'He suffers, as you would expect.'

'Then you have a duty to perform, Ruvin Ciricello.'

'And that is . . .?'

'. . . To keep an eye on our youngster for the duration of the journey. We've five, maybe six weeks sailing ahead of us. The deck of a ship is not the place to be when darkness clouds your thoughts. If Jarred suffers, he'll need help.'

'What shall I do?'

Vasco pulled at his beard, straightening the black curls as he mulled over his answer. 'Involve him in some activity; make him earn his keep. He needs to be occupied, not left alone to wallow in grief.'

'Sounds easier said than done.'

'Perhaps, but he needs a friend, Ruvin, someone to watch over him. He respects you and will listen to what you have to say.' Vasco let go of the straightened hair of his beard, and Ruvin smiled as it curled back to its original shape. 'Perhaps Tarsin could help.'

'In what fashion?'

'Ask him to teach Jarred swordplay. The lad is old enough. If he has a sword of his own and the knowledge to use it, perhaps he can defend himself when the time comes.'

Ruvin nodded, realising the benefit of having Jarred trained in swordsmanship. It would also pry his thoughts away from Salim; help him put aside his anger and frustration.

Ruvin looked to his friend and smiled, for he knew Vasco to be more than a just a captain of a ship. He was a reader of men, able to judge their mood, see their grief and feel their angst. 'I'll see to it, Captain Vasco,' Ruvin smiled, his mind less troubled. 'Consider it done.'

*

Tarsin slid his whetstone across his blade with an easy stroke.

It was late in the afternoon, a gentle wind providing enough force to see the main sail billow outwards, sending the *Lioness* slipping through the dark blue sea. He sat near the prow of the ship, alone with his thoughts. The noise of his whetstone sliding against steel was welcome, eased his mind somewhat. So too did the slap of water against the hull. Yet he was still troubled by the events in Al-Za'im.

Still troubled by Salim's death.

The lad was too young to be murdered on the street. It shouldn't have occurred. Sending him on his way, without an escort, was beyond careless. Yet that was exactly how it had been, and now regret lay like a lodestone deep in his chest.

He scraped the whetstone across his blade again.

In hindsight, he could have acted differently. Yet hindsight was merely an excuse for failed actions. He'd been taught at an early age to be particular, only on this occasion he'd been found negligent. Now he'd been asked to teach young Jarred the art of swordsmanship. Was such a request a cause of hindsight, or an admission to a failed action?

He looked to the sword lying in his lap. It was his Rykedian broadsword, the only blade of its kind as far as he knew. It was incredibly well balanced, perfectly tempered, strong and flexible. It had been a gift several years back whilst he was still in training. He was twenty-two years of age at the time, seven years older than Jarred was now.

He tilted the blade towards him, watched as light reflected from the blue steel in whorls of colour. The blade was long and narrow, its tip and twin edges razor sharp. Above the hilt was an elaborate cross guard of twinned metal, curving back on itself to attach to the pommel. It created a swept hilt of blue steel, protecting the hand as it gripped the supple black leather wound about the hilt. Along with the twinned metal of the guard, the pommel itself was also elaborately carved, mimicking the snarling maw of a large cat. It was a priceless piece, expertly fashioned.

Young Jarred had stowed it aboard the *Lioness* for him several days before their flight through the city. It was a precautionary measure, for Tarsin couldn't begin to think what such a blade in the wrong hands was capable of. But since clamouring aboard the *Lioness* they'd been reunited, and there was comfort in the reunion. With the blade in his hands he at least felt safe, despite the clouds darkening his thoughts.

The sound of light feet padded behind him.

He lifted his head and peered over his shoulder. Young Jarred stood several feet away, his arms and legs long and gangly.

'Excuse me, Tarsin, sir, but Ruvin said I should come and talk to you about learning the sword.'

Tarsin sighed and stood to his feet. Having spoken to Ruvin about the boy, he assumed he'd have a day or two to plan a regime of some sort, but it appeared training was to begin as soon as possible. He noticed the boy had strapped a short sword to his waist in preparation. It sat high on the hip and the belt was too tight.

'What hand do you use to wield the weapon, Jarred?'

'I am right handed.'

Tarsin nodded, then moved a step closer. 'Then you need to position the sword on your left side, so you can draw it forth like this,' he placed his own sword against his hip before swinging it out with a smooth motion.

Tarsin watched Jarred unbuckle his belt as he followed his advice. Once he was set, he asked him to take a seat amongst the coiled ropes. The boy tried to sit, as instructed, but his sword kept poking into the planks before he could seat himself. After several attempts to right his sword he eventually stood to his feet, his eyes downcast and his face bright red.

'I'm not exactly what you expected, am I?'

Tarsin thought of his first lesson, a lesson performed at the tender age of twelve. For the first time in his life he'd been admitted into Highcastle, ushered in by the rangy sword master Lord Henrickson. He was a tall man with blonde hair to his shoulders, an equally blonde moustache sweeping wide across his cheeks. He'd come for him in the early hours of morning, remembered the door to his dormitory opening with a whine as he'd raised sleepy eyes to see who'd woken before the rooster's crow. At first, he saw only Old Smithy, their teacher of words and numbers, but then he saw the shadow of a large man press behind him. As the shadow stepped forward a shaft of pre-dawn light slipped between the shutters of his window, highlighting a man wearing steel and a long black cape. At the time, he didn't know why he'd been chosen to accompany the sword master, but it appeared he didn't have a choice in the matter. He was allowed a minute to gather whatever possessions he cared to bring. Then they were gone, the orphanage forgotten.

As the sun crested the outer walls of Highcastle that very same morning, Tarsin found himself on his backside staring up at the swordsman. His first lesson was already over, and he hurt like hell. He'd been handed a blade of standard design. Then he was asked to attack with all his might, to swing as hard as he could to land a strike on Lord Henrickson. He couldn't even recall hearing the strident kiss of steel blades meeting for the first time. All he could feel were the numerous welts rising beneath his tunic and breeches. He'd been struck in the arms and legs, whacked once across his arse and even poked in the chest. Looking up at the smiling face of Lord Henrickson he soon realised his sword lay ten feet away from where he now sat.

He shared a smile with the lad, easing the boy's discomfit. 'You'll do just fine, Jarred,' he said. 'Here, let me help you.'

*

Jarred woke in a sweat.

For several days the *Lioness* had battled fierce winds and summer rains, cutting through swells of considerable size, her decks awash with water, the smell of brine overpowering. Jarred had endured the initial onslaught with a staunch demeanour but found the rolling ship and enormous waves too much to handle. Confined to his quarters he'd curled up on the floor, his mouth flecked with spit and his pallid skin clammy. Only thrice had he attempted to eat, but whatever food passed his lips passed them again shortly after. Nothing would stay down for long. The acidic taste of bile caused him to gag long into the night and even a sip of water resulted in sharp spasms in his gut. He wondered whether his ribs could withstand another day of heaving, or whether his belly would finally wrap itself into a knot and call it a day.

For a moment, he wondered whether his time was up. Despite offering prayers to each of the eight Dervani gods, as well as Frey, goddess of Fate and the Four winds, he wondered if any heard his feeble cries for help.

This morning, though, all was calm.

He pushed his heavy blanket to the floor, eager to crawl out from underneath its suffocating grip. The film of sweat enveloping his body was due to the heat of the day, not any sickness, and Jarred quickly wormed out of his shirt and pants, drenched as they were, before reaching for his sea-trunk and his spare set of clothes. He still felt unsettled, unsure how many days had passed since the storms rolled in to buffet the *Lioness* and her crew. Underlying all was a nagging sensation that something was wrong, that something needed to be seen too, rectified. It took a moment, but eventually Jarred realised the source of his discomfit.

He was ravenous.

With aching limbs, he climbed to the main deck, a tired arm raised to shield his eyes from the midday sun. All about him sailors and mercenaries furtively saw to the myriad tasks necessary to sail a ship the size of the *Lioness*. The sound of rough curses mingled with the hard slap of taut sails, but above it all was the constant pounding of carpenter's hammers at repair. Jarred found himself flinching at the commotion, his mind sluggish, his eyes squinting to reduce the lancing pain each sound caused.

'Jarred!'

The lad peered across the deck, knew the voice to be Tarsin's.

'Here,' a strong hand gripped his shoulder and guided him to the mainmast. He practically fell into a seated position, his energy spent. A tall shape sat next to him and offered him a cup of water.

'My thanks,' Jarred croaked as he lifted the brass cup to parched lips. He sipped the cool liquid at first, mindful of his empty stomach and the battle it waged during the storm.

'Take it slow, lad, there is no rush.'

Jarred complied, sipping the cool liquid, allowing it to slide down his parched throat at regular intervals. He brushed a strand of blonde hair from his face. 'How many days has it been?' he raised blood-shot eyes towards the swordsman.

'It has been two days and two nights, lad, with very little sleep. We are all of us tired.' Tarsin fished in a pocket, producing a dried biscuit which he offered. 'Are you hungry?'

Jarred accepted the hardtack, raising it to his mouth to nibble at an end.

'Although bland,' Tarsin said as he watched him consume the small morsel, 'it is filling. Cook said it is made from chickpea flour and spice. Unusual, I know, but then we are far from home. He said he found the recipe in Dorsa whilst we dug sand from the ruins in Bel-Afii.'

'Dorsa?'

'It's a city-state to the south-east. It lies along the coast of the Great Eastern Blue, many leagues from here. Ruvin and Captain Vasco are canny men, Jarred, and whilst we sought artefacts, Captain Vasco sought trade. Regardless of what we discovered in Bel-Afii, the *Lioness* was always going to be laden with exotic goods from the south.'

Jarred listened as the swordsman spoke; comforted by the company and relishing the sun warming his skin. 'What goods did Captain Vasco trade?'

'Timber for spices, mostly. The hold is full of pepper, cloves and cinnamon. What remained of the cargo hold was kept clear for Ruvin's findings.'

Jarred let his mind wander momentarily, which it did at the best of times. He'd seen very little of the artefacts gathered by Ruvin and his team. An assortment of vases, several statuettes and a plaque of peculiar design. There was significantly more aboard ship, though. Although it had taken almost a year to pinpoint the location of the ruined city, and perhaps even longer before they delved into darkened chambers tasting of stale air and death, there were untold wonders amongst the horde assembled by Ruvin. Most were packed and sealed in crates before being escorted by Tarsin and his men back to Al-Za'im, though, and from there to the *Lioness*. Jarred's role had been one of information, not grave-robbing, as he heard one of the men suggest. His tasks were generally bound to the city, in tandem with Salim.

Looking to Tarsin, Jarred voiced the question that had plagued him since the *Lioness* set sail. 'How did Salim die?'

Tarsin sighed, his eyes downcast. 'To be brutally honest, Jarred, not well,' he said. 'His throat was slit by a man I do not even know. It was done in spite; a tactful act to enrage and nothing more.'

'I do not understand.'

'Nor should you, but you can rest assured knowing the assassin's life was taken in return. Although to be honest a hollow feeling remains.'

Jarred was silent for some time, thinking over the times he and Salim had run the streets of Al-Za'im, seemingly carefree and innocent. Both boys knew of the inherent dangers lurking in such a city, but they'd avoided trouble as a rule, and being young, were swift enough to escape on the rare occasions trouble found them.

'How is your arm?' Tarsin's voice alerted his mind back to the present.

'My arm?'

Tarsin leant over and rolled up the sleeve of his shirt. A large splotch of yellowish skin greeted him. 'It looks good; the bruise is almost gone.'

Jarred winced as he remembered the few lessons he'd received before the squally weather overtook them.

'Master Jenkins of the Carpenters has fashioned you a wooden blade,' Tarsin continued, 'you can pick it up when you're ready to recommence your lessons.'

'Today?'

'Only if your body and mind agree. You've a great deal to learn, Jarred, patience first and foremost, methinks. You have been unwell. I dare say a day or two doing light exercises will suffice to begin with.'

The light in the young man's eyes dimmed somewhat at talk of exercises. Although the sword lessons had barely begun, he'd taken an instant liking to the discipline involved.

'Are the sword lessons a result of Salim's death?' asked Jarred, peering into Tarsin's clear blue eyes.

'Yes. It was thought a sword by your waist and the knowledge to use it would give you a fighting chance if such an encounter occurred again.'

Jarred offered a barely perceptible nod in return. Since the first day the *Lioness* had made port in Al-Za'im, Salim had been there: a scrawny boy, all arms and legs with a mop of black hair hanging to his shoulders. His skin was dark, like all southerners, but his smile was wide: a flash of sparkling white shouting joy and laughter. Almost three years they'd spent together, inseparable.

'I miss him, Tarsin.'

He felt the comforting embrace as Tarsin rested an arm across his shoulders. 'We all do, lad.'

'I wish to learn to fight like you. I want to become a swordsman, feared throughout the world.'

'It is not all it's made out to be,' Tarsin replied. 'There is no glory in dealing death, Jarred. In fact, it is quite the opposite.'

'But you have prestige, purpose. The men look up to you, some practically worship you.'

'It is fleeting, a passing phase. I fled Bastion aboard this ship to escape my reputation. Being a swordsman is not as clear cut as you think. I'll teach you to defend yourself, hone your skills, but I'll not teach you to wantonly kill.'

Jarred knew it was pointless to argue. He was young, a lanky lad without a home or a family, learning as best he could about the rigours of the world from a dozen men proficient in a dozen different vocations. All he could do was nod a youthful head in acknowledgement as he listened to their wise words.

'How did you learn to fight?' he finally asked.

Tarsin mulled over the question for some time and Jarred wondered if he could remember when he first picked up a blade.

'I learnt on the streets of Bastion,' he began, 'no more than six or seven years of age.'

'With a sword?'

'No, not at that age. Fists and feet, at first, but typically speed. If I was in a fight I could not win, I ran.'

'You ran?'

'Aye, and I was fast. No-one could catch me.' A slight smile curled Tarsin's mouth, a rare occurrence as far as Jarred knew.

'What did your parents think?'

Silence greeted his next question. For a moment, he wondered if he had crossed some imaginary line, said something out of hand. Tarsin eventually cleared his throat.

'I never knew my mother. She died when I was but a youngster. As for my father . . . well, I do not know. I am a bastard, Jarred. Tarsin Va. Tarsin fatherless.'

Jarred kept silent as he mulled over the information. He'd heard the name Tarsin Va bandied about by the men but had not understood the connotations involved. Tarsin was a bastard then; his childhood vastly different, but in some respects like his own upbringing. His own father he knew all too well. It was why he'd stowed aboard the *Lioness* in the first place, a means to escape a brutal father with a heavy fist.

'Come,' Tarsin stood, offering a hand to help Jarred stand on the swaying ship. The incessant hammering had died somewhat, to be replaced by groaning timbers and the creak of taught lines. 'It's time you saw Master Jenkins about the wooden blade, and time I spoke to Ruvin,' Jarred felt Tarsin tap him on the back to send him in the right direction. 'And remember your manners, young Jarred, lest you receive the pointy end first.'

Jarred smiled, glad to have some mobility in his legs and a stomach somewhat satisfied. Glad to also have a friend named Tarsin Va.

*

Tarsin watched as Jarred went below deck in search of the Master Carpenter before heading to the foredeck and Ruvin's quarters. Half-a-dozen of his men sat by the rail, some coiling rope, others merely sprawled on the deck as they soaked up the sunshine. The spring storm had rolled in from the south and hounded their course, and several men, like Jarred, fared poorly upon the rocking ship. Even now they appeared exhausted and pasty skinned: like deep-sea fish floundering on the deck. Only those coiling rope offered a nod as he walked by, the others oblivious to his passing. He moved on, climbed a set of stairs and rapped loudly against the wooden door leading to Ruvin's quarters. A moment elapsed before the door opened to reveal Ruvin Ciricello, a wan smile plastered across his face. The voyage had taken its toll on the old man also, his constitution not what it once was. His immaculately groomed hair was a dishevelled mess, and his eyes, so discerning and sharp, now appeared dull and lifeless.

'We need to talk.'

Ruvin nodded, moving back a step to allow him entry.

Tarsin stepped into the cabin. The quarters were spacious, as befitted the owner of the ship, and quite elaborate. A large four-posted bed occupied the central space, but there was room for a small table and two chairs, several sea-chests and a bench seat underneath a lead-glass window. Swinging from the rafters was an ornate lantern, rocking silently back and forth on a well-oiled chain. Tarsin could see charts spread across the table and floor, weighted with various objects, and a map of the known world tacked to a wall. A bowl of half-eaten stew lay in the corner, alongside an empty pitcher.

'What can I do for you, Tarsin?' Ruvin's voice lacked its usual vigour.

The swordsman walked to a chair, spun it around and sat, then waited for Ruvin to do likewise. 'I need to know what our movements will be once we reach Bastion,' he began.

Ruvin raised a hand to stroke his chin, the wrinkles about his narrowed eyes stretching like a spider's web to blanket his face. 'Most of the mercenaries will be given leave to do as they see fit, as is our custom. The bulk of the sailors likewise, once the ship has been unloaded, dressed down and the trade goods sent to my warehouse. You and I, with a handful of our men, will make for

Irongate with the relic I found. I'll then pass it on to the Brotherhood of One, for it is they who financed this quest. Why?' Ruvin asked. 'What's on your mind?'

Tarsin's eyes drifted to the bowl of stew in the corner as it slid three feet along the wall with the lurching ship, the sound of a crashing wave interrupting their conversation. Ruvin's complexion paled further, his throat bulging as he swallowed either bile, or perhaps fear. For a moment, he wondered if the fear in Ruvin's eyes mirrored his own, wondered if Ruvin could see it just as clearly.

Like Ruvin, he swallowed before taking a deep breath. 'When I joined your crew three years past, I did so to escape Bastion.'

The older man sighed, but the look of shock Tarsin expected wasn't forthcoming.

'You're not surprised?' Tarsin continued.

'It's not unusual. Many men before you have sought passage aboard a ship as a swift means of escape. What did you do, if you don't mind my asking? It's a rare thing for a swordsman of your talents to flee.'

Tarsin could see the light in the old man's eyes rekindle, the rolling ship forgotten.

'Come, Tarsin,' he continued, 'for three years I've respected your privacy and your troubled past. But you have a darker side, swordsman, a side you've kept well hidden whilst in my employ. What did you do, Tarsin Va? Who did you kill?'

'I didn't kill anyone,' he began. 'The reason I left Bastion was because I feared I *might* kill someone; someone who was once close to me.'

'You *"might"* kill someone?'

'Aye,' Tarsin wiped his brow, 'I was in a rage, furious, and there was only one man I blamed for the atrocity I'd endured; one man I held responsible for the deaths of my sword brothers.' Tarsin knew he would need to elaborate at some point, explain to Ruvin the reasons for his pain. Even now, in Ruvin's cabin, he fought valiantly to control his suppressed anger. Three years may have passed, but the red-hot coals of hatred still simmered within.

The merest mention of what transpired would be enough to fan the flames. Somewhere deep inside a voice screamed at him to unload the burden, but another voice, equally persuasive, cautioned against revelation. It told him to retain the anger, to nurture it. There would be a time and a place to unleash the fury. Now was not the time.

'I've seen you fight, Tarsin. Few men could stand against you and live,' Ruvin's voice cut through his tormented memories. 'So, who walks and breathes on borrowed time, my friend? Who have you marked for death?'

Tarsin raised cold, blue eyes to the old man, met his gaze with a steely look. He knew he couldn't contain his secret any longer, desperately needed to be free of its constricting grip now they were heading home. With a heavy heart, he opened his mouth and spoke words he'd vowed never to reveal. 'Arkos Vantos,' he said, his voice weighted with intent, 'the man who is our king.'

CHAPTER FOUR

The night sky was ablaze with starlight.

Elder Cappitus, wrinkled and white-bearded, wiggled his old frame onto a stout wooden chair as ancient as he and let out a soft sigh. He'd spent the evening with an eye to the bronze telescope before him, his gaze sweeping the firmament as he noted the celestial bodies from his roost at the top of East Tower. Resting on the small table beside him sat a sheaf of paper, a tear-drop ink bottle and a partially shuttered lantern. He leant over to write a few words with his quill-pen, his hand unsteady, before leaning back in his chair. All was silent apart from the occasional wind buffet against the timber walls. The observatory was an addition to the solid keep called Irongate, built during a period when the Brotherhood of One was in their infancy. Now it was more than two hundred years old and Cappitus often spent his nights here, alone with his thoughts as he scried the heavens in search of answers.

The observatory shuddered as the wind increased in intensity. Every evening, especially during the warmer months, a cool wind would sweep across the Bay of Pennants to strike the city of Bastion. Most often it brought a welcome respite to the populace from the summer heat, but tonight it remained a nuisance, distracting the old man's thoughts when they could ill afford to be disturbed.

With another sigh, he rose to his feet, his black robe swishing across the floor as he plunged a hand into a deep pocket. Retrieving a bronze cap, he walked three steps to the telescope and covered the eyepiece before moving to close the shutters framing the starlit sky. His hands reached high and paused, his eyes roaming the shadowed city below. Irongate, whilst old, was well situated atop a hill in the eastern quarter of the Holy City. From his vantage, Cappitus could see the glowing beacon labelled Aston's Tear, could see the monasteries, cathedrals and temple silhouettes darkening the streets below. She was a sight to behold; a melting pot for the aristocracy, an avenue for the wealthy and most certainly a destination for those with religious inclinations. To many she was a sprawling wen of paved walkways, canals and soaring towers, to others a conglomeration of the finest and most studious of minds. With her streets lined by architectural wonders fashioned by astute men, she was testament to the city's philosophy: *Labour is its own reward.* Capital of Dervae, Bastion was everything to her people. Yet her days, if Cappitus deciphered truly, were numbered.

A tap at the only door caused him to turn.

'Come in,' he offered, his gravelly voice barely loud enough to be heard.

The door swung open to reveal a solid, barrel-chested man in his late forties, an enormous black moustache prominent above a strong set jaw. His eyes were dark, although a glint of mirth resided within, and his bald pate was polished, so it reflected the light. His robes were black, much like elder Cappitus', the only difference being a silver shield emblazoned across his chest and a sword belted at his waist.

'Good evening, brother Declan.'

'Elder Cappitus,' the response was accompanied by a slight nod of the head.

Cappitus watched as Declan strode into the observatory and headed straight for the cabinet. It was positioned next to an enormous bookshelf laden with scroll cases, leather-bound tomes, charts and maps. Declan ignored the paraphernalia as he opened the cabinet door and reached inside, pulling out a bottle of wine and two long-stemmed glasses. 'Care for a drink, old man?' he offered with a wink.

Cappitus nodded ascent and moved back to his table and chair, then reached for his lantern and placed it on a hook protruding from the wall. He then shuffled his papers together and swept an aging hand across the table's surface, making room for the bottle of wine. Once placed, Declan moved to a shadowed corner to retrieve a stool, so he could sit opposite his friend.

Cappitus patiently waited for the swordsman to open the bottle and pour, accepting the proffered glass. The burgundy wine was courtesy of Otella vineyards, renown for being the finest in Dervae. Cappitus smoothed his long white beard before taking a sip, then sat back to savour the hint of black current and pepper that danced upon his tongue. He hoped it would ease his troubled mind; knew he hoped in vain.

'So,' Declan took a sip of his own wine, 'are there any new developments I should be aware of?'

Elder Cappitus sat silently for a moment, aware his words, if he spoke them, would sour the mood. 'The time has come,' he finally said.

Declan lifted his drink and gave it a swirl, then took another sip. 'Are you certain?'

'Yes, without a doubt. The signs are there if you know where to look,' Cappitus reached for his sheaf of parchment, shuffled through a dozen until he found the right one. He wondered if he should tell his friend his dire news or wait for further proof. He chose to wait. 'Here,' he passed a page to his friend. 'See the position of the comet in the constellation we call the Sleeping Bear. They're in accordance to those of the Nepharii charts, predicted some five thousand years ago.'

'What of the glyphs at the bottom of the page?' Declan raised bushy eyebrows after scanning the chart. 'What is their meaning?'

'The glyphs speak of prophesy. It is my belief the future they speak of has already arrived.'

'Can the markings of an ancient race be trusted?'

'Yes,' Cappitus took a deep breath. 'The Nepharii charts we stumbled across have proven to be incredibly accurate . . . more so than I would have thought possible. Which leads me to believe my earlier supposition was entirely correct.'

'Remind me what that was again,' Declan held up his glass to admire the wine's depth of colour.

'The Nepharii were considerably more advanced than we first believed. Their architecture, language, art and astrological charts far outweigh anything we could aspire to or replicate. You need only gaze upon Aston's Tear to know I speak the truth.'

Declan tilted his head to the side, which Cappitus took as acknowledgement. Aston's Tear, the enormous pyramid central to Bastion resided atop a red granite slab hundreds of feet thick, its four pristine walls likewise granite, constructed of equally cut white polished blocks towering twenty feet high and twice that in length. There were no doors of any description, nor any cavities boring into its depths; just an immense mass of white stone soaring towards the heavens. At its peak lay the capstone: a smaller pyramid resembling a perfectly cut diamond as it reflected the sun's rays during the day and remained alight once the sun set. Aston's Tear it was named, in honour of their sun god, although to be truthful the pyramid had been built long before the clans stumbled across the ruins and built the city of Bastion. It had been here when the first settlers arrived, dominant, striking, a beacon of hope and encouragement. To this day, after a thousand years of Dervani occupation, it remained unsullied.

'I agree, old man,' said Declan between sips. 'I'm not the only member of the Brotherhood perplexed by the pyramid's design and means of construction.'

Cappitus sat forward, 'It's the secrets she holds that I'm most interested in. There are answers hidden in plain sight: in its dimensions and its alignments. The more I search, the greater my respect for the Nepharii. I only wish the pieces of the puzzle were more accommodating. Heaven knows I am searching for something profound, yet the answers remain elusive.'

The two men paused momentarily to savour their wine. It had become an evening ritual, a chance for the two men to break from their immediate task and relax their minds and tired bodies. The time for reflection was fading fast, though. The Dark Lord, Ahriman, had risen in the north, summoned by foul witchcraft. Cappitus and the Brotherhood were aware of his temporary shift to the material plane but were still unable to locate his exact presence. Of interest were the celestial bodies in the night sky, suggesting the time was ripe for Chaos to rear its unpredictable head. The end of an age was upon them and it appeared their options were few.

Still, Cappitus believed hope remained. Years had passed since the Brotherhood of One first stumbled across a series of ancient tombs buried deep beneath the city. Tombs constructed by a hand other than man. Yet the tombs they opened contained no buried dead. There was no sign of an ancient race of scholars, no final resting place to be found. There were only manuscripts written in an ancient language: some with letters, others with glyphs. They were written by the Nepharii: a race of beings who built a city unlike anything seen before or since. It was no secret they were an enigma, many proclaiming the Nepharii as divine beings, angels paving the way for mankind. They were a mystery and their ancient city, Aos, lay deep beneath Bastion brimming with secrets still awaiting the light of day. Their greatest achievement lay in their charts of the night sky, though, detailed with incredible accuracy and often plotted far into the future for reasons now fraught with speculation. It was these very manuscripts and charts that set Cappitus on the path he walked today.

Declan reached for the wine bottle and refilled their glasses. 'Are you any closer to finding a solution . . . of any sort?'

'Hardly,' said Cappitus. 'All my findings so far point to the pyramid being instrumental in some capacity. We know Ahriman has risen in the north, and we've concluded the Nepharii knew the end of an age was imminent during our time. What that entails we've not been able to confirm. Some have speculated the end of the world, others the beginning of a golden era. To be honest, my friend, we have found little to suggest either to be paramount and yet I'm deeply concerned.'

'Yet not all the Nepharii manuscripts have been deciphered, true?'

Cappitus nodded his head. 'They are . . . difficult. Some are written in a hand that appears eerily like our own or that of the southern city-states, and there are suggestions the writings could perhaps be the progenitor of all modern language. Yet other manuscripts are awash with glyphs. The glyphs alone allude to multiple translations.'

Declan shook his head and Cappitus knew the swordsman was doing his best to grasp what he had to say. The Brotherhood of One had a single goal: knowledge in all its forms. To collate such a monumental task, four chapters were established within the Brotherhood, to best see its ideal brought to fruition. The Seekers of the Brotherhood sought out relics and treasures of the past and delved deep for such knowledge. The Scribes of the Brotherhood put quill-pen to parchment to record all knowledge gathered. The Seers of the Brotherhood spent their time creatively learning all there was to learn, including the arcane, whilst the Swords of the Brotherhood, of which Declan was a member, were the Brotherhood's protectors. As much as every member of the Brotherhood of One sought knowledge in all its forms, some members were inevitably cut from a different cloth and preferred much simpler pleasures. Whilst the majority worked tirelessly in their personal studies writing texts, deciphering ancient scrolls or reading signs in the evening sky, Declan and those under his command sought solace in the pursuit of armed combat. As he quite often reminded those of a more scholarly disposition, "Knowledge of armed combat is still knowledge".

'So where does this leave us?' Declan placed his glass upon the table. 'We've a Dark God approaching from the north, guided by a witch who craves the king's head. You know she'll not stop until Arkos and his family are vanquished. She has vowed such on more than one occasion.'

Cappitus knew all too well of Avra the witch and her vendetta against the Dervani King.

'What of Neema, have you spoken to her?'

Cappitus rose tired eyes to peer at his friend. He'd only thought of the Sister earlier this night and wondered how she and her colleagues were faring in their quest for answers. It was not every day one sought a means to destroy a vengeful deity.

'We have exchanged views on our current predicament,' Cappitus said, holding out his glass for Declan to refill. Neema, matron of the Celestial Sisters, held a position of authority just as Cappitus did within the Brotherhood. 'The Celestial Sisters are equally adept at discerning the heavens,' he continued. 'Perhaps they may find the answer we seek.'

'In the meantime,' Declan offered, 'we keep our eyes and ears open. We've a score of men patrolling the King's North Road from Bastion to Elmwood, searching for a sign. If Avra and her Dark Lord creep close, we're bound to find their scent.'

Cappitus remained silent. He knew Avra and her sorceress ways. He also knew no matter how stringent he and the Brotherhood were; if Avra wished to enter Bastion unopposed she would do so. Once here, it would be only a matter of time before she played the first hand. The signs in the night sky had drifted to herald a time of Chaos and confusion. She would be here soon; he could feel it in his blood.

He drank another mouthful of wine, any chance of savouring the liquid fading as his mind continued to ponder. There were other ails besetting the kingdom beside the approaching Dark God. Plague and its puss-filled boils darkened Benwith, killing wantonly and without mercy, whilst war in the south with Al-Za'im, now a month in duration, was an unnecessary distraction. It was hard to imagine, but Cappitus suspected such contrivances were not mere happenstance.

'Have you heard any word of Captain Vasco or Ruvin Ciricello?' Declan asked, changing the subject.

The hoary brows above Cappitus' weary eyes were knotted when the question was asked, but they relaxed at mention of Ruvin Ciricello's name. The two Seekers had been absent for more than three years, searching for a Nepharii relic in the ruined city of Bel-Afii, close to Al-Za'im. Through means available to only a few, Cappitus had been able to scry their whereabouts. They were now aboard the *Lioness*, approximately two weeks from Bastion. More importantly, Ruvin's journey was as fruitful as promised. The Nepharii disc they'd been searching for was in his grasp.

'They've been gone more than three years,' Declan continued, believing Cappitus' silence suggested no contact. 'Do you believe they'll return?'

The hint of a smile twitched the corner of Cappitus' mouth. 'Oh, they'll return, and soon. With them will be the astrological disc I've sought for so long. Five years have passed since I first read of its existence. Now it is close. Once I have it in my grasp, answers will be forthcoming.'

'What of the religious orders?' Declan asked.

Cappitus' smile wavered then disappeared. There were eight major religious orders in Dervae, each practicing the beliefs of their own deity. Aston was their chief god: the sun and creator. Next in importance came Isha: goddess of the moon and love. Then there was Eos: the earth goddess, purveyor of faith and hope; Anok: the god of mischief and his brother Eli: the god of deceit. Next was Sybis: goddess of knowledge and witchcraft; Terros: god of blood and war, and finally Hell: god of death and the underworld. The only other with a healthy following was Frey: goddess of Fate and the Four winds. And yet with so many bishops, priests and acolytes practicing within Bastion, help from their quarter was always distressingly light due to the Brotherhood's insistence on there being only one, true God.

'I have exchanged words with Archbishop Treventos, for those who pray to Aston are generally the most accommodating to our belief. Dialogue with the other orders is a waste of my time.' Cappitus scratched his beard. 'And the archbishop, upon hearing the name Ahriman, declined to offer any assistance. They simply do not believe in the one true God as we do. To acknowledge Ahriman as the shadow of God flies in the face of all they preach.'

'Is he truly a shadow of the One God, or merely some devil summoned from Hell's domain?'

Cappitus scratched his beard. 'To be honest, we have conjecture only. Whoever he is, though, his powers will be greater than ours. I have learnt that much from my studies.'

'So, there will be no help forthcoming from the religious orders, as expected. What of the secular orders?'

'It is doubtful. Most have ties with the eight religious orders in some capacity. Those who don't are quickly persuaded against any venture with the Brotherhood of One. It is madness, but until the witch and her shadow arrive, we've no proof to suggest an apocalypse is coming.'

Declan fidgeted, a sign his mental capacity had absorbed as much as it could.

'Despite the setbacks, Declan, I have hope. The Nepharii knew what was to come; I know this. I also believe they fashioned a means to survive during such a time.'

'You know this how?' asked Declan with a quizzical look.

'I have my ways, brother Declan. Whilst you play at war, we of greater intellect scry the heavens for salvation.'

Declan smiled, 'Well then, brother, if your scholarly ways are so particular, I suggest you devote more time to seeking those answers we desperately crave.'

Cappitus drank the last of his wine and sat further back in his chair, his eyes closed in contemplation. When he opened them, he met his friend's gaze and spoke in a solemn voice. 'Perhaps I have, brother, and I do not like what I have found.'

*

Declan finished his glass and noted the empty bottle. He thought to rise and procure another from the cabinet, but as much as he yearned for another drink, the mood had become melancholy. Besides, Cappitus was an old man and as much as he professed to be a light sleeper, he appeared exhausted.

'You should seek some rest, Cappitus,' said Declan rising to his feet, 'and I should be on my way.'

'Nonsense,' was the quick reply as Cappitus stood and then moved towards the far wall where his gnarled staff rested. 'The night is still young, and I've need of your strength. There is a crate by the cabinet full of scrolls that needs to be returned to the Depository. Join me for a walk, my friend. I am afraid there is more I must tell you.'

Declan knew he had little choice in the matter, and to be truthful, he felt no need to retire just yet. A walk to the Depository - the Brotherhood's Chamber of Records - would clear his head in any case, for talk of witches and dark gods muddled his mind. Once they left East Tower it was only a short walk across the courtyard to the main hall and behind that the corridor leading to the West Wing.

'As you wish,' he replied, moving to pick up the box of scrolls.

The walk was as he expected, brief but welcome, the cool breeze a relief now that summer was at its peak, a summer most weren't likely to forget. On only a handful of occasions did the patter of rain arrive during the hottest months and it barely washed the dust from the streets. Crops struggled in the field, many withered beyond salvation. More than once he'd been told the soil was hard and dry, cracked due to lack of sustenance. Cappitus was right when he mentioned there were ails other than the Dark God assaulting the kingdom of Dervae.

They reached the double doors leading into the great hall, pushed them open and stepped into a vast room capable of seating two hundred men about a dozen long tables. It was quiet now, the crackle of a single hearth the only noise apart from their booted footsteps. The Brotherhood ate their supper as the sun set, together and in silence. Three hours had passed since their repast, now the hall was empty but for a handful of hounds asleep amongst the rushes. To their left a wide doorway led to the kitchens, whilst ahead, across the hall's expanse, a corridor led to the Depository. Declan, his hands full as he carried the crate, moved past the tables and into the dim passage, his mind troubled as he recalled the words mentioned by Cappitus in the observatory.

Ahriman: The Dark Lord, God of Chaos and Destruction. The fact he was here was no longer in doubt. Declan didn't profess to understand the powers utilized by the Seers of the Brotherhood, but he'd come to rely on their astute observations in the past and when a score of his brothers mentioned they'd felt Ahriman's arrival, he wasn't foolish enough to disagree. Six months had passed since that ill-omened day, and the Dark Lord's absence, strangely, heightened the fear of his coming rather than detracted from it. The Brotherhood, along with the Celestial Sisters and even King Arkos, knew his arrival was imminent. Yet debate still raged over how to confront Avra and her summoned god. Brute force had been one option, but the outbreak of war to the south now rendered such a possibility void.

Declan thought of the dozens of temples and cathedrals situated throughout Bastion. Even if their members joined their forces, he doubted they could muster the strength to curtail Ahriman's advance. Their beliefs lay on different paths. To complicate matters, Cappitus mentioned Ahriman required the soul of a king to become flesh, a ritual unequivocally steeped in lore. So, Declan still harboured a couple of questions.

Firstly, how were they to tackle the shade of a god?

And more importantly, if King Arkos was sacrificed and Ahriman became flesh, what hope did they have against such a vengeful deity?

He walked to the end of the corridor and chose the left-hand door, then waited for Cappitus to shuffle ahead and twist the brass handle. The door opened, leading them into an enormous hall, dark at this time of night, its floor to ceiling shelves cluttered with every book, tome and scroll imaginable. Declan sighed and followed Cappitus into the Depository for the Brotherhood of One.

'Over here,' Cappitus led Declan forty feet down a narrow aisle, his gnarled staff offering a gentle glow with a word as it illuminated leather-bound books piled high, most blanketed with a thick film of dust. At the end of the aisle a solid brick wall confronted them, two dozen wooden cubicles ranged along its length. Cappitus spun to his right and reached the last in line, before pointing a long finger at the desk. 'You can place the scrolls here, brother,' he said.

Declan obliged, careful not to dump the crate atop the many charts sprawled across its breadth. He pushed some to the side, caught a glimpse of astrological maps. A number of Nepharii glyphs formed a border along one, whilst another was inked by Cappitus' own cursive hand. 'You've been busy, my friend,' Declan said as he straightened his back.

'Aye,' Cappitus reached for a scroll case from a pigeon hole above the cubicle. 'Here, I've something important to show you.'

Declan watched as he placed the glowing staff to the side, unstoppered the scroll case and drew forth an aged piece of parchment. Once spread across the desk, Cappitus used the crate to hold down one end and placed a brass candle-holder at the other. 'What have you here?' he finally asked, looking over his shoulder.

'The cause of all our worries,' Cappitus replied.

The parchment, although old, was in remarkable condition. The ink upon its surface was clear and legible. Declan assumed it had been reproduced, the letters and glyphs painstakingly copied by a Scribe of the Brotherhood sometime in the past. 'What does it say?' he asked after making a brief attempt to read the script.

Cappitus smoothed his beard before he spoke. 'It details the plight we are about to face, speaks of a Darkness and the End of an Age.'

'How can you be certain it details what's happening in our time?'

'Here,' Cappitus moved to a chart he'd tacked to the wall. 'This is a representation of the night sky as you or I would see if we stepped outside right now; wouldn't you agree?'

Declan noted several constellations, namely the Wise Owl, the Circling Eel and the Sleeping Bear. He nodded his head as Cappitus caught his gaze.

'Only this chart, although a copy, is five thousand years old,' Cappitus reached for another scroll case. He unrolled the contents with an unsteady hand. 'This, to the best of our knowledge,' he stretched the scroll above the desk, 'is a chart of the night sky during Nepharii time.'

Declan scanned the chart, unfamiliar with the lines connecting many of the stars and the constellations they formed. As he peered closer, though, he noticed the stars were in a similar position; it was just the lines connecting those formed different patterns. 'These constellations are not ours, are they?'

'No, they are Nepharii constellations. Whilst alone they do not predict the future, they do lead us to question the path of a comet we call the Eye of the Jaguar.'

Declan scratched his bald head. He trusted Cappitus like no other, understood his sometimes-unhinged intellect. Yet right now he was experiencing difficulties adhering to the old man's train of thought. 'What is your point, old man?'

Cappitus pulled the first piece of parchment from under the star chart, the one detailed with glyphs and ancient letters. "See this mark here,' he pointed a gnarled finger, 'this green tinged comet graces our night sky once every three hundred years. This time it will skim close to our sun. There is a chance it will be destroyed.' He bent close, began to read with his gravelly voice.

'And so shall the End Times fall upon the land, heralded by the arrival of Darkness: the bearer of Doom and Grim tidings. He shall strike flesh from the weak and shake the world's foundations. Drought and Famine shall be his allies, Sorrow and Confusion his blessings.

'And you shall know the hour of his arrival, for the Chaos light: the northern star, shall sit high in the evening sky. A convergence will be met with the Eye of the Jaguar and Darkness shall awaken.'

'Are you telling me this Chaos light: the northern star; is now high in the sky?'

'I am, brother Declan. The Chaos light is what we refer to as Storos, the brightest star in the evening sky. The time is now. With the aid of a telescope you can see the comet, the Eye of the Jaguar, fast approaching the sun,' Cappitus smoothed his beard once more. 'There is more, brother. Allow me to read on.'

'Beneath the Chaos light shall pass the Eye of the Jaguar, emerald bright. They will fight and the battle they wage shall be fierce. If the Eye of the Jaguar falls, Chaos shall triumph. So it is written, so shall it come to pass.'

Declan remained silent as Cappitus completed his narration. There was much to consider, and the ambiguous writing offered scant comfort to the swordsman. The only certainty he could fathom was the prospect of a battle to be waged. A battle he assumed had nothing to do with the war being fought with Al-Za'im. Mentioning the Eye of the Jaguar intrigued him, though. Arkos Vantos, King of Dervae, wore a golden crown, a polished jade stone embossed at its centre. It was referred to as the Eye of the Jaguar, a fitting analogy considering house Vantos' family crest was a rampant feline of the same ilk.

A sparkle of recognition must have twinkled in his eye, for Cappitus leaned forward, his eyes creasing under heavy brows. 'You grasp the connotations, don't you?'

Declan sighed, not sure of anything, really. 'King Arkos is the jaguar, Ahriman is Chaos, yes?'

'It is so. Ahriman needs our king's soul to become flesh. As I said earlier, the comet will pass close to the northern star for a convergence *after* it has skimmed close to the sun. There is a chance it shall disintegrate after brushing so close to the sun's surface. Such an occurrence will bode ill for all concerned. If Ahriman can claim the king and his soul, he'll move entirely onto the material plane. From that moment onward, he will grow in strength until we cannot stop him.'

'What of his sons, Prince Theos and Prince Atillus? They are men of house Vantos, jaguars both and surely capable of fighting back against the Darkness?'

The old man closed his eyes and took a deep breath. When he opened them, Declan could see sadness pool in their depths. 'There is a line,' Cappitus said, searching for another piece of parchment. He found what he was looking for, scanned the archaic words for a moment. 'Here,' he began, *Jaguars two, so young and free, now lie at peace, no longer three.'*

Declan paused before speaking, gripping the hilt of his sword with a tight fist. There were only three Vantos men in Dervae: the king and his two sons, three jaguars to rule the kingdom. He felt irked by his train of thought but spoke his mind. 'They are marked for death, then?' he snarled, knowing the two princes well.

'They are already dead.'

'What?' Declan didn't mean to shout so loudly, but the shock startled him, frightened him. 'How could such be?'

'They both rode south with the king's armies a month past, hoping to earn their stripes fighting the desert riders of Al-Za'im. Before you ascended the East Tower to share a wine, I utilized arcane means to seek them out, found both princes were . . . dead.'

'Are you certain, do you have proof?' Declan asked the question despite knowing Cappitus' ability to scry more than just the heavens.

'I would not tell you otherwise,' Cappitus lowered his voice.

Declan paced away from the desk and smashed a curled fist against a bookshelf, sending a plume of dust swirling into the air. He spun about to confront the old man. 'Why didn't you tell me sooner?'

'I needed to assess all I had gleaned, reaffirm that which I discovered. To be honest, my brother, I sought time to convince myself of its validity.'

'What of King Arkos, does he know his only two sons are dead?'

'I do not believe so, not yet.'

'Then you must tell him, Cappitus,' Declan watched the old man bow his head. He looked incredibly tired, crushed by the weight of his dire news. Whilst he may have been mistaken, he thought he saw a glimpse of fear in his eyes before he bowed his head. 'I'll stand beside you when the time comes,' Declan offered, placing a hand on Cappitus' bony shoulder.

'It is not the king's anger I fear, Declan,' Cappitus began to roll parchment, placing it in a scroll case. 'The death of Prince Theos and Prince Atillus merely highlights how close Ahriman truly is. He is coming, my brother, and he is coming on wings of hate. I fear he'll be here soon.'

'So, what do we do now, what *can* we do now?'

Another scroll case found its way into a pigeon hole, stacked with the rest. 'We protect the king,' Cappitus replied. 'If Arkos Vantos dies, then all hope is lost, it is that simple. He is the last of the jaguars, the one man who can halt Ahriman's ascent.'

'Aye, we keep him alive.'

'We do, brother. For if we fail, it will be the last thing we ever do.'

CHAPTER FIVE

Tarsin woke with a start, blanketed in a film of cold sweat.

He threw his blanket into the corner of his cabin, then swung his legs across his bed and placed bare feet on the floor. The ship lurched and Tarsin heard the hard slap of waves against the hull. He took a moment to gather his thoughts, then stood on shaking legs. Another storm had struck the *Lioness*, the men were tired, and Bastion was still two weeks away. Anxiety was burning through the veins of sailor and mercenary alike, and the wait to reach kingdom shores was close to unbearable.

He cursed as he reached for a shirt and slipped it over his head. He felt nothing akin to relief or satisfaction at the thought of returning home. There were no loved ones to welcome him, few friends he considered close enough to greet. All he felt was a raging anger boiling deep inside, an anger threatening to surface and explode. For three years he'd kept it under control, hidden under layers of doubt and fear, sealed to prevent it from seeing the light of day. Only now Ruvin Ciricello knew; knew of his hatred towards the king. Now it appeared the seals were broken, and he was unable to contain the beast dwelling within.

To complicate matters further, the dreams had returned.

He pulled his trousers on and buckled his belt. The dreams were back. He shook his head, hoping the action would crystallize his thoughts. Yet they remained sullied, clouded. The remnants of his nightmare continued to linger. A spasm clenched his jaw, twisting his neck violently to the right. The pain was fleeting yet a reminder of all he'd suffered. Random faces swam before his eyes. Faces of men he used to know.

He sat back on his bed. His head throbbed, and his stomach heaved to release its contents onto the floor. He lifted a hand to wipe bile from his mouth. A bowl of half-eaten oatmeal nestled against the wall, a wooden spoon disappearing into its congealed mass. He stifled another upheaval, then raised blood-shot eyes as voices from above whispered through planks of timber. The sound of the wind's cry startled him: a mournful lament at the storm's passing. Tarsin added his own sigh to the wail and lay back down, closing his eyes. The light of day was hours away and he still needed rest. The dreams had woken him, but he hoped they were finished. He could do with some uninterrupted sleep.

He calmed his breathing and cleared his mind using techniques he'd learnt from his sword master, Lord Henrickson, all those years ago. It worked, his mind emptied, and his heart rate slowed. Within moments he fell asleep.

And the dreams returned.

*

Tarsin opened his eyes to find himself lying on his back amongst wet grass, the swaying branches of an elm above him, twilight sky beyond. He knew he was dreaming, for he'd been here countless times before, even tried to alter the dream's path on numerous occasions. Yet he'd never prevailed, it was always the same. He looked to the sky and saw dawn was not far away. He shook his head, aware of the smell of damp earth and wild mint clouding his memories, masking his conscious thoughts. He pushed his hands beneath him only to find they were bound, likewise his ankles.

He swept his gaze from side-to-side. He was in a wooded hollow, a steep incline behind him. He remembered now; remembered the cloying scent of musk and spice, a concoction causing paralysis. At some point, he and his men were trussed like wild boar and thrown onto the back of a wagon. Only he'd fallen off during the ride, rolling off timber planks to fall with a thud before sliding down an embankment. Under the cover of darkness, he lay quiet, motionless, waiting for the effects of the poison to dissipate.

Now he was awake with anger fuelling his body. He leant over to grab a large rock, ripping it out of the soil to reveal scurrying creatures with multiple legs. Three feet below him lay another large rock protruding from the earth. He manoeuvred down, placed his feet against its flanks, then slammed his rock hard against the other. A loud crack broke the silence, startling a flock of blackbirds from a nearby tree. Thankfully the rock he held sheared in two. A moment later both hands and feet were free, his bonds cut with the rock's sharp edge.

He stretched his body and felt for any aches acquired during his capture and accidental fall. What he found was trivial, a bruise or two, nothing more. To his dismay he'd been stripped of his sword and dagger, although two throwing knives hidden in his boots remained. Without further thought, he spun and began to climb the embankment, cresting the rise to find a dirt road heading east and west. He couldn't recall their direction the night before, but as twilight faded to herald dawn's soft radiance, he could make out ruts in the soft earth left by a wagon's wheels and the clear mark of a horse's hooves. Without pausing he began to follow, his legs stretching into a run. Five of his men were still aboard the wagon headed for a destination only the depraved could fathom. He knew they were in mortal danger, their very lives at risk.

He ran harder, easing into his strides, for he knew he was their only hope.

The sun was an hour in the sky by the time he reached a small keep, a barn and several small enclosures nestled within its shadow. Twice riders had swept past him on the road as he approached, his form shrouded by bushes as he hid. He knew then that his absence from the wagon had been noticed, prayed they'd believe he'd run in fear. He calmed himself and immediately spied the wagon, the horse still held in its traces. There was no sign of his men. With caution, he knelt behind an outer fence intertwined with blackberries and found a spot where he could search out his adversaries without being seen. A minute later a man attired in scarlet robes stepped from the barn, his bald head glistening in the morning sun. Recognition flared in Tarsin's mind. He was the tavern owner: the man they trusted to stable their horses and bring them food the night before.

A vague memory surfaced as he fumed, of words spoken whilst he succumbed to the cunning folk's poison. 'This is the last of them,' he remembered one man saying as another led a horse and wagon from the rear of the tavern.

'Are you sure?'

'Aye, we were told there would be twenty-four sent to Benwith. Now they're all accounted for.'

Tarsin remembered being poked in the chest with a long staff. 'You're confident these are the ones?'

'Anok and Eli, Kepler, I can tell the difference between a swordsman and a farmer!'

'Alright, alright,' Tarsin heard a thud as one of his men was slammed onto the back of the wagon. The others followed in quick fashion before Tarsin found himself hoisted atop in an unruly manner.

That had been last night, shortly after they'd reached the tavern. It appeared even this far from their mark folk were under the influence of the Benwith coven.

Fortunately, they'd lost one during their travel. Somehow, Frey: goddess of Fate, had conspired to set him free. Now his only thought was of rescuing his men; all twenty-three of them.

He'd start by searching the barn.

He watched the red-robed man walk towards the keep and saw him push open a black door hinged with bronze. As he disappeared inside, Tarsin stood and raced across the yard, his booted feet silent like those of an assassin. Without a thought, he stepped into the barn's confines, a throwing knife in each hand, fury in his eyes.

The barn's interior was dark yet slivers of golden light streamed through cracks between the old buildings timbers. It was enough to guide Tarsin across the hay-strewn floor towards a bench where an assortment of weapons lay in a haphazard fashion. Tarsin scanned the blades; saw his broadsword amongst them. A furtive look over his shoulder revealed no hidden danger and after placing his throwing knives back in his boots, he crossed to his sword and strapped it to his waist. Reassured by its weight he moved about the barn, seeking sign of his men.

It was his booted foot upon wood that alerted him to their presence. Hay covered a carefully concealed trapdoor; easily five feet wide and three feet across. Tarsin kicked the hay aside and knelt to brush his hands across its surface. He then lifted a black iron ring, his muscles taut as he pulled the trapdoor high to reveal a rough, stone staircase below. With cautious steps, he descended into the darkness, knowing he had no choice but to search for his men. As he reached the bottom, he drew forth his broadsword, the hiss of metal a comfort in the cool, cramped confines.

He took a deep breath; saw two burning brands wedged into sconces several feet ahead. He collected one and looked beyond, noticing a stone causeway stretching away into the distance, several deep pits dug into the earth lining its flanks. With sword in one hand and a flaming brand held high in the other, he stepped forward and began to peer into the black pits to either side.

He wished he hadn't.

Men and women sat dazed amongst the dirt and mud, silent, unmoving. Even their clothes were soiled, their hair lank and greasy. Tarsin cursed under his breath. He'd seen swine in better condition.

He moved on, kept his eyes peeled as he searched for his men. They would not be difficult to find for they were strong men, tall and robust. Even with such putrid quarters, his men were taught to survive, to persevere. Yet as he walked across the causeway, his eyes drawn to the silent forms sitting in dark pits, he realized something very wrong was at play here.

He reached the fourth pit on his right and stopped as a familiar shape caught his eye. It was Cale Griffith, one of his men, red-bearded and built like a small mountain. He sat still-as-a-statue, ten feet below him. Beside him, partly obscured, sat Marco Santelli. Tarsin knelt and whispered their names, hoping they could hear him.

If they heard, they made no attempt to turn and respond.

Tarsin spoke their names louder, seeking to evoke some recognition, but the men remained silent and unmoving. At a loss to explain their lack of action, he swept his gaze to either side to find more of his men sitting in apparent stupor.

He lifted his flaming brand higher, looking for a means to reach his companions when he noticed the walls were made of glass.

He squinted, then found on closer inspection the walls were a conglomeration of mirrors arranged neatly alongside each other. He quickly moved back to the preceding pit, found it to be likewise furnished; only he noticed each of the men and women sat directly in front of a mirror, their own reflection their apparent captor.

He moved back to where Cale Griffith sat, noticed he'd dragged his body closer to the mirror in the brief time he'd been absent. Others in the pit were likewise close, Marco Santelli in the process of reaching out to touch the surface.

Tarsin screamed at his men, his concern for secrecy no longer relevant. He screamed again, louder, his voice echoing within the dark chamber. He looked to his right; fearful he might be heard, believed red-robed folk would come running at his commotion. Only the causeway remained his alone.

He spun his attention back to the pit, desperate to find a way down to the dirt floor. Santelli had shuffled closer to his mirror, his arm raised. Tarsin blinked, unsure if what he saw was real or imagined.

For one of Santelli's arms was now embedded deep inside the mirror, almost up to the elbow.

Tarsin yelled at his friend as the rest of his men began to reach for their mirrors, hands and arms, even heads, delving into their silver pools.

He yelled again . . .

. . . And again.

Tarsin woke with a start.

He cursed, then spat phlegm onto the floor and wiped his clammy brow. Sunlight sifted between planks from above. He swung his frame over the side of the bed and stood to stretch his tired body.

Moving to a small side table, he reached for a pitcher of water, drank several mouthfuls until it was empty. He then threw the clay jug across the short room, smashing it against a wall where it broke into a dozen pieces.

He remembered Captain Vasco's words the night before, when squally weather dampened spirits and strained their sanity. 'Two weeks,' he yelled across the deck, his booming voice louder than the wind, 'see out this storm and we'll be two weeks from Bastion!'

Tarsin heard the words, knew he was running out of time. He had two more weeks before they reached Bastion.

And his dreams were back.

*

Square-sails billowed on the *Lioness* as Jarred sat perched on the mast head, the morning air fresh on his cold face. Captain Vasco had asked him to "lay aloft" and look for hidden shoals at daybreak, his young eyes bright and keen and suited to the task. Jarred had done as bid, scampering up the main mast with the eagerness of a young man charged with responsibility. Now he was restless, his feet itching to pound upon the deck, or better yet, swing from the rigging. Who could blame him? His usual duties were diverse and entertaining. Often called Ruvin's "Information Gatherer", Jarred enjoyed being on the move, running the streets of strange cities and ducking into smoky taverns and loud drink halls. Now he was stuck, bound to the crow's nest and all alone. With nought but a handful of dried dates to keep him company, he sat and kept his gaze on the rolling sea.

Two days had passed since Hunters Island had fallen behind the *Lioness* but Jarred heard from several sailors the sea here was rough sailing, even during clement weather. Past Hunters Island, lying just below the water line lay Ship's Rest Shoal. It covered an expansive area, from Hunters Island all the way to the eastern shore, and in parts it clawed further out, reaching the main trade route towards Bastion itself. Careful captains gave the island a wide berth, and those with an ounce of knowledge tacked west all the way to Bastion. It was unlikely they would even come near one of the infamous shoals, due to Captain Vasco's expertise, but Jarred knew if he vacated his post such would be the case. Anok and Eli, the gods of mischief and deceit, were always on hand to remind him of such folly.

So, to keep himself amused, he watched the men below complete their tasks for brief periods whilst remembering to scan the waters from time-to-time for signs of unusual whitecaps marring the sea of blue.

As it is with the young and their oft maligned ways, though, Jarred's mind wandered far and wide, across seas and deserts and deep into the dungeons of mighty castles. For weeks now, he'd sparred daily with Tarsin, learning the secrets of swordsmanship, wearing his bruises with pride. Now he fought bravely to rescue princesses from the clutches of evil, showcasing his extraordinary skill with a blade before being feted with exotic food and wine in courts of faraway lands. Some regaled him with words of wisdom; others offered their daughter's hand in marriage. All showered him with gifts of gold and sparkling gems. Jarred obliged, his charisma infectious, his roguishly good looks irresistible.

'Ahoy there, lad, what do you see?'

Jarred almost fell from his small perch such was his fright. He'd practically daydreamed himself to sleep, and it was only his quick hand grasping the mast that prevented him from falling to the deck below. Looking to starboard he quickly scanned the blue, searching for the tell-tale sign of whitecaps.

'Nothing, sir,' he shouted back after a brief look, answering the ship's mate below. The ship bobbed atop a considerable swell, but the waves were unbroken. Nothing, so far as he could tell, represented the danger he had been asked to scout for.

'What about port side?'

Jarred smacked a hand to his forehead, aware the Captain had asked him not to forsake west of the ship. He shifted his gaze, looking down at the water, then watched as it rose and swept down, so silky smooth, its passage unhindered. Behind him he could just make out the wake stretching away from the stern, the wash colliding and then seamlessly merging with waves on either side. Again, his mind began to wander.

'Anything?' was the shout from below, reminding him of his duty.

'Ah . . . nothing, sir,' Jarred widened his eyes in a vain attempt to focus on the task at hand. He flicked a lock of his long blonde hair away from his face and spun his gaze back to starboard, but before he could return his vision to the sea his eyes caught a smudge of darkness on the horizon.

The ship's mate below must have noticed his body stiffen, for his voice rang out once more. 'What is it, lad? What do you see?'

Jarred squinted, desperately seeking clarification. Whatever it was, it was big. The *Lioness* was no poor man's sailing ship: she was a three-masted carrack with foredeck and raised quarterdeck, her length over eighty feet and able to quarter more than a hundred men with comfort. But whatever sat before them on the horizon was monstrous. 'I'm not so sure,' Jarred looked to the man below and shrugged. 'I think it's a ship.'

Within moments half-a-dozen sailors sought positions within the rigging, peering with hands held high to protect their eyes form the glaring sun. A sailor climbed the main mast to seek a vantage from the crow's nest Jarred occupied. The lad took his leave, thankful for the respite, and settled himself amidships where chaos now reigned.

'Jarred!'

The young lad spun to see Tarsin by the mizzen mast, the activity somewhat subdued towards the stern of the ship. He moved with haste to stand with the Master of Swords, careful to keep clear of the sailors scampering about the deck. 'Is it a ship, Tarsin?'

'It does appear to be so,' Tarsin said as he folded his arms and lent against the mast. 'We'll know whose ship soon enough, in any case.'

Jarred relaxed once he saw Tarsin so disinterested. If there was something to fear, like pirates from the Corphym Isles, then Tarsin would be primed for battle, his focus fixed as he sought to relax tense muscles. As it was, he looked nonplussed. Mind you, as Jarred moved to lean against the mast alongside the swordsman, he noticed Tarsin's Rykedian broadsword strapped to his belt. It was his favoured blade, expertly fashioned and honed to a razor's edge. It had been Jarred's task to stow it aboard the *Lioness* all those weeks ago whilst Tarsin stayed ashore to protect Ruvin. He once told him he rarely drew it forth, but when he did, it was sure to taste blood.

'What if they are pirates come to raid our ship?' Jarred couldn't help but ask the question.

'It is doubtful, lad. Firstly, the ship is larger than the *Lioness,* and I know of no pirate sailing such a vessel. Secondly, a large ship like the one before us requires great finances to build, as well as materials and men. The only man I know who commands such wealth is the king. I think we'll find the royal navy before us, Jarred, sailing a new ship, no doubt.'

'The king? You mean Arkos Vantos, the Dervani King?'

'I do, lad.'

Jarred nodded his head even though he felt well out of his depth. So much was occurring despite Tarsin's calm demeanour that goose-pimples were lining the skin of his forearms. A thousand questions crowded his mind, swiftly sailing past on tangents of their own, conveniently a fraction from his grasp. 'What shall we do?' he eventually asked.

'Nothing, for now; just remain calm. When the time comes, then we'll act. Until then, young Jarred, save your energy.'

Another nod followed Tarsin's wise words, but he nodded with such vigour that it took Tarsin's gentle hand at the back of his head to help him cease. He took a deep breath and held his shaking hands before him, telling himself to focus. Whatever happened, Tarsin was near, and he was the finest swordsman on land or at sea. He'd heard the men say so and he believed them.

Now he need only wait.

*

It took the smudge on the horizon most of the morning to materialize into the large ship. Tarsin watched it grow for a time, gauging her length and size. At first it was difficult, for she sailed in their direction, but after some manoeuvring it was evident the unknown ship was possibly two hundred feet in length. Not only was she considerably longer than the *Lioness*, she was four masted and twice as wide. Tarsin knew from experience that such a ship, if outfitted for war, could accommodate a thousand men on board.

By midday her colours were recognizable, the vigorously flapping pennants of black and white that of King Arkos' royal navy. Beside her sailed two caravels, similar in length to the *Lioness*, their function merely as escort, but both were armed with mangonels and a multitude of men. Tarsin wiped sweat from his brow, observing the large ship's main mast: a white square-sail with a crowned black jaguar rampant. Sailors worked furiously to trim the canvas, so the larger ship could pull alongside. Shouts and curses followed, for it was obvious the *Lioness* was to be boarded. Looking aft he saw a scowling Captain Vasco, his jovial nature absent, threats and curses rolling off his tongue. As groaning timbers collided, and waves beat against the hulls, he could finally make out the markings topside on the other ship. *Leviathan,* she was aptly named. Even with the vessels now jostling alongside each other, held by grappling hooks and pikes, he had to crane his neck to peer at the *Leviathan* amidships.

Captain Vasco and his crew formed a small circle by the main mast, many of the men carrying cutlasses by their side. Ruvin Ciricello and his mercenaries stood by, swords belted at their waist and violence in their eyes.

It took some time, but eventually a plank was lowered to the *Lioness* and soldiers, not sailors, began to board from the *Leviathan*. Amongst them strode a tall man, his chin beardless but a blonde, swooping moustache all too prominent. He wore a long-sleeved black coat with style, a white neckerchief bundled at his throat, and a tricorn hat atop his head. His white trousers sported a charcoal stripe down the side, his knee length boots were black and buckled silver, intimidating yet roguishly handsome.

'If there is a Captain Jarvis Vasco aboard ship,' said the tall blonde man with a deep voice, 'then I would ask him to step forward.'

Captain Vasco did as bid, moving easily between the men to stand alone. 'I am Captain Vasco,' he replied, standing with back straight. 'And who might I have the pleasure of entertaining aboard my ship, with your grapples and pikes and pretty soldiers to boot?'

Tarsin took a quick look at the massed ranks of men lining the *Leviathan's* decks. Balanced crossbows pointed their way, held by unflinching men wearing leather caps. Behind them stood rank upon rank of armed men, sabres held across their breasts, standing at the ready. Nearby, the caravels circled like sharks in the water.

'Admiral John Rhys of the Royal Navy,' was the quick reply. 'You've been absent from these waters for some years, Captain. Would you mind telling me where you've been?'

'Not sure it's any of your business, Admiral,' was the curt reply. 'I've papers detailing goods of trade, mainly from the south, and I've passengers aboard bound for Bastion.'

Admiral Rhys motioned several of his men to check the ship, only to have their way barred by half-a-dozen of Captain Vasco's sailors. All the while timbers groaned and scraped, the bound ships screaming their displeasure.

'I'd let the men past, Captain. There is a war underway and any ship sailing towards Bastion will be thoroughly searched and possibly quarantined, by order of the king himself. Failure to comply will result in all goods being confiscated and the men aboard imprisoned. The ship will then become property of the kingdom.'

'Over my dead body it will!'

'It can be arranged, Captain!' the Admiral's voice bellowed as a score of crossbowmen aimed bolts at Captain Vasco. 'Now stand down and allow my men to complete their task. Unless you have a noble of the realm on board who can vouch for your ship and its contents, matters will transpire at my discretion!'

Silence descended between the two parties, Captain Vasco furious, Admiral Rhys standing tall. Tarsin thought the two would come to blows, anything to release the tension stifling the overcrowded ship. Instead he pushed past his men and moved to stand beside Captain Vasco, his eyes seeking those of Admiral Rhys. 'I can vouch for the ship and its crew,' Tarsin said.

Admiral Rhys opened his mouth, the words "Who are you?" on the tip of his tongue. Only his eyes widened at the last instant, recognition almost rendering him speechless.

'Tarsin,' he finally said after a brief pause.

'John Rhys,' Tarsin watched as the Admiral looked him over, noticing the slight pause as his eyes alighted on his Rykedian broadsword buckled at his waist. The two men were of similar height, although Tarsin was broader of shoulder, but it was clear they were both swordsmen.

'How long has it been,' the Admiral uttered as he met his gaze, 'three, four years?'

'Three, or thereabouts,' Tarsin replied, watching his old friend, knowing his mind was working overtime to recall their last words together. Tarsin doubted he'd remember. Hell, he couldn't remember himself. All he could recall was confusion and blind anger coupled with fear and hatred. It was not a time Tarsin revisited by choice. 'The *Lioness* has a clean bill of health, Admiral Rhys, you have my word,' the words jolted the Admiral out of his reverie.

'Truly?' the Admiral's eyebrows inched higher. 'And what of you, Tarsin, why have you chosen to return to Bastion?'

'It's not by choice, Admiral. I'd rather be someplace else.'

'Wouldn't we all? And yet the men you see lining the deck,' Tarsin followed the sweep of the Admiral's hand as it encompassed the *Leviathan*, 'are duty bound. They cannot simply walk away when events go awry.'

Tarsin felt his heart quicken, could sense dark thoughts fashioned from despair begin to rise within. 'Leave it, Rhys,' he said, teeth firmly clenched. 'This is neither the time nor the place.'

'No, you are right, but the king needs our help, more so than ever before. We are at war, Tarsin, and if your path is set for Bastion, I'll need to know your intentions. I'll not have you swagger into the Holy City with anger clouding your mind.'

'My mind was never clouded, Rhys. We were betrayed, you know it's true.'

'Not by King Arkos, Tarsin. There are others behind the scenes, devilish foes with wicked design. Arkos Vantos would never betray his most loyal men. We swore an oath to protect him, why would he see us dead?'

'It's complicated.'

'Really? Or is that what you tell yourself, so you can sleep at night!' The Admiral's eyes were alight with intent and the hint of a smirk twitched beneath his moustache. 'Listen,' he raised a hand as he realised who he was talking too, 'we could use your skills in the weeks to come. The others would welcome you, you know that. The door will always be left ajar for one such as you.'

'Griffith lives, then?'

'Aye, he lives, and has taken command of the Sceptres, those who patrol the city's streets. We are all tasked with duty to the king, as before.'

Tarsin closed his eyes, felt the ship rock from side-to-side. The faint mutterings of his men drifted in the background and he could feel their eyes on his back. He wondered what they thought, wished he'd never agreed to return to Bastion. He opened his eyes, looked at the man he'd fought alongside for more than a decade. 'I'll not serve the king, you must know that.'

'Fine, so long as you do him no harm. We'll not stand idly by if such is your path.'

'You cannot stop me if it is,' Tarsin growled back. He could feel his blood burning in his veins despite his attempt to remain calm. He had no quarrel with John Rhys, or Cale Griffith, but neither fully understood the depth of betrayal he'd suffered.

'Is your hatred for the man so strong, then, even after all these years?'

'Perhaps,' Tarsin waved a hand. He was tiring of the conversation and sweat was beginning to bead on his forehead. 'Perhaps hatred is all I have left to hold onto.'

'What of friendship? Cale Griffith was your closest friend.'

'I have no friends, Rhys, not anymore. It's easier this way.'

The Admiral nodded, but Tarsin could see he was far from satisfied. For a moment, he wondered if he'd pushed the man too hard. Captain Vasco still stood to his left, his huge hands nervously flexing as he waited for an outcome. Tarsin didn't wish for anymore difficulties but found it hard not to vent his anger. After a minute's silence, Admiral John Rhys reached for his tricorn hat, swept it off with a flourish and wiped his brow with the back of his hand.

'You say it's easier your way, Tarsin, but life is never easy. Once you realize such a fact you'll embrace us once again. Until such time, the door remains open.' The Admiral spun to his gathered men, motioning for them to return to the *Leviathan*. As he reached the plank, he paused, turned about and shared one last glance. 'Word will be sent to Cale Griffith of your arrival, Tarsin. He'll seek you out; offer you the same advice as I. You should listen to him.' He turned his back on him, a moment later he was gone.

Tarsin remained where he was, his feet planted firmly to the deck as men raced to disengage the two ships. Captain Vasco barked orders above the din, his voice fuelled with rage. Tarsin listened to the commotion but felt a cold dread settle on his shoulders. He told Rhys his mind was clear, that it wasn't clouded. Truthfully though, he was more confused and uncertain than ever before.

'What was that all about?' Ruvin asked as he moved to stand by his side. 'You obviously know the Admiral?'

'I did once, many years ago. Not anymore.'

'But he'll let us pass; let us sail towards Bastion?'

'Aye, he'll let us pass. He fears the consequences if he doesn't.'

'And what are the consequences?'

'Death,' Tarsin said with conviction, his hand resting on the pommel of his broadsword.

Ruvin Ciricello nodded and walked away. Tarsin watched his retreating back, knew his employer disapproved. For three years they'd worked amicably together, but now their relationship was strained. As far as he knew, Ruvin hadn't mentioned their talk concerning the king with anyone else, but he feared tongues would ask questions now.

He sighed as he watched the last of the soldiers climb aboard the *Leviathan*, saw the grapples and pikes disengage. The two ships parted with a final groan and shortly after sails were hoisted to flap noisily in the wind. He turned for his quarters; hoping seclusion would bring sought after answers. Yet deep down he knew they'd remain elusive. If John Rhys and Cale Griffith believed the king's word, then who was Tarsin to deny it as truth?

He pushed his cabin door inward and fell onto his bunk.

And the *Lioness* sailed towards Bastion.

CHAPTER SIX

'Is it time to begin?'

Tarsin spun about to see Jarred standing behind him, a wild grin spread across his face. Captain Vasco proclaimed Bastion to be no more than three days fine sailing, yet the lad was still keen to continue his training with the sword; possibly too keen, he thought. Yet it was how it always began. He could remember his first week of training well enough; remember the thrill of holding a sword in his hand for the very first time. Jarred expressed the same enthusiasm, his eyes alight with hunger.

Only now the real pain of learning was about to begin.

'Sit down, Jarred,' Tarsin motioned towards the rail. They were aft of the ship, tucked behind the mizzen mast. Apart from a coil of rope and some wooden pegs, there was enough space for them to practice. As the lad took a seat he glanced towards the sky. It was pale blue today, not a cloud in sight. Perfect conditions for what he had planned.

'I'm stepping up your training as of today,' Tarsin said as he sat before Jarred. 'It's time I taught you the fundamentals of swordsmanship, beginning with you.'

'With me?'

'Aye, you and your body,' Tarsin poked the young man in the chest. 'To become a swordsman requires certain skills, one of those being strength. You also need to be flexible, have incredible endurance and be light of foot. You also need to be clever.'

'Clever? In what way?'

'In many ways, lad: in reading your opponent, in calculating your strokes and their angles. You'll need to memorize certain methods of defence, to be able to think swiftly and assess your opponent's patterns of attack.

'The object of learning the sword is primarily to defend yourself; to protect your life. You need to be able to listen to instinct and realise it for what it is. I had an instructor once, a Rykedian master named Du Weng Sai. He continually reminded us that "the sharper your mind, the sharper your sword". I still believe him.'

Tarsin saw the look of interest on Jarred's face change to one of reflection. His eyes narrowed, his mouth hung slightly agape. The fire in his eyes did not dim, though, which was a sign of commitment if nothing else.

'I never realised there was so much involved,' Jarred finally said.

'There is, lad, more than you can imagine if you wish to become skilled. I doubt there are more than a handful of men within Dervae who have endured the sort of training I've experienced. At your age, I'd been learning the sword for three years. I trained thrice daily, hours at a time, with only a single day each week set aside for rest and recuperation. On that day, I was still expected to study.'

Jarred's eyes opened wide. 'Three times daily!'

'Aye, but it wasn't all sword work. Much of what we learnt concerned strengthening and conditioning of the body. Some of which I'll teach today.'

There was a gentle nod of the head in response. Tarsin could see much of what he explained was daunting to the young man, but then it had been daunting for him all those years past. He'd also been the youngest by several years, a fact he thought would compound his learning curve. Instead he'd thrived under the added pressure of competing with men stronger than he, despite enduring taunts associated with his age. By the time he was eighteen he'd grown into his tall, lanky frame, to become strong of arm and incredibly quick. Sixty men were initially chosen to study under the tutelage of Lord Henrickson and Du Weng Sai for the express purpose of serving the king. Little more than a third would eventually be chosen for such an honour. Two years later, at twenty years of age, Tarsin was already the fastest blade in the kingdom.

'Here,' he leant over and picked up two wooden pegs. They were hollow, about a foot in length. Once placed in Jarred's hands he reached for the coiled rope. It was a slender piece and

Tarsin was able to thread it inside the pegs with ease. He then tightened each end with a knot, creating a line more than six feet in length.

'What is this for?' asked Jarred.

'It's called a skipping rope,' Tarsin grabbed a wooden peg in each hand, then stepped back two paces. 'Now, watch and learn.'

He began to skip, his wrists rotating with practiced rhythm, his feet barely leaving the wooden deck. The rope whizzed through the air, faster and faster until the line was a blur. Tarsin controlled his breathing, kept his head level, his back straight. There was symmetry in his actions. He felt at peace for the first time since Al-Za'im, felt his dark thoughts drift away.

One hundred times he flicked the rope beneath his feet. Then he stopped.

'Now it's your turn, Jarred,' he passed the wooden pegs over. The young man stood and swung the rope over his head once, but his feet caught the loop as it hit the deck. It took four more attempts before he finally completed one rotation.

'Good,' Tarsin clapped, then moved to place a hand on Jarred's back. 'Keep your posture firm, push your shoulders back. That's it.' He stepped away, allowing Jarred some room. 'I want you to complete twenty consecutive jumps before you can rest.'

'Twenty! I'll be here all day.'

'No, you won't,' Tarsin grinned. He recalled saying something similar all those years ago, only he'd been asked to complete fifty rotations.

'What exactly does skipping rope have to do with swordsmanship?'

'It will enhance your balance and coordination, increase your stamina and strengthen your wrists. It will also encourage you to be light on your feet.'

'Is that all?'

'No, it will also teach you to count.'

'I can count,' Jarred frowned, his blonde eyebrows narrowing.

'Good,' Tarsin smiled as he spun about, keen to leave the young man to his task. He waved a hand in the air as he walked away and then called over his shoulder, 'then I suggest you start counting now, you need to reach twenty.'

A sailor's curse rolled off the young man's tongue as he walked away, but it was soon followed by the slap of rope against the deck. Once, twice, three times.

Then it began again.

*

'Land ahoy!'

'Where away, sailor,' Ruvin heard Captain Vasco bellow back.

'Dead ahead, Captain, on the horizon. I can see the twinkling of Aston's Tear itself.'

Ruvin, standing near the helm, could almost hear a perceptible sigh permeate the ship as men welcomed the news. Aston's Tear, the shining capstone of the great pyramid central to Bastion lay ahead, less than a day's sailing. The men, sailors and mercenaries alike, were excited and Ruvin knew hard drink and soft flesh were at the forefront of their thoughts.

Several orders were belayed to the men, and within moments the *Lioness* became a hive of activity. Word even reached the bilge where a handful of souls kept the ship from taking on too much water. Finally, after years of labour, they were about to return home.

'Less than a day, yes?'

Ruvin jumped, not having heard Tarsin reach his side from amidships. 'Gods man, where did you spring from?'

'Your pardon, Ruvin, I did not mean to startle you.'

Ruvin composed himself, the lines about his eyes hinting at a smile, despite the fright. 'Yes,' he finally said, 'less than a day.'

Tarsin seemed nonplussed, his emotions difficult to judge, but Ruvin thought he saw a minor tightening of the jaw, as if the man's teeth had clamped firmly shut. Almost a fortnight had passed since the two men had spoken of Tarsin's vendetta against the king, and the words exchanged during that time were succinct, to say the least.

'I see you have much on your mind, Tarsin Va,' Ruvin scratched his neck, hoping his shirt wasn't infested with lice.

He'd heard men complaining earlier of their discomfit and couldn't help but feel a tingling across his skin. He'd already vowed to burn his clothes the moment he made landfall. 'Tell me,' he continued, pushing images of lice far from his mind, 'do thoughts of the king still haunt you, or is there something else I should be aware of before we make port?'

Tarsin looked out to sea, and Ruvin knew his memories were of another time. 'My last days in Bastion were . . . unpleasant,' he finally offered.

Ruvin recalled his earlier plea to Tarsin, one he'd made weeks ago. 'Do you still plan to accompany me to Irongate with the relic?'

'Yes, I'll be by your side.'

The man who had been so solid and commanding whilst fleeing Al-Za'im now appeared uncertain; distracted even. He looked tired; a man short of much needed sleep. Ruvin feared to probe deeper, but instinctively felt now was the time to ask those questions he longed to hear answers too. 'I know you're not a noble of the realm, Tarsin, and yet Admiral John Rhys left the *Lioness* as if he'd been instructed by the king himself.'

The swordsman offered half a smile, but Ruvin could see it was forced.

'So,' Ruvin pressed further, 'you were obviously tied to King Arkos in some capacity.'

Tarsin offered a stern look.

'Do not be so surprised, Tarsin, many heard your conversation with the Admiral, and putting pieces of a puzzle together is what I do best.' He watched as Tarsin's shoulders relaxed, although his brow remained knotted. 'May I ask what role you performed for the king? I may not have been a regular at court, but I am well informed. So too is the Brotherhood of One, of which I'm a member. Swordsmen of your standing do not just appear, my friend. A man of your talent is a rare commodity, but one utilized with intent. How is it that I'd never heard of you before?'

The swordsman shifted his feet with the rolling deck. 'Because you were never meant to hear of me, Ruvin Ciricello.'

Ruvin tilted his head, 'Whatever do you mean?'

The swordsman kept silent for some time, his gaze held by the faint outline of Bastion on the horizon. When he spoke, Ruvin had to remind himself what his question was to begin with. 'I belonged to an order of men, an order who pledged allegiance to the king and the king alone,' he began. 'We were not tasked with upholding the virtues of the Dervani people or required to protect them in times of need. We simply watched those close to King Arkos, watched those who came into his court. We were his eyes and ears; his sword and shield.

'We were known to only a handful of men, and to them we were called the Unseen.'

'The Unseen?' Ruvin had never heard the name, which came as a surprise.

'Aye,' Tarsin spoke with a heavy voice, 'we were a group of men trained to be the very best at martial combat, our sole duty to keep King Arkos alive.'

'How many were you?'

'We numbered twenty-four, most with secondary duties tying us close to the king and his court. At any one time two of our order was near, hidden from the eyes of the masses, but close enough to prevent danger from striking unexpectedly.'

Ruvin watched Tarsin move to starboard and grasp the rail with tightly clenched hands. He followed, standing alongside his Master of Swords as he swept his eyes across the blue sea. He was still uncertain of Tarsin's tale; found the secrecy behind the Unseen quite remarkable. Still, he had no reason to doubt Tarsin's words for the man had no reason to lie.

'What of the Palaceguard?' Ruvin wondered if the greatest knights of Dervae knew anything about the Unseen. 'Is it not their duty to protect the King?'

Tarsin lifted his eyes. 'Their duty lies in the protection of Highcastle, no matter who sits the throne. Our duty was more personal. It may come as a surprise, but there are those amongst the Palaceguard who would rather a jaguar not rule the kingdom. Lucius Vupello, cousin to the king, has declared on more than one occasion that a fox would be more aptly suited; he the obvious choice, no less.'

'Is Lucius Vupello not their Captain?'

'He is, and a fine swordsman, although the man's aspirations far outweigh his potential.'

'Does King Arkos know of his desire?'

'Aye, it is why he keeps him close. As Captain of the Palaceguard, Lucius' duties prevent him from stirring up too much mischief. Arkos was always a canny man, but as the years passed, he inevitably became a fearful one. Hence his need to surround himself with loyal, strong men: men beholden to no other who for all intents and purposes, did not exist.'

Ruvin shook his head and leant against the rail by Tarsin's side. He had no idea what sort of altercation passed between Tarsin and the king, but he feared it to be substantial. One did not flee over a simple misunderstanding. And yet his colleagues, Admiral John Rhys and Cale Griffith, did not share his view. No wonder the swordsman was confused. To compound the matter further he'd mentioned his fear of killing the king if confronted, but the possibility of his own death was likewise imminent. Few men could face Arkos Vantos alone, especially if he was fearful. He would have men on hand to lend aid if he was threatened, men such as the Palaceguard: men of steel. Returning to Bastion could very well see Tarsin put to the sword.

Ruvin certainly didn't need any complications upon arriving in the Holy City.

'Admiral John Rhys mentioned he'd send word to Cale Griffith detailing your arrival,' Tarsin nodded confirmation. 'So, what are we likely to face once we make landfall?'

Ruvin could see the swordsman muse over the question and wondered if he was truly being thoughtful, although as the minutes passed, he wondered if he really cared.

'Cale Griffith is an unknown quantity,' he eventually said. 'He is a man of inspiration on occasion, sometimes rash. He'll most certainly have eyes set upon us, but as far as making a scene, I doubt he'll bother.'

'Can you be certain of his actions?'

'No,' Tarsin sighed, 'but we were friends once, he'll believe we are still. He'll not come for me with swords and chains.'

Ruvin shifted his gaze to his cabin on the far side of the main deck, finding the elaborately carved door amongst those sailors hard at work. He envisaged the relic he'd stowed within his room, nestled in the large chest at the foot of his bed. Too much effort had been put into its retrieval for him to risk losing it now. As soon as they made landfall, he'd vowed to set out for Irongate, to make haste for the old watchtower that now served as the Brotherhood's residence.

Tarsin's past was providing more headaches and uncertainties than he cared for, though, and thoughts of setting him loose already crossed his mind. Yet the man had saved his life. He wouldn't be here, less than a day's sailing from Bastion, if it wasn't for the swordsman. He owed him. He couldn't simply cast him adrift.

'You say your order of men was called the Unseen,' Ruvin changed the subject, seeking to clarify some doubts he still harboured.

'Yes.'

'Am I right in suggesting Admiral John Rhys is a member?'

'You are,' Tarsin shared a withering look, one hinting at silence, 'although the order is no more. It was disbanded before we met aboard the *Lioness.*'

'Disbanded! Why?'

'Because the Unseen were close to extinction, Ruvin Ciricello. We were once twenty-four of the finest blades in Dervae. Then King Arkos sent us on a mission north to eradicate a perceived threat to the throne. When we returned, the Unseen numbered five.'

'Five! What was the threat?'

Tarsin sighed, and Ruvin could see the swordsman was struggling with an inner turmoil that sought to break him.

'The threat was a coven of witches residing in Benwith,' he began. 'For reasons unknown, we were summarily dismissed as the king's protectors and sent away as the king's assassins. Our task was to root out the cunning folk and put them to the sword.'

'Did you succeed?'

'Not entirely.'

'So, you blame King Arkos for your failure?'

Tarsin shifted his feet, then clenched his fists tight. 'We were ill prepared for such an encounter, Ruvin.' He wiped sweat from his brow and turned to the side to avoid the sun in his eyes. He paused to gather his breath, and when he continued, his voice was thick with emotion. 'The coven knew we were coming. They were lying in wait for us.'

Ruvin's eyes widened, 'How could they know?'

'I have my theories.'

The cool breeze sweeping across the deck did little to relieve Ruvin's florid cheeks. Like Tarsin, he turned his back on the sun and looked out to sea, tasting salt on the wind. He felt as if his senses were on fire, heightened, as it were, due to the tale Tarsin wove. Never did he envisage such a turn of events, nor expect his Master of Swords to be carrying such a burden.

'What of Cale Griffith, the man now claimed to be Captain of the Sceptres,' Ruvin saw the truth in Tarsin's eyes before he asked the question, 'was he also a member of this illustrious group?'

'Yes,' Tarsin spoke the word quietly, although it sounded like a hiss. 'Cale Griffith is one of five who returned. But I lost nineteen men in a short amount of time, Ruvin.' Ruvin could sense Tarsin needed to lift the weight off his chest before it crushed him altogether. He knew from experience such burdens had a habit of forcing a man to attempt the ridiculous and revenge, especially when clouded by anger, certainly fell into such a category.

Something Tarsin said piqued his interest further, though. 'You said *you* lost nineteen men.'

He was greeted with silence, and Ruvin felt for him then; felt like a father who wished nothing more than to help purge his son of his fear and doubt. Then Tarsin spoke, his back straight and with steel in his voice, 'Aye, I did,' the two men locked eyes, and Ruvin could see pain swirling in their dark blue depths. 'I was First Sword of the Unseen, my friend.

'I was their Captain.'

*

Cale Griffith sat back in his heavy chair: an elaborate piece carved from oak and peered about the office he'd come to call home. It was cramped, especially for a man as large as Griffith. He stood six feet three inches tall, was barrel-chested and thick of arm. A frizzled mop of auburn hair added height to his already prodigious size, and his bushy beard lent a grizzly semblance not out of place on the big man.

Yet he could feel the lines of worry creasing his aging face as he re-read the handful of reports he'd discovered piled on his desk this morning. Most concerned the war to the south in some manner; detailing reports of infiltrators caught attempting to enter the city, or the harassment of southerners openly in the streets. The last was a concern, for not all dusk-skinned southerners called Al-Za'im home and many had ties closer to Dervae than they did with the city-states of the south. Zealous behaviour of such magnitude was unwarranted in the Holy City. He would stamp it out with a ruthlessness many of Bastion's citizens had come to expect.

Another report detailed the assignment of men-of-the-watch to the gates of the city. They were to be rotated daily during times of war, their presence a necessary deterrent to those of ill repute. Patrols throughout the city would also be tripled and those manning the wall were to be reinforced with the king's own soldiers. It was to be a complete saturation for as long as it took. Griffith didn't like it, for he knew complaints would come thick and fast, but he didn't have a choice.

Yet despite the number of reports requiring his attention, a small slip of paper folded in his breast pocket continued to intrude upon his thoughts. It was a note from Admiral John Rhys aboard the *Leviathan*, sent by carrier pigeon and handed to him a day ago. He reached for it now, opening it carefully as able with his ill-suited thick fingers. The scrawling letters were barely legible, which confirmed the writing to be courtesy of the Admiral. Like Griffith, the man was born to fight, and like Griffith, his quillwork lacked elegance. Mind you, as Griffith re-read the note he realised few men could have kept a steady hand. Just mentioning the name Tarsin Va sent a shiver down his spine.

'Tarsin Va,' he said the name softly, yet felt it reverberate about the small room. Then he looked at the note once more. *Tarsin Va bound for Bastion. Lioness. Watch him.* The Admiral's initials were printed in the corner, a little flurry at the end of the *R* all the validity Griffith needed. He placed the slip of paper on the desk and scratched his beard. He didn't need this, not now. Bastion was already in a state of turmoil. With war raging in the south and talk of plague in the north, fear and confusion was to be expected. Yet now with the death of the king's two sons a fortnight past, the entire kingdom was poised to raise arms and march towards the desert. And here in the capital, as expected, exacerbation far outweighed common sense.

He pushed his heavy frame out of the chair and moved to the only window: a shuttered square allowing Griffith to observe the lower docks from above. His office was nestled within a watchtower situated near Southgate, fifty feet above ground and encased in bluestone. He pulled the shutters open and squinted until his eyes adjusted, then peered out across the Bay of Pennants.

Countless sails of myriad colour stared back at him as ships of all size and make sought either a berth or a clear passage free. For Griffith, it was chaos unchecked. Amongst it all, somewhere, sailed the *Lioness*, due to make port this day if he was any judge. He moved back to his desk, opened a drawer and reached for a flask. Then he sat back down in his chair, pulled out the cork and took a long swallow, grimacing as fiery liquid raced down his throat.

'Boy!' he yelled once he finished his mouthful. The door to his office opened with a slight screech to reveal a young freckled lad no more than sixteen years of age.

'Yes, my Lord,' Griffith saw the boy lower his eyes. He didn't expect anything less. The boys sent to run errands for him changed daily. With the war in full swing he neither cared where they came from nor what their names were.

'I need you to find Setorious for me,' he said, watching the boy nod vigorously. 'Do you know Lieutenant Setorious, boy?'

'Yes, my Lord,' the head continued to nod. 'Black hair, round face and he carries a steel-shod staff.'

'Aye, that's him. Find him for me and tell him Griffith needs to speak with him. Tell him it's urgent.'

'Yes, my Lord,' a quick bow and he was gone, the door closing behind him.

Griffith sank further into his chair and reached for his flask once more. It was early to be drinking, but he had so few comforts these days. He took another swallow then set the flask loudly upon his desk. 'Tarsin Va,' he repeated, thinking back to the man he once called friend. It seemed so long ago now. Both were hand-picked by Lord Henrickson; Griffith as a seasoned veteran, Tarsin little more than a boy but incredibly skilled. They were part of a small group of men gathered for a single purpose: to protect the king. They swore an oath and became the Unseen: men lost to society but their commitment integral to its continuation. For years they trained together, Griffith spreading a paternal wing about the lad as he matured into a man. He taught him how to fight, spoke of the hardships to come and the lessons to be learned. Treated him like the son he never sired. Then they fought together in the north; were fortunate to come home alive. Yet there were times, more frequent of late, when Griffith felt he'd be better off dead.

Now he sat in a cramped office, nearing fifty years of age, with a desk and a mountain of parchment before him. It was far from the man he used to be; far from the man he still wished to be.

His eyes roamed back to the flask. The fiery liquid called to him, enticed him. He knew he couldn't resist its sweet scent anymore, failed to see why he should even bother. He'd seen the other side of death, was cursed to relive the horror every moment he closed his eyes. Thick fingers closed about the flask as he raised it to his mouth. He was about to take another swallow when a gentle tap arrived at his door.

'Come in,' he called, placing the flask in the draw.

The door opened and Lieutenant Setorious walked in, a well-built man in his forties with an air of calm surrounding his comely features. He was attired for duty, his chequered yellow and black surcoat draping chain mail, his steel helmet nestled in the crook of an arm.

'That was quick,' Griffith saw the boy move to close the door.

'I was on my way to see you,' Setorious stepped towards the only vacant chair and sat opposite his Captain as he placed his helmet on the desk. A weathered hand brushed black hair behind an ear.

'You have news, then,' Griffith arched an eyebrow.

The look Setorious returned didn't bode well. 'Lucius Vupello has sealed Highcastle,' he began.

'He's what?'

'He claims the king's life is in mortal danger and with both prince's dead, fears an attack is imminent.'

'Where did Vupello garner such information?'

'He didn't elaborate. But he has the support of the Palaceguard.'

Griffith stroked his beard, his eyes drifting to his warhammer resting against the wall in the corner. It was a well-crafted weapon: the haft and head both cast from Herkosian steel, lending it a ruddy tinge. He'd named it *Bloodstain* long ago. Like the flask, it called to him and spoke of better times. Right now, the urge to walk over and hoist the hammer was close to overpowering. He didn't particularly like Lucius Vupello. In fact, he hated the arrogant man. The thought of smashing *Bloodstain* into his hard face was an encouraging one. 'The Palaceguard number only two hundred,' he said, knowing he could muster ten times as many in little more than an hour.

'Aye, but they've been reinforced by his own personal guard. House Vupello has been known to put more than a thousand men in the field when the need arises.'

'Anok and Eli!' Griffith cursed and slammed his huge fist down hard. 'Those men should be south fighting the war! Is there anything else I need to be made aware of?'

'Only trivial matters, nothing we cannot handle.' Setorious flexed his fingers together and cracked his knuckles. 'Oh, one other thing,' he said, 'the thieves of Bastion have been unusually quiet.'

It was not what Griffith wished to hear. The absence of thieves on the streets could only spell trouble. Whatever they were brewing could only be detrimental to the city and the folk who called her home. He looked towards his warhammer once again, longed to be out in the field with his weapon singing through the air. He craved the surge of blood in his veins, wished to feel alive. 'I'll go see the king myself,' he finally uttered, tearing his gaze away from his weapon. 'Vupello can't deny me an audience with his majesty.'

'It's a risk,' Setorious voiced the obvious.

'In a few days time it will be, but not now. Vupello will be too nervous to try anything foolish. I'll speak to Arkos; find out what Vupello really desires.'

The two were silent for a moment, their thoughts crowded. Eventually Griffith remembered why he'd asked for Setorious in the first place. 'I need to ask a favour of you.'

'Go ahead.'

'I need you and four others to tail a man for me. Don't let him out of your sight, and certainly don't confront him.'

'Is he a swordsman, then?' Griffith could see Setorious' interest piqued.

'He is, the finest I've ever seen. You'll know him, for he carries a Rykedian broadsword with a swept hilt. It's an expensive piece. I doubt there is a handful in the entire world as finely made.' He could see the details were not lost on Setorious. The man knew his blades, and Rykedian broadswords were difficult to find let alone commission.

'Where will I find this man?'

Griffith cleared his throat. 'He'll come ashore later today, having arrived on a ship named the *Lioness*. His name is Tarsin Va: tall, broad of shoulder and blue-eyed.'

'How long shall we tail him for?'

'Until I deem otherwise,' Griffith said, not knowing what to expect. His last vision of Tarsin was of a man consumed by anger as he left the king's throne room. That was three years ago. He hadn't seen him since. 'If he makes for Highcastle, send word.'

'Is he likely to be trouble?'

'Possibly, it's hard to say.'

Setorious rose to his feet. 'If he is trouble, what shall we do?'

Griffith closed his eyes, then opened them with an accompanying sigh. 'I don't know, Setorious,' he said, reaching for the flask hidden in his draw. 'I truly do not know. Just tail him for now.'

Setorious lifted his helmet and placed it on his head, then tied the strap beneath his chin. Griffith raised his flask and took a swallow, savouring the taste of forgetfulness.

'Hard night?' Setorious asked as he made for the door.

Griffith finished his mouthful and looked the man in the eye. He could see concern in his gaze, briefly wished he had the nerve to refuse the drink in his presence. 'Aye,' he said, his voice sombre as he placed the flask back in the draw, 'and it'll become harder still. Dark times are upon us, my friend, mark my words.'

Setorious offered a nod and left, closing the door behind him.

And Griffith reached for his flask once more.

CHAPTER SEVEN

The sun shone from a cloudless sky.

Arkos Vantos stood on the balcony, his private quarters behind him. He'd already stripped his robe of office from his slumped frame, discarding it along with a mornings worth of countless bickering and administrating with his aides. There was a madness creeping into Highcastle, a madness contrived by his cousin: Lucius Vupello. The closing of Highcastle to outsiders was a rash and ill-conceived idea, one doomed to fail despite the captain of the Palaceguard's assurances. Whatever hold Vupello strived for in the coming days was clearly based on a presumption. Arkos knew Vupello coveted the throne, had done so for more years than he cared to remember. He also knew his cousin had ties with the witch. In what capacity he was uncertain, but his information regarding the matter was sound. Lucius Vupello may believe himself cunning and adept, but Arkos knew the game he was playing. Whatever surprises his cousin had conjured for the coming days; he'd be prepared. He hadn't spent his time idle whilst the witch and her abomination crept close. He'd made plans of his own. As he'd told Cale Griffith and Lloyd Henrickson earlier in the day, he knew what was to come.

I know what's to come.

The thought stayed with him, clung to his mind like a blood-sucking leech. What would the people of Dervae say if they knew their king was aware of the approaching darkness? Would they ask for protection? Would they beg for salvation? He sighed, knowing only too well their reaction if told the circumstances. "Where is the proof?" they would yell. "Why should we believe you?" Or worse, they would accuse him of being mad and hang him from the ramparts. Yet the debate still raged within, even as he wondered how to explain to his people that their homes and families were in mortal danger.

Deep down he knew such confusion was tearing his sanity apart. The rage he felt, the anger at not knowing if his choice was correct, was set to erupt. It almost surfaced this very morning, with Lucius Vupello declaring Highcastle sealed from without. It had taken all his will to stay his hand, to prevent his throne room from becoming red-stained with gore.

With an effort Arkos swung his gaze away from the afternoon sun and peered down into the courtyard, taking a deep breath to calm his already frayed nerves. Below sat the Pit; a square yard hemmed in by four windowless walls and accessed by a passage from below. For close to fifteen years he'd come to stand in this very spot, watching the men of the Unseen go through their paces as Lloyd Henrickson and Du Weng Sai taught them necessary skills. It was a secret place within the walls of Highcastle, known only to those who participated in the training. Even the balcony he stood on was accessed via a sliding wall from his chamber, the twist of a brass sconce by his bedside necessary to unlock the mechanism to allow entry.

For a moment, with his eyes almost closed, he dared to dream he could see the twirling shapes of the Unseen as they paced the dusty flagstones below. Back and forth they'd step, swords held high before sweeping in practiced arcs, Du Weng Sai yelling with his thick Rykedian accent. A slight smile twitched the corner of his mouth. Du Weng Sai had been a master of the blade until the day he died. He appeared to be no more than a shrivelled old man during his time in Highcastle, his long white hair draping bony shoulders, his face creased by time and his narrow eyes mere slits of darkness. To the court delegates he was a slant-eyed advisor from the east, but in truth he was admitted to Highcastle for a dual purpose: the first of which was to mould the Unseen into the deadliest killers in Dervae.

It was some fifteen years in the making, one Du Weng Sai did not see to the end. He was an old man when he first arrived at Highcastle, a master of the blade from Rykedia commissioned one last time. Behind him spanned a generation of martial prowess; ranging from time spent as a member of the Holy Swords of Rykedia to a period of legend with the Du Qual Assassins in the south. Coupled with Lloyd Henrickson, the two shaped the Unseen into men of strength fused with finesse, their minds conditioned with killer instinct.

It had been Arkos' dream that the Unseen, when the time was right, would see an end to the vile witch known as Avra. The realization that he stood here now, on this very balcony, peering down at an empty yard devoid of his beloved Unseen brought tears to his eyes.

'I prayed it wouldn't end like this,' he said under his breath, his hands gripping the balcony rail tight. His eyes strained to see the shadowed flagstones below. Gone were the phantom shapes of his Unseen twirling in unison. All he saw now was hard, stone tiles. His feet shifted nervously. *It would be so easy to fall,* he thought. It was a thirty-foot drop. Thoughts of his wife and two sons grappled within his mind for purchase, clawing to be remembered and not forgotten. Weeks had passed since the death of his sons and he already struggled to picture their faces in his mind. A single motion would see him by their side again. He was doomed to die in any case. Would dying a day early change any of his plans? He sighed, then raised a hand to cover his breast as the pain of yearning for his family struck hard. The Pit remained below, enticing him. It would take but a moment, a leap of faith, before his head split like a melon and his worries ceased to be. Perhaps then he could feel content. Perhaps then he would see their faces one final time.

'Your majesty,' said a voice from behind.

Arkos let his white-knuckled grip of the rail ease, then spun about to see Hector, his manservant, standing silently in his white robes.

'Sire, Sir Lloyd Henrickson is without. He requests a moment of your time.'

Arkos stepped in from the balcony and waved a hand in consent, 'Send him in,' he said with a slight tremble to his voice, his mind taking a moment to swim out of darkness.

He waited until Lloyd Henrickson was ushered into the room. The man was agitated, evident by his bristling moustache, yet there was a sparkle in his eyes he'd not seen for some time.

Draped in steel with his long sword belted at his waist, the old soldier stepped forward and shared a tight grin before waiting for Hector to vacate the chamber.

'He is here,' Henrickson said once the door was closed, dispensing with formalities.

For a moment Arkos felt a shiver race down his spine, a dire prelude to Ahriman's imminent arrival.

'I saw him myself, down at the docks.'

A flicker of concern creased his face before he realized who Henrickson was referring to. 'You saw Tarsin Va?' he muttered, his voice catching in his throat.

'Aye, from a distance,' Henrickson replied. 'He disembarked an hour ago from the *Lioness*, as Cale Griffith informed.'

Arkos reflected upon the words spoken by Cale Griffith earlier in the day. The Captain of the Sceptres had barged into Highcastle like a hurricane, three hours after dawn, sweeping past the Palaceguard standing watch as if they were saplings ready to be snapped. There was anger boiling beneath his skin and his red mane seemed to be alight, but by the time he reached the throne room there were a dozen swords drawn and held an inch from his face, forcing him to halt his mad rush. With a command Arkos forced the Palaceguard to disengage, and with a look of contempt he left the throne room with Griffith by his side and headed to his private study. As they arrived he sent word for Henrickson to join them and then listened as Griffith explained the note sent by Admiral John Rhys.

Now the man he sought, the swordsman Tarsin Va, was finally here.

'How did he look?' Arkos finally asked Henrickson with a raise of his eyebrows.

'Well,' Henrickson moved to a side table and poured a glass of water from a silver pitcher. Arkos declined the drink when offered, then waited as his friend took a thirsty swallow. 'Three years may have passed, but he looks the same as ever.'

Arkos smiled inwardly; glad Tarsin Va was still the man he hoped he would be. A second passed before he met Henrickson's eyes and asked, 'Does he still carry the blade?'

'Aye, his Rykedian broad sword sits with him still, his hand never far from its pommel.'

Both men knew how important the sword was, both knew of the sacrifice made to see it fashioned. Ancient arts from lands far abroad were utilized in its construction, arts very few men were privy too. Like Arkos' twin jaguar blades, so too was Tarsin's Rykedian broad sword infused with elements beyond the ken of normal men. It was the second reason why Du Weng Sai was propositioned to help build the Unseen. Not only did his expertise lie in the martial arts, he was also an experienced practitioner of metallurgy and a sword smith of renown. Tarsin's Rykedian broad sword had been presented to him by Du Weng Sai, a gift for being his most promising student.

Henrickson finished his glass of water and poured another. 'He is in the company of Ruvin Ciricello,' he continued, 'a member of the Brotherhood of One. Apparently, they have been south, in Al-Za'im, no less, for the past three years. Upon arrival, they set out for the Oakwood and Stout, where I believe they still reside.' He finished his second glass of water. 'Would you like me to send for him? I can have him here in an hour.'

Arkos almost said yes, for it would be good to see the young man once more. Only he knew it was not to be. The visions he'd experienced suggested they were not to meet again in this life. At this point in time he feared to meddle with events he wasn't entirely sure he understood.

'No, my friend, I do not wish to see him. His path is different from mine, but no less important. I will not disrupt his journey, nor explain to him that which I so desperately wish to explain.'

'None of what you say makes any sense, Arkos. Allow me to bring him before you. You owe him that much.'

'Owe him?' Arkos swung towards Lloyd Henrickson, his blue eyes momentarily baleful, his spirit rekindled. 'I owe no man, Henrickson! All that I have done was for the kingdom, not for me. It is Fate herself who decrees I die here. Despite our kingdom enduring decades of peace during my reign, I've lived a life of fear and violence. I'll die the same way.'

He saw the simmering rage brighten Henrickson's eyes. The swordsman despised the occult and the unknown and talk of Fate and visions unnerved his sense of normality. The tall man with the straight back gritted his teeth, though, and took a step closer, his words barely above a whisper. 'I've known you for more than forty years, Arkos, and never have you accepted Fate's terms. Your life is your own; the paths you tread are yours to choose. You do not have to die here.'

'Enough!' Arkos sliced his hand through the air. 'Highcastle will be my tomb, I have seen it.'

'This is Lucius Vupello's doing, not the goddess of Fate,' Henrickson clenched a fist. 'Allow me to strike him down. No king should be kept prisoner in his own castle. I can have you away from here by this afternoon; far from here. The Palaceguard do not hold every doorway.'

Arkos listened to his friend's words and offered a brief smile in return. 'Leave Lucius Vupello to me,' he said. 'I may be old and tormented, but I still have my wits about me. Before you joined me this morning I spoke at length with Cale Griffith. Be patient. Have a little faith.'

'Easier said than done, Arkos.'

'Aye, it is.' He shared a moment of silence with his closest friend. Minutes passed, torturously slow, whilst images of a crumbling city pervaded his thoughts. 'I'd ask of you a favour,' he finally broke the silence.

'Ask away, my king.'

'I need you to leave the city, tonight, if you can.'

'And where would you have me go?'

'South, my friend,' Arkos replied. 'I need you in Aspenvale by midday tomorrow, where you'll await Lord Beaumont and his men. Once they reach you, you are to return to Bastion with all haste.' The look in Henrickson's eyes betrayed his thoughts. 'You need to trust me with this.'

He heard a grunt in return, but Arkos knew he would comply. A hundred questions might have been on the tip of his tongue, but the swordsman, for a change, didn't know where to begin.

'You will know what to do when you return,' Arkos continued. 'I cannot tell you more.'

'You'd send me south, so you can die alone?' the words were softly spoken.

'No, I'd send you away to save your life.'

'I'd rather be by your side, sire, it is where I belong.'

Arkos shook his head. 'No, Lloyd Henrickson, I need you alive. There will be turmoil in the streets when you return. Your presence will be required, for your authority will be unquestioned. You will need to make order out of the chaos and help support those who've survived.'

A sigh escaped the broad-shouldered man. Arkos could see the strain in his face, could see the extra lines creasing dry skin. He may not have grasped the connotations of their talk, but Arkos knew once Henrickson left his chamber, it would be the last time he ever laid eyes on his friend.

'What of Tarsin Va? Will he need my help?'

'He'll need men he can trust. I've already sent word to John Rhys. Most of our forces sail for Sovarto, some travel by land. Within a day half will turn about and head home. They'll be needed here.'

'What of Prince Rahesh and his forces? We've a war to fight with the southern dogs!'

'Aye, we do,' he said, 'and we shall. But if Bastion falls, then all will be lost.'

The unmistakable sound of a hundred bells chiming came from beyond Highcastle's outer walls. Arkos knew it was two hours past midday yet he had so much to accomplish. There would be scant time for rest, but rest was no longer a requirement. He could rest once he was dead. Rest eternal.

Henrickson held out his hand, seeking to grip that of his king. 'Then I bid you farewell, sire,' he said, and Arkos knew this was goodbye. He'd prepared himself mentally for this moment, told himself to be strong and commanding. He gripped the hand of his friend and brother-in-arms, met his eyes and searched for the right words. They'd spent so many years together; so many years fighting together. Only now it was over. The die had been cast. Frey, goddess of Fate, was in control.

'I don't know what to say, my friend,' Arkos shared a smile.

'There is nothing *to* say, Arkos Vantos,' Henrickson returned, his own eyes glistening. 'I'll see you on the other side.'

*

Tarsin Va adjusted his sword belt and took a seat upon a leather-covered chair.

He was in the private study of a certain elder Cappitus: a white bearded man also known to be a practitioner for the Brotherhood of One. The study was safely nestled within the strong walls of Irongate, a former outer keep perched atop a small rise, now swallowed by the ever-expanding sprawl that was Bastion. A single large table of oak was practically hidden beneath a mountain of scrolls and parchment, whilst the wall behind the table was entirely obscured by shelving straining under the combined weight of hundreds of books and heavy tomes. To his left lay a stone hearth, dry timber set, whilst to his right sat the only window, a square framed piece allowing shafts of light to illuminate an otherwise dark and dusty room. At present the elder was busy at his table searching through his papers, looking for something of importance to show Ruvin Ciricello, whilst Ruvin himself stood by his side, his hand still clenched tight about the satchel and the relic it contained within.

Tarsin sank further into the comfortable chair. It had been an eventful day. The *Lioness* had docked early in the morning, sliding into port with remarkable ease, as though she'd never been away. With Captain Jarvis Vasco in command of cargo and dressing down the ship, Ruvin had led Tarsin, Jarred and a few mercenaries towards the Oakwood and Stout, an establishment familiar to Ruvin and his men. Tarsin was hesitant at first, yet his sea legs were the least of his concern. For Bastion, the city of his birth, lay before him.

If he felt anything upon stepping ashore, it was certainly not the longing ache of separation come full circle. He was home, it was true, but his heart no longer saw it as such. Now she was simply a city of opportunity. For a moment, he stood amongst the bustling crowd, watching men in shirts of ivory and sable saunter past women in skirts of homespun, all tasked with daily chores. Encompassing all was the sound of waves breaking against stone pillars and the incessant shriek of gulls clamouring for food. Salt air mingled with the smell of decaying seaweed, which in turn was infused with the overpowering stench associated with the Southern Dock Tanneries. This was Bastion, alright; a riot of colour and smell. To many she was a city of marvels, awash with grandeur and flush with wealth as cathedral towers soared high into the sky. But to most she was simply *the* city; a city for the common people where bells in a hundred belfries rang every hour, marking the progress of Father Time.

With barely a moment to adjust to the surging crowd Ruvin led the troop through narrow streets and lanes, avoiding the main thoroughfares for fear of being recognized. Tarsin knew Ruvin's heart would be pounding with anticipation and most definitely a dose of fear. Irongate was ahead, yet their first stop was to be a drink hall named the Oakwood and Stout: a half-timbered inn four stories high with a stable out back. The sun had reached its zenith by the time the mercenaries were settled, including Jarred, before he and Ruvin continued onward to the old keep, briskly walking down cobblestoned streets.

After so long at sea the walk had been arduous, yet for all the wrong reasons. Talk at the inn revealed the state-of-affairs in Bastion, regaled by the inn-keeper with a sullen look. Dervae was at war, as they knew from their brief encounter at sea with Admiral John Rhys. What they didn't expect to hear was the death of Prince Atillus and Prince Theos. For Tarsin it was doubly troubling, for he knew both men well having resided within Highcastle himself from an early age. Granted, his contact with the boys as they grew was limited, but since Arkos had been under his protection, so too did the Unseen protect his sons. Now, like their dear mother Queen Chrissa, they were dead, victims of a sinister plot designed to undermine the king.

Tarsin felt his burning desire to see Arkos Vantos vanquished dissipate ever so slightly, replaced by doubt and a touch of regret. If he'd remained at his post and not walked out all those years ago, perhaps such an event might not have occurred. It was a sobering thought laced with self loathing, a thought destined to sour his mood.

He should have guessed something momentous was afoot the moment he set foot within the city. Countless soldiers patrolled the streets, flanked by the Sceptres in their yellow and black chequered surcoats. Ships harbouring men and livestock were leaving port in droves, obviously setting sail for southern ports in Anthos and Sovarto to supply the king's army, whilst anger bubbled amongst those left behind, as if they could make a difference in the coming conflict. Tarsin knew a war with Al-Za'im was inevitable, for he'd heard talk for months concerning trade disputes whilst in the southern city, but the death of the princes was something else. This was a calculated assault on the king and his family, one Al-Za'im could not hope to win. King Arkos, for all his faults, was a man who loved his family. He lost his wife before her time, now it appeared he'd lost his two sons. Whoever perpetrated the act was destined to regret they ever angered a man once known as the Battle-King. Dervae was a powerful kingdom. If Al-Za'im was responsible, the city-state was doomed to fall. The king would see it reduced to rubble before returning home, for such an insane quest could surely be the only thing keeping Arkos Vantos sane.

Evidence soon manifested before their very eyes as Tarsin and Ruvin rounded a bend in the road and swept onto Southgate Way. Irongate was directly ahead, yet before its old bluestone walls marched a column of mounted knights, light sparkling brightly amongst the cavalry as they pranced towards Southgate and the road to Aspenvale. Even as a child living in Bastion Tarsin could only vaguely recall such sights. War always seemed so far away back then. Yet here rode the king's cavalry, resplendent in their shining armour, sitting regally atop their sturdy mounts with a rainbow splash of colour. Their helms sat nestled at their hips, so they could see Bastion's citizens and offer a smile. Tarsin caught countless people shaking their heads in amazement at their approach. The war horses' hooves clopped loudly against the cobbled stone, their snorts and neighs alarming, whilst the knight's chainmail jingled along with harness. Accompanying the racket was the creak of leather and the slap of high-held banners. By their side walked diligent squires, gloved hands holding tightly to reins as they sought to calm the horses with soothing words. It was such a visceral display, overwhelming for many. Tears were shed by men and women alike as knights of the realm prepared to head south with vengeance in their hearts. Even the prevalence of horseflesh mingled with oiled steel and leather had Tarsin gripping the hilt of his sword in earnest.

Yet they could not stay and watch for long. Despite the surge of patriotic vigour he felt at their passing, he had a task to see through. After one final glance, he grabbed Ruvin by the arm and led him to the old keep, returning the Seeker to his Brotherhood of One.

'I'm sorry, Tarsin,' elder Cappitus interrupted his thoughts. The old man moved towards a clay pitcher and a tray of goblets at the edge of his table. 'May I offer you something to quench your thirst? The day is hot, as every day is lately, and I'm aware you have travelled far already this morning.'

Ruvin, who was scrutinizing an ancient piece of paper held aloft in his hands, peered over the rim and offered a nod of consent. Tarsin tilted his head and watched the old man pour his drink. His hands were shaking, even though his actions were slow and deliberate. He wondered if the man was nervous or excited, then assumed his hands shook due to his age.

'Your drink,' the elder said as he passed him the goblet. Tarsin took a polite sip, savouring the tart taste of cider vinegar mixed with cool water. 'It is a health tonic brewed by the brothers here in Irongate,' Cappitus explained, pouring and passing another to Ruvin. 'It keeps us strong and alert. Allows us to live longer and retain our faculties.' He finished the last sentence by tapping his head with a gnarled finger. Tarsin wondered if the old man was as sane as proclaimed.

'I have missed this drink,' Ruvin sighed after taking a mouthful. 'All we drank in Al-Za'im was cloudy water and sour goat's milk.'

Tarsin remembered the sour goat's milk: a brew named *risd*, by the locals. Whatever fermentation process was involved, he doubted it was clean. On more than one occasion he'd seen a mercenary from Ciricello's Swords doubled over in pain for the night, guttural curses accompanying flecks of spittle and vomit. Thankfully he'd declined such drink from the outset, his role as Master of Swords best accomplished with an undimmed mind.

'Yes,' replied Cappitus, 'and I can imagine drink was not the only thing you missed, Ruvin Ciricello.'

'No, the south is not as hospitable as the green pastures of Dervae. The food was . . . unusual, and often doused in spice. It added flavour, to be sure, but not every man could stomach their concoctions.'

Elder Cappitus shared a knowing look with Ruvin, and Tarsin wondered if he'd ever travelled to the desert city. After a moment of contemplation, he finished his drink and pushed himself out of the comfortable chair. 'Ruvin, your relic has been delivered, so if my presence is no longer required, I'll be on my way.'

Both men met his gaze, but it was the narrowed eyes of elder Cappitus that drew his own. 'I regret to inform you, Tarsin Va, that your presence is indeed required. A matron of the Celestial Sisters will be along any minute now. Once she arrives, Ruvin will reveal that which he found. I would like you to remain until the piece is unveiled. We have much to discuss.'

'I'm not certain my being here will add anything to your discussion,' Tarsin handed his goblet to the elder. 'I'm a swordsman, nothing more. Philosophical talk is beyond me.'

'Be that as it may, I suggest you sit until the matron arrives.'

'You'd keep me here against my will?'

'If I must.' Tarsin noted the old man's hands were no longer shaking, nor was his back stooped, his shoulders hunched. Now he stood tall and straight, his eyes alight with an inner fire. There was power in the old man yet, he surmised.

'Do as he asks, Tarsin,' Ruvin held a hand up for calm. 'The matron Neema will be here shortly. Word has already been sent.'

Tarsin sat back in his chair, his eyes clouded. So much was occurring so quickly he felt not only out of his depth but slightly inadequate. He could sense something was afoot, something greater than the king's war for revenge. He knew from his youth that the Brotherhood of One and the Celestial Sisters were held in awe with a touch of mystique. They knew things common men could only guess at. Even as a child he'd heard rumours concerning rituals performed in the dark; where lit candles whispered in vaulted chambers and men and women conversed with the dead. He wondered, and not for the first time, what it was Ruvin held in his worn leather satchel.

A loud rap at the only door startled his reverie. Ruvin and Cappitus both peered across the study as the door opened. Tarsin spun about in the chair to see a round woman barely five feet in height shuffle into the room. Matted, hoary hair framed a puffy face, whilst numerous chins pressed tight against what he could only assume was her short, squat neck. Her clothes were an assortment of brightly coloured rags sewn together in a haphazard fashion, whatever pattern they sought to evoke lost on the swordsman, whilst pudgy fingers, thick like melted candle stubs tapped hypnotically against her swollen belly.

'Greetings, elder Cappitus,' she said, her voice surprisingly clear and concise, 'I'm afraid I come bearing tidings of ill repute.'

Tarsin spun to see elder Cappitus peer with intent across his study, eyes narrowed, calculating. 'What would you tell me, Neema, that I do not already know?' Tarsin tilted his head to the side. This, then, was the matron of the Celestial Sisters. The one they called Neema. It was apparent her and elder Cappitus were obviously well acquainted.

The matron shuffled her heavy bulk further into the room. Once there was silence, she spoke, and Tarsin felt a discernible chill at her words: words of portent and fear.

'Avra Creswick is near,' she said, 'and the Darkness travels with her. We are almost out of time.'

CHAPTER EIGHT

Tarsin held his breath. He heard the words escape Neema's mouth, heard the name he feared above all others. "Avra", she said, a name synonymous with the death of his men. It was her coven he'd been instructed to eradicate all those years ago. A mission ordered by King Arkos that proved fatally inept. They were out of their depth, unprepared for the cunning folk and their mysterious ways. It was Avra's foul sorcery that eventually entrapped his companions. Nineteen sword-brothers were lost in those damned hills to the north. He remembered it well no matter how hard he tried to forget. He'd barely returned alive himself.

Now she was close, approaching Bastion.

Tarsin watched Neema shift her large bulk towards a cushioned chair and squeeze her hips past the arms. Once comfortable she beckoned Ruvin and Cappitus to do likewise, pointing to the vacant chairs next to hers. 'Sit, gentlemen,' she offered, taking control of the situation.

Ruvin did as instructed, whilst the elder simply rested against the table. Once there was silence, Tarsin sat forward. 'Would you mind telling me why I'm here,' he said, 'and what in Hell's name is going on?'

Cappitus shared a glance with Neema whilst Ruvin merely sank further into his seat. 'There is much you need to know, Tarsin,' Cappitus began, 'and some of it you will not like.'

'Why don't you start by telling me what you require of me?'

'A great deal, to be honest,' Cappitus replied. 'I know of your past with the Unseen, Tarsin. I know who you are.'

Tarsin lifted his eyebrows. 'How could you know?'

'I know because it was I who suggested Arkos form the Unseen,' he smoothed his wispy beard with long fingers. 'As to why you are here, well . . . we require your services now more than ever before.'

'My services?'

'Namely your expertise with a sword coupled with your skill at protecting the king.'

Tarsin lifted a hand to massage his temple. He was tired and wasn't expecting this, believed he was merely helping Ruvin deliver an ancient relic and nothing more.

'The king and I aren't exactly on talking terms, elder,' he finally said. 'If you fear for his life, placing him in my protection might not be such a great idea.'

'You vowed to protect him, did you not? You swore an oath.'

'Aye, I did, and then he sent us north to be slaughtered like lambs!' Tarsin squeezed his fist with the intention of diffusing his anger. For three years he'd dealt with nightmares and flashbacks of a time fraught with peril. He was witness to atrocities few could stomach, and no-one wished to hear. So he dealt with them alone and in silence, inwardly fuming at the world and the gods who ruled her.

Now he had a release. Elder Cappitus knew of his past and the men he captained. The old man knew of the king's plan. He no longer desired to keep his anger wrapped about him like a protective suit of armour. Now he could vent and rage and scream his displeasure. Now he could speak of his hurt and his all-consuming hatred.

'To put it simply, elder,' Tarsin spoke through clenched teeth, 'Arkos is the last person I wish to see right now, let alone protect.'

Cappitus bowed his head, deep in thought. Whatever ails assaulted the kingdom was not Tarsin's concern. He'd offered his services once; did his duty. Despite his best efforts, Avra the witch was never vanquished. Her coven was destroyed, it was true, but the witch was never found. If she was close to the city, then Tarsin vowed to head the other way.

Expecting the elder to plead his case, he was startled to hear Neema speak in his stead. 'There is more to Avra's arrival than meets the eye, Tarsin,' she said, 'and there is more at stake than your pride, swordsman. You may have failed in your attempt to kill the witch but failing to keep Arkos Vantos alive now could well result in the death of us all.'

Tarsin saw Ruvin sit up straight. The Seeker appeared suddenly curious.

'Avra was once a practitioner of ancient lore much as Cappitus and I,' continued Neema, 'her beliefs like our own. At some point in time she became fixated with a darker path, sought power from untapped sources. Greed was her motivation and it consumed her completely, twisting her into something only vaguely reminiscent of her former self. Eventually she was cast out of her Order, the Practitioners, and banished from the kingdom. That was forty years ago when Arkos' father, King Olin the third, resided upon the throne.' Neema looked to Cappitus, more for confirmation than anything else.

'What is her link to Arkos, then?' Tarsin asked.

'Arkos is a jaguar, Tarsin, like his father. Avra is the last of the Creswick family, her family crest a barb-tailed wyvern. For centuries, the jaguars and wyverns fought a political war. Their hatred for each other ran deep; always had. Then something King Olin did spurned the witch to breaking point and she vowed to kill every jaguar as a result. Now she creeps towards Bastion with death on her mind, but this time she has the means to exact her revenge.' Neema paused, then wet dry lips with a thick tongue. 'Avra has been busy, Tarsin, and she has summoned a Darkness to affect her wish. In her mad infected mind, she has done the unthinkable and summoned Ahriman, the god of Chaos.'

'I've never heard of him,' Tarsin scratched his head.

'Few have,' Cappitus interjected. 'It doesn't make his appearance any less dangerous. He is an ancient god, born at the world's beginning. Now he has returned a shade, although if Avra can find and sacrifice Arkos Vantos, as she claims she will do, then the shade shall become flesh and Ahriman's true power will be realized. Then we shall know fear.'

'So why tell me? I am a swordsman, not a scholar. How does my being here help your cause? What could I possibly bring to the table?'

'More than you believe, Tarsin Va.'

'Really? You may not be aware, Cappitus, but witchcraft is not a speciality of mine.'

'No,' Cappitus met his eyes, 'you are right on that score. But killing witches is. Your venture into Benwith three years ago proved as much.'

'You seem well informed about a mission few were privy too.'

'Little escapes me, Tarsin, especially when it concerns the king and the continuing welfare of the kingdom.'

Tarsin sighed heavily, aware his past would never quite go away. His effort to escape Bastion aboard the *Lioness* with Ciricello's Swords was nought but a reprieve. Now, having returned to his city of origin, he found his past had already caught up with him.

'You're talking about a witch and a summoned god, Cappitus. Don't for a minute think I'll tackle such odds with fervour. I may not be in love with life, but neither will I carelessly throw it away.' He looked towards Neema, seeing concern etched deep upon her pudgy face. 'Surely you have some arcane means to confront the witch and her god?'

'Our power lies in peace and harmony, not vengeful fury. We cannot hope to stand before her and prevail, especially with Ahriman by her side.'

'So, what do you expect me to do, cut them down with my sword?' the sarcasm ran thick off his tongue.

'We have hope from another source,' Cappitus' eyes fell upon Ruvin, sitting quietly with his satchel held tight across his chest.

'Yes,' Neema smiled, 'come, Ruvin, show us the relic.'

Ruvin untied the straps of his satchel, his hands visibly shaking as he nervously reached in to pull out the cloth-covered disc. It was still wrapped in white linen, as it had been since he found it. Leaving the satchel at his feet he stood and moved to the table, uncovering and then placing the disc reverently upon its surface.

'Incredible,' whispered Cappitus.

'Remarkable,' Neema likewise spoke in a hushed tone.

Tarsin stood and moved closer to see the relic. It was circular, in size reminiscent of a Herkosian buckler: a small shield used by the northern barbarians who strapped it to their wrist for protection. The similarities ended there. The disc itself was metal, of a hue golden-like. Upon its surface, though, were lines of silver, neatly criss-crossing the circular disc to represent the cardinal points of a compass, creating twelve equal segments. Several circular lines decreased in size from the perimeter, finishing in a bright silver circle at its centre. Amongst the wedges created by the silver lines were glyphs of unknown design, interspersed with patterns of twinkling gems of myriad colour and random bipedal shapes with ties to the animal kingdom.

'It's definitely a pretty piece,' Tarsin said over Ruvin's shoulder, 'but what good is such a relic against a witch and her dark god?'

Neema moved back to her chair, a thick finger rubbing her chin. 'We will not know immediately,' she said, 'but there is hope amongst our Order and that of the Brotherhood that truths will be realised.'

'Aye,' Cappitus likewise rubbed his bearded chin, 'the disc belonged to a race called the Nepharii, those responsible for constructing Aston's Tear. To the best of our knowledge it is greater than five thousand years old.'

'You believe hope can be found in this . . . metal disc?'

Cappitus traced a finger across its cold surface. 'I would like to believe so,' he said. Tarsin watched the old man, his gaze already far away. 'There is much to ponder, and the Nepharii manuscripts will need to be referred too.' He scratched his beard once more, a quizzical look stretching his face. 'Whatever it is I hope to find, it will not come easily.'

'By all reports, you don't have much time,' Tarsin said with disbelief.

'No, we do not,' Cappitus shook his head. 'The Nepharii manuscripts we've discovered suggest salvation to occur during a conjunction between the moon, a rare comet and Storos: the brightest star in the evening sky. It is our hope the *Nepharii*

Uranometria: the disc Ruvin so miraculously found, will provide further enlightenment.'

'I hear your words, elder, but they sound of nonsense,' Tarsin shook his head. 'Whilst the enemy circles, you sit and dither!'

'We'll not have to wait for long,' Neema said. 'Avra is close, I can feel her, and she is angry. She'll not let the death of her coven go unpunished, nor will she let Arkos slip through her fingers.'

Tarsin sat down, his mind awhirl with information. He was having difficulty comprehending all he'd been told. Even Ruvin remained subdued. It was a great deal to take in and required unwavering trust in the word of strangers. Yet he doubted the two elders would fabricate such a story for his benefit. They truly believed the words they spoke. Of most concern was their fear for the king. Somehow Arkos Vantos had wound up in the centre of an intricate web of deceit, betrayal and revenge. It was apparent his enemies were moving in for the kill. His sons were dead, his armies occupied and by all reports he was holed up in Highcastle with nought but his Palaceguard, and they untrustworthy. He needed help. He needed the Unseen to protect him once more.

He needed Tarsin Va.

Only Tarsin no longer kept vigil on the man he swore to protect.

'What do you require of me, then?' Tarsin's patience was spent. He longed to be out of Irongate, away from intrigue and the smell of fear.

'Protect the king,' both Neema and Cappitus spoke at once.

'How shall I do that? The word on the street suggests Lucius Vupello and his Palaceguard have Highcastle sealed.'

'We'll think of a way,' Cappitus replied with a twinkle in his eye. 'We may not smite our enemies with fire and brimstone, but we can manufacture disturbances and sow confusion.' He paused for a moment and then narrowed his bushy eyebrows. 'But a word of caution, Tarsin; the king is a troubled man. A man who believes he will die very soon. He sees things, does the king, for power flows through his royal blood. Yet we cannot allow such an event to take place. He is the last of the jaguars. He is our hope against the Darkness.'

Tarsin nodded, still uncertain if he should agree to help. Ruvin still sat by his side, his thoughts his own. It would be far easier to proposition the man to set sail from Bastion on the morning tide. The Corphym Isles were a thousand leagues away and more. They could settle there, far removed from this city and its troubles.

Instead he found himself asking for clarification, seeking to elicit as much as he possibly could from two vested with power and lore far beyond his ken.

'You say Avra is close, nearing the city,' Tarsin began, then watched as Neema nodded in affirmation. 'How will we know when she is here?'

'You'll know when she arrives, Tarsin. Everyone will know.'

'What of the Dark God she has summoned, can we kill him?'

'It will be difficult,' Neema squirmed in her chair before looking to Cappitus.

'The longer we keep Arkos alive, the weaker Ahriman will become,' Cappitus explained. 'He is fuelled by the souls of a thousand men and women at present, but they rebel against him, seek to escape his clutch. Once he has the soul of a king, though, he will become flesh. Then his captured souls will be confined, locked in a final embrace and unable to escape. He will be difficult to kill once he takes material form.'

'So, we keep Arkos alive and hope Ahriman withers out of existence in the meantime. Then we pray you find something of importance in this golden disc?' Tarsin asked with raised eyebrows.

'Yes.'

Tarsin felt the look of incredulity mark his face, before shifting to one of scorn. He was a warrior, a swordsman, a man of action. It was not his place to sit and wait for the inevitable. If a foe crept close, you rode out to meet him head on, with violence in your eyes and blood coursing through your veins. Instead all he saw were two old mystics putting blind faith in ancient manuscripts and pretty relics; relying on the word of a race that disappeared five thousand years ago. He was having trouble putting his faith in the same basket.

'Will you help us, Tarsin Va?' the elder asked with pleading eyes.

'I'll sleep on it,' he replied, knowing if he answered now it would be to their distress.

'There are no other options, Tarsin,' Cappitus sighed. 'If Avra succeeds, the world will fall. Ahriman is Chaos incarnate; he will destroy the world before he sits on a crumbled throne to rule. Bastion will simply be his first stepping stone to destruction.'

Tarsin stood, eager to return to the Oakwood and Stout. He was tired and could do with a feed. 'If that is all, I'll be on my way.' He shared a brief look with Ruvin before walking towards the door. 'I will see myself out,' he said, confident he could find his way through the halls of Irongate. 'As to your request,' he shared a look with Cappitus, 'like I already said, I'll sleep on it. Give me a day and you'll have your answer.'

*

Kayla admired her reflection in the oval mirror, then stepped back a pace to better observe the sparkling chain of silver she'd placed around her graceful neck. It was exquisitely fashioned: thin strands intertwined to create numerous links before being set with a finely cut emerald. She pushed her shoulders back and reached for her raven-black hair, pulling the long tresses into a pony-tail.

'It rests remarkably well on you, my lady,' she caught the older man, Roberto, admiring the emerald as it sat between her breasts.

'Do you think so?' she pouted with full lips as she let her hair fall across her shoulders. She then smoothed her black woollen pullover with delicate hands. It was tight-fitting, accentuating her generous curves.

'Most definitely, my lady,' he said with a stroke of his chin. 'Coupled with an elegant dress, few would appear as divine, methinks.'

She smiled at the compliment and returned eyes matching the emerald back to the mirror. Such comments were not unusual, and at twenty years of age she'd already become accustomed to their frequency. Beauty, so her mother taught her, had its place in society. It also had its charms.

'Is it expensive?' she asked.

'Indeed, it is, my lady,' Roberto rubbed his hands together, eager for a sale. 'The price has been set at one thousand silvers.'

'One thousand!' she pouted once more.

'The workmanship involved is flawless, my lady. Only the finest pieces find their way into my store.'

'So I've heard,' a faint smile touched her lips.

The sound of a door opening caused both Kayla and the proprietor to divert their attention. The showroom was small; a tidy room situated at the front of Roberto's living quarters where several glass cabinets lined two walls. Various pieces of jewellery sat shining within, kept from prying hands by lock and key. A single door opened onto the street, whilst another led further into his home. It was a simple setup, and she was aware only one prospective buyer was allowed entry at any time. Yet the front door had been unlocked, allowing another into the room.

'Who are you?' Roberto spoke deeply, his eyes narrowed.

Kayla watched as a young boy, no more than twelve years of age, walked into the establishment. His attire was simple: a black coat over woollen pants, shoes of aged leather. Long dark hair framed a freckled face as hazel eyes greeted Roberto.

'Excuse me, sir,' the boy's voice was high pitched, 'I have come looking for a gift for my Ma.'

'Truly,' Roberto replied, an edge to his voice, 'and I suppose you have coin?'

'A little.'

'Be off with you, boy,' he swung a hand in the boy's direction, 'you don't belong here.'

Kayla watched the young boy screw his face into a knot. Then without warning a metal rod slipped from within the sleeve of his cloak and smashed down hard on the nearest glass cabinet. Glass shattered, and Roberto shrieked, the noise reaching a crescendo as the young boy pushed a gloved hand through crystal shards to grasp a handful of gold bracelets. Quicker than aging Roberto, the thief spun about and raced for the door.

'Thief!' Roberto yelled, panic in his voice as he reached for his cane, pursuit in mind.

Kayla placed a hand on his elbow as he made for the door. 'I'll go,' she said, determination in her eyes. 'I'll run him down for you.'

Before Roberto could reply she took quick steps to the door and was gone, her lithe form twisting agilely to the right as she spied the boy amongst the afternoon crowd. Long strides began to make ground on the youngster, despite the nimble lad slipping between Bastion's citizens with ease. A shrill call sounded behind her as Roberto called for the Sceptres. She risked a glance behind; only to see a pair of men in yellow and black surcoats adding their own call to the already tumultuous chase.

One street became another as the boy veered to his left, skipping past a cart of pumpkins with both hands outstretched, a flash of gold shining in one hand. Kayla followed; aware Roberto's calls of "thief" were beginning to fade, but she was also alert to the number of Sceptres suddenly in pursuit. The two had now become six, their shouts to halt alerting those ahead. The boy, despite his brazen theft and apparent dash, was running out of options.

And still she gained.

Another corner loomed ahead, and Kayla watched as the boy's black cloak flapped out of sight. She looked to her left to see a handful of Sceptres racing towards the intersection and knew half-a-dozen toiled behind her. Then a man wearing an expensive sword rounded the corner. He was tall and strong, evident by his broad shoulders and chiselled features. Without another thought she made long strides towards the swordsman, her mind set. With so much commotion in the street he never saw her coming until it was too late. She hurtled into him at pace, swinging him round as she backed into the wall of some tavern. Breath exploded from her lungs, but she held firm, reaching a hand behind the man's neck to drag him close.

Then she kissed him.

Kayla looked into deep blue eyes; eyes surprisingly devoid of emotion despite the sudden assault. She slid a hand higher, ran her fingers through his close-cropped dark hair as she felt his hands grasp her waist and shoulder. Despite the familiarity she kept her lips pressed firmly against his. Then booted feet pounded past, accompanied by a shrill whistle from a member of the Sceptres. She leant back so she could breathe, then returned her gaze to the tall man. His eyes remained locked to hers, curious now; a minute spark of life surfacing from unknown depths. Then he looked down at the silver necklace with its emerald stone nestled between her heaving breasts.

'Are they gone?' she asked, seeking to divert his attention.

She watched the man turn his head to the side, saw his keen eyes scan the street. 'They have gone,' he said, his voice deep, measured.

'Thank you, then, for the distraction,' she placed a hand on his chest. 'My name is Kayla,' she bypassed a wooden toggle and slid her hand underneath his shirt, her nails tracing lines across his bare chest. 'Perhaps we can meet again someplace, handsome, where the streets are a little less noisy and the crowds friendlier?'

She felt a hand move to her shoulder and push her back an inch. 'Do you know of such a place?' he asked.

'Oh, I don't know. Perhaps I'll find you and we can look for it together.' She said the words with a smile. 'What's your name, handsome?'

'My name is Tarsin.'

'Tarsin,' she said the name with a husky voice, then with a twist she yanked her arm free of his tight grip. 'See you round,' she smiled and spun away, heading down a side street with long, swift strides. She travelled fifty feet and skipped down two lanes before halting beneath an overhang where the afternoon sun could not shine. Her quick hands lifted the silver-emerald necklace and placed it in a pouch at her waist. Then she sat out of sight on a shadowed step and waited.

Minutes later the young boy appeared by her side, his black cloak absent, his long dark hair now miraculously curled and blonde.

'You did well, Donal,' she gave him a gentle hug as he sat beside her.

'Thank you, Kayla,' a reddish tinge swept across his freckled cheeks. 'Do you still have the necklace?'

'Aye, I do. The Underlord will be pleased, I'm sure. It's an expensive piece.' She could see the smile stretch across his face, despite his best effort to hide it. The necklace was valuable, would see them well rewarded for their effort.

'What of the bracelets you stole?'

Donal shrugged his shoulders. 'I had to ditch them when I lost the cloak. The Sceptres were close, and the sun made them sparkle like a beacon.'

Kayla ruffled his blonde hair, a grin on her face. 'That's alright, youngster, I'm sure the Underlord will forgive you. Losing the bracelets was a small sacrifice in the scheme of things.'

'What of Reefe O'Bannon,' Donal piped back. 'Do you think he'll forgive you for kissing another man?'

Her eyes widened. 'You saw me kiss him?'

'I did. Who was he?' Donal's grin revealed irregular white teeth.

'His name is Tarsin,' she replied, still able to feel the sensation of his lips pressed against hers. 'I don't know who he is or where he comes from, though. I doubt I'll ever see him again.' The words sounded hollow, even to her ears.

'Well,' Donal said, 'I won't tell Reefe so long as you don't tell the Underlord I lost the bracelets; deal?'

'Deal,' she slapped a hand against his. The last thing she needed was a love struck Reefe O'Bannon questioning her antics. The man was . . . nice, yet he was overprotective. Kayla was young. She hadn't committed to his advances yet, often wondered if she ever would. Her father would most certainly disapprove, she knew that much.

Strangely, thoughts of Reefe O'Bannon no longer concerned her.

'Come,' she found her feet and offered a hand to Donal, 'it's time to go. Best we slink back into Undercity and seek audience with our lord.'

She saw Donal grin in agreement, then both made for the end of the street where dark shadows lay. A couple of turns saw them reach an abandoned warehouse where a plank of wood was easily moved.

A moment later they were gone.

*

Tarsin checked his pockets as he made for the Oakwood and Stout. As much as he enjoyed the close contact and the press of flesh against his body, he'd dealt with enough cutpurses and thieves throughout Bastion to understand their trade and their tactics. So, with meticulous hands he checked to see if his personal effects were all accounted for. To his surprise they were. It made his walk back to the inn less tiresome than envisaged. In fact, there was a noticeable lift in his mood as pleasant thoughts drifted languidly within his mind, replacing those swirling, emotionally charged requests from his brief visit to Irongate.

Yet they didn't last for long. Thoughts of Avra arriving in Bastion were fearful enough, but as Cappitus and Neema explained, she was not alone. Now he wondered what nightmare he'd walked into on returning to Bastion; wondered if he could escape it just as easily. He instinctively knew he couldn't. He was bred to be a fighter, it was in his blood. And Cappitus was right. He'd made an oath once, and oath to protect the king.

A shout from ahead lifted Tarsin's brooding eyes from the cobblestoned street. Young Jarred waved an arm, the lad standing at the edge of the landing for the Oakwood and Stout. 'Tarsin,' he yelled as he approached, 'can we visit the King's Plaza? I'd like to purchase my very own sword.'

Tarsin looked the lad up and down. During the time he'd spent at Irongate he'd bathed and sought new clothes. Gone were the tattered rags. Now Jarred stood before him, his blonde hair washed, wearing grey pants with a deep blue shirt. He also wore a pair of tan leather boots with silver buckles.

'Beven provided these,' Jarred said by way of explanation. 'He said once you returned you'd accompany me to the King's Plaza.' Tarsin saw the look of excitement in his eyes. 'If you're not too busy, that is.'

Tarsin lifted tired eyes to the sky. It was nearing mid-afternoon and murky clouds were beginning to roll in across the Bay of Pennants. It looked as though rain wouldn't be far away, a welcome relief from the oppressive summer heat.

'Come,' he motioned for Jarred to join him. The walk to King's Plaza would take an hour at most, but he knew where to find the best weapon smith. As much as a meal and a bathe would be welcomed, the chance to stretch his legs and clear his mind was enticing.

Jarred stepped off the landing and fell in beside him. A moment later the sound of shuffling feet caused him to turn, only to see Ruvin Ciricello reach his side.

'We're walking to King's Plaza, so Jarred can purchase a sword,' Tarsin said, the look in his eyes suggesting all talk from Irongate be forgotten for the time being. Ruvin obviously understood, for he kept silent and placed a comforting arm across Jarred's shoulders. Tarsin kept his eyes on Ruvin for a moment, and for the first time since their acquaintance he felt the older man looked lost. Gone was his leather satchel with its ancient relic, gone now was his zest for life. Now he walked the cobblestoned streets of Bastion with his head down, his footfalls shying away from the wagon-wheel ruts to either side.

Despite his heavy thoughts they reached the market in good fashion, and even Tarsin felt a sense of nostalgia as they passed beneath the enormous Archway: a set of bluestone monoliths with numerous images of knights fighting various beasts etched firmly about its flanks. Beyond spread the King's Plaza, an enormous square-shaped market ground, the Avenue of Kings providing the main thoroughfare, whilst the remainder was a honeycomb of paths and turns providing unique niches for sellers to ply their trade. To the north rested the Eosian Aqueduct with its three-tiered arches, to the south Frida's Portico with its covered walkway.

'Where do we start?' Jarred flicked his gaze from left to right.

Tarsin tapped Jarred's shoulder and walked ahead. Although some time had passed since he last stepped foot within its confines, he was certain Hinto would be placed as usual. The man was old, it was true, but he'd sold blades of every description for thirty years or more.

It took longer than expected to find the purveyor, but then Jarred made a habit of stopping to observe every oddity they happened to chance by. Wide-backed turtles from the Corphym Isles took his breath away, their size impressive. More impressive was the fact you could purchase turtle-meat skewers grilled over hot coals at the neighbouring booth. Flashes of cloth-of-gold caught his eye next, and he pleaded with Ruvin to be able to touch the smooth material. It seemed every step bought new wonders to the lad, highlighting his innocence. Brightly coloured spices from Dorsa, powdered stones of differing hue used for dyes from Herkos, and gems and jewellery of Myca, a nation to the far north-east. Elsewhere danced furry animals from the jungles of Jenzai, called *jonkeys* by their handlers and touted as being fine pets for the nobility. Tarsin saw Jarred grin as he watched the creatures gallivanting before him, whilst their owners, a bunch of stern looking men with slitted eyes and golden skin hawked their product with a heavy accent.

Eventually they found Hinto and his stall tucked into a corner, a canvas sheet stretched tight above to keep the sun at bay. Tarsin led Jarred underneath the canvas, stepping inside to look over several blades resting atop a table. He pointed towards a handful he thought suitable. As Jarred's eyes glazed at the sight of so much steel, Ruvin stepped close to Tarsin's side.

'I'm sorry, my friend,' Ruvin said. 'I didn't know such a homecoming was planned. I feel terrible for dragging you into such a mess.'

Tarsin's wry grin disappeared as quickly as it arrived. 'Never fear, Ruvin, you could not have prepared me for such an event. It's not every day you return home only to be told the world's end is nigh.'

Ruvin coughed, a weak smile stretching his lips. 'It's not as bad as they say, though, is it?'

Tarsin saw Jarred pick a blade of appropriate length and weight, then test the balance as he'd demonstrated to him whilst on board the *Lioness*. He folded his arms across his chest. 'You're a member of the Brotherhood, Ruvin, you tell me.'

Ruvin was silent, and Tarsin could see the smaller man was having trouble coming to terms with all they'd been told. Everything he'd strived for, all his arduous work, the blood he'd spilt and sweat he'd shed, was merely a prelude to Bastion's final days. Gone was the supposed glory, the recommendations and the adulation. He didn't even have his pretty disc any longer. 'I've sent word to Vasco to prepare the *Lioness*,' Ruvin finally said. 'If you're of a mind, we can sail on the morning tide and leave Bastion, never to return.'

'Do you think Avra and Ahriman will stop at Bastion?'

Ruvin squirmed under his scrutiny. 'No, Ahriman, at least, will continue to destroy. Neema suggested as much. Bastion is merely a stepping stone for the Dark God.'

'Then we stay and fight,' Tarsin clenched his teeth. 'I've no love for the king, but I'll be damned if I'm going to sit idle and await the witch. Somehow, we'll find a weakness. I've killed witches before, I'll kill them again.'

'Can it truly be done? There is also Ahriman to consider. How do you kill a god, even one as weak as he?'

Tarsin shrugged and walked over to Jarred, then ran his eye over the blade he'd chosen. It was a fine weapon, light and flexible, with twin edges and a deep fuller. He palmed a handful of silver coins to Hinto and offered a word of thanks before exiting. Rain began to fall lightly as they continued to walk the plaza. Jarred spied a leather workshop and moved to appraise the goods in the hope of purchasing a belt when a sudden squeal stopped him in his tracks. Tarsin spun on his heel as every *jonkey* in the plaza vented anguish to the afternoon sky, their small bodies squirming as they sought to break their collars and flee. The noise was horrendous and everywhere they looked people covered their ears in fright, dropping their purchased goods, their faces ashen under a darkening sky.

Then the ground shook. It was gentle at first, like a distant herd of buffalo trampling the earth, before it rapidly intensified, causing canvas sheets to flap noisily and stock to tumble from shelves. The animal screams continued, the dreadful chorus now accompanied by the peal of women and children. Dirt and grit sifted from granite pillars groaning with displeasure, and still the rain fell.

A moment later it stopped.

Tarsin breathed deep, his nerves taut, highly strung.

'What was that?' Jarred asked, his voice high pitched with fright.

Tarsin lifted a hand to shield the rain from his face. 'An earthquake,' he said. He turned towards Ruvin. The old man was clutching his chest, his skin pasty. A look of discomfit flashed across his face. 'Are you alright,' Tarsin moved to his side.

'Barely,' Ruvin whispered. He took a reassuring breath and Tarsin could see some colour return to his cheeks. 'That was . . . interesting.'

Tarsin clutched the hilt of his sword. 'They are here,' he said.

'Who is here?' he saw Ruvin's face drain of colour to become puce once again.

'Avra and her Dark God,' Tarsin said, 'Neema said we would know when they arrived; everyone would know.' He looked about the plaza; seeing distressed families and stall owners, frightened children clutching mother's skirts. He hadn't quite come to terms with Arkos' betrayal yet, but he suddenly felt his options were few. The king was a man beset by enemies, and he'd once vowed to protect him. Knowing danger was so very close, he decided he would do so again.

'They have entered Bastion,' Tarsin continued, his eyes furtively searching the plaza. 'Don't ask me how I know, Ruvin, but I fear nothing in this world will be the same again.'

CHAPTER NINE

A single candle flame offered dim light in the darkened chamber.

Avra appeared nonplussed by the lack of visibility. She sat at the bottom of a series of steps, her hands caressing the *Sawolegere:* her rusty lantern lying in her lap. The chamber, if you could call it that, was an ancient cistern beneath the city proper. Centuries ago it served as an open forum, but since Dervani occupation much had changed within the ancient city. Seated as she was at the bottom of a staircase, she couldn't see how far the chamber stretched, its end obscured by a forest of marble columns springing from watery depths. They were arranged in equally spaced rows, reaching a height of fifty feet before branching into graceful arches supporting the roof above. Marble steps led down to the water, a dozen in total, whilst those behind her ascended to the street above. She peered into the pool of water, its colour deepest blue, lit only by the glow of a single candle. A flash of light sparkled from bright scales as a foot-long carp swam past, its tail breaking the surface. It was a copper-scaled fish with eyes like pin-pricks of light. How many swam below she could only guess, but for now they were the only company she kept; apart from the six butchered corpses lying huddled at the water's edge.

Even now a set of blank eyes stared lifelessly back at her. Avra met the dead gaze, held it for several minutes as she remembered how easily she'd captured the weak-minded fools. Lured inside by the promise of carnal pleasure, they were soon betrayed by her hypnotic tongue and sacrificed in quick fashion. Now they were merely empty vessels, their souls gathered and fed to Ahriman inside the *Sawolegere.*

Ahriman, she thought, *we are here, finally, but with much to accomplish.* Avra knew now was not the time to become complacent. Yesterday's journey along North Road had been a gruelling affair. Bastion had appeared mid-morning as she rounded a bend in the road, her path now closely following the river Atvia and its wide banks. Countless fishing boats bobbed to her left, some moored at the end of private jetties, whilst others were being rowed to favoured locations. Everywhere she looked people went about their daily rituals, oblivious to the power nestled within the lantern she carried: the power of life and death. Not all who travelled the north road were so carefree, though, for many crowded towards Bastion from outlying settlements, some of which were now tasting the first horrors of plague. She could see who those families were, for their eyes were furtive, shadowed, as if they kept a great secret. It wouldn't pay to tell those who walked beside you of what you'd seen, for you were certain to be ostracized in quick fashion: quarantined until proven clean, or burnt at the stake if you were not.

Most would be burnt regardless.

Avra remained silent, urged her horse forward with a mental command. The creature obliged under duress, its ears flat against its skull, an obvious shake in its legs. Like so many others the beast couldn't refuse the witch's commands and was forced to plod onwards.

By mid-afternoon she reached Bastion proper having passed numerous outlying settlements. She could see the great grey of Bastion's outer walls ahead, an enormous gatehouse holding back the encroaching crowd. To her left, alongside the gatehouse proper, spanned Rivergate. The gate was as high as the walls on either side, battlements cresting its top, whilst two great arches allowed the river Atvia entry into Bastion, along with an assortment of fishing craft and barges from upriver. Even here guards were at work, fixing nets under water for any stray livestock or plague-ridden bodies floating downstream. Decks on either side of the waterway were set just inside Rivergate, providing an opportunity for guards to board craft and conduct inspections of their own. Like the gatehouse, a large iron portcullis rested above, ready to drop at the slightest provocation. Everywhere she looked soldiers aligned to the Sceptres rummaged through wagons and baggage, asking questions and observing the health of those seeking entry. Word of the plague had travelled fast.

Avra shifted her gaze to the wide-open maw of Northgate, looking beyond and into the conglomeration of buildings sprawling before her. Glimpses of tall towers and temple steeples reached high, some soaring above the outer walls, whilst surrounding their foundations she could see half-timbered taverns and general stores interspersed with common heather-thatched homes. Even the occasional keep with crenulated battlements could be seen, stonework old-fashioned but durable, their peaked roofs fashioned from grey slate. This was the Bastion she remembered when she was cast out more than forty years ago; crowded and noisy, a mass of heaving flesh. There was little to suggest order was maintained. It was all an illusion. Those who wished to remain innocuous would do so. Those who craved recognition simply shouted louder than those beside them.

She chanced a look above the tiled roofs to see roiling clouds coalescing in the afternoon sky, the touch of a sudden wind threatening rain. Those who chanced to remark upon its imminent arrival were oblivious to its real design. This was Ahriman's work; she could feel it. It was his way of heralding his arrival.

Darkness comes on wings of hate.

A man of the Sceptre with his yellow and black livery stepped close to the wagon, his hand reaching out to pat the horse. A heavy snort followed by stomping hoofs sent him back a pace with hands held high.

'Whoa! That's a feisty horse you have there, my lady,' he said.

Avra smiled, showing perfectly straight teeth. In fact, her appearance had morphed into that of a comely elder woman. Her flesh was no longer gossamer thin and covered in purple splotches; it was now the colour of cream and equally as smooth. She looked healthier, too, as if an extra twenty pounds had been added to her weight.

'What be your business in Bastion, my lady?'

'I am visiting family,' she replied with a smile. In truth she had no family, at least no blood relative. The closest she had to family now were those she studied with during her time with the

Practioners. The thought of seeing Neema once more, just before she died screaming under her blade, elicited a smile. Only Neema was not the only soul on her vengeful list. Cappitus of the Brotherhood was another. Both were young when she was forced kicking and screaming from the Order . . . powerful though, even back then. She knew without a doubt they were involved in destroying her coven. King Arkos, despite his ties to the occult, alone did not have the power to find her. The mystical orders - the Brotherhood of One and the Celestial Sisters - were most certainly at the forefront of such action. She would see them die for their insolence; see them squirm in fear just before she plunged her knife deep. No more would they meddle in the affairs of Avra Creswick.

She returned her attention to the guard as he cast a cursory eye over the wagon and its contents. He saw nought but a handful of timber boards and a sack of grain in the wagon itself. Next to her sat a wicker basket overflowing with chard, carrots and parsnips, along with a small sack of berries. Goods appropriated when she commandeered the horse and wagon earlier in the morning.

'How is your health, my lady?'

Avra peered down at the curious guard. 'Well enough, young man,' she caught his eye and flashed him a hypnotic smile. 'I don't have the plague, if that's your concern.'

He smiled slowly in return, as though the words she uttered were taking time to sink in. 'Good enough for me,' he finally said as he moved towards the horse and slapped its rump, startling the beast into action. Avra sat back and watched as she passed through Northgate, noting the huge iron portcullis resting above, the thick timber doors hanging to either side. Defences never meant to be utilized but present all the same. It was a necessary obligation to the citizens of Bastion: high walls and a defendable gate; whatever it took to allow citizens to sleep easier at night. Only they were never designed to keep an enemy such as Avra from breaching their defences.

Steel shod hooves clopped loudly on the cobblestones as she took in her surroundings. Once through Northgate, she found herself in Nor'wood, an area renowned for its slums. The Northern Wood, it had once been called, an area brimming with fir trees reaching high into the sky. Those same trees were cut down for building materials and the land cleared for crops as the years passed. Centuries later the ever-expanding city had encroached upon the workable land, pushing the plantations out and beyond the city's new boundary. Now an assortment of welcoming taverns lined the main street, but behind the facade sprawled a warren of ramshackle huts and abodes, hastily erected by those too poor to afford proper building materials. Many of the huts were made from warped boards due to un-seasoned timber and shoddy workmanship, with sun-baked clay crudely slapped against walls to prevent leaks and drafts. Other dwellings were barely held together by strips of leather and stolen tiles. It was a region of Bastion brimming with cut-throats, beggars and whores, where the flash of a silver coin could see you dead in an instant. Few walked Nor'wood's streets at dusk, and only the foolhardy traversed them at night.

It was exactly the type of environment Avra craved: a haven for the unsavoury where she could blend in and then disappear; an area where sudden loss of life would be nothing out of the ordinary.

A place Avra knew well, a place where she could hide.

Rain began to fall as she steered the wagon down a side street and headed for the northern cistern. *We are here, Ahriman,* she didn't speak the words, but knew he would hear them in her mind. The reply was not what she expected. Silence greeted her first, then came the howling of dogs and the scuttling of rats as they fled filthy sewers. Shouts and curses from those walking the streets followed, high pitched screams not far behind as the ground shook: a gentle rumbling, nothing more. Enough to put fear into the weak minded; enough to herald the arrival of a fearsome god.

The creak of an opening door startled her from her musing, allowing daylight to splash down the stairs and fall on her back. The sudden illumination revealed the pasty bodies by the water's edge in all their horror, vacant eyes unseeing, chests ripped opened to reveal rib cages plastered with gore. Several cockroaches scuttled across the corpses at the light's intrusion, disappearing inside cavities courtesy of her ceremonial knife. The candle by her side flickered, touched by a gentle zephyr.

'Avra,' the voice was male, although timid, 'are you down there?'

'I am here,' she croaked. Her mouth was dry. Since the last sacrifice, she'd sat unmoving, awaiting the arrival of her contact. She had sent word to her accomplice prior to entering the cistern the night before. Now, with the sun already high above Nor'woods homes, he'd arrived. 'You are late.'

Footsteps sounded as the contact made his way down the steps. 'I'm sorry, Avra, but it has been one of those mornings.'

She turned slowly to appraise the man's face for the first time. It was not what she hoped for in an accomplice. He was weak, this one, fearful and small. Avra detested small men. To compound her dislike, he was rotund. There was no strength in the man. Even his face was puffy, his hair unkempt, his nose pudgy. 'Everything is going according to plan?' she asked with a raised eyebrow.

The man caught sight of the corpses lying below, his cheeks suddenly expanding as they sought to hold back the contents of his stomach. A fly buzzed from the cistern's depths to land on his nose. He swatted it and tore his gaze away from the grisly scene, focusing on the witch still seated below him. 'Everything is as planned,' he said, a slight tremble to his voice. 'We need only await the conjunction two days hence before the king is to be delivered, alive and unharmed.'

'Good, good,' Avra almost purred as she spoke. 'What of his sons?'

'Prince Atillus and Prince Theos are dead. Both were killed in the south, as arranged. Now King Arkos is the only remaining member of the Vantos family. He is the last of the jaguars.'

Avra smiled, a hideous slash that did little to appease the man standing before her. She could almost hear the man's knees clanking together in abject fear. He continued to swat at flies as she thought of the days ahead, knowing Neema and Cappitus would be searching high and low for her whereabouts. It was paramount she remain hidden, veiled in secrecy and protected by charms against unwanted scrying. She would do well to mention caution to the little man before he left. Remind him to keep his wits about him.

'So,' he began after a period of unnerving silence, 'once we deliver you Arkos, Lucius Vupello is to become king, yes?'

'If that is what you wish,' she waved a hand. 'With Arkos dead, I care not what you do.' Inwardly a smile stretched so wide she almost burst. With Arkos dead, there would be nothing left of Bastion or its residents. Ahriman required the soul of a king to become flesh. Once achieved, he would set upon a path of destruction too frightening to behold. Little men like the one before her would be consumed in lightning fashion, nothing more than fuel for a ravenous god. In the meantime, she let them play their insignificant games of power; let them believe their betrayals had the people's best interests at heart.

'If that is all . . .?' the man practically squeaked.

Avra narrowed her eyes, noting the beads of sweat upon his forehead, the lank, brown hair and the fidgeting hands. It was warm outside, true, but not enough to make a man sweat. Not yet, in any case, and try as he might, he could not keep still.

'There is something you're not telling me?' Avra's voice became deep and purposeful.

The man squirmed, then opened his mouth only to hear his teeth chatter incessantly.

'Tell me, little man,' her tone was threatening.

Avra watched him suck in a lungful of air and wipe his brow with the back of a hand. 'The king has fled Bastion,' the words came out in a rush, 'but,' he held out his hands, shaking as they were, 'Vupello and a select number of the Palaceguard ride to meet him. They will see him safely back to Highcastle.'

'What madness is this?' she screamed, then watched as her accomplice, Kerros Gavony, ducked his head in response to her loud screech.

'It was sudden,' he began, 'a mere whim of the king, nothing more. He left before first light with Lord Beaumont of Rochdale and a contingent of his cavalry. There is talk of him seeking revenge for the deaths of his sons, but once Vupello reaches his side, he'll talk sense into the old man.'

'You mean to tell me Lucius Vupello and his Palaceguard are not with him?'

'No, Avra, they are not. Like I said, he left without warning.'

There was more to King Arkos' departure, she could feel it. She could sense the hands of Neema and Cappitus involved; practically smell their odorous touch. Although she needn't sacrifice Arkos in two days time under the conjunction of moon, comet and star, such a celestial arrangement was highly favourable.

'It is manageable, Avra. Like I said, Lucius Vupello is riding out to meet him. He knows of our plans. He will not fail us. There is a contingent of the Palaceguard riding with him, men Lucius Vupello can trust. They will do as he instructs.'

'Lucius Vupello the swordsman, cousin to the king?'

'Yes, a formidable man. Few dare cross blades with Lucius Vupello.'

'Then there is hope,' she settled, her face becoming passive. 'Although if you were in his place, Kerros Gavony,' she said with a snarl, 'I would have serious doubts concerning our success.'

'Yes, Avra,' he bowed; sweat now running in rivulets down his face.

'Leave me, Kerros, and do not return unless you have the king in tow, gagged and fettered like we discussed.'

'As you wish,' he abruptly turned and raced up the stairs as fast as his chubby legs could carry him. The clank of the door closing plunged the cistern back into near darkness, the single candle by Avra's side still offering its paltry light. The splash of carp frolicking in the water startled her momentarily, prompting her to remain vigilant, for so much depended on the coming days. Not only would she help Ahriman become flesh, she would also become immortal herself, her promised reward for unwavering devotion. Coupled with her immortality, she hoped, would be youthful vigour.

At this moment, such thoughts needed to be pushed aside. She was not certain if Ahriman listened to the discussion between her and Kerros, but he was about to find out regardless. She stroked the lantern, fearing his rage but resigned to telling him of the possible delay.

She hoped angering such an entity now whilst he remained shadow was better than angering him later, once he was flesh.

Not surprisingly, she could not fathom how powerful the shadow of a god could be.

*

Indeed, Ahriman did hear all that transpired between Avra and her contact, Kerros Gavony. Irrespective of Avra's toils over the last two decades, Ahriman had strived for centuries to arrive at his current position. He was not about to lose such an opportunity due to the foibles of man. If he could sway events into his favour, then he would do so.

He sifted forth, the lantern no longer a prison containing his shadowed form, but now a recluse to shield it from prying eyes. Six months had passed since Avra first summoned his shade to the material plane. Months spent hiding, clutching firmly to the souls she fed him. Without them he would wither to the point of nonexistence, becoming no more than a speck of darkness, a single, terrible soul desperate to experience the world he craved. He fought hard to control the souls now bound to him, a bitter fight that if lost would render him weak, helpless and once again all alone.

Ahriman was not about to lose. Flesh, once gained, would allow him to control his souls. No longer would they fight to flee, desperately seeking to plunge into newly conceived life. No, once he became flesh and blood they would happily conform to his will. Only then would they be prepared to experience life as a god and help shape the new world to come.

His coal-red eyes blazed as his shadow seeped into the shape of a man. Avra bowed her head, as expected, for she alone knew that to peer into the eyes of an angered god was to witness madness itself. The witch had no intention of becoming mad, at least not any madder than she already was. Not now, not when she was so close to realizing her dreams.

'I am most displeased, Avra,' he said, his voice encompassing the entire cistern.

'I am truly sorry, my lord,' her voice quailed, a complete reversal to moments earlier when it was she who trembled with rage.

Ahriman peered about the chamber, noting the dead bodies, the still water. 'I'll have the king return, never fear,' he said. 'I'll have him rush back into Bastion to find it broken and scarred. I'll have him gaze upon his city and not recognize its streets!'

His voice rose to such a level that ripples marred the water's surface, the carp fleeing to the furthest end. Tiny cracks, like the slightest of cobwebs, began to sift across the marble columns. 'I am the Apocalypse, Avra. Listen now as I begin to fulfil my destiny!'

He sank into the cistern, merging with the water like an oily stain only to disappear into its depths. Darkness encompassed him as he plunged deeper still, sinking further into the earth. He stretched his hands to either side: allowing them to range far, sensing the lay of the land as they crept along the bedrock. He shook the earth the day before to herald his arrival. Now, he would shake it with unsurpassed fury. With blackened thoughts, his form began to tremble, as if raking coughs assailed his body. Only it wasn't a coughing fit that provoked such spasms, but laughter. Laughter like Bastion had never heard.

*

Kerros Gavony wiped his brow and paused to catch his breath. He was distressed, noticeably so. His fine clothes: a mauve silken shirt with ivory toggles and sable pants coupled with black leather boots were incredibly expensive. He'd even polished the silver buckles on his boots himself, not trusting his manservant with such a task. Yet his dashing appearance, he believed, had been lost on Avra as he stood upon the shaded steps leading into the cistern. *So much for making a grand impression on the witch*, he thought.

Breathing easier, he began to walk once more, heading for Highcastle and his private quarters. It was still early, noon at least an hour away. There was still time enough to pen a note and send it after Vupello with haste. It was imperative the Captain of the Palaceguard be informed of his talk with Avra, and greater still, to become aware of her displeasure. A curse hissed from his mouth as he thought of the morning's events. From all reports, the king rode forth before dawn, and by the time those at Highcastle were made aware of his absence, the majority of Bastion had been bustling for several hours. Yet Vupello gathered a dozen of his Palaceguard and gave chase in quick fashion, riding their tall steeds through the streets at reckless speed and out past Southgate. There was hope they would reach the column before midday. How long it would take Vupello to convince King Arkos to return was an entirely different matter; one open to speculation and an ounce of fear. If the king refused to return, trouble was certain to ensue. For one accustomed to intrigue, Kerros certainly had a knack for avoiding the unforseen, but with a witch now plotting revenge within their inner circle, avoiding her wrath would be difficult.

He continued to fidget as he walked and for the first-time experienced real doubt concerning his current path. He was no killer, that was certain, but he did wish King Arkos dead. The man had ruled through the death of his wife and now the death of his sons. It was time for him to abdicate or, failing such a move, be assassinated. Lucius Vupello was strong, valiant and brave. He would make a great king.

And, he thought, *I will be there to guide him*.

He pressed on, his fine shirt now open at the neck, unseemly for one of his standing. Yet every passing minute saw the heat become more oppressive. Yesterday's afternoon shower had been a brief respite, nothing more. It settled the dust but failed to slake the kingdom's thirst. Even the oldest of councillors, Octavio of Elmwood, could not recall a summer so stifling.

He turned right, walking a street he knew, remembering it as a short cut to the Argosian Bridge. On the other side of the river Atvia was New City, a region of Bastion near Highcastle itself and strictly home to the wealthy. It was here nobles from across the kingdom jostled for small palaces of their own, competing with those conniving merchants who prospered in trade, lending or shipping. It was a far cry from the squalor of Nor'wood; and a welcome sight indeed. He reached the bridge and crossed with head down, his feet shuffling along as he breathed an audible sigh of relief. Ahead lay New City's paved walkways. He felt safe now, no longer fearful of Avra's cloying aura. He could begin to think clearly again, strategize with purpose of thought. It was true he was not a strong man, nor an imposing one, but he was intelligent. It was his one redeeming attribute. Avra had unnerved him, though, like those who worked for her previously. He'd only heard mention of Avra once, before he was introduced to a member of council influenced by her charms. Talk of greatness inspired him, and it had been easy to accept bribes of wealth and prestige for information. In fact, it had been too easy, in retrospect. He'd never even laid eyes on the witch until today. All the work over the years had been guided by other hands, hands that had become eerily silent of late.

The four towers of Highcastle were now visible to the west, and Kerros had reason to believe he could have his note written and on its way before noon when a slight tremor stirred below his feet. He stopped, listening to the dogs barking and howling, aware of a sudden stillness in the air. The moving of the earth yesterday had frightened him, and then he'd been inside Highcastle and its towering walls, apparently safe. Now he was out in the open and suddenly afraid, feeling small and insignificant. To make matters worse, the trembling hadn't ceased. He looked around and saw startled glances returned.

Horses suddenly reared in their traces, fighting to escape wagon and master, whilst the ground continued to violently tremble, increasing in magnitude. A blast of stifling air blew in his direction, dust choked his mouth, grit lodged in his eyes. Screams assailed him from everywhere and the sound of falling masonry became a constant staccato on the paved street. Grinding slabs of rock cracked and splintered, sounding like thunder peeling in the clear morning sky and he suddenly found himself on all fours, crawling on the uneven ground as tears rolled down his face. *This is the end*, he thought, *the world is tearing itself apart.*

Fear overwhelmed him, blanketing his reason before pounding him in the back with hardened fists. He tried to stand with a thought to seek shelter from the impossible storm, but his legs were like liquid. He coughed, sending spittle running down his chin. He could barely pry his eyes open, and when he did all he saw were his blood-stained hands, ripped silken shirt and billowing clouds of dust. A heavy boom sounded to the south, louder than anything he'd ever heard. The concussion swept over him seconds later, pushing his face hard into rock. Blood plastered his nose, his lips.

He swooned, his eyes fluttered, then with aching limbs he rolled onto his back to lie prone on the broken ground. His last glimpse before darkness overtook him was that of a falling sky.

CHAPTER TEN

The sound of a thousand bells startled Lucius from his slumber.

He opened his eyes, certain to find himself crammed into the corner of some belfry, his ears ringing due to the incessant chimes above. Instead he saw dirt and grass; heard the whinny of a horse. Dazed, he pushed himself into a sitting position and felt the sun on his face, a gentle breeze tousling his long black hair. The glint of steel caught his eye, causing Lucius to squint as he reached for his discarded blade. He couldn't remember having drawn the weapon, but there it lay, pristine, lethal. His gloved hand curled about the leather-bound hilt and dragged it close. 'Gods above, where am I?'

He didn't expect an answer and was surprised to hear a groan to his left followed by a string of curses in the Herkosian tongue.

'Jaegar,' Lucius said, believing he recognized the deep voice, 'is that you?'

A large man sat up in the grass, his blonde beard divided into two long braids. Dirt covered one side of his face, obscuring a blue eye, but his bald head remained untouched, the swirling tribal tattoos, inked black, ominously visible. Lucius watched as Jaegar found his feet and reached his full height, only a few inches below seven feet, then took two steps and offered a huge hand. Lucius gripped it tight and stood beside his comrade.

'What happened?' Lucius asked.

'Earthquake, I think,' Jaegar scanned the countryside, seeing more of their comrades, knights of the Palaceguard, as they rose from the tall grass. A handful of horses could be seen in the distance, some alone, others packed closely together. 'Are you hurt?'

Lucius patted himself down. Apart from a splitting headache and a stiff neck, he felt intact. He sheathed his sword and walked a few paces, aware his centre of balance was askew. He took a few more steps before he felt comfortable, calm in the knowledge that all was well. Whatever occurred, he must have hit his head hard on the turf. A faint ringing in his ears persisted as he walked towards his men, Jaegar close on his heels.

'You look a little green, Vupello,' a man to his right chided, followed by a chuckle. Lucius nodded, aware Owen Moor had spoken. The man was always quick with a word; quicker than he was with a sword. Lucius met his gaze and looked deep into his black eyes. There was scant respect there, but it bothered him not at all. So long as Owen Moor fulfilled his role, he had use for him.

Ignoring the comment, he scanned the rest of his men, doing a quick count to make certain all twelve were present. Despite the shock and obvious battered egos, the Palaceguard still managed to look resplendent in their silver trimmed black tabards over glistening mail, even for such a hardened crew. Strictly speaking they were knights of the realm, but they had forsaken all holdings and wealth to serve Highcastle and the King. No other could call upon them for service. 'Anyone injured?' he asked, his voice loud to his ears.

Several shakes of the head and a few grunts suggested all were well and accounted for. Lucius gave a short nod of approval and walked past his knights, heading for a small rise behind them. Once there he pulled his gloves off and placed two fingers in his mouth to whistle loud and clear. It took several minutes, but eventually a black horse, seventeen hands high and bred for battle, trotted to his side. He placed a hand on the steed's neck before running his fingers towards its ears. 'That was some fright, Strom,' he spoke softly, his hand now entwined about the steed's black mane. A handful of shouts and further whistles saw the rest of the men's horses likewise beckoned. Several minutes passed as the summoned steeds arrived and the jingle of harness and earthy clod of steel-shod hooves subsided. Whilst the men ran their professional eye over their mounts, Lucius thought back to how they came to be here in the first place. It took a moment of recollection before his mind adjusted, and only because he spied a mass of men in the field to the south. Now he remembered; now he knew why they were here.

It had been a mad dash from Bastion in the early morning, he and the Palaceguard riding fast through city streets as they headed for Southgate and the road beyond. Word had reached him after sunrise that King Arkos had fled south with a contingent of Rochdale cavalry before dawn, with the aim of joining the war. Kerros had been the one to break the news, the little man furious, and rightly so, for he had plans for the king, plans long in the making. How King Arkos managed to elude his trusted guards and leave them behind without explanation or approval hadn't even crossed their minds. All Kerros and Lucius could think of was the trouble it would take to fetch him back and the trouble they would find themselves in if they didn't.

So the chase had begun; the king and his cavalry already hours upon the road, only they were weighted down by supply wagons and squires travelling by foot. Providing he and his men travelled with care, they would reach the king by midday at the latest. True to his word, they'd arrived an hour before the sun reached its zenith, cresting a rise to see the silver column of knights and men-at-arms winding their way through a small copse of trees. Beyond lay the faint outline of Aspenvale, a small hamlet known for its logging. After a brief pause the men put spurs to their horse's flanks and rode towards the column, Lucius mulling over how best to approach the king and explain the necessity of his return to Bastion. He was still contemplating his speech when a flock of birds flew high into the air and horses reared without warning, becoming skittish. Heavy snorts and flattened ears suggested something was wrong, so he ordered his men to look for hidden snakes in the grass by the side of the road. Drawing his sword, he'd barely leant over his saddle to look himself when the ground shook and Strom reared once more, throwing him hard from his back.

Lucius raised a hand to shield his eyes from the sun as he returned his thoughts to the mass of men below. The knights and their squires were a shamble, horses fallen and scattered, supply wagons overturned. It would take hours for the column to regain its legs. He moved back to Strom and mounted, signalling his men to do likewise. 'Time to move,' he said. 'With the column such a mess, there's a chance we can convince the king to return with minimal fuss.'

'What if he refuses?' Jaegar asked what was on all their minds, his right-hand opening and closing in agitation.

Lucius pondered the question, looking long and hard at the knights scampering about the woods as they sought to retrieve their mounts. He noticed a section of trees had fallen due to the earthquake, felled as if by a giant hand. Further afield he saw the cluttered debris of a landside. He raised a hand to massage his neck and noticed a crow settle atop an old sign post to his left. It issued a caw to herald its arrival.

'Vupello?' Jaegar rode his steed alongside.

The Captain of the Palaceguard cast his gaze towards Jaegar and noticed the Herkosian had failed to wipe the muck from his face. He was a different breed, no doubt, a barbarian from the north clad in chainmail and leather and little else, although he did wear the black tabard of the Palaceguard, much to his chagrin. Lucius knew to keep such a man you needed to provide him with coin, ale and women, mostly in that order, and he was yours without question. He also knew he needed to teach the brute a modicum of respect. Clothed like the rest of the men he became part of the group and not so much an individual. Granted, he appeared far removed from the rest of his knights, being almost seven-foot-tall and hugely muscled, but he was loyal and such loyalty was hard to come by. Lucius was simply glad the enormous man stood by his side. He was a frightful sight at the best of times, doubly so when his face was soiled. He watched as the Herkosian reached for his twin-bladed battleaxe: an incredibly sharp weapon with fine engravings of northern bears tracing its length, its haft twined with leather to provide a firm grip. The Herkosians were perceived as barbarians by the majority, but they certainly crafted weapons of exquisite beauty.

'He shall come with us regardless,' Lucius returned. 'We've waited far too long to see him flee our protection now.' Thoughts of failure were far from his mind. For more years than he cared to remember Lucius had been plotting his rise to the throne. Whatever occurred today would be nothing more than a minor deterrent, the smallest of blights on an otherwise impeccable plan. Destiny awaited Lucius Vupello. It was time for a fox to become king of Dervae. 'He'll come, kicking and screaming if he must,' he snarled with venom, 'but he *shall* return!'

The remaining men of the Palaceguard urged their horses alongside their captain, ready to obey his command. They were hard men, seasoned warriors and swordsmen. All had pledged allegiance to Lucius in the last few years, one at a time as he worked on bribing them to see his vision for the future; a future where he was king and Arkos was no longer part of the tapestry. It was his destiny, so he kept reminding himself. Ever since he was a young boy his mother and father had thought to instil in him a sense of greatness. Countless comparisons with his older cousin Arkos became a daily routine, and poor Lucius was even pushed into swordplay at an early age. Not long after his lessons with the blade he was forced to learn his letters and the history of the kingdom. Houses of royalty and Houses of commerce were next, followed by the heraldry of the kingdom. Yet despite his achievements and the stupendous amount of knowledge crammed into his skull, his parents saw every waking moment as an opportunity to mock his apparent inadequacy, citing Arkos' development with apparent glee to spur him on. In time, he grew to hate his cousin and the name Vantos, just as he came to hate his mother and father. Politics bored him, and he felt family ties to be a hindrance rather than a boon. The only enjoyment Lucius experienced was with the sword. He felt immense joy in besting his instructors and their finest students, and by the age of fifteen only a handful of men in Bastion could honestly say they were his better. A decade later he was rightfully feared throughout the kingdom.

It all seemed so long ago now. He briefly wondered where the years had gone.

He shook his head to clear it of unwanted thoughts and inwardly cursed his melancholy. The knock to his head must have been harder than he first realised. It was very unbecoming for a swordsman of his standing to dwell on such trivial matters. He had a task to complete; an urgent mission that if carried out as planned would have repercussions aplenty. When the dust settled, Lucius hoped his part of the bargain would be sealed.

He looked to his left as his men fell into line and offered a grim smile. He felt a pinch of pride at their demeanour, knew they were certainly not the type to shirk duty, despite the insurmountable odds ranged against them. Not for the first time Lucius wondered how they would return if the king refused. Lord Beaumont rode with over two hundred cavalry and twice as many men-at-arms and squires. Lucius may be Captain of the Palaceguard, the finest swordsmen in Bastion, but if hostilities eventuated, thirteen men against such a force was suicide.

He swung his hand forward and his knights moved as one, the horses heading downhill towards the Rochdale cavalry. Even at such a distance he could see King Arkos moving amongst the men, his polished black armour a beacon as he issued orders with a raised, gauntleted fist. He still wore his great helm, black like his armour, fashioned to resemble a snarling jaguar. It was a fearsome piece of workmanship, but it would also be stifling wearing such protection at this time of day. The man must be roasting. He briefly wondered if he feared assassination even out here in the woods.

I would never be so fearful.

'They've spotted us,' Jaegar rumbled, his hand clenching about the haft of his axe.

'Put your axe away, Jaegar, we're not here to fight,' Lucius smirked despite the Herkosian's stupidity. 'We need only convince the king to return to Bastion. Failing that, we'll conceive another way, but for now, my large friend, we are to keep a cool head. Lord Beaumont is an aging fool, but he's loyal to Arkos. If we so much as slight the king in his presence, he'll likely pit his knights against us.' Lucius looked his men once over as he sought to gauge their thoughts. 'We're not here to fight, gentlemen,' he repeated, 'at least not yet.'

They rode forward, keeping a tight formation until several knights, having retrieved and settled their horses, mounted up with sword and shield. They formed a line across the wide road, a wall of bristling steel shining in the midday sun. Their horses stamped and snorted until a squire with keen eyes motioned to one of the knights. Words were uttered and moments later their swords were sheathed, their shields placed by their side. A knight with a green plume swaying atop his helm spurred his horse forward, halting as Lucius and the Palaceguard reached even ground.

'Greetings, Sir Lucius of the Palaceguard,' said the knight after lifting his visor.

Lucius could barely see the man's face, his silver helmet reflecting the sun like a mirror. He did notice the black wolf on green field marking his shield, though, and knew the man to be Sir Eros of Greenvale. 'Greetings, Sir Eros,' Lucius gave a curt nod, 'we are here for the king.'

The knight nodded and moved to one side, knowing it was not his place to prevent the Captain of the Palaceguard from reaching his lord. Lucius could see the surprise on his face as he passed, though, and briefly wondered if any of the men had questioned the king's departure without his loyal knights.

It took only minutes before they reached what remained of the column. They'd skirted more than a dozen overturned wagons in the process, many only now being heaved upright and some visibly in need of repair due to broken or warped wheels. No matter what their thoughts were on the matter, the Rochdale cavalry was going nowhere fast.

Eventually they rounded a cart being reloaded with barrels and spotted the king, in discussion with a few men-at-a-arms. As he and his knights approached they dispersed; sent to task. Lucius dismounted with his men and walked towards the king's towering figure.

'Your highness,' he said as he moved to stand before him.

Lucius watched the king turn about to appraise him, his eyes unreadable behind the snarling jaguar helmet. After a period of silence, the king's gauntleted hands rose to lift the black helm, but instead of the tired face of his cousin, Lucius was greeted with the grinning visage of a red-bearded man.

'Griffith!' Lucius spat the word as his hand grasped the pommel of his sword. 'Frey's Luck!' he gasped. 'What devilry is this?'

'No devilry, Lucius, just deception,' Griffith said with a hand in the air, doing his best to mimic some theatrical pantomime.

Lucius fumed. 'Cale Griffith, Captain of the Sceptres,' he said with scorn, 'why are you here, man, and in the king's armour?'

Griffith shrugged, and Lucius fought hard to stop himself from drawing his blade and plunging it through his deceitful chest. They rode half a day to reach this column, believing King Arkos rode on his way to the south.

'A request of the king,' Griffith said. 'He spoke with me yesterday, early in the morning, and asked of me a favour. You should know we spoke, for it was your men who drew their swords on me as I arrived at Highcastle.' Lucius watched as the large man smiled once more. 'I didn't ask specifics, Vupello, I simply did as I was told.'

'So where is the king?'

'As far as I know,' Griffith wiped sweat from his brow, 'he remains in Highcastle.'

'I should have you dead for such trickery,' Lucius said, his hand still firmly clasped about the hilt of his sword.

'Allow me to cut him down,' offered Owen Moor as he stepped forward wearing a wicked grin.

Griffith was about to reply when the clatter of armoured men caused him to look over his shoulder. Lord Beaumont and a score of his personal knights came to stand by Griffith's side.

'Is there a problem here, Captain Griffith?' asked Lord Beaumont. He was a bearded elderly man, nearing sixty, his muscle now running to fat. Lucius could see his three sons, all battle-hardened, by his side. Standing there in chain mail with hands resting on cold steel, they appeared eager for a confrontation.

'I do not believe so, Lord Beaumont,' Griffith smiled. 'The little man, Sir Owen Moor, was merely making a jest to lighten the mood.'

Lucius heard Owen inhale sharply and could almost feel his burning hatred. Whatever game was being played out here, it was over. He didn't have time to banter words with the Captain of the Sceptres, nor could he afford retaliation. Pushing thoughts of revenge to the side he motioned for his men to mount up. 'I'll be seeing you, Griffith,' he said, his face devoid of emotion. He then spun his horse around before spurring towards Bastion, his Palaceguard behind him.

*

'A pity they had to ride away so soon,' offered Lord Beaumont as he clapped a mailed fist atop Griffith's shoulder.

Griffith smiled as he watched the departing knights. He detested Lucius Vupello, almost as much as Owen Moor. His smile faded as he watched the departing men, now little more than a cloud of dust, before he swivelled towards Lord Beaumont. 'Thank you for your timely intervention,' he said, his voice deep, 'although it would have pleased me to have traded blows with Owen Moor.'

A chuckle rippled from the gathered men. Most knew Griffith by reputation only, but all had seen his warhammer on the morning journey. It was a large weapon, fit only for the very strong. Seeing it in action would have been a sight to behold.

'What are your plans now?' asked Lord Beaumont.

'I'll head back to Bastion; take my men with me,' Griffith looked across the field to where some of his officers helped reload carts.

'I can send an escort of knights with you, if you like.'

Griffith shook his head. 'No, my twenty will suffice.'

Lord Beaumont shifted his bulk and cursed the heat of the day before addressing Griffith once more. 'I wonder why Arkos never informed Lucius and his Palaceguard of his little ploy this morning.'

'I wonder indeed,' Griffith murmured, although he knew all too well the machinations of the king. Three years as Captain of the Sceptres had honed Griffith's mind to such devious ploys. He knew Arkos was canny enough to realize Lucius coveted the throne. Yet the deaths of princes Atillus and Theos had been the final straw. A frustrated king was bearable, but an enraged Battle-King was an entirely different proposition. If others beside southerners helped orchestrate his son's deaths, Arkos would leave no stone unturned in his quest to hunt them down.

It occurred to Griffith that this morning's deception may have been the king's first foray into turning stones.

'Time to ride, methinks,' Griffith said, followed by a heavy sigh. The ride out had been slow due to the wagons and carts, but the return journey wouldn't be so hampered.

'Then I'll bid you farewell, Griffith, at least for now. Be certain to send word of the coming events, though, I like to be kept informed.'

Griffith grinned, for he knew Lord Beaumont had become a gossip in his old age. 'I shall,' he replied, 'and gladly.' The two men clasped hands before Griffith moved to a line of horses and sent word to his men to cease their tasks and mount up. He had fled Bastion as requested with twenty of his officers, a man named Olsen his most senior.

'We're leaving,' Griffith said to Olsen by way of greeting. He was a hard man, Olsen, with short brown hair, a nose heavily askew and a day's growth always darkening his jaw line. He was as loyal as he was hard, though. 'Have the men mount up and follow me. I'll be waiting at the top of the rise,' he pointed to where the Palaceguard's dust cloud had finally dissipated.

'Is that wise?' Olsen asked with his deep voice. Griffith knew he'd watched the confrontation from where he stood. His hand would have been by his side, ready to draw steel if required.

'Not entirely,' Griffith rumbled, hoisting his crimson warhammer from the saddle. He gave it an affectionate pat. He hadn't wielded the weapon for years, at least not in combat, but today felt different. He sensed there was more to come before this day was out. He also believed *Bloodstain* would see action.

'I'll see you shortly, then,' Olsen said as he slapped Griffith's horse. The big man nodded, then guided his mount between those still at work righting wagons and reloading goods. The earthquake, for all its fury, was now a thing of the past. Yet he felt right in his assessment of the day's events. There was something in the air, something almost tangible. There would be more to this day than a broken column of knights.

A whole lot more, in fact.

For now, though, his task was to return to Bastion. He knew the pile of parchment on his desk would have increased during his short absence and try as he might he couldn't seem to whittle it down these days. Setorious would have reported in at some point as well, eager to relay his information on Tarsin Va. He would have to decide today or tomorrow on his next course of action concerning the swordsman. He'd only allow him to wander the streets for so long. For now, he wondered what his first words to the swordsman would be.

He reached the top of the rise and heard his twenty ride up behind him. They were solid men; men accustomed to dealing with the unsavoury of Bastion. They'd fought in back alleys and tavern common rooms, rumbled across the wide expanse of the King's Way. But they weren't soldiers, nor were they knights of the kingdom. If push came to shove against Vupello and his Palaceguard, Griffith knew they'd fare poorly. Still, it was a comfort to have them by his side, more so when he realised Vupello and his knights were well on their way to the city.

With a wave he gave the order and set out at a trot, keeping their pace even whilst he ordered young Miles to roam ahead and scout their path. Bastion was no more than four hours away at this pace. They'd reach her walls by mid-afternoon.

Yet hours later as the sun slid to the west, Griffith felt the cool touch of a southerly wind caress his face, and with it a sense of dread began to manifest inside his chest. At first it was more a dull ache attributable to indigestion, or so he thought, yet the pain intensified the further they travelled. Then it shifted and became a source of great discomfit. He moved his armour about, the king's armour, and told himself he lacked conditioning, nothing more.

A moment later a wave of nausea washed over him that nearly toppled him from his horse.

'Are you alright?' Olsen, riding by his side, held out a hand to steady him.

'Aye, I think,' he mumbled. 'This armour, coupled with the sun, is roasting me good and proper. I need a drink.' As soon as he said the words he knew he referred to the amber liquid back in his office, hidden away in his drawer. He could almost taste the fire running down his throat, smell damp earth and honeysuckle.

'Here, drink some water,' Olsen handed him a waterskin.

'Pah! Water is for women,' he grabbed the proffered skin anyway.

'Drink it,' Olsen gestured with a gloved hand. 'You're sweating like a pig. If you faint and fall off your horse, who do you think is going to hoist you off the ground?'

Griffith sighed and did as bid. The man was right. He'd lost a good amount of fluid, could feel it dripping down his back and running down his legs. Even his gambeson was soaked through and beginning to smell. Yet even as the cool liquid slid past his lips a nagging thought surfaced, one he was afraid to ignore.

All was confusion after the earthquake, with horses snapping their traces and bolting into the fields. Wagons full of supplies were overturned, spilling their contents haphazardly as man and beast scrambled frantically to reach a haven. Only the ground shook uncontrollably for well over a minute; violently to the point Griffith believed he was going to die. He'd rolled onto his back and looked up at the sky. Trees groaned to his left, horses screamed in the distance. Even the shouts of grown men assailed his ears, accompanied by racking sobs of fear.

Then it stopped.

His relief was palpable and within seconds men were finding their feet, offering hands to those who cautiously remained on all fours. Slaps on the back and jests about Frey prevailed. Tears were wiped from cheeks and hands were steadied with a thought. Looking back now, though, had Griffith feeling ill.

Something catastrophic had occurred; he was certain, and it wasn't just the shock of the situation.

'We've five, maybe six hours of sunlight left,' mentioned Olsen, taking back the waterskin. Griffith grunted a reply, his eyes fixed on the horizon.

'We'll reach Bastion within the hour,' Griffith said as they neared the final rise before the road headed down to the plains. The scout, Miles, was beneath an old oak tree to the left, his horse tethered to a low hanging branch. He was standing tall, a hand shielding his eyes from the sun as he cast his gaze towards Bastion. He didn't turn as the men approached.

'What do you see?' Griffith shouted as he and Olsen moved away from the road and veered over to the oak. Griffith didn't particularly wish to admire the view of the city but the shade beneath the oak would be welcome. Miles remained silent as he turned to appraise the two men. Griffith could instantly tell something was wrong. With a shaking hand, Miles pointed towards the city of Bastion, beckoning Griffith to look for himself. He did, and nearly fell off his horse.

Bastion: Holy City, had fallen.

It lay in ruins; its walls a crumbling heap, the docks underwater and hundreds of buildings aflame. Even the surrounding towns and fields were in tatters with large tracts of land heaved violently from below. The small fishing village beneath Southern Wall had vanished, nothing more than a dark smear to remember it by. To the west he saw ships listing in the Bay of Pennants, whilst others lay scattered as shards amongst the city's lower streets, thrown with impunity against stone walls and keeps. As he scanned his eyes further afield he saw a thickening pall of ash and dust hovering above much of the city, obscuring their view of the city's central, northern and western quarters.

'What happened?' Olsen was the first to speak, his voice choked with emotion.

'Earthquake,' Griffith suggested, shaking his head in amazement. 'It must have been the one we felt at midday, only Bastion felt its full wrath.' He pointed towards the Southern Wall and the location of Southgate, now a pile of rubble. 'The wall has fallen in many places,' he said. 'It looks as if water from the Bay of Pennants was forced into the lower streets.'

The men remained silent for some time, taking in the horrendous view. There was so much destruction it simply boggled the mind. Bastion was home to over two hundred thousand people. Now she lay in ruin, a shell of her former self barely recognizable to men who called her home.

Griffith wondered how Bastion could survive. She was beset upon from all quarters and now she was flattened with a single blow. How one grieving king could revive what remained was beyond comprehension.

'Let's move out,' he finally said, his voice hushed. 'We'll need to head for Eastgate, cut across the plains until we reach the Eastern Way.' It was no use following the south road, for it now lay under water and Southgate was impassable. The journey east would add an extra hour to their ride, time they could ill afford to lose but their choices were limited. Spurring his horse forward he moved into a trot. 'Come!' he yelled, gesturing towards the city, 'Bastion needs us. Let's ride like the wind!'

Behind him he heard Olsen speak to his fellow officers with his deep voice, knew he'd have his hand raised high in the air. 'You heard the Captain,' he said, and Griffith could picture his hand sweeping down with a chop. 'Let's move out!'

CHAPTER ELEVEN

Tarsin found a ladder concealed in shadow at the end of the causeway. He swung it about and lowered it into the pit where his men sat stupefied. His flaming brand followed to light the way a second later, before he descended in quick fashion, his rapidly beating heart a reminder of what was at stake. The floor, when he stepped into the pit, was mud and muck, the stench horrendous. Beyond the cloying quagmire, lining the walls, was an assortment of rectangular mirrors; some as high as three feet. Each of his men sat before a single mirror, silent and unmoving.

He reached for his flaming brand and took timid steps towards Cale Griffith, his booted feet having trouble escaping the mud. When he reached his side, he moved towards the mirror to see his friend's reflection staring back at him. His eyes were wide and unblinking. Tarsin shook his head. They were the eyes of the dead, glazed and unseeing. A quick scan of the pit revealed each of his men in a similar state. Some were several feet from their mirror; others were in the process of reaching out to the silvered surface. A few were already plunging into their magical depths.

'Griffith,' he called to his friend, waving a hand before his eyes. There was no response. 'Griffith!' he yelled this time and clapped his hands.

Nothing.

He lifted tired legs to squelch towards the mirror, careful to avoid its hypnotic reflection. He thought of smashing the glass with his sword but considered silence the better option. With trembling hands, he reached out and pulled the frame, stepping back as the mirror toppled into the muck. A gentle sigh escaped the big man behind him as the mirror fell.

'Griffith,' he said once more as he saw eyes blinking in confusion.

'Tarsin,' Griffith's voice was harsh, scraped like dried paper. 'Where am I?'

Tarsin offered a hand, helping his friend find his feet. It wasn't easy, for he'd soiled himself and stank like the muck he knelt in.

'Nowhere pleasant,' Tarsin stifled a gag and moved to the next in line, beckoning Griffith to help. It was John Rhys, his face three inches away from his reflection. Griffith pulled the man back by his shoulders as Tarsin tilted the mirror. Like Griffith, John Rhys blinked in confusion as the spell was broken.

'Come, Rhys,' Tarsin spoke quietly as he retrieved his flaming brand and held it high, looking for the next to rescue. Twenty-four men had ridden from Bastion to Benwith at the behest of the king, in four groups of six. Yet as Tarsin peered about the pit he stood in, fewer than a dozen were visible, a good portion of those already with parts of their body embedded within mirrors. He stepped towards Marco Santelli as John Rhys moved further into the shadows, ready to help rescue his fellow swordsmen. Santelli's lithe body was recognizable in the dim light, his long black hair tied back in a tail. Griffith joined him and moved his frame to stand opposite. Both of Santelli's hands were inside the silver mirror, plunged half-way up his forearms.

'What do we do?' Griffith asked with a tired voice. Behind them the voice of John Rhys spoke to another victim rescued, their steps through the muck loud as they moved towards another.

'Grab his shoulders and we'll pull him out,' Tarsin placed hands on Santelli's shoulder and elbow whilst Griffith followed his lead. They stood there a moment looking at each other, wondering what else they could do. Then with a nod they lifted their friend and walked back a pace, moving his body away from the mirror.

Marco Santelli screamed.

Tarsin looked at his friend to see blood pumping from the stumps of his severed arms. It squirted about the pit, painting the walls red as Santelli splashed hot gore into the air. In a mad rush Tarsin reached for his friend and grabbed him about the torso as Griffith sought to hold his flaying arms. Tarsin could see blood everywhere, was covered in it, could taste it. He didn't even have a cloth to bandage his friend's horrendous wounds. Even his own clothes were soiled from his time in the pit. In desperation Tarsin placed a hand over Santelli's blood-flecked mouth and spoke words to calm him, but his cries of anguish were soon joined by another. The flaming brand had fallen during the commotion to splutter feebly, casting long shadows. Tarsin could see the outline of John Rhys and someone else, then blinked as a third man on his knees toppled to the floor.

Tarsin yelled, his voice a chorus of pain.

Then he yelled again, a cry of pure anguish violently ripped from his throat.

He opened his eyes to see a hazy sky.

He was on his back lying in the middle of the street, the cobblestones hard against his spine. He rolled to his side and pushed gloved hands beneath him and stood on shaking legs. Dust sifted from his shoulders as the groans of timber drifted to him on a cool breeze. He wiped a hand across his face; saw a dark stain bloom on the back of his glove. It was apparent blood seeped from his nose.

'Frey's Luck,' he whispered, 'where am I?'

He spun around to see shattered buildings lying in ruin, segments of the street warped, entire mounds of earth heaved upward. Smoke billowed in the distance and he could hear the vibrant crackle of flame.

He shook his head to clear it of his nightmare, aware the screams in his mind still rang loudly. It took a moment before he realised the screams he now heard were the screams of the living.

He breathed deep to calm his nerves. He had no idea how long he'd been unconscious. His hands still shook with fright, his legs trembled in fear. Then in a moment of clarity he remembered the horrific shaking of the ground as the earthquake struck with Hell's own fury.

He shivered as a disconcerting thought crossed his mind, for it appeared his dreams of terror were now a living reality.

The sound of shuffling feet spun him around. A man walked past him, blood-stained and dazed. Tarsin peered down the street to see others rising from the debris. They moved awkwardly, the spark of life momentarily gone, their bodies in shock. They were listless, appeared to be unhinged: lost souls drifting through a shattered landscape. All around him were men, women and children moving in abject terror.

A muffled call for help sounded from behind him. He moved with purpose, his body suddenly fuelled by a necessity to live and to save those in trouble. A large piece of granite rested against a partially collapsed doorway. He shifted his bulk against the granite block and felt it give as his muscles strained and his breath came in shallow gasps. A scrape followed by sifting dirt saw it slide and then topple with a crash. Dust billowed into a small cloud then settled to reveal a dark recess. Fading sunlight revealed a mother and child huddled in each other's arms beneath the doorframe. Tears streaked their dusty faces. Tarsin offered a hand.

'Thank you,' the mother choked back tears as she rose gingerly to her feet, her child, a young girl, nestled in her arms.

'Are there others inside?' he asked, his voice hushed.

'No, just the two of us,' the mother wiped her daughter's brow.

Tarsin looked to his left; saw other men and women heading towards the city centre. He pointed in its direction. 'Make for the pyramid,' he said.

The lady left with her daughter clutched firmly about her neck, both bloodstained and dispirited. Tarsin watched them leave, then realised there would be thousands trapped this day. Across the street lay another large slab of granite, its irregular shape wedged firmly against a leaning wall. A single hand could be seen protruding at its base, torn and bloodied. The realisation that not all those trapped could be saved dawned on him then.

He wiped the back of his hand across his mouth, hoping to rid himself of the taste of dirt and dust. He sniffed but could do little to rid himself of the stench of death; it was everywhere. *This is how it begins*, he thought as he scanned his immediate surrounds. The city was barely recognizable. Towers and keeps lay shattered across walkways and streets, their bricks and mortar pulverised into dust and dirt, whilst timber beams thicker than a man's torso protruded from fallen homes, their ends snapped clean in half as though they were mere twigs. An even closer inspection revealed an enormous amount of jagged granite slabs lying crushed and broken amongst the crumbled houses and taverns, their irregular pieces lining every path. It was a complete saturation. How it ended up scattered throughout the city he could only guess, yet even as his mind sought a clear and definitive answer, his gaze was drawn towards the great pyramid. He looked upon Aston's Tear and saw she was no longer sheathed in white stone. Now, if his eyes were not deceived, she'd shed her outer-layer of granite to reveal a structure made of diamond.

'Anok and Eli!' the curse whispered from between his teeth. Never had he seen such a sight. For a moment, he believed it even brought a tear to his eye, before he realised it was more blood trickling down his cheek. It was apparent he wasn't as unharmed as first thought. Even now, as he flexed his shoulders and stretched his arms, he could feel bruised muscles and tender flesh. Covering his eyes with a hand he chanced a look above. Thick black clouds were already blooming to the east, the result of raging fires, obscuring much of the clear blue sky. The sun still sat high, though, reminding Tarsin it was only, at best, a fraction past midday. He'd been unconscious only a brief time.

Kneeling, he placed a hand against the cracked ground, more to steady his thoughts than for any other purpose. He'd been walking towards Highcastle when the commotion began, determined to see King Arkos for a reckoning. He needed to release the pent-up pain and anger he'd harboured for so long; needed to feel cleansed before he took up arms in defence of his king once more. For fifteen years Tarsin had done everything in his power to please Arkos Vantos, but for the last three years he'd soured his soul with thoughts of regret and failure. To the unsettling mix, when his conscience kicked in, he'd further added revenge to his blackened thoughts. It caused him to become somewhat of a recluse, to experience moods of depression. On more than one occasion he'd harboured a desire to end his own life, had come terribly close once. He still remembered sitting in the dark room in Al-Za'im, alone with the night, a sharp dagger pressed firmly against his throat. A single quick action would see the blade slice his skin, ending his torment. It would be so easy, his one chance to embrace forgetfulness.

Tarsin had closed his eyes shut in anticipation, but all he saw in the darkness was the green eyes of Du Weng Sai, burning bright with life. His former Rykedian master would disapprove, would remind him of commitment to life and the Universe. A deeply religious soul was his master, a man in tune with the world and its foibles. He understood the battle every man took internally: the battle of emotions. 'Man cannot exist with pure thoughts alone,' he would say. 'There must always be a balance. Comprehending such a balance is the first step to enlightenment.'

Tarsin recalled his lessons with the little master, sitting in the corner of the Pit with quill pen in hand and a sheaf of parchment on a board in his lap. He'd expressed concern with Du Weng's preachings. 'What of the holy priests leading their flocks?' he asked. 'Surely they are men of pure thought and action?'

'Priests are men who lead by example, young Tarsin,' he replied, 'but they are simply men who mask their inner doubts behind a facade of kindliness. Their demons may even be greater than yours or mine due to the sacrifices imposed upon them, but they are most definitely no less real.'

'What of evil men? Are they not men controlled by dark thoughts and motives, blinded to the light?'

Du Weng paused to gather his thoughts. 'It is written in some cultures that to be a great killer is to be a man devoid of emotion. Emotion clouds judgement; confuses simple solutions. Without emotion, a man can act with purpose and intent, no longer second guessing his actions or asking pertinent questions concerning such tasks. But a man without emotion is no man at all. He is just a tool, someone to be used by another, merely an object. Many evil men fall under such a banner. For them I feel sorry, for they are no longer truly living.'

'What of my doubts and fears, Du Weng? How should I deal with them?'

'With emotion, young man,' the look in his slanted eyes was piercing. 'Feel the pain of anger, experience it. If you know how it feels to be angry, in time, you will discover a means to control such anger. There must always be a balance; it is the one guiding principle of the Universe. Do not be afraid to step into the dark, Tarsin. Just remember, when it is time, to step back into the light.'

The blade at his throat still pressed tight against his skin. He could feel the cold steel; almost envisage the slice prior to the bloodletting. There was no discernible shake in his arm, he was ready.

He raced his tongue over his lips and tasted salt. *Salt? Where has the salt come from?*

It took a moment for him to realise he was crying, tears streaming unhindered down his cheeks. He breathed deeply, seeking to calm his nerves, only to feel heavy sobs rake his body. A moment later the steel blade fell with a clang to the floor, its clear strike awakening Tarsin back into the world. He opened his eyes to see a shaft of light streaming through his window; the first rays of light heralding a new dawn.

The sound of Du Weng's voice filtered through his muddled thoughts. 'Remember, Tarsin, to step back into the light.'

He'd done so then, but the more he remembered, the more he questioned his right to do so now. *Why should I live when so many of my men lie dead?* They'd been under his command. They'd followed his lead. Now they were memories too easily forgotten, memories of men and mirrors splashed with blood. Perhaps it was time he joined them. Perhaps in death he could make matters right, amend the mistakes he'd made.

Or he could redeem himself with courage and valour in the world of the living; reclaim the mantle of Captain of the Unseen and protect the king in his most desperate hour of need. Elder Cappitus had said as much last night, after he sought out the brother following the minor earthquake the day before. Ruvin agreed with Cappitus' thoughts, felt now was the time to forget the past. There were greater issues at stake right now, issues of importance far superior to those of a man consumed with his own dark past.

The brothers pressed further, reminding him that if anger clearly motivated his thoughts of revenge, then who better to seek out and destroy than the witch herself. It was she who inevitably killed his men in the foothills of Benwith. They suffered due to her design. Killing Avra would go a long way to appeasing his guilt.

In the end, he'd been swayed by their passion. Arkos Vantos needed protection. He may be king, but he was a man first and foremost, and being a man, he was subject to making mistakes. Now, like Arkos, Tarsin was keen to atone for his own errors of judgement. He could only do so if he kept himself, and the king, alive.

With a sigh, he pushed himself up from his kneeling position and began to walk in the pyramid's direction, continuing to climb over conglomerations of brick and timber and large tracts of earth. The trek took longer than expected for many buildings lay strewn across his path, and to the east he saw fires still burning out of control amongst an area known for its granaries. Even Irongate had been damaged, he saw, its observatory gone, part of its curtain wall collapsed.

Tarsin pushed on, moving slowly to avoid fallen masonry and with an ear tuned for muffled calls of help. He lost count of the people he dragged from the debris. From shattered buildings and toppled walls, he shifted stones and wooden beams, seeking those pinned or buried, his thoughts drifting to Ruvin and Jarred back at the Oakwood and Stout. He prayed they were alive and well as he climbed another pile of rubble, wondered if his men, under Bevan's leadership, were likewise safe. He couldn't bear the thought of his men suffering. An urge to return to the tavern suddenly consumed him. Yet as soon as he thought to return he crested a mound of rubble to find himself standing before the pyramid, its gleaming silver-blue walls flawless and incredibly bright as it sat atop its base of red granite. The stairs carved into the red base were cluttered with sand and quartz dust: all that remained of the pyramids former facade. The rest had been blown high and far, to land with devastating effect upon those buildings within proximity. It appeared that for many in Bastion this day, if the earthquake didn't kill you, the falling blocks of stone certainly did.

He shook his head and began to climb the steps. Countless others were already walking about its perimeter, gazing in awe as the horrors of the day were momentarily forgotten. The earthquake had been terrifying, its magnitude far above the previous day's tremor. He'd felt a moment of lucidity that he was certain preceded death. Then, so far as he could recall, he'd fallen hard to the ground before darkness took him. He raised a hand to touch the side of his head, then pulled his gloved hand back and checked his fingers. The bleeding had stopped, at least, although he'd felt a small bump near his temple.

He joined countless others now clamouring up the red steps to peer in awe at the new marvel. Forgotten were those still in dire need of support. Their faint calls were now drowned by excited chatter as eyes grew wide upon appraising the seamless flanks of diamond sitting in the sunlight. Here, despite all the turmoil, sat a wonder of hope and salvation for a people in need. It was a miracle, a sign from the gods.

Yet even as he crested the red steps and took in the wondrous view, he pondered over how many thousands perished under the avalanche of granite that once graced those very same walls.

He sucked in a lungful of stale air, then began the task of jostling past those too intent on looking upon the pyramid. The only difference he could see between their awe-struck gaze compared to the listless, dazed visages earlier was the wonder in their eyes. It spoke of life and hope, whereas those after the earthquake spoke only of death and sorrow.

He pushed through the crowd, his hand resting lightly on the pommel of his sword. It was habit only, but the noise and the press were beginning to unnerve him.

'Tarsin!' the call came from a group of black robes ahead. Elder Cappitus, his long white beard prominent, waved a gnarled staff in his direction. 'I'm glad you're here.'

Tarsin reached his side only to see doubt and confusion poorly veiled within his eyes. 'We have much to discuss, Cappitus,' he returned.

'I know, gods above do I know,' he practically choked on his words before looking to the sky with pleading eyes. It was darkening rapidly due to the fires in the east. 'There is something you must see.'

Tarsin made to reply but a commotion below the pyramid's base diverted his attention. He and the Brotherhood looked towards the noise, aware of snorting horses and their stomping steel-shod hooves.

'Who is it?' Tarsin heard a member of the Brotherhood ask as men and women offered a half-hearted cheer.

Tarsin kept quiet as he scanned the men with an assured eye. There was more than a dozen, by first count, and weary looking. Standing head and shoulders above them all was the king in his polished black armour, his snarling jaguar helmet all too recognizable.

'Do not let the armour fool you,' Cappitus kept his voice low as he spoke to Tarsin, 'for beneath the armour stands the Captain of the Sceptres.'

Tarsin raised an eyebrow. 'Where is the king?'

Cappitus sighed, and several men of the Brotherhood placed hands palm down across their chest. 'Come with me,' he said, before turning about and walking away, heading for the northern face of the pyramid. It was a brisk walk, but Tarsin kept pace until they stood looking west towards Highcastle. There was a heavy pall of dust and ash in the sky above that made visibility low, but the pyramid's silver-blue emanation offset the gloom. 'Look,' Cappitus pointed past the fallen pillars of the King's Plaza. 'It is hard to see,' he continued, 'but Highcastle is beyond.'

Tarsin narrowed his eyes to see nought but rock and shale in a wedge-shaped mound. There was no sign of the four guard towers or Highcastle's magnificent gatehouse. It lay buried, the cliff wall behind it having sheared clean from the mountain. He wondered if anyone could survive such a calamity.

'We are optimistic,' Cappitus said, as if reading his mind, 'of finding the king alive and well. He is a resourceful man, as you well know.'

Tarsin nodded, for he knew Cappitus and his Brotherhood, as well as Neema of the Celestial Sisters, all pinned their hopes on King Arkos being their salvation. If he should lie dead and buried, Tarsin feared the mystical orders would be of little help in the battle to come.

'How shall we reach him?' Tarsin kept his eyes focussed on the mound that was Highcastle.

'Through the sewers,' replied Cappitus. 'They are extensive, fashioned of Nepharii architecture. We hope they still stand.'

'When would you like me to leave?' Tarsin asked for he knew he had little choice. As much as he still felt Arkos betrayed him by sending him north to Benwith, he couldn't forsake him now. He wondered if he was too late.

'Now if you are able; we've no time to lose.'

'Will I have any help?'

'I'll travel with you,' the voice was metallic and carried a slight echo.

Tarsin spun to see a sizeable group of men and women standing behind them, consisting of the armoured Captain of the Sceptres and his yellow and black clad officers.

'If you'll have me, that is,' said the armoured man.

Tarsin shrugged as the captain raised gauntleted fists to release him of his cloying helmet.

A murmur carried briefly through the gathered crowd as those nearby realized it was not the king standing before them but Cale Griffith, Captain of the Sceptres, his red hair plastered with sweat and hanging lank across his forehead, his beard dripping moisture atop his breastplate.

'Cale Griffith,' Tarsin said, greeting the man with a nervous smile. A guard pushed himself through the crowd to reach Griffith's side, an immense warhammer tinged red by his side. He passed it to his Captain before melting back into the crowd.

'The very same, Tarsin Va,' the smile was returned, Griffith's pearly white teeth flashing from between his fiery beard. 'Shall we,' Griffith raised his helmet to point the way, suggesting Tarsin lead. He concurred, but only after offering advice to Cappitus, asking that he organize a team of men to begin the arduous task of clearing Highcastle from above. He returned his attention back to Griffith.

'Are you ready?' Tarsin asked whilst Griffith took a mouthful of water from an offered waterskin.

'Are you?' he returned, and Tarsin briefly wondered if the words carried connotations meant for him alone. He watched as Griffith drank another mouthful before he spat the water to the ground. He then hoisted his hammer across one shoulder. His other fist carried the snarling jaguar helmet.

With no more to offer Tarsin spun to face Highcastle. It would take time to reach with so much destruction hampering their path, especially with dusk approaching. Although exhausted, he vowed to plough on, for King Arkos needed him, now more than ever. The man was entombed under Highcastle, possibly alone and in utter darkness.

Tarsin needed to find him. He needed to dig his king clear and offer his hand. Then together, they could step back into the light.

CHAPTER TWELVE

Lucius Vupello withdrew his sword from the dying man's throat.

He was furious, a fact not lost on his men as he wiped his blade clean on the now dead man's shirt. 'I would say sorry, friend,' his voice was low as he glanced into the dead man's eyes, 'but you are clearly no friend of mine. Peasants should obey, not shout demands.' He stood and sheathed his sword, locking eyes with his Palaceguard as he did so. No-one said a word; which was a pleasant change. He'd listened enough to their bickering the last hour as they sought to move further into Bastion.

He walked to his horse, Strom, and stroked the steed's neck whilst his men oversaw the clearing of rubble barring their way. Two-dozen men, commoners all, slaved as they hoisted bricks from the road. Lucius was adamant the Palaceguard retain their mounts as they rode towards Highcastle, citing the need for speed, but the collapse of a building during a minor aftershock had fenced them in. Even the road behind them had become unstable and a sizeable crevice had appeared fifty feet further back, spooking the horses every time they moved near. The only path available was forward, but the fallen masonry was more numerous than first thought. What had started out as a minor task had become a gruelling affair, culminating in one commoner venting his anger at Lucius and demanding he be released so he could salvage items from his own home. Now he lay dead, his throat dark with congealing blood, his shirt soaked red.

'We're almost through,' Jaegar walked to stand beside him.

Lucius chanced a quick glance to the darkening sky; the sun was already lost behind the mountains to the west. 'Gather a handful of men and search for some lanterns,' he said, knowing the enveloping smoke would make visibility poor in the coming hours, 'or failing that, fashion some torches. We cannot afford to travel blindly, not with the horses.'

Jaegar nodded and walked away, calling a handful of men to begin searching some of the more stable abodes lining the street. There were few, Lucius noted, and not for the first time he wondered if they should have moved north towards the Eastern Quarter and not south into Guildford once they passed under Eastgate. The roads through Guildford were wider, he knew, but the Avenue of Kings was already choked with citizens fleeing the devastated city. It was thought turning south would enable them to reach Highcastle with haste. In hindsight, he was wrong. He spat to the side, anger once more boiling to the surface.

'The path is clear!' he heard Owen Moor shout from ahead.

Lucius tightened his fist about Strom's reins and walked the charger forward, quietly offering words of encouragement as he did so. The remaining Palaceguard moved to their own steeds and followed, Jeagar not far behind, he and three others carrying lanterns pilfered from an abandoned home. The commoners watched as the knights passed, then dispersed like field mice fleeing a barn owl.

Lucius and his knights led their horses with care. As far as they could see the road ahead remained void of any dark crevices, although countless piles of rubble had to be skirted. After some tedious manoeuvring, they reached the main thoroughfare of Southgate Way.

A horse whinnied to Luicus' right and he shifted to see who walked alongside. It was Sir Hector Bradford, the oldest member of the Palaceguard, once renowned for his charming good looks and cavalier attitude. Even now, at age forty-eight, his hair was more blonde than silver. He caught Lucius' eye and pointed with his bearded chin toward Aston's Tear, the pyramid having just come into view as they rounded onto the main thoroughfare.

'Would you look at that,' he said, noting the silver-blue glow emanating from its diamond-like walls.

The men, as one, halted their walk, the sound of leather and mail subsiding until only the heavy breathing of man and horse could be heard.

'What in Hell's name is going on here?' Lucius whispered. His eyes remained fixed on the marvel at the end of the street.

'Should we investigate?' Sir Hector asked, his gaze unwavering.

'I believe so,' Lucius replied, knowing if they were to reach Highcastle they would need to pass Aston's Tear in any case. The men murmured behind him, taken aback by the spectacle. 'Let's move,' he raised his voice. No-one said a word in reply; they simply followed his lead, faces raised so they could keep the glowing pyramid in view.

The walk was short, despite the crumbled buildings, and they soon reached Aston's Tear. There were only four sets of steps leading to the pyramid, one at each of the cardinal points, and the eastern face appeared most readily accessible. Once at the foot of the steps Lucius issued a verbal command to his horse to remain and began to climb, his booted feet crunching atop piles of quartz dust. His men followed.

'Look,' Jaegar's long arm jutted out to point towards the top of the steps. There, standing in awe, stood the small, rotund figure of Kerros Gavony, his back to the approaching men, his eyes fixed firmly ahead.

Lucius' mouth became crooked, the sneer not lost on Jaegar as he watched his captain. 'I'd have words with that one,' he snarled. 'Bastard sent us riding for a day chasing a jester dressed as royalty,' he spat to the side. 'I wonder if he even knows King Arkos still resides in Highcastle.' Lucius gave Jaegar a nod and sent him up the steps.

He watched Jaegar take the remaining steps two at a time until he stood towering over the little man, his large hand falling to rest on Kerros' shoulder.

Kerros did little more than sigh at the sudden intrusion.

'Greetings Kerros,' Lucius climbed the last of the steps, his men spread behind him, intimidating in their mail and black tabards. The smaller man looked a wreck, dried blood smeared across his top lip, scratches and bruises swelling his face.

'Sir Lucius Vupello!' he gasped and offered a slight bow before casting his gaze over the men, seeing stern yet tired faces. 'Where is the King?' he finally asked.

Lucius stepped forward to place his gloved hand around the small man's throat. He squeezed tight, his fingers digging into soft, yielding flesh. 'The king never left Bastion, fool,' spittle flew from his mouth to strike Kerros' face. 'It was all a ploy, a trick to root out those disloyal to his majesty.' He could see Kerros pale before his eyes. He tried to talk, but only a squeak issued forth. Lucius squeezed tighter for a moment, before relaxing his grip.

'You say . . . the king . . . is in Highcastle,' he spluttered as he caught his breath.

'Yes, he never left. It was Cale Griffith armoured like the king who rode out with Lord Beaumont,' Lucius gave Kerros a push that sent him back a pace. The little man raised a hand to massage his throat.

'That is . . . unwelcome news, I fear,' Kerros said feebly as he turned to peer at the pyramid.

'Why?'

'Come, I'll show you,' he spun on a heel and began to waddle away. Lucius and his men kept pace, pushing through men and women crowding the pyramid's perimeter, oblivious to the mournful sounds of grieving families. They rounded one side and continued until they could look over the western half of the city. A large crowd of men were already gathered, many robed figures suggesting the Brotherhood of One, along with a handful of priestly orders, were out in force.

'What am I looking at?' Lucius asked once they stopped.

Kerros pointed west, past the ruined heap of the Plaza. It took a moment for his eyes to adjust, but when they did he gasped as the devastation dawned on him. 'Highcastle,' Lucius said, barely above a whisper, 'it's gone.' He wondered if any of his Palaceguard survived. Almost two hundred of his knights were quartered there, not to mention several hundred men of house Vupello.

'Aye, and if King Arkos never left he is now buried beneath half a mountain.'

The worried glance Kerros offered reminded him of their pact with the witch. She required Arkos for sacrifice; he was the bargain she sought. But without Arkos the witch could not be satisfied.

The other thought running wild through his head excited him more, though. For if Arkos was truly dead, Lucius Vupello was next in line for the throne. Bastion may currently be a fallen city, but Dervae was an extensive kingdom. He would now be king. At least his part of the bargain had fallen into place.

He was about to mention the fact to Kerros when he caught sight of two men walking away from the Brotherhood. One was tall, with broad shoulders and a fine sword belted at his waist. The other, though, was the red headed Cale Griffith still wearing the king's armour, his heavy warhammer by his side.

'Damn Griffith is here already!' he kept his eyes on the departing figure, already dreaming about the day he could melt down the king's helmet and have it fashioned into the semblance of a fox. 'How did he arrive so quickly?' Lucius spun towards his men, even though he knew their passage through the broken city had been time consuming.

Sir Hector shrugged, 'Why don't we ask him?'

Kerros must have seen the flash of anger flicker across Lucius' face for he acted fast, moving towards several robed men and posing a question. A brief discussion ensued before the councillor returned. 'Griffith only just arrived,' he said. 'They go to rescue the king . . . if he still lives.'

'Who is the other?' Lucius asked as he looked over the shattered remains of the King's Plaza, its granite pillars no longer standing tall, the aqueduct and its arches cracked and riven.

'You don't know who that is, do you?' Jaegar cracked his knuckles.

Lucius looked up at the taller man. 'Enlighten me, Jaegar. I don't have time to play games.'

'No, you don't,' a smile pushed Jaegar's braided beard out wide. 'And I'd think twice before playing any game with those two. Few know the other man, but I recognize the sword. If the rumours I've heard are true, that man is Tarsin Va.'

Lucius was silent a moment, his eyes now resting on the other man's back. 'Are you certain?' Jaegar was right; few knew anything of Tarsin Va. The man was a mystery. Even though he was one of only a handful of the Unseen to have been identified by Kerros Gavony over the years, his whereabouts and reputed skills remained a mystery.

'Deadly certain; only one man in Bastion carries a sword like that.'

'Owen Moor,' Lucius called the swordsman over to where he stood, 'I need you and four others to tail those two,' he pointed towards their dim figures. 'Keep close, and when they find the king, you're to take charge and bring him to me. Do you understand?'

Owen Moor nodded, his nose scrunched as he breathed in deep. 'Can we kill them?'

'After they've found the king, unless you wish to find him yourself.'

Lucius could see Owen mulling over his options. The man wished revenge against Griffith for the slight earlier in the day. He doubted Owen Moor would confront him head on, the man was too big, but with others by his side he'd feel confident. 'When do we leave?'

'Now, Owen, and choose your men wisely. Do not underestimate those two; there are few men deadlier.'

Owen Moor barked his four names, calling Sirs Hector, Karl, Ethan and Darius to his side. Lucius approved, for they were formidable swordsmen. More importantly they knew how to fight together in close formation. Ethan was also heavy-set like Griffith, only not quite as tall. His strength would be of value. 'Do not fail me, Owen,' Lucius held the man's feral eyes with his own, 'I need the king, within a day if possible.'

'We'll find him,' Owen said as he and his charges moved on.

'They will not be enough, you know,' Jaegar said once the five men were out of hearing.

Lucius nodded, fearing Jaegar was right. 'They will have to be,' he finally said, 'because they are all I can spare. If the destruction of Highcastle is as bad as I fear, I'll have few men to call my own when I take the throne. The rest will stay close and keep an eye on the Brotherhood. We need to know what is happening here and further afield. You and I,' he continued, as he grabbed a fistful of Kerros' shirt, 'will seek out the witch with our councillor here.' He kept a close eye on the barbarian, knowing he didn't trust the occult. Yet he was the only member of the Palaceguard who knew of the witch's involvement.

'Why seek out the witch?' Jaegar asked.

Lucius saw the frightful glance Kerros threw his way, could almost smell his fear. 'We go not because we want too,' he explained, 'but because we must. The witch needs to know what has transpired. She needs to know the king may be dead.'

*

Kerros was sore and incredibly tired, but as Lucius Vupello whispered to him before the glowing pyramid, Avra needed to be informed of the current situation. So, having spent an entire afternoon plodding along cracked and broken streets, climbing piles of rubble and even crossing one very unstable bridge, he was again on the move. Only this time he walked in the company of the Captain of the Palaceguard and Sir Jaegar, son of Jorgun. Two very powerful men and one soon to be king if all went to plan. *If all went to plan*, he mused. The earthquake had certainly caused a major disruption to proceedings, not to mention leaving the city a broken shell. Never in his wildest dreams had he foreseen such a calamity, nor factored in a contingency plan to cope with such a hurdle. To make matters worse, the king was missing, possibly lying dead under a tonne of rubble. Kerros was not privy to all Avra's scheming ways, but he knew failure to sacrifice Arkos would be detrimental to the witch's plans. What she craved he didn't know, but dark powers surrounded her. He prayed once she attained whatever it was she sought, she'd leave. There were two plays being made in Bastion right now: one for Lucius Vupello to ascend the throne, the other concerning Avra and her feud with Arkos. Both required the king be removed, but for now, ironically, Lucius and Avra's relationship was amicable only so long as Arkos lived.

'How much further?' Lucius asked as he stepped over a corpse. Kerros could hear the anger in his words, knew Lucius detested walking at the best of times. But with so much destruction lining the streets, he'd been forced to leave his horse with the Palaceguard who remained at the pyramid.

He lifted tired eyes, unable to see far now night had fallen. Smudges of orange could be seen in the distant, remnants of fading fires, but the sky above was black as soot, devoid of moonlight and its usual twinkling stars. The lantern Jaegar carried swung on a heavy hand, casting dark shadows. He was having trouble enough picturing where they were without having to explain where they were going. He was certain they were close, though, he could almost feel her ungodly presence. 'Not long,' he said. Not that he wished to see Avra again so soon. Few situations in life had caused him such stress as his earlier meeting. 'Tell me again, Lucius,' he prodded, 'who you've sent after the king.'

'Owen Moor, along with Sirs Hector, Karl, Ethan and Darius,' he explained.

Kerros frowned, knowing they had to defeat Tarsin Va first, a dangerous man to have lurking about. For several years Tarsin Va and his men had served the king admirably, but they had been a prickly thorn in need of removal if Lucius Vupello was to claim the throne. It had taken considerable time and finances before he'd concocted a strategy to have them permanently removed. It was one of the reasons he'd fallen so quickly in with Avra's contacts. In the end, it had taken every conniving trick and ounce of wisdom known to Kerros to convince King Arkos to send his best to the north. Thankfully, the danger was real, for Avra had long been perceived as a threat to the kingdom; even being touted as such by the mystical Brotherhood of One. And her coven was growing. Kerros learnt early on in his youth that the best laid plans always contained an element of truth. For the Unseen to be sent north; there needed to be a legitimate cause. The death of

King Arkos' wife, Queen Chrissa, from a supposed witch's poison was the final piece in a puzzle some years in the making.

Only Tarsin had somehow returned from his failed foray north. Unfortunately, try as he might, Kerros was unable to discern the names of all surviving members of the Unseen. In fact, of the twenty-four men sent north, less than half-a-dozen were known to him in general. The rest went about their duty hidden behind masks of steel, or as some would have you believe, cloaked in shadow.

Tarsin Va, Captain of the Unseen, was one he knew. He believed Cale Griffith to be another. There was also talk of John Rhys, now Admiral of the King's fleet, having been by Tarsin's side. Two others survived the debacle in Benwith, yet Kerros, despite all his talent and his multitude of contacts, could not unmask them.

'Do you think those five can take Tarsin and Griffith when the time comes?' Kerros asked, peering at Vupello in the darkness.

'They're men of the Palaceguard, the finest swords in Dervae.'

'Up against the former Captain of the Unseen and the giant Cale Griffith,' Kerros returned. 'It is rumoured Tarsin is the finest blade in Bastion, better even than you.'

'Tarsin is no paragon, Kerros!' Vupello snarled. 'If I see him again, I'll cut him down myself.'

'And in the meantime, . . .?'

'There is one man,' Jaegar interrupted as he stepped over a crack in the paved ground wider than Kerros' hand, 'one man who could eradicate Tarsin and Griffith with minimal fuss.'

'Who would that be?' Kerros asked.

'Enrico Vittorio,' he said, 'an assassin.'

'Vittorio?' Kerros repeated. 'I don't believe I've had the pleasure,' he thought of all the men he did know sharing such a profession. 'How will you find such a man amongst all the chaos, Jaegar?' he asked. 'He may not even be alive after today's events.'

'If he is, he can do the deed.'

'Do you know where to find him?'

'No,' smiled Jaegar, 'but I know who to ask.'

'Then I suggest you see to it as soon as possible,' offered Kerros, listening as Jaegar grunted in the affirmative before moving ahead. He watched the Herkosian take long strides over cracked ground. He was a brute of a man: short tempered and crass, but he did have his uses every once in awhile.

The brief smile faded as quickly as it arrived and Kerros placed a hand upon his stomach, feeling it churn with discomfit. The day's events still unnerved him and despite Jaegar's assurances concerning Vittorio, nothing was guaranteed at this stage. All he could hope for was a step in the right direction. Provided plotting to kill your sovereign lord was indeed the right path to follow.

He knew deep down that his chosen path was the right one. For years he'd watched the king spiral out of control and become a bitter man. Granted, he'd suffered like few before him, but his tenacious hold on the throne should have been severed by now. His time to rule was finished. It was time for someone like Lucius Vupello to hold the mantle of king. The man was strong of mind and body, his swordsmanship celebrated throughout the kingdom. Most importantly for Kerros, there was trust between the two of them. Once Lucius was king, he would listen with confidence to the small man with the rotund body, listen to his grandiose ideas. For Kerros Gavony was a persuasive man; and whilst not king himself, he would be the man who pulled the strings.

At least that was *his* plan.

*

Avra sat quietly on the steps, her eyes closed, her gnarled hands holding the *Sawolegere*. She was still within the cistern; only the far end had crumbled inward when the earthquake struck, sending a dozen marble columns crashing to the floor. Now a large gaping hole allowed the night air to ripple across the water, but the cistern's compromised structure was the least of her concerns. Since midday she'd been aware of a series of attacks against her mental barrier, put in place to conceal her whereabouts. She was not unused to such attacks, but the repetitive nature and increased intensity was beginning to wear her down. If she lost concentration, even for an instant, Cappitus and Neema would know where to find her. Avra was powerful, at the height of her sorceress ways, but even she would struggle against the combined might of those two.

So she remained vigilant, allowing her heightened senses to alert her to any possible intrusions. But she was tiring, and the gentle lapping of water at the base of the stairs was naturally soporific. Avra could ill afford to fall asleep, not now. Especially since Ahriman was of little use.

Ahriman, she thought, *why now?* The Dark God had slinked back into the lantern some time after midday and the events of the earthquake. That Ahriman was the progenitor of such an upheaval was never in doubt. His anger at hearing word of King Arkos fleeing Bastion fuelled him with a rage few would care to witness. Even Avra averted her eyes, knowing full well what lay behind the furious facade. Yet his black-hearted anger caught her off guard. Never did she believe Ahriman could wield such magnificent power whilst only a shade. It was colossal, earth-shattering. Most of Bastion now lay in ruin, whole regions collapsed or underwater. Bridges fell, towers toppled and all because Ahriman wished it to be so.

But it came at a price. Ahriman had retreated to lie within the *Sawolegere,* no longer the dark and commanding god, but literally a shadow of himself. Avra recalled Ahriman explaining to her the constant battle he waged with the souls he'd been given. Their journey from Benwith had taken the better part of six months, and many were the times the two would converse; late at night under darkening skies. Avra knew a thousand souls were required to summon the Dark God and the soul of a king would grant him flesh. The first part of the ritual was complete, now they were close to fulfilling the second step. And although any king would do, Avra craved Arkos. She would give anything to have the Battle-King under her knife. It was his family all those years ago that had sought to ruin hers: the jaguars of Vantos. Unbeknownst to all but a few, Avra was the last remaining Creswick daughter, the last of the wyverns. Two proud families, founders of Bastion a thousand years past, enemies to the last. It was a battle that had raged for centuries; a battle about to end. Avra thought of plunging her blade deep into Arkos' chest, thought of seeing his royal blood spurt from his still-beating heart. It would be a fine way to finish the feud, a fitting farewell to a king often bathed in the blood of his enemies. Only it would be his blood this time; his so called royal blood.

Yet there was still much to accomplish and Ahriman, weak from his exertion and now locked in a furious war with rebellious souls, could offer little in return. It would take time for him to consolidate and retrieve his source of power. Once his thousand souls fell back in line, Ahriman could then lend aid in the coming confrontation. Although Cappitus and Neema had yet to show their hand, she knew a play would arrive soon. They were cunning, those two, and patient.

The screech of a door opening on rusty hinges caused her to sit upright. It came from above at the top of the staircase. No light shone through, for the night was still young, but the sounds of the street wafted in; wails of despair and the anguished cries of the fallen. At any other time, it would have been music to her ears but now, with the prospect of danger above, the noise merely mingled with the heavy beating of her heart.

'Who goes there?' she hissed and rose to her feet.

'It is I, Kerros Gavony,' the reply was timid, tinged with fear. 'I have important news, Avra,' he continued, 'news I believe you'll be glad to hear.'

She could hear footsteps, and from more than one source. Taking a step back she placed the *Sawolegere* conveniently behind a piece of fallen masonry, concealing it out of sight and shrouding it in darkness before making for the bottom of the stairs. Then she spun to confront Kerros, if indeed it was the councillor to the king, and whoever walked beside him.

'Greetings, Avra,' Kerros called out as his rotund body came into view, visible due to the flickering yellow light of a lantern. Two men walked with him: a tall man to his left and an even taller man directly behind, broad of shoulder and with twin braids for a beard. Light reflected off the giant's bald head, and Avra could see black tribal tattoos. He was Herkosian; that much was obvious. The other remained silent for now, but there was strength in the man. She could tell by the way he carried himself, the way he held his shoulders back and chest out. His right hand rested atop his belt buckle, his fingers a mere inch from the pommel of his sword. He was ready, this one; ready for the unexpected.

'You've brought company, Kerros,' Avra moved to the side to avoid the glare of the lantern, sliding close to where she left the *Sawolegere.*

'Troubled times are upon us, Avra, and the streets above are not safe. Footpads roam free, their brazen thievery a blight on the city, and buildings remain dangerously perched. It is not wise to travel without company. Not now.'

'And our guests . . .?'

'Oh, forgive me, Avra,' Kerros brushed sweaty palms across his stained shirt. 'Beside me is Sir Lucius Vupello, Captain of the Palaceguard, known as the Fox and cousin to the king.' Avra gave a curt nod, the amusement in her eyes lost to those standing on the stairs. 'The giant behind me is Sir Jaegar, son of Jorgun. He is Herkosian.'

'Well and good, Kerros, but I told you not to return unless you had the king in tow, gagged and fettered like I suggested.' A brief smile played across Avra's bone-dry lips as she watched him squirm.

'Yes . . . yes, I understand, but when I left this morning, we feared King Arkos to be riding towards the south, fleeing Bastion. As it occurred, such was not the case. Lucius caught up to the column of knights outside Aspenvale and found Arkos not amongst them.'

'What do you mean?'

'It appears he never left Highcastle, Avra. He remained within Bastion. There is a possibility he fashioned the entire charade.'

Avra considered the words, her brow furrowed. 'Such a course of action would require he know something of our plans,' she said. 'He is fearful, granted, for who wouldn't be after the death of one's sons, but such fear can make a mockery of our well-established treachery.'

'Despite the fact he may suspect foul play, with the city in chaos and Highcastle destroyed, if he is recovered alive there will be scant fight left in the man.'

Avra stiffened. 'You speak as if he may be dead, Kerros. Pray tell me what you mean.'

The councillor stifled a cough as a scream rippled through the night air from above. The sound reverberated down the staircase, distorted, but unnecessarily loud. 'Highcastle has been destroyed, Avra,' he begun, 'the cliffs behind it have fallen, crushing most of the castle. If Arkos truly is dead, then Lucius becomes king sooner than anticipated. It is what we have strived for these last years,' he said. 'The crown could soon be ours.'

Avra felt anger boil from some deep reservoir within. As ironic as it sounded, the king she hoped to sacrifice could have died early due to Ahriman's tumultuous earthquake. Without a crowned king to sacrifice, Ahriman would need to endure countless days battling his souls. Avra experienced real doubts as to whether he would survive.

'The crown could soon be *mine*, I believe,' said Lucius Vupello to break the silence.

Avra watched the swordsman step forward a pace and offer a slight bow. He wasn't handsome, she decided, even in the dim light. His face was hard and flat, with cold eyes to match. Not exactly the face of a king, but so long as he was crowned, he would be of use. It was a precarious situation for Avra and Ahriman, more so for the three fools standing before her. Either way they were marked for death. For if Arkos was truly dead, as much as it would infuriate her, Lucius Vupello would become the next sacrificial target.

'I'll be most displeased if I cannot sacrifice Arkos, councillor,' she finally said between clenched teeth. 'Our family's history is bloody, and I expect to exact revenge before all is through.'

Kerros nodded, aware of Avra's hatred for the king. It was the one binding element between the two parties all those years ago when the plan had first been hatched. Both desired the death of Arkos Vantos.

'So, when shall we know if Arkos lives?' she asked.

Kerros looked to Vupello, suggesting he speak. 'I have sent men towards Highcastle, Avra, in pursuit of two others who seek to rescue the king.'

'And they are . . .?'

'Former members of the Unseen, we believe.'

Avra hissed, knowing the men were responsible for her coven's demise. Men sent by Arkos himself to root her out and destroy her plans. She could sense the delicate touch of Cappitus at work, even now. 'I want those men dead,' she said softly. 'Do you hear me, Lucius Vupello?'

'I do, Avra, and the order has already been given. Once the king is found, alive or dead, Tarsin and Griffith shall be set upon. You have my word.'

'Tarsin, you say,' she tilted her head to the side. 'Is he not leader of the Unseen?'

'Former captain,' replied Lucius.

A cackle escaped her lips. 'And you can guarantee his demise, can you? He is a crafty one, this Tarsin,' her voice rose in volume. 'Even I experienced trouble against him in Benwith. Nearly my entire coven died due to his rage!'

The three men shifted their feet uncomfortably, sensing the power in the old hag despite her shrivelled appearance.

'I have sent a group of my knights after them, expert swordsman all, and with Jaegar's help, we'll send Vittorio, an assassin, as soon as daylight breaks.' He risked a glance towards the large Herkosian. 'Jaegar insists he can accomplish the deed. He may be expensive, but we have the coin.'

Avra rummaged through her copious garments, her hands pulling out several stoppered vials and small wooden boxes. She eventually settled on one, a triangular glass vial sealed with black wax. 'Give this to your assassin,' she said, handing the vial to Lucius, 'and tell him to smear its contents carefully over his blades. One cut is all it takes to invoke temporary paralysis. It is fast acting and will surely grant the wielder an edge. Such a token may very well bring down Griffith and the man known as Tarsin.'

Avra placed it in Lucius' outstretched hand, then watched him place the vial in a pocket.

'Now, there is one other favour I shall ask, Lucius Vupello, in return for the use of such an item.'

'And that is . . .?'

Avra smirked as she cast her gaze upon Kerros. The man was fidgeting still, his pudgy fingers working ceaselessly to find something to grasp, pull, or flick. He was an irritation, a small man with delusions of grandeur in a world fit only for the strong. 'If you are to be king, Lucius,' she began, a feral glean to her eyes, 'if you are to truly rule a kingdom from a broken city, you'll need men with not only wisdom, but courage.'

'Your words ring true, Avra.'

'You will also need to make clever choices,' Avra continued. 'Right now, you need to be clever *and* prove you are worthy.'

'And how shall I do so?'

'By killing Kerros for me!' Avra snarled.

Kerros put his back to the wall, his hands held out before him. 'No, Lucius,' he pleaded, 'this is madness.'

'Do it, Vupello,' prodded Avra. 'He is weak, a spineless cretin riding the coattails of greater men. You do not need him. Think only of this morning and his false decree concerning Arkos. Consider the time you've wasted listening to this coward!' Avra smiled, showing speckled teeth as the Captain of the Palaceguard moved to stand before the frightened councillor. He was whimpering, mewling like a child, great sobs racking his body.

'Do it now!'

The swordsman stood tall, his hand resting on the pommel of his sword. Jaegar stood behind him, impassive, his bulk preventing Kerros an egress. Then the screech of metal sounded clear as Lucius whipped his blade from its sheath, the tip sweeping towards the councillor in a blinding flash of silver. A second later the blade was resting at his side, Kerros still standing with his back to the wall. Avra watched him raise his hands and place them at his throat, saw the life drain from his face as blood began to spurt from between his fingers. It took only moments before his body slid to the floor, a timid wheeze causing his bloated jowls to quiver.

'It is done.'

Avra clapped, 'Clever work, Lucius Vupello, soon-to-be-king.'

The knight offered a curt nod, his flat face unreadable. 'Shall I remove the body?' he asked.

'Leave it. There is still time for it to be of use,' Avra reached for the *Sawolegere* resting behind the fallen masonry. 'Before you go,' she said, 'I would ask you to report on Arkos' status once confirmed.'

'Yes, Avra.'

'And make certain Tarsin and his remaining Unseen are taken care of.'

Lucius motioned for Jaegar to move up the stairs. 'As you wish,' he said, heading into the night.

Avra watched the men climb the stairs, the glow of the lantern casting strange shadows along the walls. Once the door clanged shut, she carefully reached for Kerros Gavony's still warm body. A whispered word created a ball of light above her head for her to see by, and with a deft hand she brought out her ceremonial knife from between folds of clothing. Ahriman, her Dark Lord, was currently weak and in need of sustenance.

She dragged the body closer, her small form wielding unusual strength. Then her blackened blade reached high, poised above his chest.

Moments later her Dark Lord fed.

CHAPTER THIRTEEN

The groans of a dying city subsided along with the small tremor.

Tarsin cursed and placed a hand on the ground, feeling for any further vibrations. There were none and the night became eerily quiet, as if those still alive held a collective breath, waiting to see if further destruction was imminent. He remained on his knees for some time, listening, until Griffith placed a hand on his shoulder, his armour creaking to break the silence.

'It has passed,' he said.

Tarsin nodded, knew the big man was right, but it took all his nerve to rise to his feet. He'd already lost count of the tremors following the great earthquake, but experiencing them didn't condition you to their presence. In fact, he felt more unnerved if the truth was told. He sighed heavily; weary of the day's events, tired and hungry. He could see Griffith shared similar pangs. Yet there was a need to continue, an urgency that could not be shaken. Highcastle was buried and the king could very well be entombed within his palace.

'We've a way to go, still,' Tarsin looked towards the west, unable to see far due to the night's enveloping darkness. The silver-blue emanation from Aston's Tear was dim this far out and the night sky was devoid of its sparkling stars due to the rising smoke. Despite his attempt to convince himself otherwise, he felt as if he strode through the Underworld: Hell's domain and that of the dead. Gentle winds sifted sand across paved stones, the scraping mingling with the constant moans of the dying and the wails of the distraught. He did his best to ignore the sounds and looked ahead towards the cracked pillars and shattered walls of the King's Plaza. Its entrance, normally a fifty-foot-wide arch, was now a mess of shattered blue stone. He shook his head and looked behind him to see the ruined Avenue of Kings all twisted and buckled. Before that rested Stantos Bridge, only a fraction of its ancient stones remaining, the rest swept away by an angry river, black and boiling with refuse. It had been a harrowing journey already.

'Here,' Griffith reached into a pouch at his waist and retrieved a slither of dried meat.

Grabbing the offered food, Tarsin moved to a square piece of granite lying several feet away and sat. Griffith joined him with a clank, his black armour dulled with dust, his warhammer placed at his feet with a thud.

'Why have you returned, Tarsin?' Griffith asked, his voice low. 'And where in Aston's name have you been?'

The swordsman took a bite of the meat as he mulled over the questions. Tarsin knew Griffith was more interested in why he'd left Bastion all those years ago, knew the question wouldn't be far away. In fact, he was surprised he'd not been asked sooner.

'No apparent reason springs to mind,' Tarsin said, knowing such a reply was disrespectful, especially to a man he'd saved from Benwith. Both had experienced the full horror of the north, barely escaping with their lives. As a result, they shared a bond few men could claim; a bond of life and death thrust upon them in their darkest hour. As a former member of the Unseen, Cale Griffith deserved a more complete answer.

'Sorry, Griffith,' Tarsin continued, seeing the look of hurt in his eyes. He'd been the man's Captain; had brought him back when so many others had perished. Then he'd left without a word, disappearing without a trace. Over three years had passed and now here he was again, walking the streets of a ruined city, the man they swore to protect possibly dead and buried. 'I went south,' Tarsin looked to the half-eaten piece of dried meat, 'to Al-Za'im, working for a man by the name of Ruvin Ciricello.'

'And your reason for leaving so abruptly . . .?'

Tarsin glanced towards the plaza. 'I was angry,' he finally said.

'Angry?'

'Aye, with the king, with everyone,' he returned his gaze to Griffith. 'We were betrayed, Griffith, sent to our deaths. At the time, I believed it was Arkos' doing.'

'You believed the king was responsible?'

'Aye, I did, not that you'd understand,' he rubbed his forehead with thumb and finger. 'We were compromised, Griffith, set upon before we even reached Benwith.'

'The king played no part in such deceit, Tarsin. Hell,' Griffith's voice rose in volume, 'we were his Unseen, it was our duty to do as bid. It was his life we swore to protect . . . not our own.'

'That was my point,' Tarsin stood and paced several feet away. 'We were his protectors, Griffith, not assassins. We should never have been sent to Benwith. Gods, man, we lost nineteen of the best warriors in Dervae!'

'But we accomplished our task. The coven was wiped out.'

'The cost was too high!' Tarsin's voice rose in anger. 'And we never found the coven's leader, a witch named Avra. Now she is here in Bastion, intent on seeking revenge.'

'What are you talking about?'

Tarsin moved back to the granite block and took his seat, wiping his brow as he did so. 'There is much to tell, Griffith,' he said, 'so listen carefully, for what I tell you may be difficult to comprehend. But it's the truth, my friend. Trust me when I say it is so.'

Griffith nodded and Tarsin knew the big man would believe every word. They had trained together, fought together and nearly died together. For a time, they'd even called themselves brothers, such was their bond. Then he fled without a word, sailing south aboard the first ship he stumbled across. Back then his rage had been great, his thoughts fragmented. Looking back, he told himself it was the best thing he could have done.

He wondered now if such were true.

So he sat and told Griffith of Avra's success in raising the Dark Lord, Ahriman. And then told him of her mad quest to see King Arkos dead.

'What do they hope to gain?' asked Griffith, his brow furrowed as he sought to assimilate Tarsin's information.

'With King Arkos sacrificed, Ahriman will apparently become flesh,' explained Tarsin. 'If he should obtain such a state, his power will be realized, and the world will be subject to the whim of a god. From the information I have gleaned from elder Cappitus and matron Neema, his goal is to destroy the world so that he may create one anew. Bastion will be his first stepping stone; we his first victims.'

'But if Arkos is already dead,' Griffith scratched his red beard, a sign he was deep in thought, 'will not their plans be thwarted?'

Tarsin pondered the question, wishing Cappitus or Neema were here to help explain their predicament and provide a clear answer. But they were locked in discussions of their own right now, desperately seeking a means to escape what appeared to be an inevitable conclusion. They both expressed a belief in salvation, but neither was entirely clear on how to manufacture such an event. Tarsin gave Griffith a pained look and shrugged his shoulders. 'I do not know, Griffith,' he finally said. 'Mayhaps the death of the king will thwart their desired outcome. Maybe they'll simply kill another. Vupello is primed to sit the throne should Arkos fall; perhaps they'll sacrifice him instead. Yet I fear much that's transpired involves Vupello's scheming. Being Captain of the Palaceguard, he may have gleaned information not necessarily for his ears.'

'Arkos is no fool, Tarsin, you know his nature. Keeping his perceived enemies within reach was always his way. It is why he kept Vupello close all these years. If you remained in Bastion after returning from Benwith, like I did, he would have set you up and informed you of his plans. Frey's Luck, Tarsin, he made John Rhys admiral of the royal fleet within eighteen months!'

'I know,' he replied, 'I saw him at sea aboard the *Leviathan*.'

'Aye, so you did,' Griffith pushed himself off the granite to stand tall and stretch his arms above his head. Tarsin did likewise, peering into the gloom as he sought passage through the plaza. He was about to step into the night when the sound of approaching feet caused him to turn.

'What have we here?' Tarsin peered back down the Avenue of Kings.

It took only a moment for the men to materialise, their bodies hard to see in the dark due to their black tabards, but once they moved out of the shadows, they were easily recognised.

'Owen Moor,' spat Griffith as he reached for his warhammer.

'The very same,' Owen Moor replied, a wicked grin splitting his face as his four comrades spread to either side. The armed knights walked forward a couple of paces before stopping ten feet away. The scrape of steel followed as they drew forth their swords.

'You want some of this?' Tarsin heard Griffith slap the head of his warhammer hard, saw him flex his considerable bulk. 'I knew *Bloodstain* would see action this day,' the big man muttered, stepping to the side so he had room to manoeuvre.

Owen Moor chuckled, then motioned for his men to advance.

Tarsin's Rykedian broadsword hissed from its sheath.

*

Owen Moor retained his smile.

He advanced with his men, the line fanning out to either side as they approached. They were five of the finest, men accustomed to swordplay in a brutal world, strong and commanding. Pitted against them were two men, survivors of a failed mission, one an outcast only recently returned. And the outcast carried an impressive blade, one Owen craved for himself. It would be a simple matter to kill these two, take the blade and find the king. There was no need to scurry through the dark like rats sniffing for a meal. They were the Palaceguard. They feared no-one.

He took another step forward, eager for the confrontation. Strength of arm and a mind honed to a razor's edge had provided for him in the past, it would do so again. Lucius Vupello may have issued caution, but the man was days from running a kingdom if all went to plan. His mind would be full of turmoil with so much to consider. All Owen cared for was a fine sword by his waist and the wits to use it, along with the fame and adulation one deserved when in service to the king. For him, it mattered not whether that king was Arkos or his cousin, so long as he was paid accordingly.

In truth, all he cared about was his own wellbeing. It was a simple philosophy and so far, it had kept him in good stead. Even his father, the drunken bastard that he was, would have been impressed. He often wondered how his father would have behaved if he'd known his son was a member of the Palacegaurd. A pity, really, that he'd skewered his father's full belly one night in the vain hope of seeing what cheap wine would spill from his guts.

'You've a death wish, Owen,' Griffith shared a red-bearded grin. The dim light of the pyramid did little more than keep the shadows at bay, particularly this far out, but the illumination was enough for a fight.

'Don't all men?' Owen moved towards the big man. The plan, as they'd discussed whilst trailing the two would-be-heroes, was for Hector, Ethan and himself to tackle Cale Griffith, whilst Darius and Karl kept Tarsin at arm's length. Once Griffith was down, the five would surround the former Captain of the Unseen and tear him to shreds. He may not be fearful of a confrontation, but he duelled with care. If the odds were in his favour, he'd utilize them. It was the one thing he could honestly say his father taught him. For if you failed there were no second chances. Not in this life.

He felt the wry smile as he stepped closer, his feet at right angles, perfectly balanced. Ethan moved with him, taking the middle ground, whilst Hector took the right. They were ready, eager for a kill. Nothing would sate their hunger more than to see Griffith's life blood flow across the dusty pavement.

A shuffle of feet caught his attention and he risked a quick glance to his left where Darius and Karl sought to keep Tarsin occupied. They were either side of him with swords raised, held at eye-level. Owen shifted his gaze back to Griffith and watched as he twirled his warhammer before him. The tension was palpable. He could almost taste it.

Then it began.

For all his size, Griffith was quick, quicker than he had any right to be. Without any warning whatsoever, the big man stepped to his left and swung his immense warhammer, swinging it in an arc in line with Hector. The older swordsman sought to defend the blow with his lowered sword, but the hammer smashed through his defence with ease and crashed into his chest. An explosion of air escaped his lungs as he fell into Ethan, both men scrambling as they attempted to disengage from the other. Owen had barely moved a foot towards the action when he saw Griffith's hammer rise and fall again, pounding into Hector's neck. This time the man stayed down, his windpipe crushed. Owen rushed into the fray, his sword high before bringing it down with a vicious swipe. Griffith leant back and watched the tip of the blade swoop past his nose, less than an inch from his flesh. Owen stopped its trajectory and reversed the cut, swinging it back and down, seeking to cut across Griffith's torso. The strike was true, but Griffith stepped into the cut, allowing the sword to bounce off the King's breastplate he still wore. Then he raised his hammer. Owen swerved to his left, away from the weapon, putting distance between himself and his adversary. Griffith's face had become as red as his hair and froth flecked his beard. The man was crazed, but instead of following, he swung back to Ethan who approached from behind and charged him instead. There was a loud crack as the two men crashed into each other, their weapons locked before them. Muscles strained as they pushed, the exertion audible. Gathering his senses, Owen lifted his sword, ready to return to the combat, but Griffith swivelled and threw Ethan off balance. A heavy chop of the hammer into the back of his head followed, punching the man to the ground. Hoping to reach his companion before the next blow was delivered, he raced towards the conflict, then watched as Griffith raised his hammer over his left shoulder. Then it came down, sweeping not into Ethan lying prone at his feet, but straight into his own path. He brought his sword up, its feeble blade no match for the power of the hammer's head. Then it struck. He'd already halted his advance, but the momentum of the hammer was close to unstoppable. It smashed the air out of his lungs with a whoosh and sent him flying to land in a heap. His sword clattered several feet away, now lost in the shadows. A sickening thud sounded next. Ethan had been taken care of.

'Gods,' he wheezed as he rose to his feet. He didn't even bother looking for his sword but scrambled for his dagger instead. He pulled it forth, backing away at the same time. Griffith had barely moved. He risked a quick glance behind to see how Karl and Darius fared, hoping they still had Tarsin pinned between them. But all he saw was two shapes lying on the ground, Tarsin walking casually towards him. 'Gods,' he yelped once more. He hadn't even heard them fight. He couldn't even recall a clash of blades between them. It was simply over. Two men, two of the finest swordsmen he knew, gone.

He spun on his feet and ran.

He was lithe, a warrior born. Any distance gained was a step in the right direction. It was the only defence he had left at his disposal. Never could he have dreamed such a turn of events. He was certain every eventuality had been reflected upon. But not this one, not what he just witnessed. Griffith was a madman. In the blink of an eye their supposed plan of attack was eradicated. It was incredible, really, one man against three; and not just any three. Hell, he'd fought seventeen duels to the death with hardly a scratch. Yet Griffith had unnerved them; put them on the back foot. He just kept coming, his warhammer sweeping back and forth with deadly precision, never slowing. One hit and you were down, armoured or not.

He could hear his feet pounding across stone as he fled, a hand extended for balance as he leapt over granite boulders in the dark. His breathing was even now, no longer panicked, his rhythm returned. His only thought was to cross Stantos Bridge and return to the pyramid, where glowing walls sat high above the city proper, its peak reaching for the heavens. Hopefully Vupello was still there.

He reached the bridge, now only half its original width due to the earthquake. The crossing earlier had been nerve-racking, but he'd watched Tarsin and Griffith navigate the treacherous path without falling into the river below. Crossing with haste was a different matter altogether. He stopped to catch his breath, then looked behind to see if he was followed. There was no-one there; the street was silent; the only sound that of rushing water under a broken bridge. He sucked in a lungful of air and wiped sweat from his forehead, his heart beating rapidly. He was about to spin towards the bridge and walk across when he saw a shadow detach itself from a nearby building. Its speed was phenomenal as it streaked across the ground. He remembered at the last instant to raise his dagger, but it was too late. The cold touch of a Rykedian broadsword rested against his throat.

'Going somewhere, Owen Moor?' the voice whispered in his ear. A hand grabbed a handful of his hair, pulling his head back. The blade sliced into flesh.

'Don't kill me,' he pleaded, 'I can be of use. I know things, things about Lucius Vupello. He plots against the king.'

'What of it?'

'I can tell you of his plans, inform you of his moves,' his voice quavered, his eyes flicking rapidly from side to side. He still clutched his dagger, but it was useless now. One flick of Tarsin's wrist would be all it needed. The blade was sharp, incredibly so, and it was cold, cold as death. 'Do we have a deal?'

He waited for an answer, waited several seconds. It took a moment before he realized Tarsin was no longer holding his head and the sword was absent from his throat. The man had disappeared. He was about to sigh, glad he'd been given a second chance at life when he felt a wash of warmth across his chest. He looked down . . . and never looked back up.

*

'Is he dead?'

'Yes,' Tarsin replied as he walked towards Griffith who sat wiping the head of his warhammer with a piece of cloth. The four bodies still lay where they fell.

'Amateurs!'

Tarsin moved to the granite block they had been sitting at earlier and picked up the jaguar helm, passing it to Griffith. 'They were not amateurs, my friend. They simply weren't good enough.'

'Are there any?'

Tarsin declined to answer, for he knew there was always someone out there good enough.

'You know,' Griffith rumbled as he found his feet, 'there was a time after you fled Bastion that I believed you a coward.'

'And . . .?'

'And I was wrong. I always knew I was wrong, but I tried desperately to convince myself otherwise.'

'Why?'

Griffith lifted his arm to check the strike he'd suffered across his torso. A slight dent was the only mark. 'Because it made life easier knowing I craved the death of a coward and not a friend.'

Tarsin watched as Griffith spun to stand before him, his warhammer clenched tight. There was a flicker of madness in his eyes, like a flame ready to reignite. 'Do you think my leaving sits well with me?'

'I don't know what to think. You talk of Arkos betraying our trust by sending us north to Benwith, but you betrayed us when you left Bastion without a word. How do they differ?'

Tarsin ran a hand through his hair. 'I can't change the past, Griffith,' he said, 'and I'll not lie to you. My leaving doesn't sit well with me but, at the time, I blamed the king. I now know my emotions were clouded, but what's done is done. Everything happens for a reason; unfortunately, the understanding is sometimes blurred. I made a mistake.'

'Aye, that you did,' Griffith smacked his hammer into his palm. 'You had friends here, Tarsin, friends who sought your guidance in troubled times. You were our Captain; we looked up to you, sought your counsel. Do you honestly believe you were the only one to face demons in the night?'

'I'm sorry Griffith, I once had purpose, knew who I was. Not anymore. Now I don't know who I am or what I'm supposed to accomplish. I'm a vagrant, full of anger, surviving on a rage that burns inside. It fuels me, but I cannot find a release. There are times I feel like I'm going to explode.' He looked at the armoured man he once called friend. 'If you wish to strike me, do so. I'll not stop you.'

'Strike you?' Griffith narrowed his eyes. 'I once thought to kill you, but now, why would I do such a thing? Besides, I've already smashed enough heads for one night.' He let the haft of the hammer slide through his fingers until the head hit the ground with a thud. 'To be honest, I'm relieved to have you back.'

'And the others . . .?'

'They'll be glad also . . . once they see you, that is.'

Tarsin moved past the big man, looking towards the cracked and fallen arch leading into the plaza. Beyond, out of sight for now, rested Highcastle. For all they knew it lay completely buried by rock and stone, the king entombed and irretrievable. 'We had best move,' he said.

A faint sound carried on the wind, a cry, perhaps, from a distance. 'Did you hear that?' Griffith asked.

Tarsin held up a hand and cocked his head to the side. He listened, holding his breath as he did so until the sound drifted towards them once again. 'It sounds like a child,' he looked to Griffith.

'Where is it coming from?'

Tarsin listened again and this time he heard the distinct call of "help" from ahead. 'This way,' he said as he stepped through the fallen arch and turned to his right.

Griffith shook his head. 'We don't have time, Tarsin.'

'We'll make time. I'm a killer, Griffith; it's what I've been trained to do. But when the cry of a child haunts darkened streets, I'll do my best to see them safe. We've killed men this night, now it's time to save a soul. Frey knows we need to keep the balance.'

'The goddess of Fate is fickle at best, my friend,' Griffith rumbled from behind. 'Calling her name will not aid our cause. We need to rescue the king, not some child.'

Tarsin heard the wisdom in Griffith's words, but his mind was set. 'Then we'll make it quick,' he finished by moving forward, his head tilted to the side as he listened for the feeble cry.

Griffith followed, gathering his gear and angling north as they moved down a darkened street and headed in the direction of New City. They stepped carefully, skirting fallen masonry in the dark with outstretched hands, scampering over gaping cracks in the ground blacker than Hell's bottomless pits. And every few moments the gentle call for help carried on the wind.

'Help!' the voice was close.

'Here,' Tarsin moved off the shattered road, pushing past an overturned cart and squeezing into an alleyway. Griffith followed as best he could; wrestling with the cart until the alleyway's entrance was clear. It was darker here away from the glowing pyramid. No lanterns lit street corners, nor were there stars lighting the sky. All they had to guide them was the faint call.

'Help!' closer now. It was a child's voice. The two men entered a quadrangle, a circular, three-tiered fountain at its centre. The water in its basin was silent.

'Help!' the voice sounded from the other side of the fountain. Tarsin moved, peering into the dark. It was difficult to see, but the faint outline of a small boy finally materialized, sitting with his back to them on the edge of the fountain.

'Help!'

Griffith shuffled close to Tarsin. 'Who is it?' he asked with a whisper.

Tarsin put a finger to his lips, issuing silence as he crept closer. His hand was placed firmly about the hilt of his sword. The boy hadn't moved.

'Help!'

'Who goes there?' Tarsin finally said.

Silence greeted him. The boy remained seated at the fountain. The two men moved closer.

'Boy,' Griffith called, 'boy, are you alright? Are you hurt?'

The young lad turned about slowly, seeking the two men who approached. 'I am not hurt,' he said. In the dim light, he looked and sounded like a boy of ten.

'Then why do you call for help?' Tarsin asked.

The collective sound of a dozen doors opening throughout the quadrangle was his answer. Booted feet stamped quickly across paved stones, the flicker of hastily opened lanterns bobbing before them. A score of black shapes crowded the fountain, more than half holding heavy crossbows armed with steel-tipped bolts. They were surrounded.

Tarsin moved his hand away from his blade. 'What is the meaning of this?' he sought to engage someone in conversation.

'No questions,' was accompanied by a slap across the back of the head as hands reached for his sword. Griffith was likewise stripped of his weapon, his hands pulled tight behind his back.

'Whoever you are, I don't think you know who you're dealing with.' Tarsin spat to the side as men prodded him to walk towards the far end of the quadrangle.

'No, then we are on the same page, my friend, because I don't believe you know who we are either,' the man who spoke wore a trident beard, barely visible in the poor light.

'I know who you are,' Griffith growled like a caged dog. 'You're the Nocturnals: thieves of Bastion's Undercity.'

The man with the trident beard spun to confront Griffith, lifting a lantern to better see his face. 'You are well educated, sir. Might I ask how it is that you know who we are?'

Griffith was about to reply when another man spoke in a rush, 'It's Cale Griffith, Captain of the Sceptres!'

A multitude of voices began to talk at once, then Tarsin saw the raised edge of a club. He heard a crack as Griffith was struck in the back of the head. Tarsin struggled with his bonds in a vain attempt to flee, but someone grabbed his shoulders and struck him a blow from behind. The tips of three crossbows were then levelled an inch from his chin before a hessian bag was draped over his head. The last thing he remembered seeing was the sad eyes of a young boy.

CHAPTER FOURTEEN

Jarred traced his fingers along the glowing surface of the pyramid.

He walked its perimeter having arrived with Ruvin as ash and smoke drifted above the toppled city. He was lucky to be alive. The Oakwood and Stout had trembled furiously as the earthquake struck. Timbers groaned, and windows fell clattering to the floor as the seizure continued. Men and women screamed until their yells of fear were drowned by the terrible roar of tortured earth. Then it ceased, just when Jarred believed all was lost. He'd raised red eyes to peer about the common room only to see a beam as thick as his torso smash into the floor a foot from where he'd fallen. He'd scrambled back in shock, his arms flapping for purchase until he crouched into a ball. He'd shed a tear or two then, felt hot liquid run down his trouser leg as he soiled himself. An hour passed before he dared move again. When he did, fear clung to him like flies to dung.

Several hours had now passed since the destruction. In fact, dusk had fallen to mask the horror to some extent, although the silver-blue glow of Aston's Tear added its own unique cast on the fallen city. Shifting shadows continued to reveal shaken citizens drifting towards the behemoth, drawn like moths to a flame. Jarred had sat and watched as they approached to within a few feet to stare at the diamond-like surface with its seamless facade.

Now his thoughts were many and varied. Ruvin had managed to extricate him from the tavern as the afternoon approached, prodding him out of the damaged building before it fell altogether. He remembered the curses of panicked men, heard shouts from those trapped within. Then he was out in the street, where bodies lay battered and torn, looking like nothing more than the discarded playthings of a colossal god. He'd felt sick in the stomach as he wiped perspiration from a clammy forehead, felt desperately in need of water.

He eventually found his voice and an ounce of courage as he helped drag bodies out from under collapsed buildings. Carnage was everywhere, no place remained untouched. Then as dusk approached Ruvin had lifted his eyes to see Aston's Tear shining like some beacon of hope, just like it was foretold in the days of yore. They made for it then, climbing over broken walls and shattered ground to reach the red granite base. With tired steps they reached the top, peering with hands raised to admire the startling emanation.

That was an hour past. In the time since, they discovered Tarsin was alive and heading for Highcastle to find the king. Ruvin had volunteered to follow, but the elders explained he had help from a man named Cale Griffith. Shortly after they left a contingent of the Palaceguard traced their steps, also eager to find their king. Jarred had sat with his back to the pyramid, content to rest until the Brotherhood or men of the Sceptre, or someone else for all he cared, could explain what in Hell's name had occurred. Yet their talk was nonsense to a fifteen-year-old boy, so he pushed himself off the diamond wall and began to walk around the colossal structure.

Now he strolled with his hand outstretched, his fingers brushing the southern face. It was cold, yet at the same time quite exhilarating, as if tiny bolts of lightning were striking his flesh. The soporific tingling raced up his arm, causing him to walk in a trance-like fashion, his mind aware of his actions, but oblivious to everything else. Even the constant wails of grief had subsided from his thoughts. He felt calm, relaxed, his body no longer aching from the day's rigours, the cuts and grazes lining his hands forgotten. He walked past countless people, slipping past like an unseen wraith as he rounded another corner and began to trace a line along the eastern face. A sense of exquisite freedom sufficed his body, his doubts and fears swept away as light from the pyramid bathed his form. He felt at peace, content.

Until a gaping black chasm yawned from the wall his fingers touched.

It appeared from nowhere, materializing at the centre of the eastern face, a square doorway ten-foot high. Jarred cringed as frigid air slapped his face, stale and tinged with decay. For all the beauty of the pyramid, the doorway was a direct contrast, its unforeseeable depths evoking untold fear. He stood at the entrance with shaking legs, his hands clasped before him, fear rising once again to grip his rapidly-beating heart. He heard raised voices from behind followed by shouts of alarm, but he couldn't peel his eyes away from the doorway. It stood there, dark and resolute as it towered before him, enticing yet repelling all in one.

A hand on his shoulder released a shout of terror.

'Easy, Jarred,' Ruvin's voice was soothing.

Jarred turned frightened eyes towards his master. Beside him were the dark robed figures of the Brotherhood: a collection of wispy, grey haired men, some with beards, others with dry, weathered faces, but all staring with abject wonder towards the newly found entrance.

'What have you found, lad?' Ruvin calmly asked.

'I don't know,' Jarred replied. 'I was walking, in a daze, when the doorway suddenly appeared.'

The Brotherhood stepped close to peer into the doorway's darkened depths. Little could be seen at first, but the click of fingers brought several glowing spheres into existence, their magical illumination revealing a corridor stretching far into the great pyramid's mass.

A gnarled hand rested on Jarred's shoulder as he watched the Brotherhood's magical spheres trail into the darkness. 'You have done well, young Jarred,' said a white bearded man.

Jarred looked into eyes alight with wonder.

'I am elder Cappitus, a friend of Ruvin Ciricello's,' he smiled in Ruvin's direction before pointing towards the doorway. 'Do you have any thoughts as to what we might find within?'

Jarred shook his head. 'I'm not sure I wish to find out.'

'Are you afraid, young Jarred?'

'Most certainly,' he answered, 'I've no idea what might lie within.' He said the words, but a flash of light pierced his skull to reveal patterns of gold and a door of considerable width. He shook his head to clear the image, then looked up at elder Cappitus as if nothing had occurred.

'Nobody does, lad,' replied Cappitus, 'that's what makes such a venture so exciting.'

Jarred narrowed his eyes as he watched the elder. He was smiling, the glint of passion in his eyes obvious. He may be old, but the man wasn't one to shy away from the unknown. Before Jarred could voice a question of his own, the elder barked an order to some of the Brotherhood and then called for a man named Declan. The man arrived in quick fashion, dressed in similar robes except for a shield blazoned across his chest and a heavy belt supporting an impressive longsword. His black moustache quivered as he came to stand before them, his bald head glistening with sweat. As far as Jarred knew, he was a Sword of the Brotherhood.

'We need to seal off this immediate area,' Cappitus began by sweeping his hand towards the pyramid. 'Gather your Swords and have them set up around the doorway. Nobody is to venture inside without our express permission.'

Declan nodded. 'Anything else?' he asked.

'Yes,' Cappitus raised a hand to stroke his beard, 'have word sent to Neema and the Celestial Sisters, they should be here to see what unfolds.'

'What do you think is inside?' Jarred heard Declan ask.

He could see Cappitus mulling over his answer. 'Hopefully a means to protect the city and its inhabitants,' he finally said, 'but in truth, I do not know. It could be anything.'

Declan released a deep breath before turning to leave. 'I'll return soon,' he said, 'but in the meantime, I've six Sword Brothers close by. I'll round them up and send them your way.' Cappitus offered a slight nod in return. Seconds later Declan disappeared amongst the gathering crowd.

Jarred watched as a handful of glowing spheres came bobbing back towards the waiting Brotherhood, the unusual balls of light seemingly floating on air, yet moving to the elder's subtle gestures and clicks of their fingers. A moment later they winked out of existence as the men fell into discussion, many waving animated arms as they postulated ideas concerning what lay before them. He began to feel their excitement, could feel a wave of energy flowing within, a return of the tingling sensation he felt as he walked about the pyramid with hand outstretched. Fear of the darkened doorway was now a thing of the past, a fleeting memory now forgotten. Like the Brotherhood looking with envious eyes towards the opening, he wished to step into the unknown to see what discovery awaited them. He couldn't suppress the feeling building inside of him, just like he couldn't walk away from the disaster that had befallen the city. He was here, now, with a task to perform.

'When do we venture inside?' Jarred spoke to both Ruvin and Cappitus.

The two men raised their eyebrows. 'For someone who only moments before looked like he was about to run,' said Cappitus, 'you show extraordinary courage, young man.'

'I was startled, nothing more.'

Ruvin grinned. 'We'll enter soon, lad,' he offered as he stood on the tips of his toes in a vain effort to peer past the crowding Brotherhood. 'The air is stale; you can smell it from here. The pyramid has most likely been sealed for thousands of years for all we know.'

'Possibly longer,' Cappitus pointed out. 'The Nepharii, the people who built the great pyramid,' he explained to Jarred, 'are an ancient race. How far back their civilization spanned we can only guess. I assume it to be greater than we realize.'

As the word "Nepharii" escaped the elder's lips a sudden jolt shook Jarred. He felt he'd heard the word before. Felt he knew who they were. 'So how long do we wait?' he asked, his voice edged with excitement.

Cappitus sniffed the air. 'Not much longer, young man. We'll await Declan and his Sword Brothers before we commit ourselves.'

'Aye,' Ruvin patted Jarred on the back, 'better to be prepared, lad, then to walk in blind, so to speak. You never know what may be lurking in the dark once we step inside.'

Jarred offered a wan smile as talk of things lurking in the dark suddenly manifested inside his head. He briefly patted his newly acquired sword resting at his waist, an act that did little to allay his fears. What had been an exciting adventure had once again morphed into one of danger.

The scuffling of feet diverted his attention to several men approaching from behind the gathered crowd. As they pushed their way forward he could see black robes with a silver shield across their chest and knew they were the six men Declan promised. They were strong looking and much younger than the other members of the Brotherhood. Jarred guessed they were of an age like Tarsin, thirty years or so, and equipped for combat. The clink of chain mail underneath their robes was faint, but discernible, and all carried identical longswords at their belt. With minimal fuss they approached the doorway, politely asking men and women to stand back as they flanked three to a side. There they stood with arms crossed.

'Not long now, Jarred,' Ruvin said. 'As soon as Declan returns, we'll venture inside and see what awaits us.'

Jarred cast his gaze back towards the pyramid, thinking only of the enormous size of the structure and how many corridors and passages could be contained within. Once inside, there was a realistic chance they could spend hours traversing the interior. Jarred wasn't certain he could keep his eyes open for such a duration. He was already tired, exhausted in fact.

It had been an eventful day.

*

Cappitus shook his head in wonder.

For several minutes, the elder had crept along the dark corridor after stepping into the pyramid itself. The entrance had been

214

daunting, but now, as he focused on the immense double doors at the end of the corridor, he was truly awestruck. It was extraordinarily beautiful, a true reflection of exquisite workmanship surpassing anything he'd previously observed. The doors were fashioned of metal, the myriad swirls and patterns pressed into their surface suggesting a time-consuming process from a devoted architect, and splashes of metallic colour: silver, platinum, bronze and gold reflected brilliantly as the light from the tip of his gnarled staff drifted close. He chuckled to himself, amazed at what lay before him.

He shared a quick look with those clustered behind him. Roughly a dozen members of the Brotherhood stood patiently, Declan and Ruvin amongst them. Wedged between them nestled young Jarred, his eyes wide as he sought to comprehend the pyramid's wonders. The walk along the corridor had been brief, its length no more than a hundred feet. Like the entrance itself, the corridor was square in shape, ten feet in width and height, the surface black stone polished smooth. Even the floor was of the same material, hard and level, but slick underfoot for those in a hurry.

The corridor ended here, though, before the large metal doors.

Cappitus returned his gaze, noting the band of glyphs expertly etched about its border. There was a message here, he mused, old yet disturbingly relevant. He shifted his staff high to better see the glyphs, knowing he would have need of Neema sooner than expected if they were to decipher their meaning. He wondered briefly whether to attempt opening the doors now or wait until the message was read.

'How long until Neema arrives?' he asked over his shoulder, the question directed at Declan.

'I expect she'll be here soon,' Declan answered.

Cappitus pondered what to do. He could wait, the proper course of action, or he could seek to unlock the door himself. The glyphs, despite his unfamiliarity with many, hardly constituted a warning of dire consequence. Those etched along the outer doorframe were signs of the Nepharii zodiac, he was certain.

From what he could decipher on his own, the rest were merely a reference to what lay behind the door. Besides, he doubted the pyramid would open its secrets simply to snare passersby in an elaborate trap. Every fibre of his being suggested the Nepharii temple was here for a reason; a reason soon to be realized. He didn't need to remind himself that the city teetered on the brink of an impossible abyss. If Bastion was to truly fall, the world would tremble. It was that simple.

Somehow, a means to defeat Ahriman and his pet witch, Avra, would be forthcoming. With fingers crossed, Cappitus stepped closer to the double doors, his mind issuing caution despite his call for hope. Hope for a weapon powerful enough to repel a god.

'What are you doing?' Ruvin stepped close to his old friend, his keen eyes also studying the glyphs. Cappitus knew Ruvin had gazed upon similar patterns in Bel-Afii.

'I'm opening the door, Ruvin, my friend,' a look of concentration crossed Cappitus' face, his eyebrows knotted, his lips pursed. 'Do not worry; I deem it to be safe.'

'Can you read the glyphs?'

'Mostly,' Cappitus replied. 'Not all are clear in their meaning, but I'm certain Neema, once she arrives, will be able to clarify the remainder.' He waved a hand towards the top of the door where two glyphs surrounded by squares of gold resided. 'I can make out the above, at least.'

Ruvin squinted until he saw the glyphs in the dim light. 'The first denotes a doorway, I believe, whilst the second suggests a hall, or chamber.'

'Correct,' said Cappitus, 'my thoughts exactly. I profess the above details what lies within.' He tapped a finger against the cold metal door. 'This here, Ruvin Ciricello, is what I assume to be the Doorway to the Beyond. If I'm not mistaken, inside rests the Room of Eternity.'

Several of the Brotherhood repeated the titles, their heads bowed as they reflected upon its connotations.

'The Room of Eternity,' repeated Ruvin, 'now that sounds promising.'

'Really?' said Jarred, his voice piping up from the mass of black-robed men. 'I would have thought the doorway is simply that, a doorway.'

Cappitus spun to peer down at the lad, a quizzical look in his eye. 'What makes you suggest such a thing?'

Jarred squinted as he kept his eyes on the glyphs above and Cappitus could see he was thinking his answer through. 'Because the second glyph resembles a portal, and I assume it refers to what resides within the room, not what we see before us now. The first glyph is the Nepharii symbol for beyond count, or infinity. It therefore reads Forever Chamber.'

A dozen or so members of the Brotherhood peered down at the boy with shock marring their gaping faces.

'You speak as if you know the language of the Nepharii, Jarred,' Cappitus hushed the excited men with a raised hand.

'I . . . I can see the patterns and understand the glyphs,' he said, his brow furrowed as he listened to his own words. 'I don't know how or why, though, but the pictures flash before my eyes and I know what they mean.'

The murmur increased amongst the men. Cappitus let it run its course, then watched as Ruvin placed a comforting hand on the young man's shoulder. 'How do you feel, Jarred?'

'I feel tired,' Cappitus barely heard the reply and hushed the men once again. 'My whole body feels numb. My legs and arms tingle . . . my head hurts.'

Ruvin patted his back, told him he would be alright.

Cappitus caught Ruvin's eye, nodded and spun back to the door. He gave a sudden push, both hands pressed flat against the metal. He expected the solid surface to rebuff his efforts and was pleasantly surprised to find the doors yield with only a modicum of pressure. They continued to swing open on silent hinges, the only sound a swift sigh of air as it whispered past them to travel along the dark corridor. Cappitus barely noticed; his eyes peeled as he searched the vacant space beyond the doors. The only light source came from his staff and a few of the glow-spheres created by the Brotherhood, but he sensed a vast emptiness before him.

With a thought, he sent a glow-sphere ahead with the intention of lighting the way. He then stepped forward, Ruvin and Jarred close by his side. The remainder of the Brotherhood crowded behind.

Their silent steps forward revealed a wide platform, forty feet in width. It slowly narrowed to a single path only five feet wide that stretched far into the gloom. What was most surprising was the vast emptiness that lay to either side. It appeared they had entered an enormous, vacant chamber fashioned like the inside of a sphere. Most importantly, they were positioned at its equator and could see neither a floor nor a ceiling.

'Careful,' Cappitus cautioned as he stepped further into the chamber, 'keep well away from the edge. I cannot see how far down it drops.' He spun around, noting the curvature of the chamber as he looked back at the door and the wall they stepped through. It disappeared into darkness, making for a point well above his head and beyond their vision.

'This is an incredibly large space you have found, Cappitus,' whispered Ruvin. 'But, by the One and all that is holy, what benefit could possibly be derived from such a room?'

Cappitus merely shook his head as he continued along the narrow path that lay before him. It was straight, like the corridor leading into the pyramid and fashioned of the same black material. For the moment, its end was lost as it plunged into darkness, but Cappitus boldly put one foot in front of the other, his glow-sphere leading the way, his lit staff held high. To falter here was paramount to disaster. Cappitus thought about sending a glow-sphere to plunge the dark depths to either side, but common sense prevailed. It wouldn't do to have a dozen of his Brotherhood standing on the edge, peering into unfathomable depths. The thought alone made him giddy and vertigo was not something to encourage when standing upon a narrow path in a hollow chamber.

Instead he led the group forward; one step at a time as he walked across a path he hoped spanned the entire room.

But he was wrong.

He'd travelled more than a hundred feet by his reckoning when the path before him suddenly flared to either side to become another forty-foot wide platform. Directly before him stood a lectern, four feet high and made of silver, slender like a pillar before folding outward to provide a flat surface area. Beyond was total darkness. Taking deep, calming breaths, he walked up to the lectern, his staff held close, so he could study the oddity.

'What have we here?' Ruvin was once again by his side.

The lectern was an elaborate piece up close, twined metal elegant and strong, wide enough to place either hand comfortably on its surface. At its centre sat a circular depression of unknown origin.

'Have you seen anything like this in your travels, Ruvin?' asked Cappitus as he continued to admire its design.

'No, nothing this unusual,' Ruvin scratched his chin. 'It must have a purpose, though,' he continued. 'It was certainly designed for something specific.'

Cappitus looked for Jarred and saw the young man stifle a yawn. 'Come, Jarred,' he beckoned him with his staff then placed a hand about his shoulders as he arrived. 'Is there anything you can tell me about the lectern? Can you derive its purpose?'

The Brotherhood held a collective breath as Jarred went to task. His head moved side-to-side, his eyes barely open. His mouth uttered sounds no man had heard before. Then trance-like he swayed, his eyes threatening to close before he placed his hands either side of the lectern for support.

The chamber, formerly dark and entirely secretive, suddenly bloomed into unnatural life.

It was instantaneous; the moment Jarred rested tired hands atop the surface, light began to appear, like stars in the night sky. First a cluster appeared to their left, shining like drops of gold, then a scattering of diamonds twinkled to their right, high up on the outer wall of the curved chamber. The men tilted their faces high and wide, even looked below, their eyes peeled as they watched the marvellous spectacle. The light show didn't abate, but continued to grow until the illumination was enough for the men to see clearly, to understand and reflect on the enormity of the chamber they stood in. For it was colossal. They stood inside a sphere so large that having travelled more than a hundred feet, they were not yet half way. Most impressively, their eyes were drawn towards a solid black sphere, hovering in the centre of the room. It was enormous, and even as they watched it began to flicker into primal existence. Threads of silver light arced across its surface, becoming brighter by the second, whilst nine platinum rings began to spin about the sphere, criss-crossing with a hum as they increased their rotations.

'By the One!' exclaimed Cappitus as he stood back from the lectern.

'You might be right,' suggested Ruvin as he craned his neck to encompass the chamber. The flickering lights continued to flash into existence and it took a moment of reflection, but eventually members of the Brotherhood, like Ruvin, came to the same conclusion at once.

'It's the night sky,' Ruvin said with a hushed voice. 'It's *our* night sky.'

Cappitus followed Ruvin's pointing finger, spying the constellation almost instantly. It was The Harper, exactly where he was supposed to be in relation to other signs of the zodiac. He cast his gaze further. There was the Graceful Swan, the Howling Wolf and the Sleeping Bear. Every one of the major constellations was depicted.

'It's impressive,' Declan moved alongside, keen to keep clear of the spinning rings revolving around the giant sphere before them, its silver illumination now sparkling with hints of molten gold. They were no more than ten feet away from the rings, their gentle hum now an audible whine as their rotation speed increased.

'That it is, my friend,' Cappitus concurred.

'What function does it serve, do you think?'

Cappitus ran his fingers through his long white beard, his face still raised to the heavens, gold and silver light reflecting from his glassy eyes. 'I wish I knew,' he whispered, before peering down at Jarred in the hope the lad could provide an answer. A gasp caught in his throat as he saw the young man lying in a heap at the base of the platform. He reached down and placed trembling fingers against Jarred's neck.

'Is he alive?' Ruvin asked, concern in his voice.

'He is, but he needs fresh air and water. The lad's passed out.'

Booted feet stepped forward and Cappitus saw Declan reach down and lift Jarred up. The swordsman did so with little effort. 'Where do you want him?'

Cappitus shrugged, uncertain now in such a time of chaos. Irongate was too far away and the number of abodes still standing were few. Even the cathedrals surrounding Aston's Tear were in a poor state, for they'd taken the greatest of hammerings when the granite once housing the pyramid exploded outwards. 'Take him outside and place against the pyramid wall.' He could think of no better alternative at present. 'But monitor him, my friend, and call for a priest. The lad has a gift. It would be ill-timed if we were to lose his insights now.'

Declan nodded and began to cross the spanning bridge. Ruvin rose to his feet to follow. 'I'll keep an eye on him, Cappitus,' he said.

'Please do, Ruvin, because this . . .' he gestured with his hand and staff to encompass the entire chamber, 'may be the greatest discovery the world has ever seen.'

*

Neema squinted at the glyphs lining the great double doors. She had no trouble discerning the signs of the Nepharii zodiac for she knew them well. The glyphs above the doorway were familiar also and she had little trouble reading the title Forever Chamber. Yet it was the reference to what lay within that confused her. From what she could decipher there was another doorway, or portal, on the inside. That alone was not cause for concern except the name of the portal was tied with that of the Universe, or the Great Consciousness. For Neema such a name was common, for like Cappitus and his Brotherhood of One, it was the name they bestowed upon their one true God. She shook her head, more out of curiosity than an overwhelming sense of amazement and stepped through the doorway eager to see God's Portal.

She'd arrived as swiftly as able once word reached her and the Celestial Sisters of the doorway's appearance. They were already aware of the pyramid's change; having seen her outer shell of granite blasted high and wide to reveal shining walls of diamond. As frightened as they were their surprise was masked, for they knew better than any that forces beyond their ken were swirling into existence. For days, they'd kept a constant vigil on the powers morphing about Bastion. Secretly they'd fashioned wards of protection, strength and integrity about their Celestial Tower. In hindsight, it was the right choice, for when the earthquake struck their stronghold was one of only a handful to remain standing and untouched.

Neema shook her head once more, her thoughts consumed by Avra and her Dark God. She knew the old witch was canny, knew she was sufficed with rage. It had been forty years since the Celestial Sisters and the Brotherhood of One disbanded the Practitioners by order of the king. Back then it was King Olin the third who sat the throne; large and strong, a man of power himself. Neema and Cappitus were present, acolytes at the time, raw to the ways of the arcane. Yet even they pitted their knowledge and energy against Avra and her coven, beat them down until their resistance crumbled. Then the aging witch was banished, never to return on pain of death.

With a venomous tongue Avra cursed King Olin and his line as she left, vowing to return one day and exact her revenge. The feud between the two families was convoluted at best, but it was also entrenched in bitterness and betrayal. This time King Olin prevailed, but if he'd known the price of his victory, she wondered if he would have been so merciful. She sighed, amazed at how quick four decades could pass. But she knew the time was now. The comet known as the Eye of the Jaguar already approached the Chaos star. It appeared frail and weak. Its passing close to the sun had compromised its structure and in little more than twenty-four hours the conjunction they all awaited would occur. It was only a matter of time. Whatever hand they were to play would be decided soon.

Her thoughts crowded her mind as she stepped onto the narrow path leading from the platform and stepped into the chamber itself. Aston's Tear had always evoked a sense of awe in all who stood before it, not simply due to its immense size but also due to something mystical. It was a feeling, a tantalizing hint of power, a sense of protection and perfection. The pyramid was often referred to as the Beacon of Bastion, its capstone a shinning symbol of the kingdom of Dervae and its people. It also provided a sense of hope and wellbeing.

Now it was something different, something altogether magical.

She walked carefully; following the narrow path like the Brotherhood had previously, but without the hindrance of darkness. An enormous revolving sphere at the centre of the chamber glowed silver flecked with gold, whilst several platinum rings spun hypnotically about its grand presence. Lining the concave walls of the chamber was an assortment of stars, thousands in number, fashioned to resemble the night sky in all its magnificent glory. The sparkling vibrancy resembled that of the outside walls, enabling her to view the wonder with unbridled awe. For a moment, she experienced a vague sense of walking amongst the stars of the universe, as though she traversed the heavens like a god herself.

'It's quite a sight, is it not?' Cappitus asked as he moved to stand before Neema's plump form. She diverted her attention to the tall elder, noting the excitement in his eyes and the smile stretching his mouth.

'It is, Cappitus, but it can also be a curse.'

'A curse?'

Neema waved a finger before Cappitus' face. 'You and your Brotherhood are flawed, Cappitus. As soon as you find something exciting and unfamiliar, you forget about everything else. The city is falling and darkness creeps close, my friend. Best not forget how dire our situation is.'

'We have not forgotten, Neema.'

'Then lose the smile,' she snapped, more to remind herself to remain focused than to belittle Cappitus. The elder of the Brotherhood understood and smiled warmly at the old matron anyway.

'Come, I've something to show you,' he reached out to grasp her pudgy hand and led her along the path until they reached the lectern. Neema gave it a cursory glance as she stood before it, her eyes drifting towards the silver-gold sphere. From where she now stood, at its equator, it appeared to be a sphere of vibrant energy, pulsing with unnatural life. Large platinum rings spun about its mass, criss-crossing with a hum of their own. The entire contraption hovered there, a gentle vibration sufficing the chamber, mesmerizing in its complexity.

'I have never beheld such magic before,' she said, 'nor witnessed anything so beautiful.'

Cappitus nodded, likewise entranced by the spectacle. The widened platform they stood upon still held a dozen members of the Brotherhood. Even with so many the sphere, easily a hundred feet in diameter, dwarfed them all.

'Do you have any idea as to its purpose?' Neema asked as she noted many of the Brotherhood in discussion.

'No,' he replied, 'although there is continuous speculation, as expected.'

Neema moved back to the lectern, eager to study its odd form.

'Young Jarred placed his hands upon the surface,' said Cappitus as he moved to her side, 'and the chamber lit up. First to arrive were the stars and constellations, then the sphere at its centre.'

'And what of the depression here?' she asked, pointing towards the small hollow centred in the dais.

'What of it?'

Neema turned to look at the tall elder. 'Fool,' she chided, 'like I said earlier, you and your brethren become far too immersed to observe the obvious.' Cappitus narrowed his eyebrows. 'I would suggest you return to Irongate, old man, and bring forth the *Nepharii Uranometria*. When you do, place it here,' she pointed once again towards the lectern and its circular depression. 'Then we shall see what this chamber truly conceals.'

Cappitus nodded his head slowly, his mind already working furiously as he contemplated such an event.

'See that it is done, Cappitus,' Neema sought to break him from his reverie. For all his expertise and supposedly fathomless knowledge, he was still a man, and Neema liked to remind him of such out of necessity. Like all men, she believed, they needed prodding from time to time.

'I shall,' he was almost breathless with anticipation. 'If you don't mind then, Neema, keep an eye on proceedings whilst I return to Irongate.'

Neema offered a wan smile in return. 'Don't thank me yet, old man, there is still much work to be done.' She clapped her hands together. 'Now begone, I've only so much patience myself, you know.' She watched as he began to shuffle down the narrow path. 'And Cappitus,' she yelled after his departing form, 'don't dally. Danger lurks, and we must remain vigilant.' He waved a hand in reply and then he was gone, his black robes blending with the darkness. Neema took the opportunity to appraise the walls of the chamber once more, seeing the stars of the night sky twinkling so very bright.

'So it begins,' she said softly, her eyes misting as they returned to the glowing sphere and its spinning rings, that which she knew to be God's Portal. 'So it begins.

CHAPTER FIFTEEN

Cold water splashed over his face.

Tarsin grimaced at the intrusion. Dark dreams had been swirling deep inside, looking for purchase and a chance to cause pain. Now he was awake and despite the assault, thankful. He raised a hand to wipe the liquid away and noticed shackles about his wrists. They clinked as he moved his hand to the base of his skull and pressed gingerly against a lump caked with dried blood.

'Rise and shine, surface dweller,' he heard the voice from far away, slightly slurred, he thought, although there was a ringing in his ears that made listening rather difficult. 'I said rise and shine!' the command was repeated, this time with added volume.

Tarsin opened his eyes with a wince as light from a lantern bore into his head like a red-hot lance. A dark shape moved beside him, accompanied by a groan, and he realized Griffith lay near. 'Where am I?' he asked, aware he had no recollection concerning his current location.

'Undercity,' spat the man behind the lantern. Tarsin couldn't make out his features, blurred as they were by the light, but he seemed to recognize the voice.

'Do I know you?'

A light chuckle reverberated about the room. 'Hardly,' the man returned, 'unless you call our brief meetin' last night an introduction.'

Tarsin placed his shackled hands on the floor and rose into a seated position, his back against a wall. The lantern moved and for the first time Tarsin noticed a set of iron bars between he and the man who spoke. He checked his waist but knew his sword had been removed, then saw his boots were missing. He peered about the room he now found himself in. It was small, three solid brick walls and one of iron hemmed he and Griffith into the centre where dank straw covered a tiled floor. There was no furniture.

'Boss wants to see you two,' said the man behind the lantern. 'Better wake your friend and make him lively . . . it wouldn't do to keep the Boss waiting.'

Tarsin reached over and gave Griffith a gentle push. The big man groaned and rolled over, his wrists likewise shackled. He saw a large patch of dark matted hair at the back of his head that was an obvious cause of discomfit. A moment passed before Griffith sat up, only for him to lean over and vomit across the floor.

'Nice, that is,' said the man who Tarsin assumed was the guard. There was a shuffle of feet before another bucket of water was thrown into the cell to dampen Griffith's already battered spirit. 'Clean yourself up, pig!' he snarled. 'Boss doesn't want to smell yer stink!'

'Let him be,' Tarsin spoke quietly, but his tone was menacing.

'And what are you going to do if I don't?' came the obvious reply.

He ignored the comment and leant over to assist his friend. He looked a wreck. Devoid of his armour, his trousers and beige gambeson were both stained with sweat and blood. Tarsin couldn't remember having been involved in a scuffle last night, but Griffith's appearance suggested otherwise. He helped him to a sitting position, despite his own stomach feeling queasy due to the acidic stench. 'Are you alright?' he whispered.

Griffith opened glazed eyes to peer at his friend. His lips were bloodied, and a deep bruise had formed under a cheekbone. Someone had hit the big man hard and more than once. 'I'll live,' he managed to say, his tongue racing over his teeth, checking to see if they were still present, 'but damn do I need a drink!'

Tarsin chanced a look in the direction of the guard. 'Who is your Boss?' he asked.

The guard moved away from the lantern, allowing Tarsin to finally glimpse the man. He was short and wiry, possibly forty years of age, maybe more, with receding black hair hanging in thin strips and numerous scars adorning his weathered face. When he spoke, several dark spaces highlighted his lack of teeth.

'You'll know soon enough,' he hawked and spat, obviously his way of letting Tarsin know the discussion was over.

Tarsin didn't mind, it gave him time to reflect on what had occurred. It was all coming back to him now: the earthquake, the pyramid of diamond and the race to find the king. Then he remembered the duel with Owen Moor and his men. Shortly after they came across a young boy calling for help, now they were here.

'Charming fellow,' Griffith forced a smile as he propped himself higher against the wall, the chain between his hands clinking as he did so. 'If I ever escape from here, I'll break his scrawny neck.'

'Where is here, exactly?' asked Tarsin. 'You said you knew who these people were.'

'I do,' Griffith winced as he made himself comfortable. 'They're the Nocturnals: now the only thieves' guild doing business in Bastion. I'd say we're deep underground.'

'I thought there were three or four guilds plying their trade throughout Bastion?'

'There were six when you left. But two years ago, maybe longer, the Nocturnals swept in and settled in the north-west. Before long they had control of the entire northern half of Bastion. In the following year, they pressed the remaining guilds either into service with the Nocturnals, or into service with the dead.'

'I remember those times,' snarled the guard. 'I was one of those others, but the Boss, he be good to us and we do him a service in return. One big happy family, aye,' he reached for a wooden staff leaning against the wall. 'But this one,' he used the staff to point towards Griffith, 'being Captain of the Sceptres, he causes us trouble.' The staff snaked through the iron bars and poked Griffith's bare foot.

Griffith snarled and rose to his feet before grasping the iron bars with his meaty hands. He rattled the cage, his huge shoulders bunching and then flexing like a crazed man, seeking to pull the bars out of the tiled floor. They held, though, despite his efforts, although the guard flung himself back so fast he fell in a heap near the only doorway. He was about to rise and vent forth a stream of superlatives when a shiny booted foot appeared close to his nose.

'The bear has awoken, I see,' said a tall man with dark hair and a trident beard. He was dressed in black trousers and shirt and wore a cloak that fell to his waist.

Tarsin stood to join Griffith and watched as the newcomer entered the room. Behind him were several other men attired in similar fashion, slender swords and daggers belted at their waist. Each bore a small white owl embroidered high on their chest, a mark, he supposed, belonging to the Nocturnals. 'Would you mind explaining to me what this is all about?' Tarsin addressed the man with the trident beard.

The man tore his gaze away from the fuming Griffith to appraise Tarsin. 'Sorry,' he began, 'for you it was a matter of being in the wrong place at the wrong time. No hard feelings, aye.'

'Fine,' Tarsin smiled, 'then release me from this prison so that I may go about my business.'

'And your large friend . . .'

'. . . Will be coming with me.'

Laughter erupted from the gathered crowd, and even the small guard smiled and spat in their direction. Tarsin could see there was little to be gained here, not amongst these men. He needed to speak to whoever ran the guild, the so-called Boss. It was imperative Griffith and he be released. The survival of Bastion could very well depend upon it and time was fast slipping away. He suddenly realized he didn't know what time of day it was.

'What time is it?' Tarsin spoke quickly in a vain effort to instil a sense of urgency.

'Time for you and your friend to see the Underlord,' a grin splashed across the man's face, stretching his trident beard wide. Before he could even begin to frame a question in reply, the small guard opened the cell door with a black key. Several men reached for them, grasping their chains and yanking them into the hallway. Without a word both men were hoisted towards the door, sharp daggers placed firmly against their back.

'Where are you taking us?' Tarsin heard Griffith growl in protestation.

'To see the Underlord, like I said.'

Further conversation was cut short as they were led through the only door and down a dark passage. Tarsin could see little, for the thief who led the procession carried the only torch. But a final glance showed him the room they left to be little more than an abandoned cellar, modified to hold no more than half-a-dozen men at best. It was quite possible they were only ten feet below the city proper.

They walked for almost an hour taking multiple twists and turns, always, it seemed, heading deeper below the surface. They traversed a set of stairs and at some point, the narrow pathway morphed into a boulevard that stretched away into the darkness, its walls painted with strange creatures faded and chipped. Any attempt to catch a glimpse of the artwork was met with a sharp press of the dagger at his back and a whispered word of advice not to dally. The Underlord was an impatient man and they had best not keep him waiting. Men had died for being tardy in his presence. Tarsin nodded and eventually they passed under an ornate arch leading into a vast chamber. Here the walls were lit by a score of braziers situated about its perimeter, their light reflecting the enormity of the room. Tarsin took in his surroundings, awestruck at the bas-relief walls and patterned floor of azure and jade, his eyes wide as he scanned the room with admiration. As beautiful as it was, though, the earthquake had taken its toll. A few crumbled walls were testament to its fury.

'This way,' a forceful push had he and Griffith moving swiftly again, heading this time towards the left where pale columns reared from the tiled floor to reach thirty feet towards a domed ceiling. Large bronzed doors hid amongst the shadows and the small group of men with their two prisoners halted before the first one they came across. Trident beard stepped forward and slammed a fist against the bronze. A moment later it opened on well oiled hinges.

Tarsin was shoved inside, his bare feet scraped and sore, whilst Griffith suffered a heavy fist in the ribs to move him forward. The square room they entered was well lit. Several torches burning brightly in bronze sconces lined the walls and candelabra supporting a dozen candles shone from the centre of a heavy rectangular table. Half-a-dozen high-backed chairs nestled about its perimeter, currently occupied by an assortment of men differing in size and disposition. At the head of the table stood an imposing man in his late fifties: grey-haired but straight-backed, dressed in black with a white owl over his left breast. Trident beard yanked Tarsin's chains and pulled him towards the table to stand before the seated men, Griffith led in similar fashion.

'As you requested, Underlord, so have I delivered.'

'Thank you, Reefe,' said the older man, his eyes narrowing as he scanned the two men whilst Reefe, the man with the trident beard, stepped to the side. A slight movement to his right alerted Tarsin to the presence of six dark clad men standing in the shadows, their faces obscured by heavy cowls. Daggers sat sheathed at their hip.

'Well, well,' said the Underlord, a wicked smile playing across his face, 'it appears the esteemed Cale Griffith has finally met his match.' A chuckle was heard from the assembled men, and Tarsin did his best to read their faces.

'If you call a blow from behind "meeting my match",' Griffith snarled.

The Underlord tilted his head. 'Your capture was . . . undignified, granted,' he began, 'but then Reefe O'Bannon is not bound by honour. At least not in the same sense as you surface dwellers are.'

Tarsin could see murder in the eyes of the assembled men. Whatever he and Griffith had stumbled into, it was going to take an inordinate amount of luck to wriggle out of the cesspit they now found themselves in. If he wasn't mistaken, the men before him were the hardest criminals under Bastion. Chained as he was, he doubted he and Griffith stood much chance if it came to blows. Their only course of action lay in conversation, yet neither man was accustomed to pleading for their life.

Tarsin watched as the Underlord finished his appraisal of Griffith and cast his eyes towards him. 'Cale Griffith, we all know and hate,' he said, his voice stern, commanding, 'but you, swordsman, I do not believe we've had the pleasure.'

A frown creased Tarsin's forehead as he listened to the Underlord's words. The man stood composed, almost aloof in the presence of such hardened criminals, but there was something in the manner of his speech that tweaked at memories long forgotten. 'I am no-one of importance,' said Tarsin.

'Truly?' the Underlord raised a hand. 'And yet you travel with Cale Griffith, the Bane of the Undercity. Are you friends with this man?' the Underlord finished by pointing a finger at Griffith.

'We were friends once. I'd like to think we are still.'

'Then that makes you an enemy of Undrercity,' the Underlord clapped loudly, the men seated hooting their delight at Tarsin's uneasiness.

'We mean you no harm . . . 'Tarsin began, but the men shouted their disapproval, drowning out his protestation.

A man nearest Tarsin waved a pudgy hand. He was obese; heavy jowls wobbling as he opened his mouth to talk, thin strips of brown hair matted to his pate. 'You speak when you're spoken to,' he shouted from his seat. It was almost a squeal.

'Aye, vagrant,' shouted another, a man with a thick, curled moustache and tattooed arms. 'Speak out of turn again, and we'll cut out your tongue.'

A small smile tweaked the corner of Tarsin's mouth as the men buffeted him with language from the streets. They were crass at best, downright feral at their worst. But what it highlighted was a difference between the six men at table in comparison to the Underlord. It was at that moment Tarsin recalled where he'd seen the grey-haired man before, albeit his attire had differed, and he'd worn a salt-and-pepper beard. A second later he remembered his name. What truly piqued his interest though, was his presence here amongst the gutter-trash of Undercity.

The verbal abuse simmered down a notch, enough for the Underlord to reassert control over proceedings. 'Gentlemen, how remiss of me,' he spread his hands wide to encompass the six men at table, 'allow me to introduce the Pillars of Bastion.'

Tarsin chanced a glance towards Griffith, but the big man stood in silence.

'To my right,' smiled the Underlord, 'sits Aiden Rath, Fletch Stickler and Harper Reg. To my left: Gammy the Old, Vin Hacka and Jorge Blacktooth.' They quietened at the introductions, but Tarsin could sense their thirst for blood. 'The six Pillars of Bastion, the foundation of the Nocturnals. All were guild masters, once, but now we are unified under a solitary banner: that of the white owl.'

'So why bring us here?' Tarsin sought to keep him talking. 'Do you seek to mock us?'

'Do I seek to mock you?' the old man laughed as he stood at the head of the table. 'Hardly . . . what did you say your name was?'

'I didn't. It is Tarsin Va.'

'Tarsin Va,' the name rolled off his tongue. 'A bastard then. And your profession?'

'Mercenary,' Tarsin failed to see any point in lying.

The Underlord shifted and placed his hands upon the table. 'Well, Tarsin the Bastard, you are here by association with a man many of us have wished ill these past years.' The obese man closest to Tarsin, Jorge Blacktooth, snickered as he rubbed his fat hands together. The Underlord continued, 'He has been a prickly thorn, Cale Griffith, one we have failed to extract from our nefarious operations. Now, with the city in chaos and the king likely dead, he practically walks into our waiting arms.'

'And we'll have his head on a platter by day's end, you mark my words,' Aiden Rath, a tall man with pock-marked skin and a shock of black hair stood to his feet to voice his opinion. All eyes turned towards Griffith; hopeful the big man would crack, or squirm, or plead for his life. They were baiting him, taunting him, but he remained silent.

Tarsin could only guess how the big man felt as he stood there in chains with the upper echelons of Undercity seated before him. He'd spent countless hours tracking these men, fighting these men, and doing everything in his power to thwart these men. Now he stood shackled like some circus bear, beaten and humiliated; his vision of a city free of thieves all but shattered.

'Nothing to say, Cale Griffith,' spat Vin Hacka. The man was solid with a thick neck and muscled arms. He wore a black sleeveless leather shirt to match his breeches, his arms covered in blue tattoos. At least half-a-dozen gold rings graced his fingers and Tarsin knew the man would like nothing more than to slam his fists into his friend's already bruised face.

Tarsin saw Griffith flex his arms and yank his wrists outward in response. The motion was abruptly halted once the chain of his shackles became fully extended.

'Ha,' laughed Vin Hacka with the men seated beside him, 'the once mighty Cale Griffith has nothing to say.'

'I know someone who can make him talk,' suggested Harper Reg with a smirk. His curled moustache quivered as he stifled a laugh. 'There's a gaoler of mine, Burson by name, who's whittled a little club for such a task. He claims he can jab it up a grown man's crap hole easily enough, it's pulling it out that causes undue distress. Tends to rip your insides so they're outside, if you follow. He's not the best of whittlers, you see. He leaves too many sharp edges. He makes a damn fine gaoler, though.'

More laughter erupted about the table, and Harper Reg, a man only a few years Tarsin's senior, sat back with a venomous smile full of jagged teeth.

'Gentlemen, gentlemen,' the Underlord waved Aiden Rath back to his seat and called for calm. 'Cale . . . may I call you Cale?' he asked with a smile. 'Cale is a man of honour and integrity; a man born to lead and often by example. He'll not stand here and listen to our petty rebukes and insults and waiver for our pleasure. He is too clever by half. Only by torture are we likely to see him falter before our eyes.'

'You're mad!' Tarsin raised his voice to be heard over the din. 'I thought you a better man than . . . this.' He gave him a look of disgust. 'You too once spoke of honour and integrity. I heard you with my very own ears.'

'Really,' the Underlord's lined face suddenly became passive, his eyes no longer glinting with mirth. 'And when exactly would this have been? I don't recall having met previously.'

'We haven't, but I heard you all the same.' Tarsin noticed the men had quietened; most now curiously eyeing their guild leader. 'Six, maybe seven years past,' he explained, 'in the presence of King Arkos, no less.'

'Preposterous.'

'I think not, Lord Derrick Tolston of Deepwell,' Tarsin saw the blood drain from the Underlord's face.

'Is this true?' Harper Reg pushed his seat back, the wood scraping loudly across the tiles.

'Calm yourselves, gentlemen,' the words were accompanied by a stern look, but the Underlord's face remained ashen. 'The bastard merely seeks to create a schism between us, his last vain attempt at survival. He's a canny one, alright.'

'It is the truth. Why would I lie?'

'Enough!' the Underlord's hands slammed hard atop the table. Movement along the wall caused Tarsin to divert his gaze, but the black clad men who stood there remained. 'I believe it is time to rid Bastion of its scum.'

Strong hands suddenly gripped Tarsin and Griffith from behind, dragging them back a pace. Both men struggled, but with their wrists bound and two sets of hands gripping them tight, they found it difficult to find any sort of leverage. It took mere seconds for the doubt creasing Harper Reg's face to morph into raucous laughter. Coupled with Aiden Rath, it sounded spiteful and the flickering torches highlighted the animalistic glee in their eyes as they waited for the perceived deaths to follow. A quick turn of the head showed Tarsin a set of iron rings placed halfway up the wall, rusted chains hanging silently to the floor. Reefe O'Bannon and his men dragged them closer. 'You cannot do this!' Tarsin shouted back at Lord Tolston, giving him one last look of desperation, trying in vain to swing his arms free.

'I already have.'

They were several feet from the wall when Reefe hissed under his breath for them to cease. Tarsin planted his feet firmly on the tiles and shook his head. Lord Tolston, the Underlord of the Nocturnals, merely smiled before giving a slight nod. From the shadows of the room drifted the black clad men, six of them, silently stepping forth with curved daggers glistening in their hands. But instead of moving towards where he and Griffith struggled, they headed straight for the table. Tarsin watched helplessly as black gloved hands reached for the Pillars of Bastion and yanked their heads back with force. A second later silver blades scraped across their throats, leaving each with a final blood-red smile. There wasn't even time for the men to scream. They simply bled, their heads unceremoniously left to plonk atop the wooden table as fountains of blood pumped forth.

Where there had been wild laughter and ribald jests was now an ever-increasing crimson pool.

Tarsin shifted his feet, seeking to pivot and throw his captors, but their hands were strong, hard fingers clamped tight about his shoulders and upper arms. He looked back at Lord Tolsten, 'What madness is this?' he shouted across the room. The old man heard his words, for his face lifted momentarily, still pale, but now flecked with dozens of ruby-red droplets. Tarsin watched as he licked his lips and saw the spark of satisfaction in his eyes.

'Hardly madness,' he returned, although Tarsin wondered if he replied to his question or merely spoke to himself. 'They were the last of the guild leaders,' he said, 'the last to speak ill of the kingdom and those it harboured.' The Underlord, Lord Tolsten of Deepwell, took several steps around the table, his boots stepping over the burgundy stain pooling at his feet. 'Now it is done, yet I feel no joy. Why is this?'

Tarsin shared a look with Griffith. 'Is he talking to us?' he asked him.

Griffith shrugged, then flung his head back sharply, cracking his skull into a man's face. The sound of breaking bone was drowned out by the man's howl of pain, his hands instantly seeking to cover his wound. The movement allowed Griffith to swing his massive frame about and shake free in an instant. He kicked out with his left foot, striking one guard in the midriff before clasping his hands together like a club and swinging to collect the other guard across the shoulder. Thinking on his feet he looped his chain over the man's neck, and a quick step around his would-be-captor had Griffith at his back, his chain now pulled tight against the guard's throat.

'Stand back!' Griffith growled as a handful of the dark clad men moved to intercept. 'Step any closer and this man dies.' The men halted their advance, looking to Lord Tolsten for guidance.

'You've nowhere to go, Cale,' Lord Tolsten shook his head. 'If you seek to walk out of here, your friend Tarsin dies.' Reefe O'Bannon and another still held Tarsin in a tight grip, and the dark clad men with their crimson blades sidled closer. A spluttering cough alerted them both to the man with the broken nose returning to his feet, a dagger in his bloody hand. 'Now release your hostage.'

'I cannot. I'll not die here, Tolsten, in some hole in the ground. Not to the likes of you.'

Tarsin saw Lord Tolsten grin but gone was the malevolence he spied earlier. He now appeared relieved, like a weight had miraculously been lifted from his shoulders. Even the colour in his face returned. 'Who said anything about you dying,' Lord Tolsten returned, 'certainly not I.'

The smell of death was beginning to permeate the room as Tarsin felt the hands holding him relax, then release him. He spun about, only to see Reefe O'Bannon and his comrade walk back a pace with hands held high.

'I did not bring you here to kill you, Cale Griffith,' Lord Tolsten moved to stand before the big man. Cale Griffith still bristled, his breathing heavy, but the chain about the man's neck was loose enough for his captive to breathe. 'I brought you here to present you with an offering.' Both men followed Lord Tolsten's outstretched hand as it encompassed the former Pillars of Bastion lying slumped at table. 'All those you sought to capture in the past years are now gone,' he continued, 'and the thieves of Bastion are now mine alone. Although as of yesterday's destruction, they are mostly dead, I fear.'

The confusion Tarsin witnessed on Griffith's face mirrored his own, he was certain, but the words rang of truth.

'What you said earlier, Tarsin Va, about honour and integrity still holds true,' he clapped a hand to his chest, momentarily covering the embroidered white owl, and it was then that Tarsin remembered it being the sigil of House Tolsten. He looked back towards Griffith. 'For five years I've toiled down here in the basement of the kingdom for the king, before even you, Griffith, took upon the mantle of Captain of the Sceptres. Whilst you kept the streets above safe, we sought to clear the streets below. It has been a taxing time, gentlemen, but one I would gladly commit to again should the king so command.'

'So, you are here on king's business?' Griffith asked, taking the chains from around his captive's neck and pushing him aside.

'Since day one,' Lord Tolsten sighed, and Tarsin could almost see his mind reflecting on the journey. 'It has been difficult, as you could well understand. Supplanting the previous thieves' guilds took cunning and cost many good men their lives, but once begun we could not cease. There was too much at stake and so little time to waste. We were propositioned with a dual purpose, gentlemen. First, we were to eradicate the guilds under Bastion, a task the king and I both agreed upon.'

'What of the second task?' Tarsin asked the obvious question.

'It was the more important of the two, although to be honest, the first was coupled with revenge at the time and felt equally relevant. But a group of men called the Brotherhood of One,' he said with pride in his voice, 'also requested the thieves be removed. I am a member of their order, a Seeker of the

Brotherhood. The reason we needed to clear Undercity, was so we could operate without the threat of prying eyes. In short, gentlemen, we were tasked with finding an entrance into Aston's Tear.'

CHAPTER SIXTEEN

A copper haze hung over the city of Bastion like a pall of dread.

Jarred stirred and woke, unsure of his surroundings until he noticed the pyramid's shining wall. He saw other survivors of the previous day's horror waking to gaze upon a living nightmare. Fitful sleep had taken away the memory of a fallen city, but now, with the sun attempting to shine through smoke from a hundred fires, the terrible devastation was viewed with sorrow. With such realization came the tangible loss of loved ones. Jarred could already hear the lamentations of the women, the distress in their wails a clarion call to herald a day of pain and misery. A day many of them, if given a chance, would wish away.

He placed hands on cold stone, noticed a brass cup of water by his side. He took a sip, savouring the clear liquid, hoping it would take the cloying taste of ash and dust from his mouth.

'You are awake, young Jarred,' a voice crackled.

Jarred looked up, shielding his eyes from the rising red sun to see an elder of the Brotherhood stooped over him. His face was like dry leather, his eyes clouded.

'Do you feel better, now that you've rested?'

Jarred shrugged, then squinted as he moved his raised hand. 'I feel . . . awake.'

'That is good,' a wrinkled hand drifted to pat him on the head. 'I am Fratelli, an elder of the Brotherhood, as you can tell by my robes,' he stepped back a pace to pat his black garments. 'Ruvin asked if I would keep an eye on you. You passed out last night, whilst in the Nepharii chamber.'

Jarred sought to remember, vaguely recalled a glowing sphere of silver-gold and spinning rings. He delved deeper into his memories; saw a doorway leading into a chamber surrounded by glyphs. A yawning black space appeared next, gaping wide as it sought to engulf him. He was startled, the shudder he experienced reminding him of the corridor leading into the pyramid.

He rose gingerly, saw the gaping doorway twenty feet from where he'd rested. Half-a-dozen Swords of the Brotherhood still manned the entrance. They appeared worried, their expressions dark and fearful. It was not difficult to see why. So many citizens now crowded the pyramid, most emotionally distraught. It appeared the apparent safety of a dreamless sleep could not eradicate the hurt one felt upon awakening.

With pangs of hunger he made for the doorway in the hope of finding Ruvin. He expected the Seeker to be alongside the elders, frantically collating the information they'd found, that *he* had found, so they could discern its purpose. Deep inside Jarred knew what to expect. Somehow, he'd managed to become a vessel of knowledge in a time of need. He could read the glyphs left by the Nepharii, could understand their connotations. No longer were the messages ambiguous or poorly deciphered. Still, he needed to be inside the chamber to help with their next step.

The Swords guarding the doorway let Jarred pass, so he moved quickly, aware Fratelli was doing his best to keep up. The walk along the corridor was a walk amongst shadows, for several braziers were positioned along its length to keep the darkness at bay. Yet Jarred was determined not to dawdle, for he felt claustrophobic and short of breath. Thankfully two members of the Brotherhood had positioned themselves beside the great metal doors at corridor's end, solid looking staves held in iron grips, their end alight with a magical glow. No words were spoken as Jarred and Fratelli passed them by and entered the immense chamber. Inside hovered the silver-gold sphere with its twirling rings, reached by a slender path he recalled from the night before.

He and Fratelli walked to the centre, aware of nervous chatter between brothers, priests and sisters.

'It's inconceivable,' said a black robed brother, 'the chamber's proportions are mind numbingly vast. Whatever magic was employed is beyond our comprehension.'

'And I would hazard a guess the sphere itself is a power source of some magnificence,' said another. 'It is quite possible the

Nepharii were able to harness the power of the sun, for I believe the sphere is a representation of our solar orb.'

'Nonsense,' replied a white-haired priest of Aston, resplendent in his red robes. 'One does not harness the power of a sun, my friend, not even your mythical Nepharii.'

'How would you know?' several brothers asked in unison.

Jarred saw matron Neema shuffle towards the squabbling men. 'Listen,' she spoke calmly, but her voice was raised to pierce the din, 'your suppositions are many and varied gentlemen, and entirely plausible, but they are getting us nowhere.' She took a couple of steps to stand before the lectern where the *Nepharii Uranometria* had been placed atop its surface. 'Here lies the key,' she pointed at the scintillating disc, 'but unless we can unravel its mysterious nature, I fear we may be stymied in our pursuit for knowledge.'

A collective nodding of heads ensued as the men and women turned their thoughts inward, hoping to elicit an understanding concerning an item they were unfamiliar with. As the debate continued Jarred saw Ruvin Ciricello approach to stand by his side.

'Did you sleep well?' he asked.

'Yes, and no' Jarred replied. 'It is morning outside.'

'Really,' Ruvin scratched his chin.

'There were five more tremors during the night,' Jarred sighed as he spoke, mentally fatigued more than anything else, 'and the fires still burn. When will it end, Ruvin?'

The older man sighed, his eyes full of concern. 'I do not know, Jarred. For all we know it could be the beginning. There are powers at work here beyond our comprehension, lad, and the earthquake was quite possibly the stirrings of a vengeful god.'

'So, what can we do? There are people dying in the streets, I can hear them.' Jarred wiped his eyes, the toll from spending a day listening to those trapped under crumbled buildings had caught up with him. His hands were blistered and grazed, his nails cracked, and his stomach continued to growl. He needed food. The smell of ash outside had been close to overwhelming and the stale air inside the pyramid was only marginally more tolerable. Right now, he'd give anything to be able to dip his head in a bucket of water to wash away his doubts and fears.

'Listen,' Ruvin placed both hands on Jarred's shoulders, 'whatever slim thread of hope we have resides in here, I've no doubt. Bastion has fallen, make no mistake. We can flee the city if that is your wish, but I'm afraid the journey would be one of constant pain and suffering, and eventually death.' Jarred saw Ruvin's eyes mist over and knew at once he thought of Captain Jarvis Vasco and his ship, the *Lioness*. He instinctively knew any hope they survived was slim at best. 'Ahriman the Dark God has arrived, Jarred. He has two goals that we are aware of. The first is to become flesh; the second is to destroy. We have already experienced a taste of what is to come.'

'What can we do against a god?' Jarred's eyes widened in fear. He'd heard words to a similar effect the day before, discussed amongst those of the Brotherhood vested with such knowledge. He found their talk irksome at first but having witnessed the earthquake he felt inclined to believe their discussions were truthful.

'All that we can,' Ruvin sighed. 'There is power here, lad, we need only discover how to utilize it. Mayhaps it will be enough to send the Dark God back to whatever hole he crawled from.'

'What if it isn't?'

'Then death awaits, young Jarred,' Ruvin looked to the stars above. 'But do not be so fearful, for death awaits every man.'

A few brothers overheard Ruvin's talk of impending doom and hurriedly set about their appointed tasks, invigorated by the overwhelming fear that gripped not only the men and women within the chamber, but those who even now scurried about the broken streets of Bastion looking for survivors. Jarred simply watched as brothers pointed shaking hands at constellations in the artificial night sky. And basking all in its metallic glow was the silver-gold sphere, spinning within its surrounding rings, an elaborate contraption that defied every Seer's effort to explain.

Jarred moved with Ruvin to study the *Nepharii Uranometria*, positioned on the lectern in what Neema hoped would be a revelation. Only nothing occurred when the disc slipped into the hollow other than settle perfectly into place with a click. If the elders watching expected something profound to materialize, they were sorely disappointed. But looking at it now, Jarred could see why Neema thought it would be perfectly placed. The disc itself was a series of concentric circles surrounding a silver dot at its centre. Twelve lines traced away from the centre towards the outer rim, creating twelve segments that further separated the concentric circles. Within each panel were ancient glyphs coupled with patterns of stars representing constellations in the night sky. The constellations depicted were those of the Nepharii, not those of the Dervae. But Jarred knew them well, for he'd seen the exact same signs replicated about the doorway they entered through. The detail was incredible, lines of silver, gold or platinum highlighting their shape. Jarred heard a voice inside his head call out the names as he shifted his eyes across their representations. First there was Tyrranus: the dragon, then followed Enlil: the eagle. Next was Venati: the hound, Ophidia: the serpent and Taurus: the bull. His eyes traced the circular relic until he saw Panos: the deer and Sable: the panther, then flicked past Corvus: the crow, Eloki: the fox and Trich: the rat. The last two were Ursa: the bear and Lupus: the wolf. Twelve constellations formed to reside in heaven and rule the Nepharii night sky. Countless gems of myriad hue also graced the disc, embedded seamlessly into the construct to lend a sparkle of ruby, emerald and sapphire-blue. Ruvin was still tracing his hand over a series of humanoid glyphs when Jarred reached out and touched the silver dot at its centre. It depressed with a click . . .

. . . And a deafening clap of thunder boomed within the chamber.

'Heavens above, what was that?' elder Cappitus was the first to speak. The thunder reverberated about the chamber for some time, with many clutching hands over ears to keep the sound at bay.

Jarred was about to respond when another sound, more like a screech than a whine, diverted their eyes towards the silver-gold sphere. The nine revolving rings had noticeably slowed, now lazily whooshing past as their speed decreased. All eyes were transfixed on the spectacle. Jarred felt his heart race, for he knew his gentle touch of the silver dot was the cause, but he also knew the phenomenon wasn't a mere coincidence. His action hadn't stalled the magic contraption. If anything, he'd moved the procedure along. There was purpose coupled with a hint of power to come.

A handful of minutes passed before the rings slowed their rotation and eventually settled into a position about the sphere's equator with a terrible bang, one after the other. The noise was horrendous, forced every man and woman to fall to their knees as the sound ripped through them easier than an icy wind. A minor shock wave followed, blowing over their stagnant forms to sweep past with a numbing sensation. Finally, with the ring's motion having ceased, the men and women were able to see the rings had now created an extension of the platform leading to the sphere itself. Several elders at the forefront of the crowd took a tentative step towards the new path, only for the sphere to flicker maddeningly as all traces of silver became swamped with molten gold. A crackle of energy could be heard before the chamber was silenced.

Then the gentle murmurings of men and women blossomed into a cacophony of noise as they jostled towards the rings and the now golden sphere. Ruvin grabbed Jarred's arm and dragged him forward, the Seeker intent on seeing what new wonder was about to be revealed. Jarred allowed Ruvin to escort him, aware of the revelation lying before the countless mystics and priests converging at the rings perimeter.

Ruvin bent close and whispered in his ear. 'You haven't by any chance broken the contraption?'

Jarred smiled, an act that put Ruvin's fear at ease. 'No, Ruvin,' he said. 'If anything, I've prodded the device into revealing its true nature. Come, let us watch and learn.'

Elder Cappitus pushed his way to the front, his tall frame squeezing past some of the more rotund gathered along the platform. He reached the edge and noticed the outer ring sitting flush with the path, not even the tiniest gap visible between the two. What was of more interest was the outer ring itself. To left and right it appeared to be smooth and unmarked, its platinum surface reflecting the stars above, but directly before Cappitus lay a segment five-feet wide. It revealed three etched glyphs about a circle, with three smaller circles randomly placed beyond its outer diameter.

'What do you think it details?' Ruvin asked, whilst Jarred pushed to the front of the assembled men and women.

Cappitus thought about the question as he raised his eyes. Everything within this chamber spoke of a presence within the universe. The golden sphere at its centre appeared to be a representation of the sun, the thousands of twinkling dots lining the inside of the hollow chamber were the stars in the night sky. Looking down, Cappitus knew the large circle on the outer ring represented a planet circling through the night sky, the smaller circles denoting moons surrounding the celestial body. He rose to his full height and stepped onto the ring, moving towards the next in line. Like the first, it was marked with a large circle with seven smaller circles surrounding its shape, two of them quite minute and one rather irregular.

'Each ring represents one of the planets in the night sky,' he said to Ruvin, 'the smaller circles are their moons.'

An understanding passed quickly amongst the gathered men and women. Cappitus heard a multitude of questions thrown his way, but he kept his head down, his eyes focussed on the task ahead. Out of the corner of his eye he saw young Jarred nod in affirmation. He took a few seconds to cast his eye over the boy. Outwardly there was no discernable change in his appearance or behaviour. Although inwardly he knew something profound had occurred. Whether it was his early contact with the pyramid he could not say, but the lad knew things few should be able to realise. With a shake of his head and a careful step he moved on, easing past three more rings, their planets large and their moons many, until he reached the fourth from the sphere. It bore a planet with a single moon, a glyph in the left corner reminiscent of the Nepharii glyph for life. Two humanoid etchings were standing next to a tree, its branches reaching high to crowd the right-hand side.

'I would suggest this to be our world,' he said aloud. He scratched his beard after voicing the words, for he could see three more rings ahead of where he stood, yet to the best of his knowledge and that of the Brotherhood, only two more inner planets should be orbiting their sun. He cautiously moved forward, aware he was standing on rings that hovered unaided in the middle of a large empty space. The etchings on the next two rings were as he thought; small planets without moons. The final, innermost ring was something altogether different.

It was an elegant piece, really, the smallest of the rings with a segment before him as wide as the path he followed. A single glyph of an eagle encompassed the uppermost area. Below the glyph sat a world circled by a single moon, two humanoid figures etched in stunning detail in the far-right corner.

'It is Enlil,' Jarred spoke as Cappitus knotted his brows. 'It is the eagle, the second Nepharii constellation in the night sky.'

Cappitus knelt and placed a hand on the cool surface. The glyph was indeed a large eagle, expertly fashioned, its splayed talons reaching for the world and the moon lying beneath it. He knew the Nepharii zodiac signs; recognised the pattern. What intrigued him now though was its placement directly before the golden sphere. With such a thought crowding his mind he swivelled his head to the right, then left, hoping to see if there were other glyphs to either side. To his delight he could see glyphs etched atop the curved plantinum ring, and despite not being able to see them all from where he stood, he knew without a doubt all twelve symbols of the zodiac would be represented.

With a smile Cappitus shifted his gaze to the enormous sphere pulsing with life not more than fifteen feet away. There was a dark chasm between the inner ring and the golden sphere, a vacant space ten-feet wide threatening to swallow any soul who stepped too close. The energy coursing through the artificial sun was palpable even from where he knelt, not so much an experience of heat, rather a sense of vibrant, unforgiving power. Sudden spasms of liquid flame coupled with pulsating surges of white light caused the old man to retract his vision, his eyes hurting if he looked at the display for too long. He took a deep breath and noticed the sphere still created a harmonious hum, barely perceptible, but its faint signature permeated the area.

He returned his vision to the inner ring, chancing his eye over the two figures etched upon metal. They were men in every sense of the word except for their heads. Their heads, in every aspect, were those of an eagle.

'I am confused, I must admit,' Cappitus spoke loud enough for Ruvin and Jarred to hear.

'Confused or not, the enormity of this device suggests it has purpose,' Ruvin replied. 'One does not construct something of such magnitude merely to appease the eye.'

Cappitus knew Ruvin's assessment was logical. The magic required to fashion the pyramid appeared to be god-like. And this chamber was certainly created by beings beyond their comprehension. He briefly wondered what purpose it was built for. He knew the Nepharii were aware the end of an age was coming. Scripture said it was so. They also expressed concern for the wellbeing of mankind; hinted salvation was possible if they only knew where to look. Cappitus knew the great pyramid was central to their belief; knew the pyramid would be central to their survival.

'What about this . . . solar orb?' Ruvin swept a hand towards the sphere of shining light pulsing before them. 'There is power there, more power than I have ever witnessed. How do we utilise it?'

Cappitus couldn't even begin to speculate how to harness such power. He came here looking for a weapon of enormous capability, something to send the Dark God back from whence he came. Yet as he peered about the chamber he saw nothing to suggest a weapon was in the offering, although the power coursing through the sphere was frightening. He feared to touch the surface; even if he could reach across the dark chasm.

The bustling shape of Neema squeezed through the press of men and women to reach his side. She appeared flustered, her cheeks rosy from sudden exertion. As she knelt by his side he could hear her wheeze, obviously short of breath.

'Are you well?' he asked, his eyes showing concern.

'Well enough,' she paused to gulp some air, then smoothed her hair back with a sweaty palm. 'The heat outside is oppressive and I fear I don't travel well these days,' he lowered his gaze to encompass her massive form. She was heavy, severely out of shape. Cappitus feared for her then.

'Do you have any insights regarding these figures?' Cappitus asked, diverting her attention to the segment before them.

'Interesting,' Neema traced a thick finger across the eagle-headed forms. Whatever craft was employed to etch the glyphs and symbols, it was unknown to them. The markings were not made by any tool they were aware of.

'Are they gods, do you think?' Cappitus reached out to follow Neema's lead. 'Is it possible we may call upon their aid?'

Neema shook her head. 'There are a few gods to the south, amongst the city states that share an eagle's features. None look exactly like this, though.' Neema pointed towards the left creature. 'This one appears to be female for there is a slight bump across the chest, curved rather than chiselled. The right one is also a fraction taller. I would say you have a male and a female here. Are they gods?' Neema held out her hands, 'Who can say?'

'Perhaps they are Nepharii,' Ruvin leant in close. 'We have no records concerning their appearance, at least nothing substantial. What we do have is conjecture only.'

'You're right, old friend,' Cappitus scratched his beard, deep in thought. It was true. They'd never encountered the Nepharii in any capacity, for their records were blank regarding their appearance. The Brotherhood of One once spent three years searching for ancient Nepharii burial sites deep below Bastion in a hope to glean something about the enigmatic race. It had been to no avail. Apart from corridors and chambers of unusual design and construction, no corpse had ever been discovered. Cappitus, along with his brothers, believed the Nepharii to be immortal beings: beings who abandoned a once great city to travel someplace else. He often wondered why they would do such a thing. At other times, he'd discussed where they might have gone. Perhaps the chamber they now crowded could provide an answer.

'So, what we have to the best of our knowledge is either a pair of gods, or a couple of Nepharii,' Cappitus could hear the scratching of quill pen on parchment. 'As to the chamber, all I can safely assume is that it represents our solar system.'

He could see the disappointment in the eyes of his brethren. Like he they expected answers to be forthcoming, not hints to sate the appetite and riddles to occupy their time. They needed answers now, and quickly.

'Somebody, look at this!' a brother's voice shouted from across the chamber.

Cappitus lifted his weary head. The brother was calling from the lectern. A sudden flurry saw the gathering disperse back across the rings, sandaled feet slapping hard against the platinum surface until they reached the cold metal of the platform. Then he saw the bent figure of Fratelli. He was an astute old soul, despite his age, and still surprised many of the younger brothers with his uncanny memory.

'What have you found?' Cappitus asked as he rounded the lectern to stand beside him.

'Look for yourself,' he rasped.

Cappitus did as bid, gazing upon the lectern where the *Nepharii Uranometria* resided. It still lay as he placed it, only now the inner sections of the disc were moving in a clockwise direction, slowly, he noticed, but moving all the same. 'When did this start?' he looked at Fratelli with eyes suddenly alive.

'Not so long ago,' Fratelli said. 'I wasn't certain that what I saw was real, or simply my tired eyes playing tricks, but I eventually saw the pattern.'

'The pattern?'

'Yes,' he continued, 'the inner ring spins fastest, and once a full rotation has been made, the second outer ring begins to turn, one segment at a time, whilst the inner ring continues. When a full rotation of the second ring is complete, the third outer ring will shift one segment at a time, and so it continues. What you have here is a timepiece.'

'A timepiece for what?' Cappitus asked.

Fratelli shrugged and lifted his eyes to peer back at the golden sphere.

Cappitus followed his gaze and saw Jarred still standing at the inner ring with hands held high, his palms facing the artificial sun.

'What is he doing?' several voices asked at once.

'Jarred!' Cappitus shouted to alert the boy to his presence. He heard him, for he lowered his hands and spun about, his eyes glazed and unseeing. He stood there for several seconds before a shake of his head bought him back to the realm of the living. Moments later Ruvin raced to his side. He consoled the lad, draping an arm over his shoulders as he led him back to the lectern. As he approached Cappitus could see fatigue dragging him down, his arms hanging limp, his eyelids heavy.

'Are you alright, Jarred?' Cappitus could see he was barely conscious. Whatever ailment the boy suffered, he was finding it difficult to shed.

'I am well,' he slurred, 'just tired, is all.'

A murmur spread through those assembled. Cappitus ignored the muttering and focused on the boy. 'What did you see, Jarred, when you stood before the golden sphere? What did you see that we did not?'

Silence reigned for several heartbeats as everyone awaited the boy's answer. Ruvin supported his sagging frame, then motioned for help as Jarred's dead weight became too much for the smaller man to bear.

'Jarred?' Cappitus asked once more.

His eyes opened. There was life sparkling within their depths. He took his time to appraise those standing around him, his face now shining with vitality. When he spoke, every soul in the chamber listened.

'I saw what I wished to see,' he began with a clear voice. 'That is all one sees when they peer into the *Kardiversum*.'

'The *Kardiversum*?' Cappitus held up a hand to stall any further comments. 'What exactly is the *Kardiversum*, Jarred?'

'It is the Heart of the Universe,' Jarred explained, his face awash with innocence and joy.

Cappitus mused over the unusual reference. 'What does it do, lad?' he eventually asked.

'It leads to salvation, if that is your wish,' he smiled; his arms held out wide. He then turned his attention towards Neema. 'You called it "God's Portal" did you not?'

'I did,' replied Neema. 'The glyph above the doorway reads such.'

'No, Neema,' Jarred spoke so everyone could hear. Cappitus frowned; for he believed Jarred's voice was not that of the young boy, but someone else. There was a noticeable difference in the inflection of his words and something alien about his manner and stance. 'It does not read, "God's Portal",' he heard Jarred continue. 'The *Kardiversum* is the Heart of the Universe.

'It is a Portal *to* the Gods.'

CHAPTER SEVENTEEN

Lord Derrick Tolsten, formerly Baron of Deepwell, sighed heavily as he sank into his plush, red leather chair. He was in his private study, a small, square room with enough space for a table, several chairs and a single book shelf. Behind him, opposite the only doorway, stood a painted wall depicting an elaborate display of man-like creatures with heads resembling those of a crow, blue-black feathers running down their arms and across their torsos. It was an interesting piece of artwork, faded now, a segment closest to the floor completely bare. It was reminiscent of the work he and his colleagues had long ago associated with the mysterious Nepharii.

He shifted his gaze from the wall to peer at the men now taking a seat. There were four others, apart from himself. Jack Boyd, his aide and confidante and the most stable and trustworthy right-hand man he'd ever known. Reefe O'Bannon, a thief of Bastion with a trident beard and a self assurance in his own skills, and two men from Bastion's crumbled surface, looking rather haggard, but formidable all the same. A dozen black-clad guards were arranged outside his study door, no more than several feet away should he but call. They were his Shadow Brethren: his dark knights. But here, in his private study that once belonged to a race of men few deemed to know, he felt safe. The two newcomers, Cale Griffith and Tarsin Va, were warriors in every sense, without a doubt killers. Both had been stripped of their shackles, their wrists no longer chained, although their effects had not yet been returned. He'd dealt with such men before, though, and knew these two were men of their word.

'I need my armour back,' Griffith spoke as soon as he sat. 'It's expensive, and it doesn't belong to me.'

Lord Tolsten smiled. 'It belongs to King Arkos, does it not?'

'It does,' the big man's eyes still simmered. 'And I'll need my weapons . . . our weapons,' he looked at Tarsin, 'and our boots if we are to be on our way.'

The old man nodded understanding, but the smile remained. He liked Cale Griffith. He was gruff, that much was certain, and short tempered, as per his reputation. He was also strong, loyal and likeable. It was a pity their paths, whilst essentially the same, had proven to be worlds apart. In only a short amount of time Tolsten already felt the stirrings of kinship, despite Cale Griffith's impatience. 'Where exactly are you headed, Cale? I may be able to help. Before yesterday I could have sent men to escort you to almost any place in Bastion. Now,' he held his hands out, a frown knotting his brow, 'we are limited. So many of our pathways and tunnels lie in ruin, whole sections of our network, including the sewers, are now buried. Still, wherever you're headed, we'll do our best to see you there.'

Griffith and Tarsin shared a look. 'We seek Highcastle and the king,' Griffith's voice was a low rumble. 'We hope to find him alive.'

Silence descended amongst the assembled men at Griffith's words. Jack Boyd fidgeted, as did Reefe, for they knew, like he knew, that Highcastle was a disaster. The better part of half a mountain fell atop its spires when the earthquake struck. Word had reached Tolsten's ears late in the afternoon as to its misfortune. The entire inner ward lay buried as far as they could tell, the outer curtain wall sundered in half-a-dozen places. The only structure remotely intact was the garrison for the Palaceguard. Yet even it suffered at the hands of the earthquake, its crenellations toppled, its peaked tiled roof now open to the elements. From all reports, and there had been many, Highcastle was finished. If Cale Griffith and his companion, Tarsin Va, thought to find their king alive, they would have one hell of a task in front of them.

'Can it be done?' Griffith asked to break the silence.

Tolsten shrugged. 'Nothing is impossible.'

'You obviously hold little hope for the king,' Tarsin offered, concern in his voice.

Tolsten looked to the swordsman and noted his broad shoulders and straight back. He reminded him of his younger self, only

Tarsin was taller. That and the sword they had taken from his person. Reefe had shown him the blade early in the morning, a Rykedian broadsword of impeccable design. To possess one spoke of skills beyond the norm, skills Tolsten never shared. A lesser man would have it stripped from him in a duel or stolen out of hand. Either that or be killed outright. Not Tarsin, though, which led Tolsten to believe him an expert swordsman. Yet a man with such a sword would be required to have a reputation, except he'd never heard of Tarsin Va before. For a man reputed to be the centre of the Nocturnals, the greatest guild of thieves in the history of Bastion, and a member of the Brotherhood of One, such a fact was slightly disconcerting.

Now, as a show of good faith, he was required to hand the sword back. Reefe would be most displeased.

'The news we have received is . . . not good, I'm afraid.'

He watched Tarsin shift in his chair. 'Still, we must attempt the rescue, we have no other option. Too much rides on King Arkos' fate to walk away.' Tolsten tilted his head as he listened to the man's words. 'We, too, are on a mission for the Brotherhood of One. We must see it through.'

'You work for the Brotherhood?'

'We do,' Tarsin answered. 'Elder Cappitus himself requested our services. To put it bluntly, it's imperative we find the king. If we fail, there is a chance Bastion will cease to be. And when I say, "cease to be", I mean completely destroyed.'

Reefe O'Bannon curled his hand into a fist and coughed; a none-too-subtle attempt at masking his disbelief. Tolsten remained impassive though, his thoughts his own. The comment appeared incredulous at face value but Tarsin certainly didn't look the type to fabricate such a story. There was no purpose for such a wanton lie. Not here. Not now. Tolsten may not have garnered their complete trust, but neither did he believe they'd think him a fool. Both parties had connections with the king and the Brotherhood, and secrets between the two would never hold for long.

'Would you care to explain yourself?' Tolsten asked, only to see Reefe shake his head. He ignored the man. He had proven useful these past years, a trusting hand during a time of sudden transition. He was an accomplished swordsman, albeit headstrong at times and quick to anger, but his loyalty was unquestionable. It was a pity his mind lacked subtlety and common sense. Then again, he doubted he'd ever master such traits, so he ignored Reefe's conspicuous protestations and listened as Tarsin began to tell all he knew.

The tale took time and when Tarsin finished he sat in silence, his mind running through the events mentioned concerning the Unseen. There was a great deal left to the imagination. Not all that occurred was relayed during the tale. He saw anger upon his face at certain points, knew he'd experienced pain and humiliation. Still, he'd outlined the course of events clearly enough for him to understand what was at stake. Provided the tale he wove was true, of course.

Yet Tolsten had listened intently and read the truth in the swordsman's eyes. He was an astute reader of men, always had been. If Tarsin swore a witch named Avra had summoned a god named Ahriman to help crush Arkos Vantos, then he would trust his instincts concerning the validity of such a tale.

After a moment of reflection, Tolsten decided he believed every word.

'You speak a tale of woe and deceit, young man,' Tolsten offered when Tarsin finished.

'It is true, I grant you that much. Much of what you heard are the words of elder Cappitus himself.'

'And you're a surviving member of the Unseen,' it was a statement.

'Not just a surviving member,' offered Griffith, 'he was First Sword of the Unseen. Our Captain, if you will.'

Tolsten sought Griffith's eyes. 'That would make you one of their rank, Cale Griffith, if you are to call Tarsin your Captain.' Griffith sat unmoving, 'And this witch, Avra . . . is she responsible for the destruction to befall Bastion yesterday?'

'It is possible,' Tarsin replied, 'although the destruction is likely a product of Ahriman. At least Cappitus tends to think so. Avra would not be foolish enough to risk harming Arkos before sacrificing him. She craves his death, yearns for it. Ahriman, on the other hand, might not harbour such reservations. Cappitus believes they need Arkos' soul to grant Ahriman flesh, but there is also a possibility that should Arkos die; the next king to take the throne will prove to be as beneficial.'

Tolsten nodded sagely, yet he felt the weight of a city literally fall back upon his shoulders. Eradicating the Pillars of Bastion had been an impulse, an act manifesting due to the chaotic nature of the day before. Never had all six remaining leaders been present in a room together, but the collapse of much they called home prompted them to seek out Tolsten, their Underlord, to discuss future options. He took their lives because he needed to, because he'd been ordered too. The king had set him a task and Tolsten was a man of his word. With their deaths, he believed his part in this grand charade would be over. Now Avra and her summoned god had become a bane to the city. From what Tarsin mentioned, Cappitus believed the pyramid was integral to their salvation; along with a king who was alive.

'So, once you find Arkos, then what?' he watched Griffith shrug his massive shoulders.

'We keep him alive, if we can. Take him far from here, out of harm's way.' Tarsin appeared to be more optimistic than his friend.

'And if he's dead?'

'Then we move on, seek a way to nullify Avra's power and prevent her from claiming the next king to sit the throne.'

'With the king's son's dead, Lucius Vupello is next in line if I'm not mistaken,' Tolsten said.

'How do you propose to accomplish such a thing?' Reefe finally weighed into the conversation. Tolsten had wondered if he'd been listening at all.

'With greater minds than yours, boy,' Jack Boyd voiced his own opinion, and Tolsten was thankful his old friend was beside him to put Reefe back in place. Tarsin, on the other hand, took the question at face value.

'The pyramid, Aston's Tear, is our hope and salvation. Already it has changed as you have no doubt seen. Given time, the Brotherhood will discover its secrets; unless you've discovered them already, of course?' Tarsin said.

'We have not,' Tolsten sighed, knowing he'd spent an inordinate amount of time during the past years seeking a way to breach her walls from below. The process had been tedious, more so when secrecy was paramount.

'In the meantime,' Griffith almost snarled, and Tolsten could see the big man was restless, 'we do our best to stay out of Avra's way. The Unseen could not face her and survive, lad, so I doubt you and your bunch of misfits would fare any better.'

Reefe shared a look with the Captain of the Sceptres, but it was brief. Men of greater stature than Reefe had fallen under the swing of his hammer and the smaller man knew it. *Maybe*, thought Tolsten with a smile, *the lad is starting to learn some common sense after all.*

A loud rap at the only door suddenly had the men sitting on the edge of their seats. Muffled voices could be heard outside, but they were quickly silenced as the door swung open to reveal one of Tolsten's Shadow Brethren standing with a quizzical look on his face. Before he could say a word, a figure, tall and lithe, pushed past him.

'Daughter?' Tolsten tempered her outburst before it even began by offering her his undivided attention.

'Father,' she replied, taking a moment to observe her surroundings and catch her breath. She was breathing heavily, as if she had been running for some time.

'You have news, I take it?' He looked her up and down, frowning at her close-fitting black leather pants and cotton shirt.

She looked back towards the door, obviously waiting for it to be closed before she addressed her father. Tolsten waved his dark knight away, watched the door close then offered his daughter the last remaining seat. She sunk into the chair, cushioned like his red leather one, and exhaled deeply as she gathered her thoughts. Beside her, Tarsin Va began to fidget, apparently uncomfortable at her proximity.

'I do, father,' she said matter-of-factly, suddenly remembering to take a moment to see who else sat at table. Tolsten watched as her emerald eyes swept over Jack Boyd and Reefe O'Bannon, then saw her eyebrows knot as she spied Cale Griffith's unruly mop of red hair. 'What's he doing here?'

'He is here to help, I think,' Tolsten replied. 'Or perhaps we are here to help him.'

She didn't question his presence further and cast her eyes towards the man sitting next to her. Their eyes met . . . and held.

'Gentlemen,' Tolsten cleared his voice, 'I'd like to introduce you to my daughter, Kayla Tolsten of Deepwell.'

Griffith mumbled something under his breath, but it slid past unnoticed as Tolsten kept his focus on his daughter. Eventually she and Tarsin tore their gaze away from each other and after wiping her brow with the back of her hand, Kayla returned his look and said, 'And this is Tarsin. We've met.'

*

Tarsin sought to control his emotions, fought hard to keep his mind clear as he listened to the talk about the table. He still sat within Tolsten's study, a small repast of bread and cheese lying half eaten atop the polished wood, an empty jug of water pushed to the side. They'd initially been offered ale, but it was Griffith, under duress, he noted, who asked for water instead. He appeared to be battling demons of his own, just as Tarsin did concerning the king. He didn't wish any of his former comrades to experience the pain of doubt, regret and fear that he felt, but as Griffith had mentioned to him previously, he wasn't the only one who suffered on returning from Benwith. He blinked to refocus his attention towards the maps stretched across one end of the table, a couple of tankards keeping them flat. Jack Boyd stooped over one, a gnarled finger pointing toward a straight section with flowing words scrawled beside it.

'It is here that our best hope resides,' Jack Boyd said with his monotone voice.

Tarsin chanced a look but like Griffith, he was tired of sitting and talking. He needed to act. For over an hour he had listened as Kayla reported her urgent news, telling of several cave-ins close by, which were alarming, but also speaking about the collapse of several walls revealing chambers of unusual design. Like her father, Kayla was privy to some of the information concerning the Nepharii, due only to her father's association with the Brotherhood. What she found was ancient in origin, but right now of little practicality.

So, having discussed their options, talk had finally swung back towards rescuing the king. Their effects had been returned, begrudgingly, it seemed, especially concerning his sword, but it now rested by his side once again. Armed and armoured, they had hoped to depart, only to be cautioned against such a move due to the instability of the tunnel network.

That and because Griffith was still a marked man.

Despite the leaders of the Nocturnals having been assassinated, many of the thieves still harboured resentment towards the crown, and Griffith was the embodiment of such an entity. It was he and his Sceptres who had chastised them, locked them up, and occasionally hanged them. There was little love for the big man and it was feared their mission would be compromised if he was to be let loose in Undercity.

Instead they discussed routes towards Highcastle whilst Tolsten's most trusted men sought to clear a passage.

As they sat, Tarsin couldn't help but think of Arkos Vantos lying bloodied and bruised under a tonne of masonry.

'How do we know if the path is clear?' Griffith asked, his hand gripping his warhammer, *Bloodstain*, as it rested against the edge of the table.

'We don't,' Kayla returned, 'but there are secondary paths here, and here,' she pointed to two narrow blue lines intersecting the main tunnel. 'If we find our way barred, we'll simply back-track and move around.'

'We?' queried Tarsin as he watched her intently study the map.

'Yes, I am coming with you,' she held up a hand to stall any retort. 'Because you'll need a guide and I'm the best there is.'

'She is,' Tolsten nodded, 'but Reefe O'Bannon will also accompany you, along with young Donal, I think.'

'Donal?' Kayla looked up from the map.

'He is young, granted, but he reads a map better even than you, my dear. Besides, his small size may help in a tight situation.'

Kayla accepted her father's council and returned to perusing the map with Jack Boyd. Tarsin immediately wondered what use Reefe O'Bannon might provide but thought it best to let it lie. Trust was hard earned from his experience and Tolsten was doing an admirable job as it was without him complicating matters further. In any case, his added muscle might prove the difference if they had to dig their way through, or possibly dig someone out.

'How long until Reefe returns, do you think?' Tarsin was struggling to keep calm. Reefe had left earlier with a dozen men to oversee the securing of a path out of Undercity. The path towards Highcastle was convoluted at best, unlike many of the thoroughfares employed by the Nocturnals. To reach the palace from below would require a significant journey. Regardless of their current delay, coming up through the cellars of Highcastle would be their only means of finding and hopefully rescuing the king.

'He should not be long now, gentlemen,' Tolsten sat back, his eyes tired. He reached for his tankard and took a swallow. 'Don't expect any deference from Reefe, though. He is strong-headed, I'll not deny it, but he's also able-bodied. He'll also make certain Kayla is kept out of harm's way.'

'I can take care of myself, father,' Kayla's lips were pursed as she stared down the old man.

'You can, but you'll also forgive a father his anxiety and allow him to send someone to keep an eye on you.'

'It's settled then,' Tarsin stretched and then swivelled his torso from side-to-side, flexing the muscles across his back and shoulders. 'As soon as Reefe returns, we head out.'

Griffith lent over to grab a large sack placed on the floor. Inside was his helmet, a skin of water and some bread and nuts. He then watched as Kayla rolled up the maps and placed them in a cylinder before turning to meet his eyes once again. 'Agreed,' she said, 'as soon as he returns.'

*

Reefe O'Bannon sighed as he rounded another bend in the tunnel. He was already exhausted from having been awake all night, and he'd spent the last hour gathering armour and weapons belonging to the two surface dwellers before overseeing the clearance of a path out of the Nocturnal's main hive of activity. Now he was returning to the main hall to gather his own possessions . . . and to meet an accomplice.

He sighed again, recalling the Pillars of Bastion, remembering how their deaths unnerved him. For years he'd done his utmost for the Underlord, hoping to one day wear the mantle of Pillar of Bastion and be in command of his own minor guild. This morning's deaths had struck fear into his heart, though. He very well could have been one of the six now lying in a pool of blood. Whatever crime they'd committed he was none the wiser. He was told only what he needed to know and then very little by all accounts. Even Kayla knew more about what was occurring and she was a woman.

Thoughts of Kayla leapt unbidden into his mind. It was hard to keep her out and he rarely did so. He'd forgotten just how long it had been since he'd fallen for her beauty. He instinctively knew it was barely a year, but in truth it felt a lifetime. Tall and slender like a willow, he often thought, she was a vision to behold. Long hair the colour of midnight cascaded beyond her shoulders and her emerald eyes, so large and inviting, merely hinted at the treasures they were likely to unveil. Reefe had tried every trick he could conceive to win her heart, had even attempted a few suggested by the other men, but all to no avail. Yet he knew she cared for him for they were often assigned together. Once he'd mistakenly believed their continuous partnership a design of her feelings towards him, but after several advances he'd ended up sprawled on his back from a vicious right hook. The fact she could defend herself so admirably did little to dampen his longing; in fact, he believed it heightened his desire.

Since this morning's activities he now felt an altogether different sensation, a burning in the pit of his stomach fuelled by a passion he'd not experienced before. He saw the look Kayla shared with the swordsman, Tarsin. He saw the flicker of light in her beautiful emerald eyes, the sparkle associated with a quickened heartbeat. He heard her words, heard her say they'd met before.

Reefe slammed his left fist into the wall as he moved down the passageway. His right hand held a flickering torch, its orange light wavering with his gait, illuminating only a short distance ahead. He wondered where they had previously met; wondered whether they'd met on more than one occasion. Anok and Eli! He'd never even heard of this Tarsin fellow before today. And he was a bastard! What could Kayla, daughter of the Underlord, see in such a man?

His mind drifted suddenly to the sword. It was a beauty: a Rykedian broadsword with a swept hilt of polished blue steel, bound with the softest black leather. Balanced beyond anything he'd ever handled before, it was also light and flexible, the blade itself honed to a razor's edge. Reefe doubted anyone could best him in a duel if he possessed such a blade and it had almost been his. Yet by midmorning he was asked to return the weapon to a man he believed besotted with the woman he loved.

He cursed once again, wondering how a night of promise and prestige could descend so rapidly into a day of disappointment and regret. When he had first captured Griffith and his unknown friend, visions as a member of the Pillars of Bastion had sufficed his waking thoughts. Surely a reward was in order beyond the claiming of the Rykedian broadsword for his part in capturing the Captain of the Sceptres. Surely Kayla would see his bravery and cunning as a mark of his greatness.

Now his visions of grandeur were reduced to running errands like some gutter rat, no different to young Donal as he traversed the tunnels of Undercity.

Thoughts of claiming Kayla's love still lingered though. Whilst Tarsin and Griffith lay cold on the cell floor in the early morning a man had drifted into the tunnel network cloaked in shadow. His eyes were black to match the colour of his long-curled hair, but they were deadly all the same. Talk had been brief for he spoke an unfamiliar name, requesting a person's whereabouts. With uncaring shrugs on their behalf, the stranger had moved on and not a single man sought to bar his path. No-one knew who he was and the coldness in his eyes prevented any from asking.

Reefe sought him out now, though, for the name mentioned earlier was suddenly familiar. Moving into a wide, columned chamber, he spied the man in discussion with several thieves recently returned from the surface. As he stepped closer to the man he noticed the light of his torch did little to sweep away the shadows surrounding him.

Excusing himself, he spoke quickly and in a hushed tone, fearful of betraying his nervousness to one so deadly. When he was done, Ruvin walked back the way he'd come. He didn't need to look behind him to know the man with the deadly eyes followed.

*

Tarsin slapped his hands together in frustration. 'Time is not on our side, Tolsten. We can sit around and await your man Reefe, or we can leave now and to hell with whoever steps in our way. Seriously, we can take care of ourselves.'

Griffith grunted ascent and moved towards the door. With the king's armour returned Griffith now looked even more impressive, although moving through narrow tunnels and tight sewers was going to test his nerve and patience. 'I agree, and you said yourself Kayla was the best guide,' Tarsin could see Tolsten's frustration at hearing Griffith's words, but he knew the old man would consent. There was very little he could do about it in any case. If Tarsin and Griffith chose to walk out the door, his dark knights would not stop them. 'He can catch up later, if he ever finds his way back here.'

Kayla grabbed the cylinder containing her maps and followed them out the door. After leaving the main chamber they entered a narrow hallway that led to another room with bas-relief images skirting the walls. Like those Tarsin saw previously they were folk of fable, their bodies carved with exquisite detail, their heads resembling wild creatures. In the centre of the room rested a lit brazier, its orange light highlighting three separate doorways, dark and sombre under arches of ivory.

'Which way?' Tarsin asked Kayla as they milled in the chamber. Tolsten and his Shadow Brethren jostled behind them, prepared to see them on their way.

Kayla shifted her gaze to their left and stepped forward a pace to lead the procession when movement caught her eye. She turned to her right to see Reefe exit a doorway, a torch in his hand. Young Donal paced by his side, a lantern held tight. 'You're late,' she snarled, unable to contain her anger, 'we should have left an hour ago.'

'I had some unfinished business to attend,' Reefe's trident beard split into a smile as he crossed the dusty floor. Donal followed, his curious face assessing the two warriors he saw before him. Tarsin swore under his breath as he realized the blonde-headed boy Donal was the bait that led them here. 'I brought a friend,' Reefe gestured behind him where another figure exited the same doorway. He was a head shorter than Tarsin and cloaked in black: his breeches, shirt and boots likewise dark. The cowl of his hood revealed only a few curly locks of the man's long midnight hair. At his waist rested a sabre.

'I do not know this man,' Tolsten moved to address Reefe.

'Nor should you, Underlord,' Reefe spoke sharply, with what Tarsin could only assume was repressed anger. 'He arrived early this morning whilst many were asleep. He too has been sent to search for the king. I thought it prudent to ask him along. You never know when an extra set of hands will become useful.'

Tarsin met the newcomer's eyes, barely seen beneath the cowl of his hood.

'If there are no objections to his presence,' Reefe said, 'I suggest we move on.'

'The more the merrier, I say,' Griffith was done with delays.

'Good,' Reefe forced a nervous smile as the man stepped forward and offered a bow. 'Then allow me to introduce Enrico Vittorio.'

CHAPTER EIGHTEEN

Fetid water sloshed about their boots.

Kayla ignored the stench as she carefully moved ahead. Young Donal was at her side trying his hardest to keep up. He still held his lantern, a single shutter open to allow a stream of light to mark their way. Kayla felt for the boy. As much as she knew he would have followed them regardless, for such was his nature, he was in for some gruelling hours ahead. As her father pointed out before they left, at least this way they could keep an eye on the boy. For one so young, he'd developed an infuriating habit for seeking adventure. Kayla knew that in Bastion's Undercity, one didn't need to look far to find it.

A passage crossing their own caused Kayla to halt momentarily. She looked over her shoulder to see how the men fared. Tarsin followed directly behind her, unfatigued by the look of him, despite them having travelled for close to two hours. Behind him stomped Griffith in the king's armour. His heavy breathing and constant curses had intensified as the walk progressed and she wondered what possessed the man to wear such gear. He appeared so large in the dim light of the passage she could neither see, nor hear, Reefe and his companion Vittorio. She judged their lack of presence to be fortunate. Having lived and breathed the last year in Bastion's underworld, she'd met, spoken to and worked with countless unsavoury characters. Never had she felt such coldness emanate from a single person before. Vittorio's deep black eyes, when she peered into them, sent shivers racing down her spine. Whoever he was, Kayla held grave doubts concerning his intentions. Where Reefe found him, she could only guess.

Despite her misgivings the men appeared to be making ground, so she moved forward, stepping softly into the passage crossing their own. Her booted foot searched for solid purchase, feeling for stone under the ankle-deep water that inundated the sewers. Such a junction had to be trodden with care, for the water's depth could easily become waist high in a single step, often with an undertow capable of carrying the unwary away. With one hand pressed firmly against the brick wall to her right she ventured out. The passage was deeper, but only by a foot.

She crossed with relative ease, then took a moment to peer ahead. For half-an-hour they'd held an almost straight course towards Highcastle. She knew that was about to change. Ahead lay a series of vast caverns and underground cisterns, many linked to forgotten canals from the days of Nepharii occupation. Kayla knew they weren't fashioned by man, for the stonework was too fine, the enormity of the scale too overwhelming. Whoever the Nepharii were they were incredible builders. Derrick Tolsten, her father, had studied what little information the Brotherhood of One had deposited away in Irongate. Kayla, being a woman, was not privy to their secrets but her father was easily persuaded to share what he knew with his only daughter, especially when his daughter showed such genuine interest.

She smiled at thought of her father. He was a remarkable man, an intellectual of some renown. He'd been a general for the king years ago, a tactical genius, so it was said. Together with King Arkos they'd led forces against the northern Herkosians, battled the barbarians for eight years until they were forced to bend the knee. After the war Lord Derrick Tolsten became a respected, but also feared, man. Having shunned the usual endorsements offered to a kingdom's saviour, he drifted back to his estates and sought solitude with the Brotherhood of One. For more than a decade he kept himself busy, always professing to know so very little, constantly cursing the lack of hours in the day.

He'd been content, though. With a loving wife, two sons and a young daughter, he rightly assumed life to be grand.

Until one day his eldest son, Jarrick Tolsten, was murdered in some alley in Bastion's southern docks.

One month later lord Derrick Tolsten led a contingent of hard men into the Undercity with a design to set up their own guild. With him were his most loyal knights and men-at-arms, along with his remaining son, Will Tolsten, and some of the king's best infiltrators. Their task was to eradicate the growing boldness of the thieves' guilds and supplant them with one of their own, controlled by Derrick Tolsten and governed secretly by the king.

That was five years ago. In the time since, Derrick Tolsten had wiped out the Cloak and Daggers, the Misfits, the Shadow Men and the Dockland Bruisers. Whoever remained of the Scarlet Hand was no longer a problem, and the remnants of the Black Widows were rumoured to have set up home in Anthos, two hundred leagues south of Bastion.

The only thieves' guild to rule under Bastion now was the Nocturnals. As of several hours ago, the last remaining ring-leaders to have ties to their former guilds had been slain.

Kayla felt a sense of satisfaction at their demise. She knew some of the men: the despicable Aiden Rath, the obese Jorge Blacktooth and the sly Harper Reg. Even though Kayla had been in Bastion's Undercity for barely a year, she'd heard terrible stories concerning those men. It was why her father had balked at her joining him in the first place and why he tried in vain to send her back when he found out she was here. If it hadn't been for the untimely death of his wife and Kayla's mother, Lady Jayne Tolsten, she may never have set foot in Undercity at all.

Holding out her hand, Kayla grabbed Donal's loose jacket and hauled him up the last two steps so that he stood once again by her side. With Tarsin already stepping into the moving water, she peered down the tunnel she now found herself in. The ceiling was no longer straight and square, but arched, sitting atop walls six feet high. The water underfoot had also dispersed, a layer of muck all that remained, its stench just as imposing. She could hear muttered curses as the rest of the men fell in behind, their voices muffled by the continuous sound of water dripping from dank stones above. By her reckoning, the tunnel ran straight. Onwards she walked, her hands pressing against slippery walls, only to abruptly stop before a circular cistern a handful of minutes later. Across its breadth lay another tunnel like the one they were in, two others to their right and left. Donal joined her at the edge and both looked down to see black water twenty feet below. An iron ladder was bolted to the wall to her right which led to a ledge five feet above her current position. It was narrow, but if one walked about the perimeter they could reach any one of the tunnel entrances provided they didn't lose their grip and plummet into the cistern's depths. It was risky, but they had no other means of crossing the vast space.

Kayla jumped as a gentle hand rested on her shoulder.

'How do we cross?' Tarsin said, having crept up behind her.

Kayla cursed inwardly; alarmed she'd not heard his approach. 'Up the ladder,' she explained once she regained her composure, 'then along a ledge to the other side.'

Donal placed his lantern on the floor and sat with his back to the wall. Kayla could see he was tired. He'd barely spoken a word since they began, and he kept silent now. She admired his stoicism but feared he wouldn't last the journey. There was still considerable ground to cover before reaching Highcastle.

'How far do we still need to travel?' Tarsin asked another question, and she briefly wondered if he could read her very thoughts.

'Still some way,' she replied, 'and it is difficult. Few venture this close to Highcastle for fear of being discovered. I don't need to tell you what would become of a thief caught this close to the royal court.'

'Are you truly a thief, Kayla Tolsten?'

A wry smile splashed across her face, but she turned her head slightly so Tarsin couldn't see. 'Perhaps,' she said the words softly, remembering their encounter in the streets of Bastion. 'Perhaps I just play the part.'

'You play it well.'

The sound of Griffith clanking down the tunnel diverted their attention, and Kayla took the opportunity to lean out and grab the iron rung of the ladder and swing out into open space. Quick steps saw her booted feet carry her up and onto the ledge and seconds later she was walking the narrow path, one hand sliding along the curved wall, the other outstretched for balance. She'd reached the midway point when she stopped and turned to face the men now crowded about the tunnel opening, 'Are you coming,' she asked, 'or do you need me to hold your hand?'

She watched as Tarsin reached for the ladder and began to climb before offering Donal his support. Donal obliged and fell in behind the swordsman and by the light of the lantern she could see the smile on his face. He was a handsome man, strong, and for a swordsman, surprisingly well mannered.

She watched for several seconds before spinning back to her task and moving on. By the time she reached the opposite tunnel, Reefe O'Bannon and the man named Vittorio were walking the perimeter. Tarsin had spoken to the man named Enrico Vittorio briefly when they first set out, a quiet conversation that did little to dispel her fears of the stranger. And yet like Tarsin, Vittorio moved with consummate ease, his balance perfect, cat-like even. Kayla spent a moment watching his progress. *Who are you*, she thought, studying his movements, *and what's your true business down here?*

*

Reefe O'Bannon flung out a hand to steady himself, his booted foot having slipped on damp cobblestones. He shook his head, thankful he hadn't dropped his flickering torch and pushed on, placing one tired foot in front of the other. He could see Vittorio ten feet beyond him, the hulking form of Griffith even further ahead. Of Kayla, Donal and Tarsin he was blind to their whereabouts. For all he knew they were traversing another tunnel on the other side of Bastion. With the constant dripping of water and the sloshing caused from booted feet he couldn't even hear them. He just followed the dark form in front, one foot at a time.

He thought of the man before him, Enrico Vittorio. He knew little concerning his reputation or how it originated. That he was skilled was beyond doubt, for he carried himself with staunch belief and his movements and manner did more than hint at what he was truly capable of. Still, there was scant gossip detailing his exploits. In fact, very few guild members were even familiar with his name, let alone his perceived reputation.

Yet to take a glance at the heavily cloaked man nearly always resulted in a cold shudder. Whatever skills he could harness seemed to have coated the man with ice. Reefe wondered if Vittorio's dark eyes had been cold his entire life, or whether they were merely a product of his villainous existence.

He arrived at a series of steps and began to descend. This was their third descent in the last half hour. The depths they had plunged seemed far greater than any sortie Reefe had taken before. He hoped Kayla knew where she was headed, although with Donal by her side he doubted she'd become lost. The boy had an uncanny knack for reading maps; and not just the everyday assortment utilized by the Nocturnals. Donal could read the ancient maps just as well, a feat few could replicate. He'd heard the Underlord talk of the maps being priceless, remnants from another age. Locked up behind a clear sheet of glass they were, all three of them, in a private chamber few were privy to. Donal had pictured them up close, though, and by all reports he could remember all he'd seen. Apparently, he was gifted with some memory trick where he could look at something once and always picture it in his mind. Reefe scoffed at such nonsense, although he had to admit the lad could find his way about Undercity with disturbing accuracy.

The torch sputtered and hissed as water dripped from the ceiling. Looking up Reefe saw the architecture had changed once more. The stones here were older, shaped differently to those used for the building of Bastion a thousand years ago. It meant they were deep underground in a section few dared to venture. Nepharii was the word used throughout Undercity from those brave enough to delve so deep. A handful of the older thieves had professed to know something about the ancient race that once dwelt here, but in truth they spoke sparingly of such times. Reefe doubted anyone really knew anything about the buildings and walkways buried under Bastion; most were myths coupled with fanciful tales employed to scare young children. Right now, he could see a token of the marvel those few men so enlightened spoke about. The stonework was incredibly precise, almost seamless. Reefe hardly thought of brick walls as being beautiful, but now, as he gazed upon the ancient stones, he could sense symmetry beyond anything he'd witnessed before.

He was about to reach out and sweep his hand across its surface when he took a step and bumped into the stationary form of Enrico Vittorio.

'Careful,' Vittorio spun and whispered the word, his eyes searching out Reefe's.

Stepping back a pace Reefe offered a feeble, 'Sorry,' before looking past the man to see the remainder of the party gathered about a wide opening. As he watched he heard Kayla instruct Donal to hold up his lantern. The lad did so, only to be accompanied by the sharp intake of air.

'What is it,' Reefe called out, attempting to peer over Vittorio's hooded head.

No-one paid him any heed for they all stepped forward instead, allowing Vittorio and then Reefe to shuffle onward. He reached the end of the tunnel and opened his mouth wide.

A vast rectangular chamber lay before him, its walls damaged in parts, its floor covered with bricks and mortar. It was thirty feet across and twice that in length, and as Reefe chanced a glance at its ceiling he noticed a portion had caved in. At its far end an arched doorway continued into darkness, their obvious route out of here. Yet to their right lay a completely crumbled wall, its structure compromised by the earthquake, various bricks and slabs of stone having fallen to lie strewn about the floor. The opposite doorway was still accessible if one crawled over the piled masonry, but it was not the exit they were so excited about.

It was the vast chamber behind the wall that stifled their conversation.

It took mere seconds before Griffith's booming voice broke the silence. 'Gods be damned,' he said, 'what have we here?'

Reefe watched open mouthed as Kayla and Tarsin moved towards the tumbled wall. He could see their intention, knew they'd clamour over the mess to see clearly the wonder revealed within. Donal likewise scrambled ahead, his small frame scampering atop bricks piled high, causing the rubble little discomfit whilst he took a seat and rested the lantern in his lap. Seconds later he opened the shutter wide to aid visibility. Reefe closed his mouth and walked closer, joining Vittorio and Griffith as they sought to follow Kayla and Tarsin's lead.

'What have we found?' Reefe asked as he stepped over shattered stones to tread lightly on a dust covered mosaic floor.

No-one answered him yet Reefe felt no disrespect for he knew everyone was inwardly asking the same question. The room they entered was circular, curved walls lying to left and right surrounding a circular dais. The room was perhaps a hundred feet across, maybe more, for it was difficult to judge with such poor light. A quick glance revealed a domed ceiling resting above, its facade a patchwork of murals now faded with time. He looked past his companions to see the room devoid of furnishings, a fact causing angst for the allure of hidden treasure had already crossed his mind. Still, the mosaic floor and the painted walls were a treasure in themselves, especially if the room was equated with the ancient Nepharii. From the abnormal figures depicted upon the walls, he felt the room held promise.

'Have you ever seen anything like this before?' Tarsin addressed Kayla as they moved towards the centre of the circular room.

'Yes,' she replied, leaning over to study something of interest on the floor. 'This chamber is almost identical to the two we found earlier today, before I came to report their presence to my father. Only the paintings on the wall are . . . different.'

'How so?'

'They are like all Nepharii artwork. They like their men and women to be bold and colourful, their heads to be animalistic. The chambers I found earlier were reminiscent of eagles and lions. This one,' she narrowed her eyes as she appraised the wall, 'appears to have men and women with scaled heads.'

Reefe paid Kayla's words no heed as he made for the circular dais, believing if anything of value was to be found it would lie there. He walked up several steps to reach its smooth surface, then bent his knee so he could wipe a hand through a layer of dust, revealing polished granite below, not the mosaic patterns blanketing the rest of the room. Reefe guessed the dais to be forty feet across, its position perfectly aligned with the centre of the room. Wiping his hand through dust once more, he gasped as a filament of gold reflected the dancing flames of his torch.

'What is it?' Kayla asked as she moved to his side.

Reefe placed his torch on the ground and scrambled on hands and knees, blowing more of the dust away to reveal a circular ring of gold, ten feet in diameter, now bathed with lambent flame. 'Gold,' he lifted his head and smiled at those gathering round.

'There is more over here,' Donal's piping voice invaded their thoughts. Reefe, already giddy with excitement, sought out the boy. He'd made his way into the room behind the others and now stood along the wall, looking intently at a spot on the floor.

'There is a band of gold here as wide as my finger,' Reefe listened as the boy raised his voice, 'and it forms a circle about the entire room.' Donal began to walk the perimeter, slowly stepping past the fallen bricks, then quickening his pace as he moved alongside the inner wall.

'What is its purpose?' Griffith had sat on his rump, the big man keen to take a respite from the arduous journey.

'I'm not about to sit here and guess,' replied Tarsin. 'We've still a task to see through. So long as Kayla and Donal know how to trace their steps back here, we can leave our philosophising for another day.'

'I say we dig out a portion of the gold,' Reefe wasn't about to leave empty handed, 'a token only, more as a reminder of what we've left behind.'

'No, we must press on,' Tarsin was adamant. 'Your antics last night have already delayed us considerably, Reefe O'Bannon, don't test my patience a second time.'

'You do not lead this party, Tarsin Va, it is Kayla's decision.'

'Fine, stay here and I'll take the boy to see if our king still lives.'

Kayla stepped between the two men. 'That won't be necessary. Reefe, on your feet,' he obliged, not through deference, but for practicality. If there was to be an argument, sitting on the floor was unlikely to see his words taken seriously. 'We'll move on, as Tarsin suggested. There will be time after we have searched Highcastle for us to revisit this place.' She cast her eye about the room, looking for something, he was certain, but with a question poised on his lips she spoke. 'Besides, if father catches you defacing this chamber, Reefe, he'll likely cut off your hands.' She said the words jokingly, but the look in her eyes suggested it was far from a jest.

Reefe nodded consent, knowing whatever he said now would only divide the group further. He didn't trust Tarsin any more than Griffith. Both men looked ready to be rid of him and he honestly thought he could do little to stop them. He was an able swordsman, strong of shoulder and with a constitution typical of a thief. Yet he feared his only real hope lay in the hands of the silent Vittorio. The cloaked man seemed indifferent as he peered about the room and Reefe wasn't certain he'd taken any notice of the words spoken. Still, the man could tip the balance his way if the situation turned ugly. Then it all depended on Kayla and who she would support if blows were traded.

Then again, Vittorio's agenda was not yet clear. Perhaps it would be Reefe O'Bannon lending a hand, for if he'd guessed correctly it was Tarsin he was after. It had been Tarsin's name mentioned in the halls of Undercity when he first arrived. Surely the swordsman had been marked for death. If so, Reefe would do what he could to help. There might even be a reward involved for any part he was to play.

With nothing further to search or discuss, Kayla motioned for Donal to lead them out of the room and continue the walk to Highcastle. Reefe bent to retrieve his sputtering torch and followed, Vittorio stepping to his side. Reefe didn't know what to make of the move at first, but with his mind working over-time he figured it a gesture of support in the battle to come. A line had been drawn and the pieces were set. Soon, very soon, there would be a confrontation between the men.

*

Tarsin paused to await the others.

He was in a narrow hallway constructed of brick, a line of muck snaking its way between his feet to drip into the sewers behind him. For some time, he'd followed Kayla as they climbed closer to the surface, the prospect of Highcastle above lending strength to their aching limbs. Now he strode ahead, alone, seeking tunnels beneath Highcastle's dungeons.

He shared a smile with the burning brand in his outstretched hand, for it appeared he'd found what he was looking for.

The soft patter of light feet sounded behind him. He spun to see Kayla reach his side. She was exhausted, he could see it in her emerald eyes, but she was also glad to see him. A faint smile tweaked the corner of her mouth as she rested a hand on his shoulder.

'How are you faring?' she asked, taking a moment to catch her breath.

'To be honest, Kayla, I'm anxious,' he replied. 'We are fast running out of time.' He was about to ask after the others when he heard Griffith's deep voice cursing in the dark. After several minutes, the remainder of the group filed up the hallway to stand huddled about the flaming brand.

'There should be a stairway at the end of this hall,' Tarsin addressed the group, then motioned with his eyes along the length of the hall towards an area cloaked in darkness. 'If we follow the stairs up, we should bypass the dungeons and the lower store rooms before reaching the kitchens. From there it is but a short walk to the throne room. The earthquake struck close to midday, so I'd suggest we look for him there.'

'What if he is not in the throne room?' Reefe almost sneered as he spoke the words, an act not lost on Tarsin.

'Then we look elsewhere, thief,' Tarsin replied, his feet already moving towards the end of the hall. Now they had reached Highcastle, Kayla no longer led and fell in behind the swordsman, Donal with his lantern walking beside her. Begrudgingly, Reefe followed, Vittorio and Griffith bringing up the rear. For several minutes they walked in silence, until the light from his burning brand revealed a staircase leading up, its steps covered in dust and fragments of stone. Beyond lay another hallway, several doors leading to store rooms, before yet another set of stairs sent them upwards once again. They reached the top of the stairs only to find a smear of congealed blood on the landing, almost black but still sticky. The wooden door, iron bound, had been sheared in half, a stone pillar lying amongst shards of wood. A single body lay crushed underneath, an arm and leg visible on either side. It was a grisly sight and Tarsin moved to shield Donal from stepping too close. Then he ushered the lad through the shattered door and into what remained of the kitchen. What had survived was scant indeed. Where a baker's oven once stood now sat an assortment of tumbled bricks, a large wooden beam having smashed down from above to lie amongst the ruin. Shelves lay toppled on their side, their contents spilled across the floor leaving the kitchen a ghostly white as flour lined the surface like freshly fallen snow. Tarsin lifted his torch high, to better see the carnage. Another body could be seen behind an overturned table, several pots and pans scattered close by, whilst a pool of deep crimson bloomed beneath the head. He stepped towards the body and knelt, placing fingers along the neck to check for a pulse. The body was cold to touch.

'Is he alive?' Kayla had stepped quietly into the kitchen.

'No,' Tarsin moved further into the wreckage, then looked to the ceiling to judge the stability of the room. Flagstones from above had slid into the workspace, crushing tables with their prodigious weight, along with another body. Flour sifted about his legs as he spun to find a way out. Crossing to a space between two cupboards, their contents disgorged upon the floor, he found one of several doors leading out of the kitchen. It was buckled, bent under the weight of a leaning beam, its hinges shorn. 'Griffith,' he said, 'I'll need your help.'

Griffith made his way to where Tarsin stood and assessed the doorway. The beam was wedged tight between the stone wall on one side and the shattered ceiling above, most of its mass resting atop the lintel. 'You're thinking of opening the door,' Griffith stated, stepping forward to place his hands beneath the beam. He gave a gentle push to see if the beam would move. 'It seems to be safe,' he said, 'although forcing the door open may change the dynamics.'

'That's why you'll stand here and hold up the beam while we walk through,' Tarsin leant against the door. Although the hinges were sheared, the wood had warped. It would take some heavy blows to knock it clear; heavy blows that could topple an unstable doorway and the ceiling above. He passed his torch to Reefe as he prepared himself.

'I'm ready when you are,' Griffith bunched his muscles and pushed up while Tarsin leant back and then slammed his booted foot against the wooden panels. There was a loud crack as wood splintered from the strike and three more kicks saw a panel spin clear. 'Use my hammer,' Griffith suggested, looking down at where he'd placed his weapon. Tarsin obliged and after two solid hits the door fell outward with a crash.

An eerie groan sounded as the door settled, like stones grinding in protest. Tarsin stood completely still, his heart racing and he could see Griffith's face lined with a sheen of sweat in the dim light. 'Can you hold it?' he asked his friend.

'Aye, I can,' he offered a feeble smile, 'but I'm not sure it'll survive if I let go. Quickly, pass through.'

Tarsin did as bid and called the others through in succession until they all stood in the adjoining room. Griffith came last and for a fleeting moment he expected the doorway to crumble as he released his hold, only to be pleasantly surprised to see it remain. 'We have a way out, at least,' he said to no one in particular, thankful the structural integrity had not been compromised.

Griffith stretched his shoulders before taking his warhammer back. Once again it was difficult to see about the room, for much lay broken, but another door could be seen opposite from where they gathered. 'Through that door,' Griffith pointed as he spoke, 'will see us climb another set of stairs towards the Hall of Kings. From there only a set of bronze doors will bar our entry to the throne room.'

'Provided the Hall of Kings hasn't collapsed,' Reefe uttered to the side.

'Provided the Hall of Kings hasn't collapsed,' repeated Griffith.

Tarsin moved forward, eager to reach the king. There was an urge within him burning greater than he thought possible. Three years ago, he left Bastion for the open sea having walked out on his sovereign lord; disgusted, betrayed, and as far as he could fathom, cursed. Now he'd climbed through sewers and ancient passages below the city to reach the king's side, perhaps eager for atonement; perhaps for retribution. He wasn't certain, for his thoughts were a shamble, his heart racing. What he did know was that he desperately needed to lay eyes on the king. He reached the far door and opened it without any difficulty, hitting the stairs two at a time as he raced upward. He could hear Kayla and Donal climbing behind him, the light from Donal's lantern casting shadows before him, his own shadow always one step ahead.

'Ahead lies the Hall of Kings,' Tarsin was sweating profusely, rivulets sliding down his cheeks. 'I do not know what lies beyond the throne room doors,' he said, 'but be prepared.'

'Prepared for what?' Reefe placed a hand upon the pommel of his sword.

'The unknown,' Tarsin moved, holding his torch high as he swept his gaze from left to right to take in the enormous statues of Bastion's past kings, the marble sentinels lining the wide hallway. Even in the dim light of the torch they were impressive, statue-still but commanding all the same. Tarsin watched as flickering orange light cast fearful shadows across their stern features. Few were allowed to traverse its length and most only to pay their respects. To walk its length unsummoned, especially at night, was said to do strange things to a man's mind. The old kings looked down upon those who passed, casting silent judgements of their own, it was said, causing doubts to linger and then fester in the unworthy.

As Tarsin walked his thoughts turned inward, quickly swirling into a maelstrom of doubt. He was a cursed man, like all the Unseen and yet here he was in Highcastle, striding towards the throne room, his doubts and fears following him like some twisted shadow. What could he possibly do to make King Arkos forgive him? Pulling him clear of Highcastle was not going to be enough. The king would require more from the man he once named First Sword of the Unseen; much more. More importantly, if he did rescue the king, could he truly protect him from the likes of Avra and her god? Would he last more than a heartbeat if he came face-to-face with Avra's summoned creature?

Tarsin couldn't know for certain and the not-knowing was sending his mind spiralling into a pit of despair.

'Tarsin,' Griffith placed a hand on his shoulder. He looked around and saw the remainder of the group gathered close, then saw the bronze double doors leading to the throne room partially open before him. He hadn't realized he'd reached the end of the hall, nor how long he'd been standing there. 'Shall we?' Griffith asked, his hand sweeping towards the doors.

'Aye,' he found his voice and wiped moisture from his brow, 'let's do this.' A gentle shove was all it took for the doors to open wide, revealing the enormous throne room of Arkos Vantos, King of Dervae.

'Anok and Eli!' Tarsin heard Griffith call upon the gods of mischief and deceit. The room was destroyed from top to bottom; its fluted columns flanking the main thoroughfare cracked and splintered, in some cases completely toppled. Stained glass windows were now dark voids of splintered glass and the main entrance was a mess of tumbled beams and piled rock. Flagstones lay scattered about the floor, some areas no more than gaping holes of darkness. To their left, where the throne itself had sat for almost a thousand years atop a raised dais of marble, could be seen nothing but rocks and dirt, bricks and marble. Even shards of blue-grey tiles from Highcastle's roof could be seen lying randomly atop the conglomeration.

Kayla moved a step closer to Tarsin, her hand reaching for his arm. 'No-one could have survived this,' she said. As soon as she said the words he felt tears swell in his eyes. 'You could not have saved him had you been here. You too would have died under the falling mountain.'

'I should have been here, though,' the words came out barely louder than a whisper. 'Honour dictates I should have been close by. Only I wasn't; I'd run away like a spoilt child, too afraid to say what I needed to say, too afraid to tell the king my fears.' Tarsin peered deep into Kayla's searching eyes, not knowing what he would find there. 'I returned to Bastion two days ago,' he said, 'look what has happened to our city in that time.'

'I would hardly call you responsible for what has occurred,' Kayla offered, shaking her head.

'Then who else?'

'The witch and her demon god,' Griffith slapped his meaty hand atop Tarsin's shoulder. 'Stop beating yourself up, swordsman. You survived Avra once, you'll survive her again. We'll survive her again,' he quickly added.

'How can you be so sure, Griffith? We barely escaped with our lives the last time, and now she is stronger. She also has the help of her shadow god. What can we possibly do to keep them at bay?'

'All that we can.'

'Really? I'm struggling to find the faith you so effortlessly adhere to,' Tarsin shook his head in reply.

'It's Frey's Luck, my friend,' he said, calling on Fate. 'Listen,' Griffith grabbed his jaw and spun his head, so he could meet his eyes, 'you are First Sword of the Unseen, the greatest swordsman in Dervae. You are a leader of men. You made a mistake . . . once, but that is over. Now it's time to make amends.' A shuffle of feet alerted both men to Vittorio moving behind them. They turned, only for the cloaked man to smile.

'We should search where we can,' he said, pointing towards a darkened area of the throne room, near what remained of the king's dais.

Donal and Reefe immediately held their light high, looking towards the section indicated as they bathed the dusty pile of rock with an eerie glow. It took only seconds before a bright splash of lime-coloured cloth could be seen amongst the rubble. Keeping a wary eye on the unstable floor and its surroundings, they made their way across the throne room and began to gently lift rocks from the body. It was trapped at the periphery of the landslide, but once free of the confining rocks and dirt, dead all the same. Reefe flipped the body onto its back. It was an elderly man, crushed and broken.

'Do you know who it is?' Kayla asked.

'Lord Fenrick of Avenwood,' Griffith sighed as the torch's flame flickered over his pale features. 'He was a good man, loyal.' Tarsin winced at the word loyal, dark clouds threatening to engulf him once again. No matter the validity of Griffith's earlier words, he couldn't shake the impending doom he felt at his betrayal. If King Arkos lay buried under the mass of stone, he vowed he would find him.

'There,' Vittorio pointed further into the darkness.

Tarsin watched as the man drifted away, his movements sleek and graceful. The rest followed until Donal's lantern light fell across a fallen column, white shards littering the marble floor like fragments of ice. Donal stepped around the fallen column itself, his lantern illuminating the darkness beyond.

'Tarsin!' he yelled, his voice high pitched.

Tarsin ran towards the boy, rounding the column to see a man lying in a pool of blackened blood, his arm crushed beneath a slab of rock. White hair, lank and lifeless lined a wizened face, leathered by years in the sun, and a neatly trimmed beard covered his square jaw. If the hard face and broad shoulders didn't tell Tarsin who it was who lay before him, then the cape of royal velvet and the golden circlet resting atop his brow certainly did.

'It's King Arkos,' Tarsin knelt by his side and reached out to place his hand across Arkos' chest. It was damp, slightly sticky. Tears rolled down Tarsin's face.

'He fell with the rest of his court,' Griffith said in a solemn tone. 'Despite his greatness, even Arkos could not escape the destruction.'

Tarsin lifted his hand from the king's chest and moved it up to his cheek. It was like touching ice. He blinked back tears as he realised his fear to return was entirely centred on Arkos and his perceived disappointment. The man who pulled him off the streets at an early age and offered him direction was now dead. He'd betrayed him; having ran away in a fit of fear and anger. Arkos deserved better from his First Sword. He should have been by his side at the end.

He bowed his head for a moment, then stood and wiped tears with the back of his hand. He looked to his silent companions; found he couldn't say a word. Arkos Vantos was dead, they all knew it.

Like everyone else standing within the throne room, he suddenly realised hope for Bastion was fading fast.

CHAPTER NINETEEN

Cappitus scratched his scraggly white beard as he watched the *Nepharii Uranometria* rotate within its place on the lectern. A selection of priests from various deities gathered nearby, along with an assortment of Brothers and Sisters. Together they were a collective of some of the greatest minds in Bastion, called upon to help decide the city's fate, but in truth fixated with a timepiece about to finalize its latest rotation.

Seconds passed, accompanied by a ticking sound reminiscent of a clock as the rings continued to spin. Cappitus knew such pieces were incredibly detailed. He'd seen firsthand the intricacies involved with Federico Garelli's Water Clock when it was incorporated into the Eosian Aqueduct. So many minute gears all turning with purpose, powered by the constant drip of water from the aqueduct at its rear. Yet this Nepharii disc was something else. The level of expertise was far beyond anything Federico Garelli could have envisaged. When the timepiece reached its cycle's end, an audible click could be heard by those standing near the silver lectern. It was immediately followed by a resounding bang as the platinum ring surrounding the enormous sun-like, golden sphere, spun to another segment.

'Like clockwork,' Cappitus murmured. Those beside him paid him little heed. Instead they moved as one to see the new segment at the end of the path leading to the golden sphere. 'How long?' asked Cappitus.

Elder Fratelli looked up from where he sat with his hour glass. 'Two hours exactly,' he croaked. 'Like the past two complete rotations. It appears each of the twelve signs of the Nepharii zodiac remain in place for two hours, spread evenly across our twenty-four-hour day.'

Cappitus offered a nod of thanks before making his way to the inner ring hovering about the artificial sun. Since they first saw the constellation of Enlil with its eagle-headed bodies on the inner ring, each new segment had differed from the first. All appeared to be human-like: two arms and two legs, yet their heads were fashioned to resemble animals associated with each zodiac sign. Eagles were first, for such was Enlil, then hound-like beings for Venati, followed by serpents representing Ophidia. Each had been finely etched in platinum. Many still insisted they represented the Nepharii themselves; although since Jarred's revelation earlier, most now likened the images to gods. Despite their many conjectures, no-one truly knew for certain. They sought to ask Jarred for clarification, but the boy was asleep once again and could not be roused.

Cappitus shook his head and walked towards the bunched elders, listening to their muttered words as they began to counsel one another as to what the new image represented. As he peered at the platinum segment, he saw the two figures etched in the right hand lower corner, their heads representing a bull, the larger of the two accompanied by a set of curving horns. The image was as expected, for Taurus was next in line in the Nepharii zodiac.

'Is there a pattern here?' asked Ruvin as he looked up from the segment etched onto the inner ring.

'Only the obvious,' Cappitus scratched his beard once more. 'Eagle followed by hound, then serpent and now bull. To the Nepharii we have seen Enlil, Venati, Ophidia and Taurus. The only connection is that of the zodiac.'

Ruvin nodded then spoke. 'Perhaps the images are simply the male and female aspect of a deity. Each image is joined by a world and its moon. We know many gods are representations of celestial bodies.'

'True, but they are not ours,' Cappitus shook his head. 'Neither are they familiar in shape or form. To be honest, my good friend, I am at a loss. Bastion has fallen and here we are contemplating the etchings of a race we barely know.' He sighed. 'We should be preparing our defence; we should be seeing the survivors to safety.'

'There have been no reports of Avra anywhere within the city. What if she became a victim of the earthquake?'

'We cannot afford such speculation, Ruvin Ciricello. No, the witch will have survived, and she'll be planning her next move.'

'What of the king . . . there has been no word? I would have expected Tarsin to have returned by now.'

Cappitus walked back to the lectern to see if the *Nefarii Uranometria* continued to spin. It did, which meant in approximately two hours another segment would slide into place about the golden sphere. 'He'll be here soon enough, Ruvin. He's certainly capable. My only concern is whether King Arkos will be by his side. I have grave fears concerning His Majesty. First his sons perish, now the father is in mortal danger. I've scried the ruins on three occasions since the earthquake struck, but for the life of me, I cannot see into Highcastle.'

'You mentioned he is last of the jaguars.'

'He is. If Arkos should fall, House Vantos will be no more.'

'Such an outcome is of greater concern to you now, is it not?' added Ruvin.

'It is. There are words written in the Black Book at Irongate, written by a hand far older than ours. They appear to be mostly nonsense, but there is mention of a time when the jaguars are few and Bastion is falling.'

'What else does it say?'

Cappitus sighed, already weary beyond belief. 'It says if the last of the jaguars was to fall, so too would Bastion. They are entwined, the city and the jaguar.' Cappitus stroked his beard. 'Mind you, it also mentions dragons sleeping under Highcastle. So, read what you will in that regard.' Cappitus paused, remembering another passage he thought might be of relevance. 'There is also a verse concerning Bastion being reclaimed.'

'Reclaimed?' queried Ruvin, his heavy eyebrows knotted. 'That would imply it had been taken, would it not?'

'Reclaimed, rebuilt; they could be one and the same,' offered Cappitus. He was too tired to argue further. Prophesy and strange humanoid figures had suddenly lost their appeal. 'Come, Ruvin, let us find some rest. We'll be no good to anyone if we continue to avoid sleep. I'm mentally and physically exhausted.'

Cappitus gave Fratelli a nod and began to walk away, his steps leading him across the narrow path and out of the Forever

Chamber. Regardless of where he lay his head he knew whatever rest he might find would be brief. There was simply too much to organize and so little time. He'd also promised to speak with Declan concerning the deployment of his Swords, whilst rumour had flitted in concerning the Palaceguard. Apparently not all perished when Highcastle fell. He would need their expertise in the coming hours and he would need it soon. The greater the number of swords surrounding Aston's Tear the better. He couldn't risk any man becoming complacent. It was imperative they *all* remained vigilant.

He passed the double doors that led out of the chamber and saw a dark corner to the side, cool and inviting. Without a word to Ruvin he walked over and slumped to the floor, his head resting on his hands. He was asleep in minutes, his last thoughts of King Arkos lost somewhere within Highcastle, alone and wandering a realm of grey.

*

Kayla looked down at the old man.

His visage was that of a tired monarch: lines of worry etched deep into his aged skin, his features softened but somehow still regal. There was power in the man when he was alive. Power she remembered well on the few occasions she'd appeared in court to see her father speak with the king. She also remembered the time she sat on his knee as a five-year-old, her eyes wide as she pointed to his golden crown. King Arkos had been a colossal to the small girl. He was strong and commanding, his manner of speech firm, yet fair.

She touched her hair, recalling the king patting her on the head as she leapt off his knee. There was affection in the man despite his kingly appearance and royal manner.

Now he was dead, his throne room buried, his city destroyed. Whatever fight the old man had left was now dust on the wind.

Kayla moved away from the corpse, uncertain what the group's next action would be. They'd travelled far already for no reward and she knew the prospect of returning would be met with stern disapproval. They needed rest, time to recuperate. Even as the thought crossed her mind she saw young Donal curl up on the floor, his head cushioned by his jacket atop a slab of marble, his lantern no more than a foot away. Behind him she saw Tarsin, now sitting in the shadows, his thoughts his own for now as he stifled a yawn.

She took one last look at the dead king and moved to Tarsin's side. 'Is there anything we can do?' she asked as she sat on the broken floor and pulled her knees close to her chest.

'No,' Tarsin replied, a note of sadness in his voice. 'Arkos has gone and the one chance I had at redemption has fled with him. Now I'll never know his thoughts, never know if he truly cared.'

Kayla listened to his words but understood little of what he said. Talk of redemption was beyond her; she didn't know what history Tarsin and the king shared; couldn't possibly understand the connotations of his ramblings. He'd spoken of a witch and a summoned god whilst they journeyed towards Highcastle, expressed his desire to see the king safe under his protection. If there was a link between the two she was none the wiser.

'He is safe, at least. From the witch, I mean.'

'I would think so,' Kayla saw the swordsman raise his head and peer about the shattered throne room. From their vantage, they could see only one accessible entrance, the one they'd appeared from. The Hall of Kings was the only way in or out.

'So, what do we do now?' She could see he was out on his feet. He needed rest as much as anyone, they all did. They might not be able to see the sky outside, but dusk couldn't be far away.

Tarsin pointed towards Donal, the lad lying on his side, 'Let the lad rest, in fact we could all get some sleep,' he said. 'Then we'll need to return to your father and alert him to what's transpired. After I speak to him I'll need to seek out the Brotherhood.'

'Then you rest first, for your journey is more arduous than mine.'

He was about to decline but Kayla gave him a stern look, the one she used most often on her father. Instead he unbuckled his sword belt and put his back to a pile of rubble, then closed his eyes whilst his hand rested on the pommel of his sword that now lay across his chest. She watched him for some time, tracing the line of his jaw with her green eyes, noting his sun-kissed skin. He was a handsome man. Tall and well muscled, broad of shoulder. She thought his short black hair lent him an air of respectability, of confidence and control. It wasn't difficult to picture him leading the king's armies into battle, or if he chose, leading a lady onto a dance floor. He was all grace and good looks. She briefly wondered if it was Frey's Luck that sent her racing into his arms the other day, whether there was a connection between the two of them.

Whatever it was, she liked what she felt.

It took only a moment for her to dismiss such thoughts. Tarsin was a warrior. He would never have time for one such as her. Not now, not with Bastion destroyed. What life could they ever hope to fashion? From what she'd heard there was more pain to come. Every man was now primed for war and bloodshed, not love and happiness. No matter where she looked, the future was dim.

So what chance did love have to flourish in such terrible times? Where would the laughter spring from?

She looked at Tarsin once more and heard the gentle sigh of his breathing. He looked to be already asleep, peacefully unaware. Moving quietly, she gathered her long legs under her and stood, then made for the dead king twenty feet away. She wished to pay her respects one last time. Reefe and Vittorio watched her, but she paid them no heed. Kneeling, she saw nought but a man at peace with himself, an aged man no longer carrying the hard lines of leadership. She reached out a shaking hand to feel his flesh, touching him lightly on the cheek. She pulled her hand back at the sudden touch.

Arkos was cold and smelt of death.

*

Arkos Vantos walked a grey path, his faculties sound, his injuries no longer present. Yet he had no idea where he was.

He stopped walking and looked to his left, then right, before raising eyes to the sky. It was slate-grey and devoid of clouds.

He scanned the horizon, looking for a sign, seeking something to follow. All he saw was stunted trees wrapped in gloom and clumps of grass resembling slivers of steel. There was no sun.

So, this is it, he thought, *the afterlife: the result of all my toils, my battles and my victories; a lifetime of labour for a realm void of life.* He walked on, moving down a gentle slope as he headed for a valley as barren as the windswept hill. A dry creek bed wormed along its length, cracked earth and dust its only companion. The only movement to catch his eye were a couple of dust-devils twirling briefly before disappearing into thin air.

What role do I now play? The thought stayed with him as he made for the dry creek bed. All his life, it seemed, he knew what his path was, where it would take him. From an early age, he'd been groomed for leadership, his father his teacher and mentor. Everything had been planned, his existence an elaborate tapestry where his life journey had already been sewn.

Now he felt alone and for the first time in an age, afraid. If this was all there was, in the afterlife, then he'd rather not have died. Surely there was more to his continued existence than a barren wasteland so grey and forlorn. He sat upon a slab of conglomerate protruding from the earth on the side of the path. It was neither cold nor warm, a fact that did not surprise him. He sat still and closed his eyes, remembering the last moments of his life, remembering the pain he'd felt as the column knocked him down and crushed his arm and chest. As painful as the memories were, their vividness touched a chord in his soul. Pain coupled with love, suffering with laughter, life and death. Without one you could not have the other. Life was a cycle, yet it was also an eternal struggle of peaks and troughs, an equilibrium always sought. Here in this grey wasteland Arkos wondered if the same rules applied.

'Arkos Vantos?'

He spun around. Behind him, walking down the path he'd trod only moments earlier came a man wearing a scarlet shirt and trousers of cerulean. His shaggy black hair bounced as he walked, the man apparently full of vitality. He reached the rocky slab Arkos sat upon and halted with a bow.

'Your Majesty,' he said with a smile, 'I've been expecting you.'

'You have?' Arkos replied, his voice surprisingly loud.

'I have,' the man continued to smile. 'Allow me to introduce myself. I am . . .'

'. . . You are my father,' Arkos interrupted.

The man sighed. 'No, I am not, even though I wear his image. You see, I am merely a product of your consciousness, an apparition, if you will. You must have thought of your father just now and hence I am here, your mentor and confidante. I am here to help.'

'How can you help me if you're already a part of me?'

'How can I not?'

Arkos narrowed his eyes. In his time as king few would dare banter words with him in such fashion. He'd been known for his wisdom, in the end, but he'd never been one to profess patience. 'Speak plainly, man-who-is-not-my-father.'

'I am you, Arkos. When you were alive, I would speak to you from within, but here, in this realm, I can walk beside you if I so choose. I was, and am, your sub-consciousness. Nothing here is impossible; you need only free your imagination.'

'Free my imagination?' Arkos narrowed his eyes, not quite sure he understood. 'Where is "here" exactly?'

'This is the shadow world, where reality is a concept forged in the dark. It is an in-between place. A crossroads, if you like. Many make a small journey before the end, especially those who have suffered trauma or sudden death. For those who are aware it is a time of reflection. For those unaware, it can be eternal damnation. They have a choice, an opportunity, if you will, to make the correct decision before the end.'

'The end,' queried Arkos, 'what is "the end"?'

'The final destination,' the smile remained, 'the return to the Great Consciousness.'

'What if I do not choose to return to the Great Consciousness?'

'Then you will either wander these grey plains for eternity if you are most unfortunate, or worse, you will be consumed by the Darkness that is rising.'

Arkos frowned, 'How do you possess such knowledge of this place?' he spread his hands out wide.

'Because you and I have been here before,' there was a twinkle in his eyes, sparkling with mirth and excitement. 'We are part of the Great Consciousness, Arkos, and having travelled this path before, an infinitesimal portion of our soul remembers the journey. This is not your first life. I remember, Arkos. That is why I am here.'

Arkos closed his eyes as he contemplated the words of the Apparition, for that is what he'd decided to call him, and knew he spoke the truth. When he opened his eyes a moment later his mind was clear . . . and he remembered.

'What if I have unfinished business?' he asked.

'In the realm of the living?'

'Yes,' Arkos scanned the grey sky as he spoke, sought to remember his last moments once again. 'There is a man, Tarsin by name, who I must talk too.'

The Apparition frowned and lost his smile for the first time. 'It will be difficult.'

'I thought you said nothing is impossible in this realm?'

'In this realm, yes, but you're seeking to communicate with someone from a different plane of reality. It can be done, but you'll need to be lucky.'

Arkos shared a broad grin with the Apparition. 'You should know, since you are a part of me, that I was born lucky.'

The Apparition cocked his head to the side and smiled once again. 'You are right. Follow me.'

The journey was quicker than Arkos expected. The Apparition led him back to where he'd first arrived in the grey realm. He then asked him to sit.

'Now you'll need to concentrate hard, Arkos, and picture the man you wish to talk to. It will be difficult, for your appearance will be ethereal and his mind will doubt that which it sees. He may even run away. If he does, then your chance will have passed. So, concentrate Arkos, and prepare your thoughts.'

Arkos did as he was bid and sat cross-legged on the ground with his hands on his knees. He thought of the young man, the swordsman named Tarsin Va. He pictured his face, saw his sapphire eyes and his stern mouth, then shifted his gaze to see his close cropped black hair. Then he remembered his Rykedian broadsword, thought of the time Du Weng Sai handed the blade to him, placing it in his hands as a gift. The air before him shimmered, as if the sun beat down upon hot dessert sands. Dark colours began to manifest, swirling before Arkos, and then flickering wisps of orange torchlight seeped into the realm of grey.

'Keep concentrating,' the Apparition's voice could be heard as if from far away. Arkos clenched his jaw and called Tarsin's name repeatedly in his mind.

The swirling air before the king took shape and Tarsin Va lay before him, apparently asleep. Beyond him Arkos could see his shattered throne room. It took his breath away momentarily. Tarsin had come for him.

'This is good,' the Apparition was again by Arkos' side, 'for whilst he is asleep, he will believe he dreams. Instead of seeing him on his plane of reality, you can now summon him here. Go,' the Apparition gave him a nudge, 'wake him up.'

Arkos leant over and gave Tarsin a gentle shake. The swordsman woke immediately, his eyes flicking from side-to-side, his hands clenched about the sword across his chest.

'King Arkos,' he said, sitting up. A bewildered look marred his features as he took in his appearance. 'You're alive!'

'No, lad, you are merely dreaming,' Arkos smiled and looked to the side, expecting to see the Apparition. But he had vanished. 'I would speak to you, if you would listen,' he said as he returned his focus to Tarsin.

A flash of pain crossed Tarsin's face and his eyes lowered. He could see Tarsin harboured doubts, could see the frustration in his tightly curled fists.

'What would you say?' Tarsin replied through clenched teeth.

'Many things,' Arkos returned, 'although I'm afraid our time is short. I now remember much of what transpired before my demise and in doing so my sight is clear concerning certain . . . entities. I would pass on some of that knowledge, Tarsin. I will do what I can to help your cause.'

Tarsin rubbed his eyes and cast his gaze beyond, seeing the grey wasteland in its entirety. 'Then you are truly dead?'

'I am.'

'Where are we, exactly?'

'In another realm, Tarsin, but one where I can show you what it is you are to face.' He gestured behind him. 'See the valley and the mountain beyond it?' Tarsin nodded. 'Then watch,' he said as he began to concentrate. At first nothing happened, but gradually the air shimmered until a curtain of gossamer thin material appeared, light and breezy, shifting before their eyes. Arkos swept his hand across the substance and suddenly they were sitting atop the mountain's peak, hard rock beneath them. Their vision was impaired to their left by the mountain's continuous ridge, but otherwise they could see . . . everything, it seemed. 'Look,' Arkos pointed to a smudge of darkness in the distance, twirling over barren plains.

'What is it?'

'It is that which you will eventually face.' He watched Tarsin scan the horizon.

'Can we travel closer? I can hardly make out its form.'

Arkos nodded and repeated his earlier process, concentrating on an outcropping far away and moving them there in a heartbeat. The dark smudge was now considerably larger: a whirlwind of dark energy swirling and convulsing as it moved across the grey terrain.

'Gods above, what is that . . . thing?'

'It is the Dark God, Ahriman,' Arkos replied, 'and he grows stronger, Tarsin. Even as we sit and watch, his tendrils snake out to grasp as many unwary souls as possible. With each soul gathered he becomes more powerful. With the fall of Bastion, he suddenly finds feeding all too easy.'

'How can he be here and in Bastion at the same time?'

'He is not truly in Bastion; at least not fully. He needs the soul of a king to grant him flesh. Only then can he come fully into the material plane. Flesh will enable him to keep control of the souls he now gathers. It will bind them to him with the force of life. Without it, he'll fight every waking minute to keep them chained to his will. Once he is flesh, he'll seek to exert his influence over a terrified populace, until he has dominion over your world.'

'I thought you said he needs the soul of a king. Are you not afraid he'll reach out for you?'

Arkos shrugged as he watched the whirlwind inch closer. 'He senses me, Tarsin, but my soul will not be here when he comes for it. He knows he has lost his chance concerning Arkos Vantos. For Ahriman to become flesh, certain rituals need to be performed before a king's soul becomes his.'

'He'll await the next king and seek him out, then?'

'He will. That is why I show you Ahriman now, so you can fully grasp the horror that is coming for you.' He sought out Tarsin's eyes. 'You are now the last of the jaguars, Tarsin. You alone remain Bastion's one, true hope.' If he expected shock or surprise to flare from Tarsin's grim face, he was disappointed. He simply sat, head bowed, his thoughts his own. When he finally raised his eyes, Arkos could see the hurt.

'I knew I was your son, Arkos.'

The king was stunned. With a blank look he simply said, 'How?'

'I have known since I was twelve, when Lord Henrickson appeared one day at the orphanage and summoned me to Highcastle. I had never seen or heard of the man before, but here he was explaining the rigours I was to face once I joined the ranks of an elite force of men, specifically chosen to protect the king. I'd never held a blade before that day, now I was suddenly chosen from amongst a city of noble swordsman and a thousand knights. I knew something didn't quite add up and when I reached the castle and was ushered towards the garrison I saw you watching from a balcony. We locked eyes and I knew.'

'And yet you said nothing.'

'What would you have me say? I was a bastard and you already had two healthy sons. I was told my mother died when I was young, so I was sent to an orphanage. Never did I imagine I would be anything of note and then suddenly I was to be trained to fight, to wield a sword and to be garrisoned in Highcastle.' Tarsin raised a hand to stroke his chin. 'I was twelve years of age and given every young boy's greatest dream. You gave my life purpose. I knew you were my father, but I also knew you had a wife and two young sons. I kept my silence out of respect, believing you'd tell me when the time was right. Only you never did, Arkos. You never said a word to suggest I was your bastard son.'

Arkos sat in silence. He'd felt turmoil for three decades concerning Tarsin, his one and only bastard. Born before he'd met his queen, he'd always sought to keep an eye on his welfare. Even when his queen bore him two beautiful, healthy boys, he saw fit to keep him close. He was a bastard, one only a handful of men knew existed, but he was his son; a son of a jaguar. And the jaguars always looked after their own.

'Then why did you flee Bastion?' asked Arkos, shifting the subject to Tarsin's sudden departure three years earlier. 'If you knew who you were, why leave without a word?'

'Because at the time I believed you'd betrayed me. Prince Atillus and Prince Theos were both of age and suddenly I was sent north on some fool's mission against a coven of witches we knew nothing about.' Arkos could sense the anger brewing behind his sapphire eyes; could see the storm clouds forming. 'So here I was, First Sword of the Unseen, no longer a protector of the king but an assassin for the king. Once my men began to die, it was hard not to assume I was never meant to return. Gods above, Arkos, we hadn't even reached Benwith before we were set upon!'

'It was not my doing.'

'What of the Unseen? Were we sent to die?'

'No, never that,' Arkos shook his head. 'Only a handful knew of your existence. We believed if we were ever to succeed in destroying Avra, you were the greatest option available. In hindsight, we were wrong.'

'You were more than wrong, you were compromised! We were compromised!' Tarsin raised his voice, his anger evident. 'We never even reached Benwith! They knew we were coming. I heard them say so myself. Someone informed them of our task. Someone knew of the Unseen other than you!'

Arkos sighed, aware of the frustration coursing through his son's veins. He remembered the day he returned, his face haggard, his eyes simmering. He'd charged into the throne room with a hessian bag slung over one shoulder, madness in his eyes. Then he dumped its contents onto the floor. Arkos watched as men and women of the court gagged and sought to stifle heaving stomaches. Half-a-dozen severed heads rolled onto the marble floor with a wet slap, their faces unrecognizable due to the decaying flesh. 'Some men of the coven!' he'd practically screamed, his hand now reaching for his sword. 'In the future, my king,' he'd spat on the floor to emphasise his point, 'if you wish me dead come face me yourself!' Then he spun on a heel and stormed out of the throne room, pushing past the four men he'd returned with, their faces unreadable behind steel masks. He learnt later that their mission had been a disaster, albeit Avra's coven had perished in the conflict. It was small justification for the loss they'd been dealt. When Tarsin and his men first entered his throne room he'd felt a moment of cathartic relief, but his emotions turned sour once he learnt how deceptive his adversary had become. Always attempting to stay one step ahead of Avra and her machinations, this time, with his bastard son's life at risk, he'd been outplayed. More importantly, the man who was his son felt betrayed.

'I am truly sorry, Tarsin,' Arkos looked up to see eyes flickering with hatred. 'I made an error in judgement, one that could have cost you your life. As a result, you lost men dear to you . . . and to me. I never intended to see any of the Unseen die. You must believe me.'

'It has taken three years of contemplation, Arkos. Three years dredging up a past full of hurt and regret, wondering why as a young boy I never had the opportunity to leap into a father's arms full of love and protection. A boy needs a hero and I had no-one. You denied me that experience. You eventually sent for me, though, and I was old enough to know you gave me all that you could. So yes, it has taken time, but I believe you.'

'Well, you have returned to Bastion to find yourself heir to the throne,' Arkos began once he saw Tarsin's anger subside. 'With Atillus and Theos slain you are the last of my bloodline. Lucius will seek to become king, but it is you who shall lead.'

'What if I don't want the crown?'

'You don't have a choice. If you refuse, Lucius Vupello will ascend the throne. You cannot allow him such privilege. In your absence, Tarsin, we've discovered much concerning Benwith. Lucius Vupello is heavily involved; we believe his actions may have influenced the abduction of the Unseen. If you have issues to resolve, then it's with my cousin. It is he who betrayed you. How he found out about the Unseen is anyone's guess, but his treachery is unquestionable.'

'So why has he not been brought to justice?'

'Because he and a handful of others have ties to Avra, and if we are fortunate, he'll lead us to her whereabouts. Trust me; we were close before the earthquake struck. Mayhaps we'll be close again in the days to come.'

Tarsin thought of the Captain of the Palaceguard, knew he'd deal with him when the time was right. 'No-one will believe I am of the blood.'

'Perhaps, but you need to look into the mirror, son, realise who you are.'

'I don't look into mirrors anymore, Arkos . . . not since Benwith.'

Arkos felt a twinge of regret at the words, inwardly cursed himself for his slip of the tongue. 'It will not matter,' he waved a hand before him. 'There are documents proclaiming you as heir in a mahogany chest in my private study. It remains intact despite the earthquake. There is also a suit of armour I wish you to take, along with my twin blades hanging above the hearth. You must also take my crown. It will become useful in the days ahead, a symbol of our kingdom and a sign of hope.'

Both men sat in silence for some time, watching the black whirlwind as it swept ever closer. It was strange, for neither imagined speaking so openly before. Now there was a companionable silence. Arkos wished it could last forever.

'We need to leave here,' he finally said. He regretted saying the words, but they were necessary. 'If Ahriman sweeps any closer, he'll sense your worth. It would be beneficial if he were to stay in the dark concerning your bloodline.'

Tarsin nodded understanding and seconds later they were back on the hill, where they first met.

'Can we defeat Avra?' Tarsin voiced the question he feared to ask.

'I will do what I can to help,' he replied. 'I may be dead, Tarsin, but I still have a part to play. The jaguars and wyverns have fought for longer than I care to remember, our life's tapestry fashioned of bloodied fabric, but I've one strand left to manoeuvre. If I succeed it will unravel the tapestry so completely no-one will remember our vengeful feud.

'What of the Dark God, can I kill him?

'I cannot see how,' Arkos grimaced, 'and I sense an evil other than Ahriman fast approaching.' He reached a hand towards Tarsin's shoulder. 'What I do know is that you need to stay alive, son. So long as a jaguar lives and breathes, there is hope. But you must leave the depths of Highcastle as quickly as able. Retrieve the items I mentioned and flee.' He wiped his brow with the back of his hand, 'I don't know how I know, Tarsin, but I sense the city is about to awaken.'

'Awaken?'

'Aye, as if she has slumbered for thousands of years. She has been hibernating, waiting for an appointed time. Believe me when I tell you, her depths were never our own.'

'What of Bastion?' Tarsin asked. 'Can we save the city?'

'Perhaps, do what you feel is right; Anok and Eli know you are more than capable.' Tears welled in the king's eyes, but he couldn't hold them back, nor did he feel the need. 'I wish I could tell you more, son,' he motioned for him to lie down, 'but it is time for you to wake.' He watched Tarsin lay back, his hands clasped about the sword across his chest.

'Fare you well, Arkos Vantos,' Tarsin shared a smile with his father.

'I shall, Tarsin, for my wife and boys await me,' tears rolled down his cheeks as pure light began to shine from his chest, a soft radiance of gold, warm and comforting. 'I can hear them calling my name, but I've so much work to accomplish.' He leant over to rest a hand on Tarsin's brow, saw his body shimmer as it began to disappear. 'Know that I'll always keep an eye on you, son . . . the Eye of the Jaguar.'

    Tarsin closed his eyes . . .

    . . . And woke.

CHAPTER TWENTY

Kayla leant over and gently shook Tarsin's shoulder. His eyes had been closed for no more than several minutes. 'Tarsin,' she said as she gave him another shove.

The swordsman opened his eyes and Kayla watched as they adjusted to the poor light. 'What is it?' he asked, sitting up.

'Should we not find someplace safer to rest,' she looked over her shoulder at the king lying cold upon the tiled floor. 'It smells of death in here.'

'I know,' Tarsin replied as he followed Kayla's gaze. Vittorio, still cloaked in black, knelt by the king's side whilst Reefe paced a few feet away. Griffith and Donal were both lying on the floor. 'Listen, I know it sounds strange, but I spoke to the king just now. I spoke to Arkos Vantos in a dream.'

'But you were asleep for no more than a few minutes.'

'It happened all the same,' Tarsin rose to his feet and re-positioned his sword belt. 'We need to move from here and find his private study.' Kayla stood and watched as Tarsin moved towards the double doors, giving Griffith a kick to rouse him off the floor as he passed. The two spoke quietly in the hallway for a minute or more. She couldn't hear their words but could see by their posture they were alert. She took a step and nudged young Donal, still lying asleep by the lantern.

'Up, Donal,' she said, 'I think it's time to move. There is nothing more we can do here.'

'Actually,' Tarsin had returned quietly to her side, 'there is work still to be done.' He reached Arkos' body and knelt to retrieve the king's crown, a golden circlet inlaid with an oval stone of jade. It was polished smooth and known as the Eye of the Jaguar. He handed it to Griffith who placed it in the sack he had strung about his torso. 'I take it Arkos' private study hasn't moved since I last stepped foot in Highcastle?' he spoke to Griffith; the big man lost in thought for a moment as he paid his last respects. When he did raise his eyes, Kayla saw they glistened in the torchlight.

'It's where it's always been, Tarsin,' his voice was choked with emotion, heavy and saddened.

'Then let us be on our way.'

'What of King Arkos?' asked Vittorio. 'Will you not bury him?'

Kayla saw Tarsin share a look with the men about him. 'No,' he said after a moment's pause, 'the man who was Arkos no longer resides here. Trust me on this,' he said, gathering their attention. 'We need to move.'

Griffith shrugged his shoulders and lifted his warhammer, turning to walk back towards the Hall of Kings. The rest followed, and Kayla found herself walking beside Tarsin as they left what remained of the king's throne room. She chanced a look at his face and saw it was hard, devoid of emotion. 'What do you hope to find in his study?' she tentatively asked.

He was silent as they passed the bronze doors and began to walk the Hall of Kings. The flickering torch light did little to keep her fear at bay as they passed the marble statues and once again she quickened her pace. As they reached the end, he turned to face her. 'A couple of items,' he said. 'Firstly, his swords, for they are too valuable to be left buried under a pile of rubble. Secondly, some documents of equal value.'

'Do you know where to find them?'

'I do. Like I said, my dream-talk with Arkos was . . . unusual, but it was real. I'd stake my life on it.'

'What else did he tell you?'

She saw him peer ahead towards the doorway the others had passed through. To the right lay a narrow stone-walled passage leading into darkness. As a group, they headed towards it.

Kayla grabbed Tarsin's elbow, 'What . . .'

'. . . I'll not talk of it here,' he whispered, looking towards Reefe and Vittorio a couple of steps ahead.

She ceased asking questions and remained silent as she walked beside the swordsman. She was content, glad to be close. It was small comfort, here in the dark, but it was welcomed. They took several more turns and climbed down one set of stairs before Griffith banged his hammer against an oak door.

'This is Arkos' study,' Griffith said as the men milled about.

Tarsin strode up to the door and looked at the iron lock. He tried the handle to no avail.

'I can help,' Donal said as he squirmed to his side. Tarsin looked down to see the young boy fishing in his pocket. A second later his hand emerged with a selection of metal picks of varying length and shape. With a raised eyebrow, he watched as Donal stepped past him to place the first of his picks into the keyhole.

A minute later the door swung open.

*

Tarsin moved past Griffith and entered the study to reach the large mahogany desk in three strides. Papers and scrolls lay scattered about the room, the only book shelf lay face down on the floor. There were no windows to the outside world here, for the room lay deep under Highcastle. But there was a single hearth with a mantle holding an assortment of trinkets from neighbouring kingdoms: statues and carvings, mostly, although several knives and jewelled daggers were present. A handful of lucky charms had fallen during the earthquake to lie strewn across the floor, resting on plush rugs and various animal skins. Reefe entered, his flaming brand lending light which allowed him to see just how many trinkets were scattered about the room.

Diverting his eyes from their odd nature Tarsin looked above the hearth to see the twin swords of Arkos Vantos. They were still resting in their brackets, as promised. He crossed from the table and reached for them, lifting them with care. His hands tingled as they wrapped about the leather-bound hilts. Like his own sword, they were Rykedian made, the blades a blend of Herkosian and Dervani steel, folded and beaten hundreds of times by a Rykedian master sword-smith. Men would sell their own daughters for such a blade, and Tarsin now held three.

'What else are we here for?' Griffith cast his gaze about the small room.

Tarsin stepped back towards the desk and began to look for the mahogany chest. 'Anything you care to take,' he said. 'Once we leave here, I doubt anyone will be coming back.'

Vittorio and Reefe suddenly became active, heading towards the book shelf and attempting to heave it upright, whilst Donal sorted through the scattered papers as he sought anything of interest.

'Kayla,' Tarsin asked, 'help me find a small chest, about so big,' he held his hands a foot apart. 'It should be amongst this mess somewhere.' She did so, moving quickly to assist him, sweeping parchment from the desk before looking under the table. Within seconds she found it, nestled against the leg of a chair. She handed it to him. A simple latch was easily flicked to allow the chest to open. Inside were a handful of scrolls; bound and marked with the king's royal seal. 'This is it,' he closed the lid and fastened the latch.

'Tarsin,' Griffith's voice cut through the noise of books being stacked and furniture scraping across the floor, 'you need to see this.'

Tarsin crossed the room, stepping over Donal who still sorted papers on the floor. Griffith stood in the corner and stepped aside as he approached to reveal a suit of armour displayed on a wooden cross. It was exquisitely fashioned, a hauberk of fine chain links over black leather with a breast plate, gorget and a set of over-lapping plates forming spaulders to complete the ensemble. It was the breast plate that caught everyone's eye, though, for it was embossed to resemble the face of a snarling jaguar, savage and primal. With utmost care Tarsin passed the chest and swords to Kayla, then reached out with trembling hands to touch the mail. It was cold, as expected, but there was a feeling of invincibility coursing through his veins as he admired the suit.

'I'd suggest you take it and put it on,' Griffith smiled as he spoke. 'It looks to be your size; Aston knows it won't fit me.'

Tarsin did as bid, lifting the gorget and placing it to the side before removing the breast plate. He wore only a shirt, sweat-stained with dust and dirt, and this he quickly covered with the leather gambeson and chain. Griffith then helped buckle on the breast plate and gorget before strapping on the spaulders. 'There,' Griffith said as he walked around him, admiring his handiwork, 'you look the part.' Tarsin held his arms out. The chainmail reached his wrists, but there were no vambraces, nor gauntlets to cover his gloved hands. Still, it was better than nothing at all, and the entire ensemble rested like a second skin. In fact, it was remarkable how comfortable it felt to wear.

Having gathered all he was required, and more, Tarsin made one last sweep of the room, reminding Vittorio and Reefe to be quick before ushering Donal up off the floor. The lad had an assortment of papers clutched in his hands, maps, mostly, and a small ornate box trimmed in silver. Apart from the armour, Griffith had found a small stash of coin in a pouch and had placed a jewelled dagger at his waist. Reefe and Vittorio both placed an assortment of items into their pouches, most ranging from mundane ornaments worth a small fortune, before placing the more practical daggers into their belts.

'Come, we need to leave,' Tarsin said once he'd taken the swords and chest from Kayla's hands. She quickly bent and gathered a handful of trinkets and charms lying atop the animal rugs. Many were made of silver or gold, fine pieces fashioned by expert hands, and a number even held small twinkling gems: amber, ruby, amethyst and diamond entwined amongst their delicate threads. Without a backward glance, they filed out of the study, torches leading the way as they delved back into the darkened corridor. It took some time for them to make their way back to the kitchens, and half as long again before they descended back to the convoluted depths beneath Highcastle.

Physically exhausted, the group trudged ever forward. Yet despite the urgency they all felt, the rigours of the day were taking their toll. Donal could hardly put one foot in front of the other and even Griffith was labouring. It appeared only Vittorio, beside himself, retained any stamina for the path ahead. Even Kayla appeared exhausted as she led them down a gradual incline before waiting for everyone to reach her position. 'We need to rest,' she considered his face as he reached her side.

'I know, but we needed to put Highcastle behind us,' he peered over his shoulder, watching as Griffith walked with heavy steps, young Donal by his side. 'We'll make for the circular chamber, the one we stumbled across on the way in and rest there till morning.'

He saw Kayla nod in agreement, then waited for Griffith to arrive so he could take the waterskin from his sack and hand it around. Even though Kayla had mentioned nightfall had arrived, it remained hot and humid in the tunnels beneath the surface. He could see the effect the heat was having on Griffith with his plate armour, felt similarily stifled with the extra steel he now wore.

He motioned for Kayla to press on and watched as Vittorio and Reefe passed before falling in himself. He chanced a single glance back the way they'd travelled, taking a moment to recall the rooms, halls and corridors of Highcastle. During their entire travels within, not once did they hear the cry of a survivor, nor see another living soul. Highcastle was now a tomb with only the dead in residence. With so much destruction above and below, the thought of Highcastle and Bastion being forsaken was a distinct possibility.

And with Arkos dead, he now had to deal with Lucius Vupello.

*

Kayla rolled onto her side and peered about the shadowed chamber. The sound of heavy breathing permeated the room, all the men lying on their backs snoring loudly except for Donal who slept in silence. They were arranged in a circle about a selection of bricks taken from the crumbled wall, piled high with the last remaining torch wedged into its centre to provide the illusion of a warm fire. Apart from the brand's infrequent flickers, all was still. Standing, she moved away from the sleeping forms and crept towards the dais with its gold ring embedded in granite. She had just reached the top step when she saw Tarsin's dark form resting on the fallen bricks at the entrance to the chamber. She stepped across the dais on light feet to where he sat, taking care not to wake the others.

He turned as she approached and in the dim light she could see his forced smile.

'Why are you not asleep?' she asked, her voice low.

'Someone needs to keep watch,' he sighed and placed his hands on the rock he sat on, lifting his tired frame. He'd taken his armour off when they arrived, in a vain attempt to relax.

'Have you slept at all? She pressed him, 'I can keep watch for a time.'

She saw his hand rise to rub at tired eyes, but he shook his head all the same. 'No, I'm finding it hard to sleep. My thoughts are troubled.'

It was dark out here by the broken wall and the empty room. What light they did have was on the far side of the circular chamber. Still, she could sense the anguish in his words; almost feel the tension in his body. She sat next to him and placed an arm around his shoulders, then moved her hips along the stone seat until she nestled against him. 'I can keep you company, if you like?'

He breathed deeply but did not refuse her offer, and for some time they sat in silence. Eventually Kayla rested her head on his shoulder and smelt the remnants of leather and oiled chain. Then, without a second thought, she cupped his chin with her hand and leant in close, brushing her lips against his.

And they kissed.

Kayla couldn't tell how long they kissed, for all sense of time and place faded into obscurity. All she felt was a longing for a man she barely knew, a swordsman, tall and handsome, who currently felt burdened by the death of his king. All her life she'd been taught etiquette and fine manners, the daughter of a baron, high born and proper. But with the death of her mother, and then her elder brother Jarrick, the Tolsten's family dynamics had changed considerably, and for the past year she'd spent her time traversing the streets of Bastion both above and below. Suitors had come and gone, most at her father's behest, and Kayla, never one to spurn her father's most stringent wishes, remained a novice in the game of love.

'I want you,' she heard herself murmur, running a hand through his close-cropped hair. He kissed her harder, passionately, before abruptly pulling away.

'Should we be doing this?' he asked, and Kayla could see his eyes searching for hers in the poor light.

'Why should we not?' she gasped. 'The world is in turmoil, about to end, and you would deny our feelings for each other. The opportunity might never rise again. I don't want to die having never known a man, Tarsin.'

'What of your father?'

'What of him? You can't ask for his consent out here,' her voice was husky, her breathing quick. 'I'm certain he expects nothing less than a dashing young prince to come sweep me off my feet.' Kayla felt a shudder ripple down Tarsin's spine, but then his hands settled on her shoulders and they embraced. Seconds later his mouth found hers before he lifted her up and stepped towards a dark corner. She felt his hands race over her body, over her hips, across her breasts. Her nipples hardened, straining against her shirt, and then his fingers were untying laces, searching for flesh, squeezing, caressing. She lifted a leg to hook about his waist and let out a soft moan.

Sometime later she lay beside him with their clothes beneath them, spread across the stone floor. Her hand rested across his naked chest, gently rising with his every breath. She couldn't see in the dark but instinctively knew he dreamed a dreamless sleep.

She thought of their lovemaking. It had been passionate and fierce, not soft and gentle as she'd always imagined. But the energy they exuded was intoxicating and the release, when it came, was exhilarating. Regardless of what was to come and despite all her father cautioned her against, she felt content and at peace with the world.

She even dared to believe she was in love.

An hour passed before Tarsin stirred beneath her hand and propped himself on an elbow. 'We'd better dress ourselves,' he said, 'before the others wake.' He leant forward and found her mouth, kissed her again. 'Thank you,' the words were softly spoken.

Kayla grinned then began sorting their clothes. It was difficult in the dark, but they eventually managed. Just as they were about to move towards the circular chamber Tarsin reached out to grasp her hand.

'There is something you should know, Kayla, something you should hear from me first.'

She leaned in close. 'What is it?'

'I . . . I spoke, as I told you, with Arkos whilst I slept.'

'Yes.'

'And although he mentioned several concerns about the future and what we faced, he also revealed to me a truth I'd been waiting to hear for a very long time.'

Kayla remained silent, allowing Tarsin time to gather his thoughts.

'I am a bastard, Kayla,' he eventually said, 'but I am the king's bastard.'

A sudden rush of air whistled past her teeth before she composed herself. 'What does this mean?'

'It means I am blood of the jaguar and thus heir to the throne. There are documents within the mahogany chest detailing my validity and Arkos' plan for my succession.' He paused to allow the information to sink in, for them both, it seemed. 'It appears your father was right after all.'

'What do you mean?' she asked.

'You're being swept off your feet by a prince.'

'You're no prince, Tarsin Va,' she said quickly, moving to stand directly in front of him, her hands wrapped about his neck.

'No, I guess you're right,' she could see the light in his eyes fade, 'and I never truly will be.'

'No, you won't, fool of a man,' Kayla smiled, 'because with Arkos dead . . . you are king.'

*

The sun sat high in the sky as Jarred stood before the shining pyramid, his feet atop the blood-red granite. He spun around and then walked to his left until he found a side bathed in shadow. It was cooler here and he could see without squinting. He lifted his gaze out across Bastion, looking for the landmarks he knew. Only Irongate was nowhere to be seen, nor was Highcastle to the west. Even the cathedrals surrounding the pyramid were eerily vacant. He did notice the red-granite base he stood upon was larger, set higher from the ground below. It was two levels now, resembling two enormous steps. But the steps carved into their side remained, leading down to bridges spanning water and manicured gardens blooming with colour and life. Beyond lay strange buildings of unfamiliar architecture, their graceful lines and intricate embellishments a wonder to Jarred as he marvelled at their walls of polished marble. Interspersed amongst the structures wove paved walkways, spreading from the pyramid like twisted branches, irregular yet strangely hypnotic to peer at. Verdant patches of grass, like neatly placed quilts, pockmarked the city, home to swaying willow trees sighing to the caress of a gentle breeze. Amongst the landscape spun four circular canals, sparkling under the sun's golden light, their clear blue waters reflecting unblemished sky. The first, directly below the pyramid, was fashioned into a moat, whereas the second became a wide expanse of water separating the inner city with the outer. The third and fourth circular canals were almost too far away for him to see clearly, but the bridges spanning the third were easily recognizable, whilst the fourth and last circle of water was noticeable due to the twelve small temples neatly positioned along its perimeter. Each was reached by an arrow-straight path through the city proper, all originating at the pyramid, fashioned to resemble the spokes of a wheel.

It was an incredible sight. He knew where he was for Aston's Tear sat behind him in all its magnificent glory, but a voice inside told him what he saw was from a different time. This was not Bastion: capital of the kingdom of Dervae. This was Aos, city of the Nepharii.

He stood here at a time five thousand years past.

He cocked his head to the side as he sought to listen to the voices he'd come to know. He was dreaming, of that he was certain, but there was purpose to the dream. For now, he listened to the pleasant sound of nature's gifts as he sat on the hard-red granite, seeking to rekindle the voices from within.

He knew his deft touch along the pyramid was the spark of his newfound intellect. The people who created the wonder were many, their combined will god-like. He also knew the Nepharii could confer the essence of their being into the structure, leaving memories that remained. Somehow Jarred's caress stirred the memories into life. The tingling in his hands was the transfer of information and knowledge. He smiled, the irony not lost on the young man. For five years he'd been Ruvin's information gatherer for Ciricello's Swords. Yet he never imagined he'd garner so much knowledge with such a simple gesture.

He concentrated by closing his eyes, then sought to relax his mind and bring forth the numerous images he'd come to know. Glyphs of the Nepharii appeared, detailing everything he saw. The ones he knew to be of utmost importance were the glyphs representing the zodiac. He found them and watched as they drifted past his field of view, seeing each of them matched to one of the twelve temples surrounding the city. There was power here. Like the canals before him, fed by the river he knew as Atvia but here named Wyst, the temples were fed by the glowing pyramid, its silver-blue vibrancy life-like. Small spheres of light rested at the peak of the temples, balanced atop spires of gold. Jarred could sense their harmonic beat from where he stood; could feel the connection. The entire city hummed with vitality.

Then he saw the pattern; knew Ruvin's relic, the *Nepharii Uranometria*, was an exact replica of the circular city named Aos. It was their key to salvation, their last hope to escape the Dark God.

He began to walk around the pyramid, memorising the temples and their place, assigning each a symbol. Eagle, hound, serpent, bull, deer and panther were the first six, balanced with positive energy. On the negative side were crow, fox, rat, bear, wolf and dragon; a balanced wheel about the Heart of the Universe.

As he scanned the city with admiration a voice popped into his mind, its language ancient but its whispered words clear. It spoke of the inherent danger associated with the *Nepharii Uranometria*, spoke of the danger that could come from beyond. Jarred tried to listen to the words as he sought to understand their connotations, but an incessant voice, old and gravelly, kept intruding upon his thoughts. A violent shake of his shoulder caused his vision of Aos to waiver. Then the voice was accompanied by another, more familiar, asking him to wake. He sought to hold on to the dream state, wishing he'd grasped the words whispered to him. A minute later his vision of blue sky and golden sunshine faded and the temples with their balls of light disappeared.

Jarred woke to find himself lying on the floor of the Forever Chamber, Ruvin and elder Cappitus hovering above him. Both wore expressions of confusion, although there was an element of excitement twinkling in their eyes.

'Jarred!' Ruvin shook his shoulder once more.

'I'm awake,' he replied, rubbing his eyes as he sat up. He looked past the two men and immediately saw the golden sphere pulsing in the background. The fabricated constellations in the night sky remained.

'You need to see this, lad,' elder Cappitus stood tall, looking over his shoulder. Jarred followed his gaze. A dozen or more members of the Brotherhood crowded atop the platinum rings, peering back every minute or so as they divided their attention between the inner ring and old Fratelli who watched an hour glass set upon the lectern. Cappitus offered his hand and Jarred reached for it. As they crossed to the innermost ring a wave of excitement could be felt trembling through those assembled nearby. Something was happening and Jarred was eager to see what it was.

'What has happened?' he asked, although as they pushed forward he caught a glimpse of the new oddity.

'It is a bridge, Jarred,' replied Cappitus.

Jarred shifted his body and eased to the front to see a golden bridge spanning the ten-foot space between the sphere and the innermost ring. It was eerily transparent, yet strangely appeared solid. A minute later he realised its transparency was fast fading. He looked down at the glyph, knew it was the sign of the wolf: Lupus to the Nepharii. Turning to peer at Cappitus he asked a question. 'How long have I been asleep, elder, and how many signs of the zodiac have you seen?'

'You have slumbered for almost a day, Jarred. We have tried to wake you, but your body refused our call,' he scratched his beard as he spoke. 'As to the latter part of your question, the wolf is the eleventh sign we have laid eyes on. There is only one more.'

Before he could speak further, old Fratelli called out. 'Two hours is almost upon us!'

The men and women chattered as the allotted time crept close. Jarred heard their excitement, realised they'd watched the inner ring spin about the sphere a segment at a time for nearly a day, perplexed as to its design and function, but aware that once every two hours the platinum ring would rotate a single segment to reveal the next sign of the zodiac. Strangely, in the last hour a golden bridge had materialised, connecting the inner ring to the source of power swirling at its centre.

'Jarred,' Ruvin said over the bubbling enthusiasm.

Jarred spun to see his master, his eyes dark and serious. 'Ruvin, what is it?'

The small man leant close, 'Do not lose sight of the fact we are in dire straits, young man. The excitement here is illusory; has no substance. The real problems lie outside.' A nod from Cappitus standing next to him showed the old man had heard Ruvin's warning. 'We must remain vigilant, Jarred, and any insight you might possess will be greatly appreciated.'

Jarred felt both men grab an elbow of his and move him forward a step, so they stood an inch from the inner ring surrounding the sphere. A shout from Fratelli was quickly followed by a booming sound as the ring rotated one segment, its resonance reverberating for several seconds before fading. The movement was disconcerting and Jarred almost lost his balance owing to a bout of vertigo. But with Ruvin and Cappitus holding tight to either side, he remained upright. Seconds later the animated gossip ceased as necks strained to see the last of the Nepharii constellations.

'We may be wrong, Ruvin,' Cappitus' voice was grave as he scanned the new segment. 'Perhaps the real problems we face may indeed be in here.'

Jarred shuffled closer to Cappitus; then looked down upon the new glyph with its sign of the zodiac. It appeared like all the others: its constellation fashioned into the image of a beast, a world and its moon directly below. To the right stood two humanoid figures also representing the zodiac sign. Old Fratelli called out, his old voice strangely clear above the sudden silence. 'What is it, what do you see?'

Cappitus pointed a gnarled finger. 'Those,' he said, squinting as he peered at the image of two humanoids with clawed hands and bared fangs, 'are men with the heads of dragons!'

CHAPTER TWENTY-ONE

Reefe grimaced as fire flared in his belly.

He'd woken minutes earlier, momentarily disorientated as he peered about the circular chamber, their make-shift fire casting dreadful shadows about the room. He rubbed sleep from his eyes and searched out his companions sleeping forms, and immediately noted two were missing.

Kayla and Tarsin.

He cursed under his breath and scanned the rest of the chamber as he sought them out. With his eyes adjusting to the dim light he finally saw two huddled shapes near the entrance. And they were embracing.

Reefe almost drew his sword in fury but stayed his hand and watched covertly instead. His trust concerning Tarsin Va was negligible and his only reason for accompanying Kayla on this fool's quest was to keep an eye on her welfare, a promise made to her father. Now she'd fallen into the swordsman's arms, through weakness or some trickery, he didn't know, but he was adamant the ruse wouldn't last long, especially once he mustered the courage to plunge his sword into Tarsin's back.

With careful, silent movements, Reefe crawled to the curved wall, pressing his back against the cold surface. He could still make out Kayla and Tarsin, their heads close, but he was certain they wouldn't see him if they looked his way. Again, he was about to draw his sword, but a movement amongst those asleep cautioned him. Griffith snored loudly, Donal beside him, but Vittorio had rolled to his side. Reefe watched him, wondered why he hadn't taken Tarsin yet. He was certain the man was an assassin, and there'd been ample opportunity during their travel. Yet Vittorio remained as impassive as ever as he followed orders and kept quiet at the rear. Any effort on Reefe's behalf to include the man in conversation was futile, for his silky voice offered short answers and then silence.

Seeing no further movement, he left the sleeping assassin and inched along the wall. *To Hell with Vittorio, and to Hell with*

Tarsin Va, he thought. *I'll kill them both*. The thought was intoxicating, but then he realized he'd have to answer to Griffith, and he wasn't so cocksure concerning the big man. His only real chance was to kill them in their sleep, noiselessly, an observation that did little to steel his confidence. He wished he'd never fallen asleep in the first place, but with Kayla and Tarsin now awake, his opportunity had passed.

Now the two of them were close, creating another obstacle for him to overcome.

He was contemplating his next move when the room suddenly shimmered, like a thousand motes of light flickered before his eyes. He held out a hand to steady himself, vertigo swamping his senses, threatening to send him crashing to the mosaic floor. He staggered once then righted himself, alert now to a gentle hum thrumming from everywhere at once. Even through the soles of his boots he could feel the energy, a constant drone encompassing his entire form. He peered about the chamber and saw the golden ring lining the outer wall glowing bright as it leant colour and illumination to the previously dark room. A second later Tarsin stood by his side, his Rykedian broadsword grasped firmly, his eyes wide as he too gazed upon the marvel.

'What did you do?' Tarsin asked, motioning Kayla to wake the others. He needn't have bothered for the noise had woken them already.

'Nothing,' Reefe replied. Both men looked towards the dais, noting the golden hue rising from the polished granite. It was like liquid gold, snaking up towards the domed ceiling, fiery tendrils swirling and then expanding. Sharp twinkles of ruby, aquamarine and emerald pierced the gloom from within, and diamond sparkles soared high. A moment later the golden substance reached a height of ten feet and then spun back into itself with a bulge, producing an ellipsoid of swirling matter. A tremendous boom finalised its creation.

'What in Aston's name is this?' Griffith's loud voice was heard above the hum, his hands pressed to his ears. Young Donal stood by his side, his mouth agape.

'Stand back,' Tarsin said as Reefe took a step towards the remarkable oddity.

'The Hell I will!' he snapped. 'Look at this thing, its liquid gold swirling with gems. We could all be rich beyond our wildest dreams.'

'You don't know that, thief; it could be witchcraft for all we know.'

At the mention of witchcraft Griffith reached for his warhammer lying atop his plate armour. Reefe saw him hold it tight, his face suddenly pale. For several minutes, they simply observed the swirling patterns within the ellipsoid, unsure of their next step, before Tarsin moved towards his discarded armour.

'Help me with this,' Tarsin said to Kayla. Reefe saw her cross to his side, her hands helping him with straps and buckles as he wriggled into his chain mail and jaguar breast plate. Griffith took the same approach, quickly buckling his greaves about his legs and working his way up, fastening his breast plate with Vittorio's help. By the time Tarsin had finished, the golden ellipsoid had been present within the chamber for some time, still humming gently, endlessly spinning atop the dais.

Then, surprisingly, a dark shape materialized within the ellipsoid and stepped into the room.

Donal screamed; his high-pitched voice a clarion call of fear. Reefe barely heard the boy, for his eyes were fixed upon the creature now standing ten feet away. It was large, easily several inches above six feet, as tall as Griffith. But it was not its size that caused a sudden intake of breath, but its features. For it was no man that stood before them, but rather a demon: scaled and fanged with yellow eyes staring from a head resembling a giant lizard. Reefe blanched at the sight, blinking rapidly to assure himself he wasn't hallucinating. Sallow skin stretched across the creature's upper torso, visible beneath leather straps, before culminating in vermilion scales across its shoulders and head. Splotches of maroon surrounded the eyes and a darker marking, almost black, streaked back over the skull. Its attire consisted of a leather kilt embossed with steel rivets and a belt of hardened leather covering its belly and sides. Sharp protrusions could be seen at its shoulders and elbows, whilst its feet were scaled and clawed. Broad bands of steel ringed its ankles and wrists, vibrant drops of colour alerting Reefe to the gems embossed within.

'Gods above!' Griffith was the first to utter a sound after Donal's scream.

The demon stood as transfixed as they, unmoving apart from its flickering yellow eyes.

'Do you speak?' Reefe heard Tarsin ask as he took a step forward.

Reefe saw the demon tilt its head to one side, its eyes now fixed on the swordsman. Large, clawed hands flexed, the red scales stretching to show cream-coloured palms. Then it raised an arm over its shoulder, grasping the hilt of some weapon. It pulled it forth with a hiss, the blade heavy and wide, one edge serrated and the other razor sharp. Its mouth moved, but the words it spoke were foreign, disjointed.

But the tone was recognizable.

Reefe moved a step towards Kayla, seeking to protect her from any sudden rush, but it was unnecessary for Tarsin carried the naked steel of his Rykedian broadsword in front of him, light from the ellipsoid bathing it gold.

'Is this wise?' Griffith motioned Vittorio to quickly finish buckling his armour, then reached for his warhammer. The smaller man worked as fast as he was able, strapping the last pauldron in place. As Griffith rose to his feet, the hiss of Vittorio's blade quickly followed.

'Probably not,' answered Tarsin as he circled the demon.

Reefe reached out for Donal, beckoning the boy to run towards him and Kayla.

'We need to send word to elder Cappitus, Griffith,' Reefe heard Tarsin raise his voice, then saw him wave his blade to either side, watching as the demon took a step in his direction, 'and we need to send it now.'

'I'm not leaving you here,' Griffith rumbled.

'Nor am I,' Kayla's voice cut through the hum.

Reefe grabbed Donal and stepped further back from the confrontation. If they were too stupid to do as ordered, he would go himself and take the boy. Someone had to protect him. He was terrified.

The demon stepped off the dais, its blade swinging back and forth with a whoosh. Then it charged.

Reefe gasped as Tarsin shifted to the side, the demon's heavy blade smashing into his own and knocking him back several paces. The demon was strong, it seemed, and quick. Snarling it swung again, and again, seeking to knock Tarsin down, battering him with blows in quick succession. But the swordsman deftly stepped out of harm's way, twisting first to the right, then to the left as he found his rhythm. Then the clash of steel rang throughout the chamber as swords screamed upon meeting each other, one broad and heavy, the other slender and light. Reefe found himself wondering if Tarsin's sword would break, for it seemed inconceivable that it should withstand such tremendous blows, but not only did it hold its own, blinding sparks of blue were resulting in large chips scoring the heavier blade.

'Help him!' Reefe heard Kayla shout across the room, signalling Griffith who stood armoured and ready. The big man shrugged, for the two combatants were moving rapidly, spinning in circles too fast for him to enter. Reefe understood his hesitancy, knew an ill-timed move could prove fatal. Tarsin was focused, his mind clear. He didn't need another distraction.

A moment later the demon struck him with a vicious backhand. The strike was brutal, the sound like a clap of thunder. Tarsin staggered back three feet, shaking his head as blood streamed from his nose. The demon stepped in swiftly, sniffing at the scent of blood, its shoulders bunched for a killer blow. Kayla screamed as Tarsin fell back onto the dais, his sword raised to protect his neck from a descending blow. Sparks flew as metal screeched, then Reefe watched as Tarsin pushed his feet underneath him and backed away once more, the golden ellipsoid behind him.

With the demon's back exposed Griffith raised his warhammer and charged, bounding across the room with its neck in his sight. The beast moved just as swiftly, though, and hammered another blow towards Tarsin's midriff before it charged the swordsman, seeking to overpower him.

The attack was brutal and well timed, Tarsin barely quick enough to defend and instead of standing his ground he fell back. The demon followed, the two tumbling into the ellipsoid with a pulse of white light . . . to disappear from the ancient chamber.

*

'I need Neema here and I need her now!' Cappitus shouted the order to anyone who cared to listen. His usually calm demeanour had evaporated at the sight of dragon etchings on the segment before him. As Ruvin had accurately mentioned whilst pointing towards the golden bridge, "A bridge was an extension of a path, and a path traditionally led somewhere". Cappitus agreed, which caused all manner of unlikely scenarios to manifest inside his head. Scenarios he didn't quite have time for. All their energies appeared to have been wasted inside the pyramid to date, with no grand weapon capable of destroying a god in evidence. What they had most likely found though was a path to . . . somewhere. The consensus was that it housed the realms of the Nepharii gods, although Cappitus thought such a destination unlikely. Gods were fickle entities at best from his understanding, popping up in droves in some cultures, whilst others paid homage to a few. From the sophisticated nature of the Nepharii, he doubted they ever needed divine inspiration. If anything, the figures depicted at his feet were the varying forms of the Nepharii, for he attributed them with god-like powers. Yet even he felt himself questioning such a conclusion.

To complicate matters, young Jarred, the boy who previously offered insights beyond their wildest dreams, had nothing to say concerning the golden bridge. His silence was most unusual, and Cappitus feared he knew something, but couldn't quite grasp its meaning. That, or he couldn't interpret the signs.

He took long strides to where the *Nefarii Uranometria* sat, its discs still revolving, the hour glass recording the time. In little more than an hour-and-a-half the inner ring would move once again, this time bringing the segment containing the eagle-headed figures of Enlil in line. Only now the golden bridge was solid, connecting the sphere with the path, waiting for some brave soul to cross on purposeful feet.

'I'll go,' the voice was clear, resonant. Cappitus spun to see his old friend, Ruvin, standing with his back straight.

'The Hell you will!' Cappitus snapped. 'I need you here, for your expertise is second to none.'

'There is nothing here for me, old man. I'm a Seeker of the Brotherhood,' Ruvin gestured with a hand towards the golden bridge. 'This is what I do, my friend. I seek the unknown. You know I'm the best there is.'

Cappitus sighed as he heard his friend's words. He knew the Seeker spoke truthfully. Whatever was occurring here, they needed a clearer picture. Too many questions were being left unanswered.

'If it is a portal, as you and I believe it to be,' Ruvin continued, 'then I should be able to travel through and back again in a short amount of time.' Cappitus saw him sweep his gaze towards the contraption. 'I have more than an hour. I can do this.'

Another sigh escaped Cappitus, but he saw a smile stretch across Ruvin's weathered features as he placed a hand atop the pommel of his sabre. 'I can protect myself, you know.'

'I know, old friend,' Cappitus said, 'and I wish I could walk beside you.'

'No, I'll do this alone.'

'You'll not even take Declan and a handful of Swords?'

'No, we don't have time, and I'm not intending to stay for long.'

'Then go and be quick. I want you back as soon as possible. I needn't explain to you how important this journey will be. Whatever lies beyond will either be cause for celebration or cause for fear. My instinct tells me the latter.'

He watched Ruvin nod in understanding and clasped hands with him. The Seeker then offered a short bow to the assembled elders watching silently to the side. With a slight adjustment to his belt he walked the path and crossed the platinum discs until he stood before the inner ring. On the other side sat the golden bridge, fashioned by light but mysteriously solid.

Cappitus watched as Ruvin paused and sucked in a lungful of air, then walked with purpose across the span. A flash of light flared then Ruvin, Seeker of the Brotherhood, was no longer amongst them.

*

Tarsin felt the air blast out of his lungs as he fell backward. He hit stone, hard, then rolled left, putting distance between himself and his adversary. The thud of a large object hitting the ground alerted him to how close the creature was, and in desperation he jumped to his feet, his sword poised for battle.

Then he blinked, clearing his vision of the blinding white light as he saw the golden ellipsoid to his right, its gentle hum almost soothing. Beyond the ellipsoid was open sky, azure tinged scarlet as a foreign red sun crested barren plains. The soft touch of a warm zephyr caressed his bloodied face, promising heat like he'd never experienced before. Sweat already beaded upon his brow as he quickly stepped back to observe his surroundings.

'Anok and Eli!' he called, but he knew no god of his would heed his call.

A growl was the only response he received as the demon that followed him crouched with blade at the ready.

Tarsin met its yellow eyes and saw the hunger residing there, could almost feel the lust. He didn't know where it sprung from or why it wanted him dead. For a moment, he believed the fell beast to have been summoned by Avra, come now to finish the task she began back in Benwith. If that were the case, where was he now? He certainly wasn't in Dervae. And if the beast wasn't one of Avra's minions, why did it want him dead?

He took a deep breath, tasting heat as it scorched his throat. Sweat ran in rivulets down his face, dripping from his bloodied nose. He couldn't believe how hot it was, couldn't tell if the blood-red sun was rising or setting. He felt all alone, standing on stone blocks a world away with his father dead and his city a ruined heap. Now a witch and her Dark God were close, apparently intent on killing his people. Whichever way he looked, Death seemed to be glaring back at him with a sparkle of recognition in his eyes.

Only Tarsin wasn't prepared to die; at least not yet.

He slid his left foot back and shifted his weight so that he was evenly balanced. Then as the demon rose to its considerable height, he raised the tip of his blade to point directly at its eyes. A flick of his wrist prompted the demon to step forward and engage.

The demon's sudden rush was exhilarating.

The clear call of steel striking steel pierced the air as the two combatants twirled, their blades whipping back and forth as they sought to find an opening in the other's defence. Tarsin kept his footwork controlled, adjusting to a rhythm he'd not encountered before. The demon was large and strong, its shoulders broad, the sweeping arc of its blade tremendous. To counter such an advantage, he needed to step within the demon's range, duck under its heavy swings and force the beast to defend repeated short, sharp thrusts to its midsection. The danger here was the demon's greater size and strength, as he'd found out the hard way when backhanded earlier. But now he was prepared, focused, fighting in a foreign land with nothing to lose but his life.

He stepped up his attack, his blade deftly working low then high, forcing the demon to keep changing its balance. Being large and strong had advantages, but Tarsin knew he could fight all day, even in the stifling heat. Three years in Al-Za'im had conditioned him to such extremes.

A wicked snort escaped the demon as Tarsin sliced his blade across its snout. The demon was tiring, its heavy shoulders slowing as its breathing became ragged. Blood splayed across its torso, crimson red against pale scales. Tarsin stepped up his attack, his sword-work quickening until it was almost a blur of silver light. Sweat drenched his body, but his mind was oblivious to the sensation, his reasoning masked. The fight had become not one of survival but one of anger, and the beast crumbling before him was bearing the brunt of his pent-up aggression. Three clawed fingers sailed through the air with a carefully timed sweep of his sword and a howl of pain escaped the demon before its head slumped and it fell to its knees. The sound of its fallen blade as it clanged against stone was enough to bring Tarsin back to his senses. He ceased his furious attack and stepped forward to place the tip of his sword under its chin, forcing the beast to look him in the eye.

'What manner of creature are you?' he asked with a raspy voice, his eyes maddeningly wide.

The demon returned his look before shifting its gaze to the left. Tarsin followed its line of sight to see a horde of demons crouched not sixty feet from where he stood, staring at him with baleful eyes. Like the one he fought they were attired for battle, leather straps and cured hides covering their arms and bellies, a few even wearing caps of steel atop their scaled heads. All wore kilts of boiled leather studded with metal and rings, and wide blades rested at hip or shoulder. They were of differing colours, their scales verdant green to vibrant orange, scarlet and indigo and even brilliant blue. At first glance, he guessed there were close to a hundred present. As he returned their gaze they flared their nostrils and bared their fangs, and in that moment Tarsin felt all hope vanish.

His momentary lack of concentration almost cost him his life.

The demon before him lunged, a needle-like dagger plucked from its belt screaming for his abdomen, its silver point shining. Instead of attempting to step out of harm's way Tarsin swivelled to the side and brought his sword down with a sweep, then lifted his knee high. The sword took the demon's arm off at the elbow, gouts of hot sticky blood rushing forth to spill across the stone, whilst the knee cracked into its head, shattering bone.

The demon fell to its side, its yellow eyes now vacant.

With his heart still rapidly beating Tarsin spun to greet his new threat.

He looked across rusty grass to where the demons crouched. They hadn't moved; their expressions were unchanged. He didn't know whether to laugh or cry. Felt like doing both. He took a deep breath as he focused on what occurred, then wiped sweat from his eyes as he risked a quick glance of the land.

It was . . . vast. He appeared to have arrived atop a hillock affording him a view over a barren plain. The soil was sun-blasted, dry and parched. A grey-green smudge on the horizon suggested plant-life of some description flourished, yet close to where he stood was little more than corroded grass growing in large clumps. The only other sign of life was the crouching beasts. They hadn't moved, remained a group of silent, scaled flesh that looked ready to pounce. Behind them, if he wasn't mistaken, the sun was beginning to set.

He looked back at the ellipsoid of gold; knew he needed to step back within its light. He couldn't risk being here after dark. His only concern was whether the assembled demons would follow. He prayed they'd remain, but instinctively knew they would not. The ghost of Arkos mentioned the depths of Bastion would awaken. Now he knew what his king meant.

Tarsin turned to glance once more at the demons before stepping towards the ellipsoid. He was about to place a foot within when a flash caused him to raise a hand to protect his eyes. A second later a dark shape fell his way.

'Ruvin,' Tarsin couldn't believe his eyes. The Seeker blinked, as Tarsin had earlier, then stood upright.

'Tarsin Va?' Ruvin said, by his tone bewildered. 'What in Aston's name . . . where are we?'

'No place pleasant,' Tarsin grabbed the man's shoulder and spun him to look at the waiting demons lining the grass. They remained where they were, but their eyes were beginning to hunger. He couldn't begin to understand their culture, but he felt they waited out of respect. A duel had been fought, a fair one by all accounts, but curiosity was causing some to become agitated.

'Hells Fury!' Ruvin swore as he spied the horde, then diverted his gaze to the dead beast lying only feet away in a pool of blood. After a moment of curious inspection, he returned his gaze to Tarsin, and the swordsman could tell by his wild look that he noticed his bloody face for the first time. 'You killed it?'

'I had no choice; it attacked me in Undercity. We fought, then fell into this glowing . . . thing, and ended up here.'

'It's a portal,' Ruvin's eyes were wide, and Tarsin knew he was attempting to remember all he could about their location. Tarsin watched as his eyes traced the horizon, noting the bloated red sun hovering above barren plains. Ruvin then took note of etched stones at his feet forming a pattern about the golden ellipsoid. Wiping sweat from his forehead Tarsin caught his concerned look. 'We need to return, now,' Ruvin said, his voice fearful.

Without another thought Tarsin used his sword to steer Ruvin back a pace, casting a wary eye towards the demons at the temple perimeter. A number crept forward, watching, fangs dripping saliva as blue tongues flicked forth to taste the air. Not one to tempt fate, Tarsin quickly grabbed Ruvin's arm and stepped back into the portal.

*

Ra'tor could taste blood on the wind. So too could his brood, who were becoming increasingly impatient with his inactivity. Every one of them had seen the mysterious creature with the dancing blade cut down one of their own, only to be joined by another. Despite his age he was speechless as to who they were and where they'd come from. Pale skinned and heavily clothed, they appeared weak and insignificant. But Ra'tor saw with his own eyes how deadly they could be. The one clothed in blue steel had been quick and nimble. He wondered if the creature was a god.

For if he was not, who then was responsible for the golden ball of light shining from the temple dais.

He unclenched a mighty clawed hand, aware of a dull ache in his shoulder, his muscles tight. He rolled his arm over his head in a vain effort to lessen the pain. The brood took it as a sign to race forward and examine the kill. Ra'tor let them, content to

327

watch, knowing his wisdom would be needed in the coming days. Cerato, Storm Lord of the Highborn and magister of Varos, had spoken to his subjects of a coming change. "Ill winds of cosmic origin have swept our world, brethren," he had said, "and those who would seek to harm us will appear when we least expect them." The words sounded of nonsense a moon ago, now they seemed eerily prophetic.

Ra'tor snorted once, remembering how surprised he and his brood were. Until yesterday they'd been involved in a hunt as they tracked the large mountain wolves they knew frequented the area. Now the temple of Unifying Light, once a solid, primal place of worship, lay in ruin, its facade having crumbled to reveal . . . what exactly? No-one knew, least of all the Patriarchs who now dithered amongst the fallen stones. To excite the masses further, an ellipsoid of golden light appeared amongst the ancient dais within, pulsing brightly to attract their attention. It was enough to distract his brood from the hunt, an event, he recalled, that had never occurred before.

'Do we share the blood?' He'd walked towards the temple, his clawed feet stepping atop the ancient stones. With narrowed eyes, he looked down to see Tysta flicking his tongue from side-to-side.

'Do you believe it right for us to do so?' Ra'tor asked in return, his voice a hiss.

The bloodling stretched his neck as he thought, and Ra'tor noticed for the first time that his purple scales were finally brightening to a deep copper. From adolescence to maturity took twelve cycles amongst the Deios. Tysta's maturity was closing fast.

'He fought with honour,' Tysta's teeth clicked, 'and he did not show fear. So yes, I believe the sharing of his blood would be accepted by the One.'

Ra'tor nodded his large head, his yellow eyes blinking his agreement. Tysta turned and moved towards the fallen Deiosian, clearing a way for him to follow. He reached the body to find a perfect circle of twelve in attendance. They stepped aside to allow him space to inspect the deceased.

The wounds Shyxt suffered were numerous and deep. Arterial blood, thick and black had pumped unhindered onto the stonework, and slashes about his face, shoulders and torso had sliced scale and flesh with consummate ease. Ra'tor reflected on the dead Deiosian's journey, a journey whose duration was far from complete. But then he knew Shyxt's reckless nature was bound to catch up with him one day. Ra'tor stood to his full height of seven feet after his inspection, stretching his heavily muscled shoulders and arms. His emerald scales shimmered as he turned to address his brood. 'Share the blood,' he commanded.

A couple of Patriarchs jostled to the front and began to administer lines of blood to the young and eager. It was a ritual steeped in lore from the *Beyond*, a period of existence so far back that only primal urges of such actions remained. One-by-one the Deios crouched, their heads bowed to allow blood to be smeared across their cranium. Death was never far from the Deios, and to carry the blood of one who fought valiantly was an honour.

Ra'tor moved away from the ritual. He needed no blood to survive in this world, for he was old, his emerald scales already kissed with gold. At best, he would live another score of years. At worst, he would be challenged and killed by a Deiosian from another brood.

Thoughts of fighting another of his kind were fading by the minute, though. An enemy had appeared before their very eyes, sleek of movement, bold. What Shyxt was doing at the temple he would never know, but he saw him die at the hands of someone, and god or not, the Deios would fight to protect their own. Honour dictated they should do so.

Tysta walked towards him and sat on the edge of the temple stones, his clawed feet scraping against the smooth rock. For the first time Ra'tor noticed faded patterns etched into the rock's surface, faint, as if eroded by the hot winds of time. 'I feel empowered,' Tysta grinned, his sharp teeth glistening. 'The blood is good.'

'It is good,' Ra'tor also smiled. He liked Tysta. He had an energy, a vibrancy often missing amongst the young. Too many remained cautious these days. Mind you, Shyxt displayed the same energy and now he was dead.

'So,' Tysta said with a hiss as he looked to the blood-red sun sinking to the west. It left a smudge of indigo to light the sky, light enough for the Deios to still see by. 'Do we continue our hunt?'

'We do,' Ra'tor said, 'only not here.'

'Then where?' Tysta looked confused.

'Through there,' Ra'tor pointed a clawed finger towards the golden ellipsoid still pulsing atop the dais. Even from where he stood he could hear the gentle hum emanating from the oddity. 'Honour demands we seek retribution for the death of one of our brood. No matter who stands in our way, be they god or not, we shall see justice done.' He clenched a heavy fist tight and closed his yellow eyes as he thought of what lay ahead. He would need help, he was certain, and there were several broods close by who would heed the call. 'I do not know what lies beyond, Tysta, but we are hunters, one-and-all. It is time we sharpened our blades.'

Tysta fidgeted atop the ancient stones, his eyes seeking the swirling, golden oddity. 'What happens when justice has been served?' he asked.

'Then we shall drink their blood,' Ra'tor replied. 'Honour demands it.'

CHAPTER TWENTY-TWO

Reefe cursed and spat as Donal let out a wail of grief. Tarsin had disappeared with the demon-beast, thankfully, into the golden light. No-one knew if he was dead or not, or whether some foul witchcraft was at play. Griffith paced like a caged bear, grunting and swearing, his warhammer, *Bloodstain*, swinging back and forth. Even Vittorio seemed agitated, which he took to be a sign of displeasure at losing his mark.

Then there was Kayla.

An almost silent whimper was quickly silenced as she fought to hold back tears. A hand covered her face to shield her eyes from the golden light, but she didn't falter as he believed she might. Perhaps her proximity to Tarsin earlier wasn't all it was made out to be. Mayhaps he still had a chance at winning her hand.

He thought quickly, a trait he wasn't particularly adept at, but one he was finally beginning to harness. Derrick Tolsten wanted Kayla kept alive and clear of danger. Whatever just transpired was clearly dangerous, possibly fatal. Instinct told him to run back to the Underlord and report their findings. As Tarsin had yelled before he vanished, others needed to know what was occurring down here. He could act as herald and save Kayla in the process. Given time, she may remember the deed as heroic and view him as a man of valour.

'We need to leave,' he raised his voice above the hum permeating the room. He at least expected a response from those gathered, but all he received was silence apart from Donal's sobs. He raised his voice higher, 'I said we need to leave!'

'Damn you if we're leaving!' Griffith growled back as he circled the ellipsoid. He looked as if he was about to jump into the light.

'He's gone, Griffith, finished. There's nothing more we can do here,' Reefe looked to Vittorio, hoping the assassin would listen to reason, but Kayla pushed past him to stand beside the armoured Griffith.

'Has he gone?' Kayla asked, placing a hand on Griffith's forearm to stall his pacing.

Griffith shook his auburn mane, 'No, he can't be, not Tarsin. There is more to him than meets the eye, Kayla. His life will not end like this. I'll not allow it.'

Reefe saw him take a step towards the light, his face bathed in gold, his armour shinning like a star fallen from heaven. For an instant, he appeared like a crazed incarnation of Terros: the god of war. It was frightening.

'Don't go, Griffith,' Kayla pleaded, 'what if you can't come back?

'I'll not stand here wondering,' he snapped. 'He needs me. I should be by his side. I owe him that much.'

Reefe hoped the big man would go. It would be one less to deal with on the road back to Undercity. He briefly considered walking forward and giving him a push.

Before he could act the portal flickered and two dark silhouettes materialized within. A moment later they stepped out of the light and into the circular chamber side-by-side.

Reefe's shoulders slumped as he saw Tarsin. And instead of the demon-beast by his side it was some grey-haired old man, his face pallid as he gripped the hilt of his sabre.

Seconds passed as everyone exchanged a look before the swordsman spoke, 'We have a new problem,' Tarsin lifted a hand to wipe blood from his nose. 'We need to leave . . . now!'

*

Neema walked with a purposeful gait, her patchwork cloak now replaced by the white robes of her order as she pushed her heavy legs up the red staircase. Aston's Tear still pulsed brightly as she approached the marvel. Its silver-blue light was welcome for the streets of Bastion were dark this early, their corners unlit and uncannily silent considering dawn was no more than an hour away. So many people had died in the past couple of days and so many more lay buried and irretrievable. Those who survived were battered and bruised, their morale low, their minds frayed. Many were at a loss as to why such a catastrophe occurred and

Neema knew nothing she said could provide clarity. Many blamed the gods, expressed their doubts with raised fists and harsh words. But the Dervani gods were false, mere figments of a kingdom's imagination. Either that or they were the archetypes of the one true God; nothing more than his differing moods and personalities. She didn't particularly care, for she'd stopped believing long ago. Aston and Sybis, Anok and Eli, Isha and Eos; and who could forget Hell and Terros. The Eight, they were called, strong gods for a strong people, governed by Frey, goddess of Fate and the Four winds.

Neema knew they were not responsible for the destruction, nor could they prevent the calamity. If they existed at all, they did so merely as observers.

Yet the one true God did exist. He was known as the Great Consciousness: the Universe in its unfathomable entirety. It was He Neema believed in, for He was life.

Yet there was another god now by the name of Ahriman. Neema had doubted his existence to begin with, scoffed at the idea when Cappitus first sought her counsel. It was no secret the Celestial Sisters and the Brotherhood of One differed on a great many things. As much as both Orders professed knowledge of the one true God, their beliefs were never aligned. A symbiotic relationship between the two orders was desperately sought when they were founded, but animosity quickly severed whatever whimsical ties they'd established. The Brotherhood sought knowledge, believed it was the only path to God. The Sisters followed a different mantra, though, one based on nurturing life in all its forms. Hence conflicts between the two were a common occurrence over the years, and at her behest the Brotherhood were monitored both within and without. For she feared the path the Brotherhood trod. Knowledge, in all its forms, was a dangerous proposition. Avra herself followed a similar path all those years ago.

Only now, with the emergence of Ahriman: god of Chaos, doubts in her own beliefs surfaced. If there was only one true God, then where did Ahriman fit in?

The answer remained elusive, much to her chagrin. As the months passed and Cappitus' insistence intensified, she succumbed to the knowledge of Ahriman's existence. As she focused her eyes to the heavens for answers, she came to realize who he really was. He was god-like in his power, it was true, but when comparing the Dark Lord with the Universe, there was no comparison. Ahriman was merely a shadow of the Great Consciousness, a sinister thought, perhaps nothing more than a discarded nightmare.

He wielded power, though, power far beyond anything man could replicate; power enough to destroy an entire kingdom.

Neema wondered now as she made for the pyramid's dark entrance what succour the citizens of Bastion could expect. They were distraught and discouraged, and those who remained to loiter about Aston's Tear clutched at false hopes from fabricated gods. What future awaited her people now? Where now was the spark of life?

Neema didn't know, couldn't offer any words of wisdom or uncanny insight to any who asked. She'd already spent the better part of the night tending the wounded and consoling the emotionally distressed. As much as elder Cappitus proclaimed answers would be forthcoming, the Celestial Sisters were concerned more with aiding those who survived. Finding a solution to all their immediate problems was pointless if the population ceased to exist.

With troubled thoughts Neema stepped into the square corridor and walked its brazier-lit length after a nod from the two brothers standing guard. They were weary-eyed, yet their shoulders remained square, their gauntleted hands resting atop the pommels of their unsheathed swords. Neema could see the strain in their eyes, though, saw it as a reflection of her own.

She reached the main entrance to the Forever Chamber and stepped inside the enormous, hollow sphere, before turning about to scan the door from the inside. She'd placed wards of power across its breadth before leaving the night before, more as a precaution. The words of young Jarred had frightened her the previous day. The lad knew things she deemed impossible to know, but she couldn't refute his words nor disbelieve his hypothesis. On closer inspection, she'd found him to be possessed, although it was like nothing she'd ever witnessed before. Apart from excessive sleeping patterns and the occasional fever, he appeared to be coping rather well. What did alarm her was the entity, or entities, residing within the young man. She didn't know if they could come and go as they pleased or were fixed, firmly entwined about Jarred's soul. Therefore, she'd created a set of wards to monitor any unusual ethereal activity, placing them at the only entrance to see what passed during the night.

With a deep breath Neema knelt beside the door, pulling a small vial stoppered with cork from her voluminous white robe. With her eyes neatly shut, she opened and then tipped the contents into her mouth, forcing herself to swallow the bitter brew. A spasm shook her prodigious frame, her numerous chins jiggling from side-to-side. Then she opened her eyes, fixing her gaze on a spot not far from the floor. She found the pattern of light she sought, then traced its length to the doorframe's opposite side. Then she followed the lines of power back and forth in the hope of discovering what magical entity, if any, passed in the last twelve hours.

What she found was completely unexpected.

She traced her lines of power once more, double checked the emanations still present. Then she moved further to the side, looking back at the wards from a different angle so she could see the image of the intruder clearly defined. It confirmed her suspicions and justified her fears.

She pursed her lips before cursing under her breath.

Neema took a step back as she thought about what she'd discovered. There was a problem here, a problem greater than first perceived. With a visible shake in her body, she lifted her eyes to seek out elder Cappitus. He was easily recognizable; his tall, thin body stooped over someone's shoulder as he peered down at whatever piece of information they'd brought him.

Behind him sparkled the golden sphere, spinning slowly, whilst further back a thousand stars provided an incredible backdrop. Then an unusual flash of gold caught her eye and held it. It was barely glimpsed, a sudden flare of pure light between black robed figures. She focused on its location and saw it again. With tired arms, she pushed herself to her feet and walked across the spanning bridge to where Cappitus and a handful of the Brotherhood conversed.

'Neema,' Cappitus saw her as she crossed towards him and held a hand high.

'Elder Cappitus,' her voice was subdued as heavy thoughts crowded within. Then she focused on the elder, only to see his face drawn tight. There was something amiss here, something not quite right. 'What have you done?' she asked before he could speak.

'I . . . I'm not sure where to begin,' he looked over his shoulder, too afraid to meet her eyes. She traced his line of sight; saw him peer at the golden sphere.

'Then start at the beginning,' Neema replied.

He nodded slowly, his white beard scraping against his black robes. He motioned her forward and walked towards the sphere. She watched as those Brothers surrounding the Portal to the Gods stepped back. When they did she saw with her own eyes the golden bridge connecting the platform with the portal.

'What is it?' she asked with a husky voice, although she knew as soon as she opened her mouth what it was.

'A bridge,' he replied, 'although where it leads we have no idea; at least not yet. Our best estimate suggests another world, but we'll know soon enough.'

'What do you mean?'

He sighed heavily, placing his hands into deep pockets by his side. 'We sent Ruvin Ciricello into the portal,' he finally said. 'When he returns we shall know what lies beyond.'

'How long has it been since he left?'

'More than an hour,' he nervously glanced at old Fratelli. 'I had hoped to see him return by now.'

'What of the golden bridge,' she asked, waving a hand towards its location, 'how long since its manifestation?'

She watched him shake his head and count a handful of numbers on his gnarled fingers. 'It has been solid for no more than an hour, but its existence began a couple of hours prior to that.' He looked down at her, his eyes narrowed. 'Why would the timing of its existence be of interest?'

Neema's pudgy hand grabbed a fistful of his robe, dragging him close. Then she whispered in his ear so no other could hear. 'I placed wards across the entrance before I left last night,' she began, 'more as a precaution than a whim. But someone cloaked with spells of concealment passed them several hours ago. I need not spell it out to you who that someone was.'

'Avra!' Cappitus hissed the name.

'Aye, the very same.'

'Damn me for a fool,' the elder spun on the spot, his fingers clawed, his nose scrunched tight. She could see the anger surfacing, briefly wondered how dangerous the old man could be if pushed to the edge. She knew he was powerful. She just wasn't sure *how* powerful. He eventually calmed himself down and tapped a finger to the side of his head. 'How long ago did she enter?'

'The emanation of her passing was weak. I'd say six or seven hours at least.'

'The bridge did not exist back then.'

'No, but the sphere was here. Avra has dealt with portals before; she'll know what she saw.'

'Maybe, although there is a chance she hasn't fully grasped what it is we have before us.' Neema heard the words but knew even Cappitus didn't fully believe them. 'What is it?' he asked.

'You *hope* she doesn't fully understand what lies before us, but if she does . . .'

'What . . . what new danger could she possibly pose?'

Neema sighed, and it appeared her form deflated as she did so. 'Ahriman is by her side, Cappitus. If she enters here with the Dark Lord, how many souls do you think he may have at his fingertips? What strength will he garner with twelve extra worlds to plunder?'

'Hell's Fury!' Cappitus flinched as he grasped the connotations.

*

The sound of stones crunching underfoot heralded someone's approach. Avra peered into the gloom from her seat, not bothering to rise. If the man who approached was the one she expected, she would show him no courtesy. In fact, he would be most fortunate to leave unscathed. It all depended on whether she could contain her anger and frustration.

His shadowy form stepped forward, bowing under a leaning pillar as he walked into the room. She smiled a wicked smile. She no longer resided in the city's north, bunkered underground with only the dead for company. Now she took residence in an abandoned villa in the eastern quarter, only a stone's throw from Irongate and even closer to the pyramid Aston's Tear. The relocation had been necessary, not only due to the instability of her former retreat, but for the distinct purpose of being able to reconnoitre Bastion's central district. The pyramid was now a gathering place for all those who survived, and those in power were utilizing their skills to organize a city on its knees.

'You're late,' she said, holding the black stub of a candle in a frail hand. 'I thought I asked you to be here by midnight, Vupello?'

The Captain of the Palaceguard shrugged. Avra could see hard lines and dark rings about his eyes. Like many in Bastion, he looked as though he'd barely slept the past two days. 'Your messenger did not reach me until well past midnight, Avra. I've been scouting Highcastle with my men, searching for our king.'

'How goes the search?'

'Not well, I'm afraid. The outer curtain wall collapsed and finding a way into the inner courtyard took time. Once we did gain entry we were met with another obstacle.'

'What was that?' she snapped.

Vupello peered at his dirt-stained boots, usually polished bright. 'The remains of half a mountain barred our path, sealing the throne room completely. It will take weeks to hammer it clear.'

'We don't have *weeks*, Vupello, we have less than a day!' Her impatience was palpable. 'I thought you mentioned your men would find the king for me?'

'I did,' he said, 'only it's difficult to complete a task when you're dead. Their bodies were found before the King's Plaza. They never reached Highcastle to begin the search.'

'Who killed them?'

'Impossible to say with certainty, although my guess would place Griffith and the man known as Tarsin Va as the two most likely responsible.'

Avra sunk back into her chair. The man before her was next to useless, despite his fearsome reputation. He might be able to wield a sword with uncanny precision, but when it came to practicality and resourcefulness, he was found wanting; which is why she'd taken matters into her own hands. Empowered with her own dark energy, she'd morphed into the guise of a Celestial Sister and slipped into the pyramid's bowels.

What she saw within the chamber was astonishing and having summoned creatures from planes other than her own, she knew a portal when she saw one. Only this portal was powerful beyond comprehension, controlled and precise. Her only thought right now was how to steal the contraption and utilize its magnificence.

She diverted her attention back to Lucius Vupello. 'Men of the Unseen killed your knights, you say?'

'Yes, it appears to be the case.'

She mused over the words, remembering her attempt to eradicate the assassins sent by the cowardly King Arkos. She was aware a handful escaped, but not knowing their identities she found finishing them off an arduous task. Besides, the attempt on her life had been foiled. She found more interest in offering the souls of the Unseen she *had* captured to Ahriman. It was so nice of Arkos to send such worthy men.

'Where are they now, these men of the Unseen?'

'I believe they're looking for Arkos still. We did not see them at Highcastle, but they may have found a way in. When they surface, we'll take them, including the king.'

'Provided Arkos is still alive,' she added. 'If he is dead, I'll be most disappointed.'

She watched Vupello straighten his back. 'His death could hardly be construed as my fault, Avra. It was your god who shook the earth, not mine. If you have a grievance, it's not with me.'

He was right, she knew, but how could she chastise a god for being overzealous. Ahriman craved the flesh of the living and would do all in his power to accomplish such an end. He knew a king was needed for the final rite, and a king he would have. Only she yearned for Arkos to be under her sacrificial knife, not some . . . other. Still, if Arkos was to die, Vupello would be destined for the altar. It was why she'd originally coveted his services. He was her contingency plan. If all else failed, his sacrifice would suffice.

And although she knew his death would never be as gratifying as that of Arkos Vantos, she would enjoy it all the same.

'Is there anything else?' Vupello asked as he looked over his shoulder. She could see the night sky tinged with blue behind him. Dawn was not far away.

'Yes,' her tone was commanding, 'I want those men of the Unseen dead by day's end. I'll not have such dangerous swords so close. Should they catch wind of my presence here in Bastion, matters could become complicated.'

'Surely the esteemed Avra is more than a match for mere swordsmen?' A faint lift of a lip hinted at a condescending smile.

'Watch your tongue, Lucius Vupello, lest I cut it out and feed it to my Dark God.' She saw him take a step back, the hinted smile vanishing in the blink of an eye. 'Go now and complete your task. I want Arkos, and I want the Unseen dead. Do not fail me.'

'I promise you, Avra, you shall have that which you desire. In return, I'll have my city and the kingdom of Dervae.'

Avra nodded once as he offered a short bow and then spun on his heel. As he passed out of the room and into pre-dawn murkiness, she leant over and hoisted the *Sawolegere* into her lap. She stroked its surface, her frail fingers tingling as raw energy sparked at her touch. 'Did you hear his words, my lord?' she spoke softly, timidly, 'by day's end we shall have the king. He promised. And if he lies, we shall have him instead.'

*

Donal did his utmost to keep pace.

They'd left the circular chamber in quick fashion, Tarsin introducing Ruvin, Seeker of the Brotherhood of One, as his new comrade once he stepped out of the golden portal. The man was older than Griffith, possibly mid-fifties, but his thin frame and tied-backed grey hair lent him an air of confidence. Yet even he appeared flustered after returning from the unknown. The men, especially Griffith, thanked various gods as they stepped from the illuminated dais, but it was Tarsin who ushered them with fervour out of the chamber, citing a need to be well clear as soon as possible.

'What did you see? Where did you go?' Griffith was full of questions as they hurried over fallen brickwork.

'I saw a world that was not our own,' Tarsin said with all seriousness, 'with a blood-red sun and heat shimmering across barren plains. It was hot, hotter even than Al-Za'im.'

'What of the demon,' Donal heard Reefe shout from the rear, 'what became of it?'

'I killed it,' Tarsin said as he peered back over his shoulder. In the dim light of the torch Donal could see the red welt across Tarsin's cheek, the dried blood below his nose. Donal was no expert, but he assumed they fought ferociously.

Hopping over an uneven section of floor Donal fell in behind Kayla who led the party back the way they'd travelled earlier. She knew the tunnels and corridors, knew the sewers and cisterns as well as anyone apart from himself. But then he knew he was

341

different to everyone else. From an early age, he'd acquired a knack for reading and writing and most of all, observing. Somehow, unexplained to him so far, he could recall all that he saw and heard. Many said it was a gift from the gods, although he couldn't recall that experience. He simply saw things differently and memorized those events.

Now, having travelled with the swordsman Tarsin and his large friend Griffith, he was beginning to feel not only overwhelmed by all he had seen, but frightened by the situation. He was a very smart lad, the Underlord had told him so, and his mind couldn't simply shut itself away from what he'd seen but felt obliged to probe for answers. Right now, as he scampered behind Kayla and watched her long legs eat up the miles without pause, a thousand questions swirled within his head, clamouring to escape.

A sound to his left caused him to turn his head. He saw Ruvin smile as he reached his side, before offering to take hold of the lantern he carried. It flickered as he passed it over, and for a moment he felt a sense of relief to suddenly have both hands free. 'Where did you come from?' Donal asked, his voice barely more than a squeak.

'Aston's Tear,' Ruvin replied, 'from inside the pyramid. There is a portal there, twenty times bigger than what you saw in the chamber we just left. I stepped into it, found Tarsin on another world, and now I am here.'

Donal watched Kayla wade through calf-high water and swish across a small expanse before stepping onto higher ground. Two entrances gaped ahead, one leading left, the other right. Kayla chose left. It was the correct passage. 'So why are you with us in the tunnels beneath Bastion and not back in the pyramid?'

He saw Ruvin shrug, the action causing the lantern's light to drift. 'I've been asking myself the same question, lad.'

'So, what are your thoughts on the matter?'

A smile caused Ruvin's eyes to squint. 'Many and varied,' he said, 'and better left to men who crave such conundrums. I'm a Seeker of knowledge, boy, and an astute observer. Having said that, I believe the sphere in the pyramid is the power source, with a number of lesser sources of power surrounding it serving as pathways between . . . whatever or wherever we went.'

'I've seen three other circular chambers like the one we left.' Donal had no regrets telling the man what he'd stumbled across in the wee hours of morning. The earthquake had opened great fissures in the ground, causing some tunnels to be sealed off, their walls unsafe, whilst other walls tumbled to reveal hidden avenues in the dark, lost secrets now laid bare. It took him no longer than half-a-day to find his way about an area previously inaccessible. The wonders there were mimicked here, except for the shining golden light. 'They contained no portal, though,' he said as Ruvin helped him up a flight of slippery steps.

'From what I have observed in the pyramid's chamber, I've a feeling the portal is operational for two hours at a time. Then it moves along to another, and so on. There are twelve different segments, suggesting twelve different destinations.'

'Two hours!' Donal heard Tarsin's voice from behind. 'You're telling me that portal will remain open for two hours!'

'Less, now, obviously; perhaps an hour,' Ruvin appeared certain of his claim. 'There is a ring surrounding a sphere within Aston's Tear. Twelve segments are etched about its perimeter, changing every two hours. The one currently before the sphere is fearsome looking, I might add. It looks like a man with the head of a dragon.'

'The creature was definitely fierce. Only I have never seen a dragon before to compare,' returned Donal.

'No, neither have I, but there were creatures in the past who once roamed our world,' Ruvin answered. 'We have fossilized remains at Irongate, some incredibly large.'

'What does it all mean, old man?' Reefe had fallen in behind Tarsin, and Donal could see Vittorio's shadow skulking only a few feet away. He could hear Griffith's trudging and the clink of his mail but could not yet see him.

'It means we need to keep up the pace,' Tarsin beckoned them all to keep moving. 'I may have slain a demon on the other side, but at least a hundred others sat not sixty feet from where I stood.

They are like nothing I have ever seen or fought. They are strong, and they are quick. I want you to fully understand what I am saying when I tell you few men could stand alone against such creatures and live.'

'But you fought one,' Reefe sneered, 'and you are still alive.'

'Aye, but I'm the best there is, Reefe O'Bannon, and it will take more than an overgrown lizard to bring me down. You, on the other hand, would not fare so well.'

Donal saw Reefe stiffen at the jibe, his eyes narrowing, his breathing deepen. The flickering torch added an evil cast to Reefe's features. 'I'm a more than capable swordsman, I'd have you know.' Donal could see Reefe's hand flexing near the hilt of his sword.

'Capable, yes; deadly, no,' Tarsin replied. 'Only killers can hope to stand against such beasts.'

'Are you saying I'm no killer?'

'I'm saying exactly that, Reefe. If you doubt me, draw your sword. I promise you, you'll last less than a minute if you cross blades with me.'

Donal could read Reefe's face like an open book. First the glare of hostility and resentment, then the realization of Tarsin's honest words. It took him time, but eventually he moved his hand away from the hilt of his sword. He knew Reefe better than he did himself. He may not be a-great-many things, but Reefe was a survivor who liked to keep his skin intact.

Seeing the situation defuse itself, Tarsin continued. 'If I'm any judge, we may have more than a hundred beasts swarming these tunnels any time soon. I doubt they'll take kindly to seeing one of their own slaughtered before them. I saw lust in their eyes before we left.'

'He's right,' Ruvin added, 'never have I seen their like. If you think the demon he slew was impressive, trust me, there were others taller by a foot and more savage than you could imagine. I also doubt they'll sit idle. They are hunters, killers; beasts attired for battle. It will only be a matter of time, but eventually they will seek us out.'

'What happens when they do?' Kayla stood within the mouth of a tunnel, darkness behind her.

'When they do,' Tarsin repeated, 'they'll come for blood.'

*

A bright flash followed by a slight dizziness completed his passage through the portal. Ra'tor stood on cold stones, his feet firmly planted as he waited for the vertigo to pass. It took only seconds and then his eyes adjusted, his pupils expanding in the shadowed chamber. He narrowed his eyes and peered about the room. It was circular, and a central dais bloomed with golden light at its centre, the door-between-worlds he'd just stepped through. A score of his brood were already spread before him, searching their surroundings, sniffing the stale air. By the looks of it, there was very little of interest. It was also cold.

Sensing no danger, he walked towards a group of Deios flicking stones from a pile and saw another chamber beyond. 'What have you found?' he asked.

The Deios bowed in deference as he approached. 'Nothing of substance,' the Deiosian who spoke rose to his full height of seven feet. His name was Rax't, and his frame was almost as intimidating as Ra'tor's. 'There is an unusual stench emanating from the passage,' Rax't indicated the dark opening. 'The creature's smell,' he slid out his tongue, 'you can taste them.'

Ra'tor followed suit, his tongue darting out to taste those who were previously here. It was faint, certainly, but it was unmistakably there. There was also something else, a mere trace that set his nerves firing. 'I can taste blood,' he said.

The rest of the Deios nodded, knowing his words to be truthful.

He turned towards the door-between-worlds, not understanding how it came into being, or why, only that he'd been given an opportunity to hunt. When Bhral, the Blood-god, sent you a sign, you followed. It was that simple. Ra'tor was wise enough to follow; only he would do so in number. Tysta and another, Ryv'k, had been sent to find other broods. They would explain to them what had been found at the old temple and remind them of the importance of following Bhral's wishes. Ra'tor was confident they would come. Within an hour he hoped to have three hundred Deios in these tunnels. Within a week he dreamed of having thousands. It was an ambitious assumption but one he knew to be right. One of his kin had been openly slain by an outsider. Now they sought revenge.

He was shaken from his reverie as Rax't placed a large hand on his arm. 'Do we hunt?' he asked, his voice a hiss. Ra'tor looked over his shoulder; saw the yellow eyes of his brethren burning with anticipation. They were hungry, and they could smell blood. He thought of waiting for the other broods, it would be wise. They were in a foreign place, on an unknown world. For all he knew there could be thousands of the pale-skinned creatures waiting just around the corner.

But the Blood-god had sent them, and if there was one thing Ra'tor trusted above all else, it was He.

'We hunt!' he snarled, his ivory teeth, so long and sharp, reflecting the golden light. 'Gods or not, we know they bleed, and I have a taste for flesh and blood!'

A deafening roar greeted him, shaking the very walls so that dust and mortar sifted from the domed ceiling, a noise so loud it carried half-a-league down twisting corridors and half-submerged tunnels before it reached a small group of men, a woman and a boy.

The noise, when they heard it, chilled them to the bone.

CHAPTER TWENTY-THREE

Tarsin cursed as he slipped on the wet floor, a hand slapping hard against the bas-relief of a man with bull-like horns protruding from his skull. It was an eerie visage, dimly seen in the corridor they travelled, but it was apparent enough to cause him concern. Every new turn they took revealed some grotesque form chiselled from stone, larger than life and powerfully built. He didn't know who they represented, or why their forms were so prevalent, but it was easy to assume the Nepharii were responsible.

Tarsin pushed on, sloshing through ankle-deep water, his feet sodden. Dark and damp, he yearned for the light of day to bathe his face. It felt like an eternity since he'd last felt the cool touch of a wistful breeze. Down here in Undercity, life was beginning to become more than a little claustrophobic. It was also becoming rather crowded.

'I can hear them still,' Griffith's voice cut the air like a knife.

Tarsin risked a backwards glance at his friend, several feet behind him, last in line. Griffith's breathing was rapid, the air whistling past his lips as he drove his body forward. Heavy armour weighed him down, his gait ungainly as he powered forward as quickly as able. For a man so large, Tarsin thought Griffith's effort admirable. He knew the big man would also feel the need for clean air and room to stretch. The surface of Bastion couldn't come quick enough.

And the demons weren't far behind.

The first roar they heard had been deafening, shaking the walls until Tarsin believed they would collapse. Young Donal froze at the sound, too frightened to take another step. All Donal could see were dark passages and long corridors surrounding them, shadows crawling back and forth, always at the edge of their torchlight. Now the sound of scraping claws and blood-chilling roars echoed below, their source difficult to judge, causing confusion and disorientation. The boy felt Death's fingers snake about his throat.

In the end Tarsin ordered Reefe to pick the boy up and carry him, kicking and screaming if he must. One thing they couldn't afford was to waste precious time. Tarsin knew the beasts were behind them. Their only requirement was to keep pushing towards what Kayla called Thieve's Retreat.

From what he could gather the retreat was the Nocturnal's hideout, a series of rooms and hallways all interconnected and able to accommodate a thousand men, women and children. The Underlord, Kayla's father, kept his council chambers and private study within hailing distance of the abode, a place he and Griffith had already graced with their presence. Kayla pressed towards the retreat now, moving nimbly through the passageways as she sloshed past sewer pipes and drains dripping filth.

After an hour of scampering through sodden halls the sound from behind became infinitely louder, the roars more frequent as the beasts closed in on those who fled. If they didn't find the retreat soon, panic would overtake them before the beasts surely did.

'How close are we?' Tarsin gasped as he reached Kayla's side. She'd stopped at an intersection, waiting for the group to catch up, her breathing ragged. Donal sat at her feet shaking like a leaf, whilst Reefe doubled over as he sought to catch his breath.

'At the end of this corridor we'll reach a series of steps,' Kayla panted, 'then a ladder leading to a chamber above. Once through the trapdoor, it's a short way to an elaborate arch. Pass through and we're in the great hall named Thieve's Retreat.'

'How long to travel this corridor?' Tarsin looked down its dark depths.

'If we run hard; ten minutes.'

A deep sigh from Griffith was the only response. Tarsin looked at his friend. He carried his warhammer slung over one shoulder, a rucksack containing the king's crown, his twin swords and other oddities over the other.

'Here,' offered Tarsin, reaching out to take the sack, 'I'll lighten your burden.'

'I can carry it,' Griffith said with a grimace.

'I know you can, but if the beasts catch us, you'll need hands free to swing your hammer. You're last in line; they'll reach you first.'

Griffith nodded and passed him the sack. Tarsin then took a second to appraise the corridor they were about to flee down. It was wide enough for three men to walk abreast, just wide enough for Griffith to swing *Bloodstain* if pressed.

'Let's go,' said Kayla, moving once again. Reefe picked Donal off the wet floor and urged him to run. The rest followed.

Behind them the sound of claws scraping against stone stalked their very thoughts.

No more than five minutes later, half way to the steps Kayla promised at corridor's end, the thump of a heavy body sounded against a solid wall. A screech, high-pitched and sinister, chased their heels.

'They're behind us!' shouted Griffith, still bellowing as he ran.

'Move it, people!' Tarsin added his voice to the din. Blood-curdling screams echoed behind them, drowning the sobs of a terrified Donal.

They ran, their single lantern lighting the way as they fled down the tiled corridor, its bas-reliefs now a blur. It seemed they ran for an eternity before the steps came into view, but when they did, Kayla scampered up like a cat, quick and agile, followed by Vittorio and Ruvin. The older man was labouring, one hand pressed tight to his chest, his eyes wide with fright. Reefe climbed next, Donal's hand holding his. At the top of the steps sat a ladder, its bottom rung five feet from the floor. It climbed for nearly twenty feet before it reached a trapdoor. Tarsin waited for Griffith before he began his ascent, and by the time he did, Kayla had pushed open the door above and was crawling through.

'Come, Griffith, we're almost there.'

Without a word, he ushered Griffith before him, forcing him to climb the ladder. As the armoured man's boot stepped off the bottom rung, one of Tarsin's hands reached for it, the other grasping the sack. He climbed, his eyes tracing the dark path of the corridor as he watched for any sign of the demons. A moment later he reached the top rung and pulled himself through the hole. He moved with haste and slammed the trapdoor shut. Before he did so, a set of yellow eyes glared up at him.

'Run!' he said, looking for a bolt to lock the trapdoor. There was none, and nothing of substance to keep it closed. Everyone apart from Griffith had fled towards a great arch, a sculptured piece of exquisite beauty and flowing design. Any other day he would have stood and admired its composition; its flawless lines, its elegance. It was a delicate piece of work sculptured by delicate hands, but right now it was his only egress. Beyond, he could see milling men and women: the thieves of Bastion, his companions running into their ranks with flailing arms and warning shouts.

The trapdoor behind him shattered into a dozen pieces as a clawed arm slammed against the wood, sending shards and splinters flying in every direction. Tarsin's sword hissed free as he passed the sack to Griffith and urged him to flee. The big man did as bid, heeding the orders of his Captain. One step saw Tarsin reach the trapdoor and then his blade swept down to slice across a scaled face. The beast screamed in pain, its clawed hands reaching for its eyes. Without a thought Tarsin stomped a boot atop its head, forcing the beast to fall into darkness. He then turned about and ran.

He passed through the arch and saw a well-lit hall, lanterns hanging from wall brackets revealing a quadrangle, a flowing fountain within a circular basin at its centre. A painted canopy curved above, doming the area beneath. He crossed towards the fountain, its tinkling water subdued by a cacophony of raised voices. Lord Derrick Tolsten strode towards his daughter whilst behind him walked Jack Boyd and his Shadow Brethren. They were armoured in chain and wore long swords at their waist, as silent as their leader was boisterous.

'What in Hell's name is going on?' Tolsten barked.

'We need to evacuate Undercity,' Kayla raised her voice, so everyone could hear. Reefe immediately began ushering those standing around open-mouthed towards the exits on the far side.

'Beasts spawned in Hell have been snapping at our heels,' she
said, 'and if you stand here any longer, you'll see them yourself.'

A roar answered her proclamation, accompanied by another
from beyond the archway.

'Aston preserve us!' Tarsin heard an elderly woman utter, a
finger tracing a protective symbol in the air. She looked to where
Reefe sent others scurrying towards the exits and made to follow.
Lord Tolsten moved to stand before Kayla, his Shadow Brethren
drawing their swords.

'Is what you say true?' he asked, disbelief in his eyes but
caution in his words.

'It is, father.'

'What of the king?'

Kayla shook her head. 'We need to move,' she pleaded. 'The
beasts are here, and they are fearsome. Never have I seen their
like. We must flee to the surface, tell the Brotherhood what we
have seen,' Tarsin saw her look over his shoulder. She stiffened,
and for a moment he believed they'd arrived. As he turned he
saw not the scaled hide of a towering beast, but the huddled,
petrified body of Donal pressed up against the outside of the arch.

'Donal!' he yelled, seeking his attention. The boy looked his
way, his eyes glassy even from this distance. The sight brought
distant memories back to haunt him.

Before he could wave the boy forward the sound of heavy feet
preceded the arrival of three demons charging into the hall.

They were seven feet tall and scaled bright red, each wielding
a huge cleaver that swung back and forth. Ivory fangs glistened
in the faint light as they cast baleful eyes about the room.

'Gods above!' several voices yelled at once.

Screams of fright rent the air as men and women saw the
powerfully scaled beasts with their sharp teeth and flexing claws.
Hurried footfalls slapped against tiled floor as they beat a hasty
retreat, heading for stairs that lead to the surface above. Tarsin,
his sword still bloodied, moved towards the three in a hope to
draw their attention away from young Donal. Yet as he strode
towards them he felt himself no longer in the Undercity of

Bastion. For Tarsin, all he could see was young Salim standing on the docks of Al-Za'im, a black clad assassin with a silver dagger at his throat. Dust swirled about him, the heat was oppressive. Grit lined his mouth. He clenched a fist about his leather hilt, testing the balance of his sword. Shouts of fear and caution assailed him, but all he heard was the sapping song of a summer breeze. He couldn't help Salim from the assassins, for an expanse of water barred his way. But here, now, he stood only thirty feet away from his antagonists. Blood surged through his veins, causing them to swell. He felt invigorated. He was strong, powerful. He was lightning.

And so was his sword.

He crossed the thirty feet in an instant, in silence, his mind focused. The demons spun to face him, tongues flicking to taste the air, yellow eyes wide with anticipation. Behind them stood Donal, not five feet away. They raised their cleavers: heavy weapons capable of cutting a man clean in half, and fanned out, putting distance between each other so they could swing their arms wide.

A moment later Tarsin hit them like a tornado. He ran straight towards the first in line, his blade snaking out faster than the eye could follow as it dived for the beast's throat. A heavy blade sought to halt its plunge, but it was too late, for the tip of his blade sliced through scales and flesh and sank deep to sever the jugular. A quick twist of his wrist saw his blade slice out the side of its neck, hot blood arcing across the room to splatter against pale tiles. Then he was moving, ducking a vicious blow aimed at his head, pirouetting, side-stepping and deflecting another with a sharp clang of his sword. He was a whirlwind of movement, his anger evident as revenge fuelled his mind. The demons never stood a chance. Two lightning thrusts saw blood bloom another beast's chest, then he spun behind to send a reverse cut into a hamstring. A second later he twirled to face the remaining demon, his sword clanging against steel in quick fashion, its razor-sharp edge sparking blue-fire as it beat against its blade. The beast fell back, its snout raised towards the ceiling as it howled in pain from half-a-dozen cuts, Tarsin's sword repeatedly piercing its defences. A brief pause followed as yellow eyes sought him out before Tarsin ran in and lopped off its head.

Silence descended across the hall.

He flicked his blade to send ruby droplets of blood to the floor, then raced towards Donal. He bent and picked him up, then slung him over a shoulder before moving back to where Lord Tolsten and his men stood in shock.

'Move now if you intend to live,' he was done being tactful as he placed Donal on the floor.

'Are there more of the beasts?' asked Tolsten, still shaking his head at what he'd just witnessed.

'Another hundred at least,' he caught Griffith and Ruvin's attention, signalling for them to leave. 'There are many larger than the three you saw just now. I'll not lie to you Lord Tolsten, they are formidable. They won't be easily killed.'

The old man looked to his Shadow Brethren, judging their strength. He knew their character, had no doubt as to their devotion. 'We'll stay and hold them,' he said, 'my knights and I.'

Tarsin counted, 'You've half-a-dozen knights, Tolsten. You'll not stand long against such odds.'

Tolsten nodded agreement. 'I know, Tarsin, but we'll stand all the same. My people need time to flee. You need time to flee. Besides, more of my Shadow Brethren will heed the call when it is made.' He looked towards Reefe who stood alone, still breathing hard. 'I see you made it back alive, lad.'

Tarsin saw Reefe's confusion, his face blank. Then a spark of enlightenment pinged behind his eyes. Like the rest of the men, he'd been startled as Tarsin raced towards the beasts, more so when he saw him kill them with such efficiency. 'I . . . I guess I didn't do anything too stupid whilst I was gone,' he said.

'Then you're still of use,' Lord Tolsten beckoned him forward. 'Go now and round up what remains of the Shadow Brethren. Tell them their Underlord calls.'

'Yes, my lord,' he bowed, backing away, and then raced towards the exit.

'Will they come?' Tarsin asked.

'As fast as they're able,' Tolsten's tone suggested he expected nothing else. 'Sixty of my finest blades will be here. We'll hold them long enough for you to escape.'

'Why?' Tarsin asked. 'Why not flee with us?'

'I am leader down here,' Tolsten explained, 'and as such it is my duty to protect. I took the lives of six men yesterday. You saw me do it. They were evil, vicious men; men of violence and hatred. Yet I murdered them, murdered them for the perceived benefit of Bastion. Now, it seems, it is my turn. Now *I'll* die for the benefit of Bastion.'

'It doesn't have to be this way?'

'It does, Tarsin. These are the choices we make. Hard choices made by hard men. It is the way of things. Arkos knew it, which is why he made such a great king. As a life-long friend of his, I'll sacrifice my life to do the same.'

'I'll stay by your side if you'll have me,' Tarsin said, feeling a kinship with the older man.

'The hell you will!' Tolsten scoffed. 'They'll need you above, boy. I've seen you fight. With Arkos dead, there will be few who can lead. Gods, man, nearly all our forces are south or at sea.'

Tolsten was right. Not only was Bastion teetering on the brink of an abyss, she was practically helpless. Apart from Griffith's Sceptres and four score Swords of the Brotherhood, there were few seasoned soldiers ready to heed his call to arms. Bastion had lost her king and her dignity, it seemed. If they weren't careful, she could soon lose everything else.

'Besides, you need to see my daughter to safety; I'll not have her lost down here in the dark, and you're the best damn swordsman I've ever seen. I'll trust her safety with no-one else.'

'I can take care of myself,' Kayla said, but she moved closer to Tarsin's side as she spoke the words.

'I do not doubt you, daughter, but this is life or death we're talking about.' The sound of boots hitting hard against the tiled floor caused them all to turn. Black clad knights began to pour into the room, a score at least, the first Shadow Brethren to heed Tolsten's call. 'Well done, Reefe,' he said quietly, before turning his attention back to Tarsin. 'Go, lad, we'll buy you time.'

Tarsin tilted his head and offered his hand. They gripped tight and shook before parting ways. Tarsin then headed towards the surface with his group, whilst Tolsten took a moment with his daughter, planting a solitary kiss on her brow to send her on her way before moving to stand with his knights. As Tarsin passed under a doorway, another roar sounded from beyond the arch.

He instinctively knew that whatever occurred in the great hall, it would happen soon, and it would be bloody.

*

Lord Derrick Tolsten heard the roar reverberate within the hall. Two-score of the demons, terrifying to behold, had entered via the archway, their tongues flicking from sneering maws as they sensed spilt blood on the tiles. They slowed to a walk, their clawed feet clicking, their massive weapons hanging limp at their sides. The sight of three of their own lying dead had stalled their mad rush. Choice words were spoken in a tongue alien to Tolsten, rough, like the splintering of rocks accompanied by a scraping hiss. There was little chance of him understanding their words, but the connotations were obvious. The feral glean to their yellow eyes intensified as they appraised Tolsten and his gathered knights. Little more than thirty men stood huddled together, grossly outnumbered and undersized. The beasts bunched huge shoulders and flexed heavy arms as they prepared for the onslaught. Sharp teeth clanked together with ominous bearing.

Tolsten watched as they advanced; his mind clear, his thoughts somehow peaceful. What he'd told Tarsin had been the truth concerning the Pillars of Bastion. They were evil men, men without a conscience, without heart. He expressed no regrets concerning his order to have them killed. If anything, he wished it had been finalised sooner. It was to have been his final task in Undercity.

Yet the Pillars were canny, as deceitful men seem to be. Gathering them all in one place had been difficult to near-on impossible. Only the sudden destruction of Bastion had seen them muster in strength. It was to be their final act of camaraderie.

Now, as punishment, it seemed, Death was staring him in the face in the form of a demon.

Tolsten drew his sword, the long blade sighing as it slipped from its sheath. His newly arrived Shadow Brethren followed his lead, and the hall sang with the hiss of steel. Tolsten found himself remembering the words he spoke to Tarsin before he left. "Hard choices made by hard men", he'd said, and it was true. He was adamant a weaker man would listen to his conscience and seek an alternative. In the process, his mind would offer conflicting scenarios, express doubt, possibly even fear.

In doing so, the enemy would gain an advantage.

As the first of the demons strode towards him with a blade held over a shoulder and a snarl showing teeth as long as his index finger, he wondered if they were truly evil or simply following some animal instinct. He would have liked to believe they were more beast than man, but the armour they wore: the kilts of hardened leather embossed with steel and the assortment of bracers and greaves told him otherwise. As he locked eyes with the enormous leader, he saw intelligence residing within.

For Tolsten, it made his final stand all the more worthy.

'Gentlemen,' he said as the demons began to race across the hall, 'now is the time and this is the place. You have served me and my family well. Now let's send these demons back to whatever Hell spawned them!'

The men matched the beasts with a roar of their own as they stepped forward, the clank of steel and booted feet a precursor of things to come. The charge followed a second later, the clash of bodies deafening. Scaled flesh pounded into the line of knights, swords rose and fell, and gouts of crimson splashed through the air as men fought like savages and demons fought like men. Tolsten raised his sword to block an overhead swing, his knees buckling under the force of the blow. A heavy fist smashed into his face, causing blood to pool in his mouth and his eyes to water. He felt himself fall back, knew his time was up. Death had come calling and it appeared he was in a hurry to do business.

A clawed foot came crushing down on his leg, snapping bone with force. Tolsten howled in pain, dropping his sword to clutch his knee. Despite the agony he managed to peer to his left, spent several seconds watching his men fall under the brutal attack. They were no match for the demon warriors. Half their size and outnumbered two-to-one, their bodies were being carved in two, their blood splattered recklessly about the hall. How Tarsin killed three was inconceivable. Perhaps the answer would become clear when Death finally claimed him. A dark shadow spread over his prone form and he looked up. A scaled lip curled back to reveal glistening teeth arranged in a smile; mirth, or possibly hunger, evident in the creature's eyes. A clawed hand reached for his throat, lifting him off the floor like a child's straw doll. Fetid breath stung his nostrils as his face was brought close. He cringed as foreign words were whispered in his ear. The noise was grating, corrosive. It was the sound of death.

Silence descended within the hall. His men were dead, their bodies strewn in ungainly fashion, butchered to the last. He couldn't tell if any of the beasts succumbed. He knew there wouldn't be many. He struggled to breathe, could feel the life being choked from him. With his last strength, he looked the beast in the eye, only to see its deadly maw open wide to envelope his head.

A tremendous grinding sound was accompanied by splintering bone as Lord Derrick Tolsten's head was crushed, the skull finally popping with a squelch as gore oozed from numerous cavities. Thankfully, like the rest of his loyal knights, he was already dead.

*

Lucius Vupello rode his horse through the streets of Bastion, Jaegar, son of Jorgun, riding beside him. Three men of the Palaceguard followed, their armour no longer shining bright, their countenance suggestive of their tumultuous past days. It was early morning, the sun desperately trying to pierce the ashen pall hanging over Bastion with minimal success. The city was in mourning, he knew, shrouded in darkness and no longer vibrant. He wondered if becoming king was now such a great idea. It was never meant to happen like this. His ascension was to have been an impressive step as he replaced a grief-stricken Arkos Vantos. Now he led his horse past cracked and broken streets towards a fallen plaza, the few citizens he saw staring blank-eyed, their spirits shattered like the city they called home. Braziers smoked as pots of oats bubbled on the side-walk, battered folk holding small wooden bowls in trembling hands as they waited to break their fast. It appeared only the weak, old and stubborn had chosen not to flee. He couldn't help but think there was nothing left for them here. In fact, there was little to entice even the most ardent of citizens. Yet here he was, holding on to his dream of being king, hoping for a future of promise.

Lucius knew the future he'd envisioned was far from reality. He could sense the nagging thoughts surfacing: of deceit and lies, of undermining family and friends, of compromising his integrity. He was no longer a man of honour; he doubted he'd *ever* been a man of honour. Yet he'd always dreamt of being king.

He shook his head, aware it was too late to change tack now. He was in too deep. He'd promised the witch, Avra, she would have her king, and he feared crossing her, feared disappointing her. He knew the power of her curse; had been witness to several of the Unseen's demise. Better for him to do his task and then decide his future. He could always walk away from the city and travel to Anthos and set up court. Bastion was far from finished, but she needed a great deal of work before she'd be named Holy City again. Now, she was simply the Fallen City.

A scream sliced through the morning air, cutting through the early heat of day like a sliver of ice. He found his hand gripping the pommel of his sword and saw Jaegar reach for his axe.

Another scream echoed the first, crisp and clear, followed by loud shouts and panicked voices.

'What trouble brews this early in the morning?' he held a hand above his eyes.

Jaegar shrugged his broad shoulders, and Lucius knew that was all the answer he was likely to receive. The Herkosian was generally not his best in the wee hours, a habit stemming from his uncontrollable urge to drown his sorrows each evening. What ailed him he did not know, but it was a recurring nightly routine. If he thought it difficult to pry words out of his mouth when he was sober, it was practically impossible after a night of drinking. For the briefest of moments, he wondered where the barbarian had even found a flask of wine.

'Look,' Lucius pointed towards a leaning, half-timbered building where a handful of shadowy figures disgorged onto splintered pavement. Their number continued to increase; men, women and children running out of the structure and away, fleeing along the clearest route available. 'What do they run from?' he asked, looking to Jaegar.

The barbarian narrowed his eyes, but his face showed no sign of enlightenment. The three Palaceguard moved their horses alongside, and for several minutes they simply sat and watched as the exodus continued. Finally, the movement of bodies ceased.

Lucius kept his eyes peeled. He was interested to see what caused so many people to flee in panic. He hadn't felt another tremor, but it didn't mean the building was safe, either. The sound of crashing masonry was forever prevalent since the earthquake. Every few minutes another building toppled to the ground amongst billowing dust and broken stones. It was feasible the half-timbered structure was groaning even as they walked towards it.

At least he thought so until another group of figures exited onto the street.

There were six of them: four men, a woman and a boy. For an instant, they raised arms to shield their eyes from the morning sun, looking about them in bewildered fashion. It was a curious gesture, one he found of interest until he noticed the hulking frame of Cale Griffith at the rear. A quick inspection revealed Tarsin Va beside him. The woman, apart from being attractive, was unknown to him, likewise the boy. That left a brother robed in black and another attired in similar fashion.

'Vittorio!' he cursed as he saw the assassin. 'I thought you said he was the best,' he accused Jaegar as he swept a furious look towards his companion. 'His orders were to kill both Tarsin Va and Cale Griffith, were they not?'

'They were,' Jaegar spoke begrudgingly. 'Maybe he'll do so now.'

Lucius couldn't see how the assassin could be so brave, not in the open, unless he had the help of others. Without a second thought he urged Strom across the broken ground, Jaegar's horse a step behind him. He'd remembered the words of Avra, knew now was the time to deliver. 'Well, well,' he said as he sat atop his mount, his eyes fixed on Tarsin Va, 'if it isn't the vainglorious bastard we've all heard so much about.'

The first movement he saw was Tarsin's hand drifting towards the hilt of his sword. 'Lucius Vupello,' the swordsman replied as he stepped to the front of the group. Griffith eased his bulk alongside, whilst Vittorio surreptitiously moved to the side.

'We've been looking for you two,' Lucius said as he noted their ragged appearance and Tarsin's blood-stained armour. 'I know Owen Moor was looking for you a couple of nights back. You didn't by chance happen to run into him?'

'We saw your man,' Tarsin's face was blank.

'And ...'

'And we dealt with him. But then you already knew that, Vupello,' he watched as Tarsin wiped sweat from his brow. 'Is there anything else, or shall we be on our way? I'm tiring of this conversation.'

'Really, and what of the king, Tarsin Va, did you find him? Where is Arkos when Bastion needs him most?'

'King Arkos is dead,' Lucius saw Tarsin motion towards Griffith and the sack he held. The big man threw it to the ground before Tarsin leant over to rummage through its contents. When he rose, he held Arkos' golden crown in his hands.

Lucius dismounted in quick fashion, one hand holding the reigns to his horse, the other beckoning. 'With Arkos dead,' he licked his lips, 'the crown now belongs to me. I am next in line for the throne.'

'Not while I'm still alive,' rumbled Griffith.

'You'd deny the rightful heir to the throne, fat man?' Lucius spat, anger flaring. The three knights of the Palaceguard dismounted to stand beside him, along with Jaegar. Griffith and Tarsin were formidable, it was certain, but they were two men against five. Six if Vittorio played his hand; and it was obvious they were unaware of Vittorio's intentions. Unlike Owen Moor, Lucius respected the men he now faced. And unlike the former knight, he feared no man with a blade. 'Give me the crown, Tarsin Va, and bend the knee. If you do so, I may let you live.'

Griffith swung his warhammer from over his shoulder, resting the heavy weapon in his hands. At the same time Jaegar likewise loosed his battle axe. The scrape of three swords being drawn told him his knights were ready.

'I don't have time for this, Vupello,' Tarsin's tone was flat, his face devoid of anger. He looked like a man who didn't care. 'If you want the crown, take it,' he tossed it high, and Lucius watched its flight, saw the feeble rays of the sun strike its golden surface. It shined bright, despite the gloom. At the last instant, he flashed out a gloved hand and caught it.

'With this crown, I am now king of Dervae!' his face was alight with the promise of power as he admired the golden circlet. It was heavy in his hand, but at the same time reassuringly comfortable. He could do this, he *could* be king. He *would* be king.

'With that crown, you are nothing. A crown doesn't make a king,' snarled Tarsin.

'Says you, bastard!' Lucius sneered. 'You'll bend the knee, or I'll see you dead.'

'And who will you send to strike me down?'

'A king need not raise his sword in retaliation. He has other means, secret ways unseen by lesser men.'

'Really,' a smile crept across Tarsin's face. 'Who do you have at your disposal?'

Lucius laughed and drew his sword, flourishing it in a wide arc before settling it on the assassin now standing by himself, well clear of Tarsin and Griffith. 'Allow me to introduce Enrico Vittorio, gentlemen, an accomplice of mine and an assassin by trade.'

A crooked smile teased his mouth as he heard the woman's sudden intake of breath. She looked towards Vittorio with frightened eyes, clutching the young boy tight. He laughed out loud, saw her back away and head down the ruined street in fear. The old brother in his black shirt followed her, his sabre now in his hand as he stood protectively by their side.

'You see, all is not as it seems, and a king, even one newly crowned,' he paused to place the golden circlet on his head, 'commands greater respect and reverence than you could possibly imagine.'

With the crown set firmly atop his head, he watched as Vittorio unstoppered a small vial and began to sprinkle an oil-like substance across his unsheathed sabre. It was the potion Avra had given him, which he in turn passed on to the assassin. One scratch, Avra had said, was all it would take to incapacitate a man. Then you could do with him as you wished. Tarsin might be rumoured to be the greatest swordsman in Bastion, but with the assassin lined against him, chances were high he would be struck, even with Griffith by his side.

'As I said earlier, Vupello, I don't have time for this,' Tarsin kept an eye on Vittorio's movements, 'take your crown and be gone. Be a king, for all I care, just let us be. We have business to attend.'

'Oh, I'll be king, have no fear on that count,' he smiled before taking a step closer to the swordsman. 'As my first act, I believe I *will* have your head.' He felt the smile broaden his face even as he felt the tension in the air. It was tangible. He could almost sense a storm cloud coalescing overhead, a clap of thunder imminent. He licked his lips, moistening dry skin. 'When you're ready, gentlemen,' he finally said, exchanging a glance with Jaegar and the assassin as his Palaceguard spread wide to either side.

'Kill the bastard!'

Enrico Vittorio paused to look at the grey sky, his face feeling the sun's gentle touch even as it sought to pierce the clouds. The warm caress heightened his senses, invigorated tired muscles. It soothed his soul. For a split second, he forgot about the tumultuous flight from Undercity, forgot about the scaled demons with their heavy blades and glaring, yellow eyes. He shifted his gaze to the broken street and watched as dust swirled in lazy circles, caught by a zephyr that refused to let go. Gone now were the sounds of a prosperous people living a life of order and structure. The streets were practically deserted, devoid of life. Bastion was now a city lost, a scarred shell, a remnant of her former self. There was nothing left to govern, little to salvage. If Lucius thought to be king, he'd be a king ruling nought but ash and stone.

'Kill the bastard!'

The words were said with venom, Lucius' order issued with hatred at its core, his mouth frothing with anticipation. Vittorio considered his wild eyes and saw madness radiating unchecked. He was sufficed with power, the crown on his head gleaming in the feeble light. He could see Lucius wasn't about to relinquish his hard-won gains.

For a moment Vittorio sought to place the hatred. He'd never heard of any feud between Lucius and Tarsin, but when it came to men with swords and reputations, little was needed to cause sparks to fly. Both men were at their peak, efficient, deadly. Few men in Bastion would be foolhardy enough to cross Lucius, but then Tarsin wasn't like most men. He certainly wouldn't cower from an encounter.

There was also the matter of the Rykedian broadsword Tarsin carried. It would rest nicely by Lucius' hip should Tarsin be vanquished. Many would covet such a blade, more than the crown, in fact. There was certainly an upside to killing Tarsin Va.

The scuffle of feet swung Vittorio's head towards Tarsin and Griffith. The brother, Ruvin, had moved to their side, his sabre gripped tight. His face was stern, a mask made of stone. It appeared he would stand with them, fight alongside the two warriors. Vittorio expected nothing less. Behind him stood Kayla and Donal, crouching in the shadows of a crippled building, fearful and tear streaked. After all they'd endured, the light of day wasn't about to offer any respite.

Vittorio returned his attention back to his blade. Shimmering oil snaked along its length, the light refracting into a multitude of colours, almost hypnotic in its simplicity. The mere thought of being struck with such a poisoned weapon was unnerving, would send fear to burrow deep into the psyche where it would plant the first seeds of doubt. One scratch was all it took to render a man helpless, for him to lose all articulation, to become nothing more than a slab of meat lying on the ground. It took away a man's dignity, stole his right to fight, to challenge for his life. No swordsman would choose to die in such a fashion.

Vittorio lifted his eyes to see men with naked blue steel standing in a street bathed red. It brought memories flooding back from a time of fear and loathing. Reminding him of what he'd lost, reminding him of what he'd always feared to lose.

His mind drifted to recall another time and place. He could smell muck as it clung to his boots. It was thick, cloying, but the stench was the last thing on his mind as hands lifted him off his knees. There was scant light to see by, merely the flickering orange glow of a sputtering torch lying on the damp floor. He could make out the tall frame of John Rhys as he stooped beside him.

'Gods, man, where are we?' he said the words as he gazed about the pit, seeing mirrors staring back at him everywhere he looked. Then realization hit him.

'Come,' John Rhys waved him forward, 'we need to rescue the others.'

Vittorio looked over his shoulder and saw Tarsin Va and Cale Griffith surrounding Marcos Santelli, the man's arms almost embedded up to his elbows in the mirror before him. They were about to lift him out as he spun to see John Rhys move to someone's side. He trudged a few feet to help him, then saw the man was no other than Vincent, Enrico's younger brother, the man he'd vowed to protect.

He mimicked John Rhys and stepped to Vincent's side. He'd fallen to his knees, his hands firmly plastered amongst the muck. But his head had slumped to fall into the mirror, completely encased within its magical entrapment.

'What do we do now?' John Rhys croaked.

'We grab his shoulders and pull him out,' Vittorio replied. 'Let's do it fast, use all your strength.'

John Rhys had nodded his head, and with a quick look behind to see Tarsin and Griffith doing the same for Santelli, they yanked young Vincent Vittorio from the ensorcelled mirror with all their might.

The blood from a headless corpse bathed them red.

Vittorio blinked back tears as he watched Lucius step forward, his sword leading towards Tarsin's throat. He acted instinctively and stepped quickly to smash his own blade hard against that of the self-proclaimed king, knocking it down before reversing its motion to slice the tip of his blade across his cheek. A crescent of blood appeared as the newly crowned madman stumbled back in shock.

'What in Hell's name!' he shouted, his free hand clutching his face.

'Back away, Lucius Vupello,' Vittorio's voice was soft, barely more than a whisper. 'It is you and I, now. You have much to answer for!'

'Traitor! I'll have your head for such insolence.' He flicked blood from his gloved hand and lunged, his sword snaking towards Vittorio's chest. The assassin beat a hasty retreat, his sword clanging against Lucius' continued thrusts as he sought to push his sword out wide. A horse reared in the background, its hooves flailing in the air before bolting down the street. All but Lucius' horse followed in quick succession. 'Damn it, Jaegar,' the mad king screamed. 'Kill them!'

Vittorio gave himself space as the tall Herkosian hefted his heavy battle-axe. To his right Tarsin drew his Rykedian broadsword in one smooth motion. Then the three members of the Palaceguard moved forward to engage. Within seconds the sound of steel rang clear and vibrant, followed quickly by the dying groans of butchered men.

'Anok and Eli!' Vittorio heard Lucius curse as he stood back to survey the carnage. All three of his knights were down, Tarsin and Griffith having dispatched two, the other falling under the heavy axe of Jaegar. Vittorio saw Ruvin standing firm, but his eyes were constantly shifting between Jaegar and himself.

'Stand down, Lucius,' Jaegar said with his heavy Herkosian accent. He stood over one of the Palaceguard, his axe-blade bloodied, the man's chest ripped open despite his protective breastplate.

'Frey's Luck, Jaegar, what are you doing?' The madman's face was etched with confusion.

Jaeger's tattooed head tilted to the side, his blonde-braided beard unable to contain his mirth. 'I'm rejoining my Captain,' he said with his rolling northern accent.

'Your Captain?' a shadow of doubt swept across Lucius' face, his eyes narrowing.

'Aye, apart from Admiral John Rhys, we four are all that remain of the Unseen,' Vittorio smiled as he watched Jaegar point towards Tarsin, Griffith and himself. 'Tarsin was our Captain.'

'He still is,' shouted Griffith, 'and we need to move, Jaeger, for Death approaches. We're running out of time.'

Vittorio moved to stand before Lucius, now all alone, his kingly aspirations in tatters. He may have crowned himself king, but he had no loyal subjects to call his own.

'You'll pay for your insubordination with your lives!' Lucius cursed, his eyes wide once again, his mouth flecked with spittle. A twitch creased the corner of his mouth and Vittorio wondered if the poison was taking its toll. He'd cut him once across the cheek already. It was a minor scratch, but it was enough. 'I'll cut your god-damned hearts out and slam your heads upon spikes!'

'No, you won't,' Vittorio spoke calmly, his sword held out straight, its tip level with Lucius' wild eyes. He stepped forward a pace, his sword leading. 'Instead you'll pay for your crimes against the Unseen. You betrayed us, Lucius, sold us out to the coven in Benwith. Now you'll die.'

The cousin to the late King Arkos swung to stare at the assassin. 'Do you seriously think you can best me with a blade, traitor?' he sneered as he flicked his sword to clang against Vittorio's.

Vittorio shared a quick glance with Tarsin, only to see him nod ever so slightly. He was giving him this chance, giving him a chance to put Vincent's death behind him. He looked back at the madman crowned king, said words he truly believed. 'I know I can.'

He lunged, seeking to catch Lucius off guard. His sword pierced the air, screaming for his face. At the last instant Lucius faded back a step and slapped his own blade hard against his own, sending the plunge wide. A quick riposte saw Vittorio hastily lower his blade to point vertically towards the ground, sweeping to block three well timed thrusts. For several seconds, the ring of steel sounded like a clarion call from some monk's belfry, splitting the morning silence with harsh ferocity and tempered regularity. Back and forth they stepped, their foot work beating a steady staccato against the cobblestoned street, as both men sought an opening. The duel was fierce, the tempo frantic. If Lucius felt the poison burning into his cheek he masked it well. Vittorio hoped its onset would be soon, though, for Lucius was pressing hard, his skills sublime. Without administering the poison, he doubted he could best Lucius Vupello. From what he knew and now experienced, very few could.

He swatted aside a calculated lunge and hastily stepped forward, crowding in close to Lucius as he pushed his blade high. The move was dangerous, and he expected the slice across his shoulder before it even landed. At the last moment, he ducked to his right and presented his left shoulder high. Vittorio winced in pain as the sword bit deep but held his nerve and brought his own sword up to plunge through chain mail and into Lucius' stomach. The two men were close, laboured breaths fouling the air between them. Raw hatred bled from Lucius' eyes as he stared down at Vittorio. The assassin grinned, even though his sliced shoulder felt aflame, blood already trickling from his fingertips to fall upon the dust covered stones at his feet. With a grunt, he planted his foot against Lucius' stomach, next to his blade, and withdrew it with a squelch.

'Dangerous move . . . assassin,' Lucius gasped as he sought to stem the blood flow, 'next time . . . I'll take your head.'

'There won't be a next time, Lucius,' with an effort Vittorio stood tall as the newly crowned king stumbled back in a desperate bid to keep his feet. He then watched the man's sword fall from nerveless fingers to clatter against the cobblestones. Seconds later he slumped forward, his hands barely lifting to halt his fall. He walked over to where Lucius lay, incapacitated, literally unable to move a muscle, blood blossoming beneath his fallen body. Vittorio knelt to wipe his sword with the man's cloak, then whispered in his ear. 'Rot in Hell, Lucius Vupello,' he said with angst, 'it is where you belong.' He then spun on a heel and rejoined his companions.

Lucius remained where he was, slumped in the middle of the street, the golden crown lying askew atop his head. It glittered faintly, its lustre dimmed like the man who wore it.

*

Tarsin looked behind him and offered a smile towards the wincing assassin.

'I'll make it,' Vittorio puffed, still clutching his shoulder.

'You didn't have to engage him, you know. I could have fought Vupello.'

'Aye, you could have, but I needed to avenge Vincent. It was Vupello's betrayal that cost him his life. Now he can rest in peace. The deed is done.'

The words rang of truth. Tarsin couldn't begin to imagine the anguish Vittorio felt when he lost his brother, but once again he realized how badly he'd failed his own men by fleeing Bastion. 'It's good to see you,' he finally said.

'Aye,' Vittorio wiped his brow then placed his hand over his wound, 'and it's good to have you back where you belong.'

Tarsin shrugged and pushed on, sharing a glance with the heavily armoured Griffith labouring beside him. Ever since they left Lucius Vupello lying motionless upon the ground, they had raced through Bastion's vacant streets towards the great pyramid. How far back the dragon-men were, he could not tell, but several roars of aggression had ripped through Bastion's streets since. His instincts told him they were close and as Vittorio suggested after his duel, he needed to act with haste if they were to organise a force equipped for retaliation.

'Jaegar,' Tarsin slowed his pace so he could talk to the Herkosian, the tall man running last in line, 'how many men patrol the pyramid's perimeter?'

'Of the Sceptres, possibly no more than two hundred,' he replied, his deep voice a delight to hear after so many years, even with its northern accent. 'A number of Arkos' Palaceguard survived Highcastle, though. Nearly sixty climbed out of the wreckage yesterday afternoon. Some are injured, but you know they'll fight regardless.'

Tarsin nodded, unsure if the numbers would be enough. He'd explained to Jaegar the potential danger chasing them as soon as they began to run. The Herkosian was doubtful when told, but he trusted him, always had. If he saw dragon-men with his own eyes, that was good enough for Jaegar, no matter how fanciful or unrealistic.

'How many of the creatures follow?' Jaegar asked.

'Difficult to tell,' Tarsin could see Aston's Tear ahead, her silver-blue walls visible, shining through the red haze, 'but there could be a hundred at least. Even with every available man armed and armoured, it will be some encounter. I doubt they'll take a backward step. They're taller even than you, Jaegar, and stronger.'

'What do they seek?'

Tarsin kept his gaze fixed on the pyramid and wondered if the temple was their objective. But then how could they possibly know of its existence, let alone its importance? His first encounter revealed they were just as surprised to see him as he them, and from whatever realm they hailed, they certainly didn't appear to be equipped for a prolonged invasion. It was a chance encounter, nothing more. His first impression was one of shock coupled with disbelief, his feelings reciprocated within the dragon-man's yellow, slitted eyes. He looked up at the tall man. 'I've no idea, Jaegar, but whatever it is, they'll not let us stand in their way. For beasts as vicious as the ones I've faced, there'll be no compromise.'

He and Jaegar slowed to a walk as Kayla, Donal, Ruvin and Griffith wormed their way down paths now crowded with people. The vacant streets were now a thing of the past. Here, close to the pyramid, countless people jostled back and forth, crowding its base, the folk forlorn and disenchanted. White tents flapped in the morning breeze, erected as a buffer against the relentless sun to house the wounded and dying. The sound of men and women mourning loved ones lost in the tragedy pervaded the area, their wails bitter as tears left dark trails upon ashen faces. Amongst them could be seen the white robes of the Celestial Sisters and the ubiquitous brown habits of the clergy, tending as best they could. 'We cannot fight the creatures amongst such a crowd,' Jaegar said, his height enabling him to see far over the bobbing heads of the populace. 'We'll have to evacuate them out of the city.'

'I doubt we'll have time,' Griffith huffed as he moved to stand with the two men. 'The roads out of Bastion are shattered and twisted and already crowded.'

'They'll need to go somewhere; we can't leave them here to be butchered,' Tarsin wiped sweat from his brow.

'Tarsin,' the voice was that of Ruvin, 'I need to speak urgently with elder Cappitus about what we've seen. When I saw him last, I was stepping into a sphere of light with the belief I was entering another world. He will be awaiting my return, keen to learn of my discovery.'

'Now is not the time for philosophy, Ruvin. We need to solidify our position, make a stand.'

'And you shall do so,' the old man breathed deeply, 'only I need to see elder Cappitus. It's imperative I speak to him.'

'Then go, Ruvin, and take Kayla and Donal with you.'

'No,' said Kayla, gripping his arm tight, 'I'll stay with you. I'll not leave you.'

Tarsin grimaced. 'It's not safe out here, Kayla, at least it won't be,' he shifted his gaze to the glowing pyramid. 'Besides, I need to gather my men, as do Griffith and Jaegar so we can organise a defence of the city. You'll be safe inside Aston's Tear.' He traced a finger across her cheek before peering into her emerald eyes, spoke with a hushed voice. 'I'll come for you when the time is right, I promise.' He then rummaged inside the hessian sack and pulled forth the twin swords of Arkos Vantos. 'Take these, Ruvin, and look after them.' He then passed the small chest to Kayla.

'Why are you giving me this?' she asked.

'Because you'll know what to do with it,' he replied.

Ruvin stepped forward and offered his hand to Kayla. She took it and saw only grim faces in return. 'Who are you people?' her eyes swivelled to encompass the towering Jaegar and the bleeding Vittorio.

'We're the Unseen,' explained Griffith.

'The Unseen?'

'We are the king's personal guard: the shadow behind *his* shadow.'

'What of Lucius Vupello? He was Captain of the Palaceguard. Why kill him?'

Tarsin shared a look with Griffith and gave him a nod. 'Because he knew of the Unseen's existence, even if he didn't know our identities. The man betrayed us; witnessed many of us perish in Benwith several years ago. His actions made him responsible for the death of Vittorio's younger brother, Vincent, amongst others.

We would have gladly killed him sooner, but he was our only link to Avra the witch.'

Tarsin saw confusion mask Kayla's face. Her knowledge of Avra was limited and he didn't have time to explain.

'Frey's Luck!' Jaegar's deep voice drowned out further questions.

'What is it?' Tarsin narrowed his eyes. The Herkosian looked agitated, his teeth clenched firmly together.

'Avra!' he spat the name as he met the eyes of his companions, his huge hands twisting about the haft of his axe. 'I know where she is.'

*

It was the sound of someone sniffing that woke him.

Lucius had lost consciousness shortly after Vittorio left, his mind reeling from the burning pain flaring in his stomach. The wound was severe, possibly fatal, especially if help wasn't found soon. For some time, he felt a numbness sweep throughout his limbs that rendered him helpless, disabled and unable to move. It was the poison on Vittorio's blade, the poison he'd handed the assassin.

Now he lay in a stupor because of his misjudgement.

Still, the pain in his stomach had fled, chased away by the toxic, numbing oil. That alone was a blessed relief. He'd prayed for help, at least until he'd lost consciousness. How long he lay on the street he'd no idea. Hopefully not long, for he knew his life-blood was staining the stones below. Someone was now close, though, he could hear them sniffing, and he knew it wasn't his horse, Strom.

Heavy, rough hands flipped him onto his back. He opened his eyes, ready to plead for his life, hoping his entrails weren't piled high on the cobblestones. He so desperately wished to live and be king. There was a great deal to accomplish, so much to prove. His journey to the throne had been fraught with difficulty but he'd arrived. It would be a shame to see it end so soon.

He opened heavy eyes to see who lay hands on the fallen king . . . and saw his worst nightmare staring back at him. A demon peered from above, yellow-slitted eyes scanning his body, flared nostrils drifting over his bloodied stomach. Clawed fingers lifted his chainmail, so the beast could examine his wound with an unnatural curiosity. Other demons crowded in close, likewise sniffing, ivory teeth, long and sharp, snapping hard with what appeared to be dissatisfaction. For a moment, he believed he'd fallen into Hell.

A chorus of jarring words scraped forth from demonic mouths. He felt the blood seep from his face, knew his skin would be almost translucent due to his loss of blood. Sweat dotted his brow, his hands were clammy. Then the beasts rose to their full height of seven feet, towering over his prone form. He didn't know who they were or where they'd come from, but he remembered hearing Griffith's words as he departed, telling Jaegar Death approached quickly. Now he knew what he meant. Now he could see with his own eyes what they fled from.

It was horrifying.

Yet even as he thought this was the end the beasts moved away, turning their backs to reveal huge, wide blades of steel strapped across their shoulders. Steel bracers lined their forearms and leather kilts hung to their knees. He'd never seen their like, nor heard of any beasts resembling such a vision. Yet despite their menacing visage and horrific appearance, they appeared to be leaving him alone.

For several minutes he lay still, watching as dozens of the creatures moved past him, most smelling the air until their heavy footsteps faded down the street. He could feel sweat trickling down his neck, and a distant pain began to manifest in his stomach. It grew with each passing minute; solidifying into what he feared was bound to occur. The poison was wearing thin and his nerves were regaining their ability to sense. He didn't know which predicament was worse: being immobile but free of pain; or sharing mobility with horrendous discomfit.

With timid motions, he sought to place his right hand over his injury, hoping to stem the blood flow. The beasts had confirmed one thing; at least his entrails were tucked safely within his stomach. The wound was clean, a straight cut into his abdomen, even though it sliced through chainmail and leather. He was lucky the poison had slowed his heart rate, an act compounded by his losing consciousness. Now all he needed was to find someone with the skills to administer a healing compress after stitching him up. A feat exacerbated by the already dwindling populace in the fallen city.

With considerable effort he lifted his head and looked about for Strom, seeking the warhorse amongst the empty street. Then he remembered the beasts and knew his mount would have fled with haste once he caught their scent. He was too weak to even whistle for his mount and he was resigned to the fact he would have to crawl to reach whatever solace he could find in this broken city. He thought of the temples close by, wondered if any priests or priestesses were in attendance before he realised Avra was equally close, hunkered down in the cellar of a crumbled villa not far from where he lay. She was a witch with powers of the occult. She could do things few in this world could even begin to fathom. Surely healing a wound as grave as his would be child's play to one of her expertise?

He rolled over, grimacing as pain stabbed through his body like the sting of a thousand fire ants. Tears rolled down his cheeks as he sucked in a lungful of air tinged with ash. He kept his hand placed firmly against his belly and lifted his legs beneath him, then pushed against the hard stones and slid himself forward a couple of inches. It was excruciatingly difficult, taxed him of all his reserved energy, but eventually he slid through the streets to find his way outside Avra's abode. With exhaustion plastered across his face and a hand covered in gore, he pushed open the green door and crawled into the dark room beyond. He found the stairs at the rear of the establishment that led down to the cellar, and with short, sharp breaths, he descended as quickly as able before falling in a heap on the bottom flagstone. With a feeble cry, he called out for Avra, his hoarse call barely above a whisper. He hoped it was enough, hoped she could perform the miracle he craved. His last thought before he passed back into unconsciousness was one of fear; fear Avra had left on some clandestine errand of her own design to leave him to his own bloody fate. It was a discomfiting thought, but thankfully there was movement to the rear of the cellar, and moments after he passed out a shadow crept forward to encompass his immobile form.

*

Avra peered down at the comatose swordsman, noting the blood-soaked hand lying limp across split chainmail, his pallid skin gleaming under the light of her lantern. She could see his wound, despite his best effort to hold it together. Blood was everywhere, caked thick between his fingers and congealed into dark clusters, almost black. She knelt and pressed a withered finger against his neck, feeling for a pulse. It was faint and erratic. Whatever happened to the fool he was near the end. She wondered if he was even worth the effort.

Then she noticed the golden crown circling his head.

How she'd missed its bright glow she couldn't say. Perhaps it was the severity of his wound that caught her attention, blinding her to the obvious. Now she could see it: Arkos' crown, the crown of the king. She lifted her finger from Lucius' neck, touching the cold metal and tracing a line to the circular stone. The Eye of the Jaguar. After countless years warring with Arkos, it had finally come to this. The man she hated with all her soul was dead; his crown already planted atop the usurper's head. Her dreams of sweet revenge were already forgotten, their dark, dire means intangible, elusive. A shiver raced up her spine. 'Lucius, you fool of a man,' she whispered, 'what have you done?'

She placed the lantern by her side and reached into one of her many pouches hidden within the voluminous folds of her cloak. A small pear-shaped vial appeared in her hand, stoppered with blue wax, its contents swirling grey smoke. A sharp, lengthy fingernail pierced the seal before she tipped the vapour into Lucius' gaping mouth. It slid into his throat like liquid ash, disappearing in an instant. A second later he convulsed, his chest rising as he breathed deeply, his eyes flaring wide.

'Easy, Lucius,' Avra was already working the seal off another vial, this one round and squat. She poured the contents over his wound, the sound it made reminiscent of steaming water. 'There will be no pain, Lucius,' she said as she watched the blood wash away. He murmured something unintelligible, his eyes rolling back, but a sharp slap across his cheek focused his attention. 'Don't die on me, fool,' there was a tone to her voice that dared him to disobey; 'I've a number of questions for you to answer before I decide what shall become of you. Try not to disappoint me.'

He nodded feebly, the effort almost too much for the swordsman.

'Now,' she began, 'tell me where Arkos is, and explain to me what happened to our beloved king.'

The words stuttered forth at first, his mouth parched, his body drugged. Avra sat by his side, patiently coercing. Lucius' tongue eventually began to function with a modicum of success, at least enough for her to discern his speech. It was as she feared, Arkos dead, buried under Highcastle. She could lay the blame at no-one's feet but the Dark God she worshipped. She was old and wise enough to comprehend the complications involved if she chose such a course. Ahriman was not a forgiving deity, nor one to grieve over something as trivial as the death of a king. So long as the next in line could be found and sacrificed, concern was minimal. What did concern her, though, was the survival of the Unseen. Vittorio's subterfuge and betrayal were galling, but to have Jaegar mimic his actions was as subtle as a blow to the head with the barbarian's axe. It was not the transition into power Lucius sought. Not that she particularly cared. Now she knew Arkos was dead and Lucius, already crowned, was next in line, she could begin what she'd envisaged months ago. With Lucius at ease and immobile, she tucked a hand back into her cloak.

Out came her ritual blade, splotched purple steel wickedly curved. It was deadly sharp; a powerful blade bound with arcane force the likes not seen for an age. She reverently held it above the inert man, showing him its hideous design. 'It is time,

Lucius,' she said, ominous words she'd uttered countless occasions before. The poor fool couldn't move, even his tongue had swollen to become thick and useless. A pitiful grunt was all he could manage before she turned her blade towards his chest and raced its tip across his chainmail. The links parted easier than a whore's legs when offered silver, slipping away from his torso to lie crumpled to either side. The leather gambeson was next, allowing Avra to lay a cold, wrinkled hand atop his naked chest. A gentle caress, just to the left above his beating heart followed. 'I have waited for this moment a very long time, Lucius Vupello.'

The man who would be king fainted, the whites of his eyes shining bright beneath the golden crown as they rolled back in his head. She chuckled, then began to make her preparations. The ritual was not difficult, for Ahriman was already summoned. This was simply the decisive step: the step needed to grant her Dark God flesh. Soon, very soon, the material world would be his to conquer.

Avra smiled, for no matter what occurred, she planned to be by his side every step of the way.

She moved to the rear of the cellar and retrieved her *Sawolegere*, the ancient lantern both a focal device for the coming ritual and a protective abode for the shade that was He. She'd left it in the corner sitting atop an old wine barrel, the rust on its iron surface resembling blood leaking from within. A dark aura surrounded the *Sawolegere*, a mystic shimmer of pure evil pulsing with frightful intent. Even Avra paused momentarily before gripping the handle tight, her knuckles white as she carried the relic across the room to rest it above the head of Lucius. Once settled, she withdrew a piece of chalk and carefully marked the floor surrounding the unconscious man. The finished circle was elaborate and precise, a mystical ward to prevent Lucius' soul from escaping back to the Great Consciousness. Unseen to the naked eye, a sphere of rippling energy was now in effect.

She then placed the knife against his chest, murmuring the first words of an incantation best forgotten, but one she had memorised years ago when her spiral into the abyss began. They were hideous words, flecked with sinister tones, comprised of a language only a handful of the truly depraved understood. At their conclusion, she pressed the purple blade into Lucius' flesh. A thin, crooked finger inched forward to rest in the blood. She held it there for some time, allowing it to soak in the plasma until she pulled it away all sticky with gore. She then traced a mark upon Lucius' forehead, a mark of Chaos.

Finally, she turned her attention to the knife. This time she straddled Lucius with her bony legs and pushed down with all her might, sending the blade deep. Feverish words danced upon her lips, fearful words that conjured a miasma to pervade the cellar. The witch was lost to the stench and the death that preceded it. Her head swung from side-to-side, her mangy white hair flinging back and forth, a high pitched keen issuing from her throat. Then she ripped out her knife, dripping red, and licked the blade with a pointed tongue. She swallowed, and the light in her eyes dimmed, as if a Darkness had descended to engulf her slight frame. Her vision swam; multi-faceted lights appeared before her eyes. Knowing her timing to be critical, she pushed her right hand deep into the cavity she'd created in Lucius' chest. Her fingers squelched as they gripped vice-like about his heart. A tremendous yank found the organ oozing blood inches from her face, sparkling droplets flicking across her nose and cheeks to settle like innocent freckles, before she reached out to place it atop the *Sawolegere*. It settled with a hiss and a cloud of violet bubbled above, which grew with each passing second. As the heart continued to sizzle, her warped vision spied the minute golden ball of light as it floated from Lucius' form. It was his soul, bound by arcane magic and confined within the sphere she'd constructed. It could not escape.

A second later the sound of rusty hinges reverberated throughout the room as the lantern's shutter swung open. The dark shade of Ahriman leached onto the floor, an inky substance that began to congeal and grow, morphing to greater heights, pulsing with energy and life. Avra watched, mesmerized, her blood-stained mouth hanging slack as Ahriman's inky hand reached out to pluck Lucius' soul like a golden berry from an almost barren tree.

A moment later it was over.

She blinked, her eyes adjusting to the gloom as she gazed not upon a dark shade but a naked man of flesh. 'My Lord,' she lifted a leg over the lifeless Lucius and pressed her forehead to the ground. *One thousand souls to summon the Dark Lord*, she thought to herself, *and the soul of a king to grant him flesh.*

'Avra,' the voice was deep, sepulchral, 'you have committed yourself well, and you shall be rewarded.'

She lifted squinting eyes to look upon Ahriman's naked body, not daring to meet his gaze. It was well proportioned, strong, his bronze skin totally devoid of hair. It was everything she dreamed it would be. Her eyes roamed across his abdomen as she caught sight of his rippled stomach, before spying his thick manhood hanging limp across heavily muscled thighs. A quiver raced along her spine. 'You're very handsome, my Prince of Darkness,' she purred.

'Am I?' queried Ahriman. 'I feel strong; Avra, but I sense something amiss.'

She sought out his face, looking for any abnormalities but saw only hard lines of perfection. Even his arms were toned, chiselled as from stone. 'You appear perfect, my Lord, as a god should be.'

She saw his pursed lips falter, his bald head tilting to the side as if contemplating something profound. 'No, something concerns me,' he finally said, and Avra watched as a terrific shudder assaulted his body. A cry of pain escaped his lips, followed by a heavy grunt as arms twisted and bent out of shape, contorting into positions not humanly possible. Spasms rippled across his torso and twitching muscles knotted, cramping Ahriman's legs and sending him crashing to the floor. Avra screamed herself, but the sound was drowned out by a wail of grief as her god's heaving body thumped repeatedly up and down. It lasted no more than a minute, but it seemed an eternity.

When it ceased, she took a deep breath and waited for Ahriman to raise his once flawless head.

It was his eyes, when she finally saw them, which revealed to her a terrible truth.

'This . . . man,' he wheezed, looking past her, 'is not . . . king.'

She peered over her shoulder to gaze upon the prone form of Lucius with his golden crown. 'He has to be,' she stumbled, 'there is no one else.'

'No, there must be . . . another . . . next in line,' she could hear his struggle for words, his own breathing ragged. 'He is not the one. His blood is tainted, and I am now . . . crippled!'

Avra returned her vision to her stricken god. He lay there helpless, his body twisted out of shape, his fingers clawed. Even his face was screwed into a hideous mask of pain. 'How can such be?' she questioned herself, her mind racing. 'With Arkos' two sons' dead, there was no other to claim the throne. Lucius Vupello was next. He was the king's cousin.'

Ahriman shuddered after a raking cough burst forth from his throat, a wad of phlegm spitting from his mouth. Sticky strands fell across his misshapen hands.

'Can you walk, my Lord?' Avra probed. 'Do you still retain your power?' Her voice quivered, despite her best efforts to conceal her fear.

'I can walk,' he placed his hands on the floor. His arms were still colossal, despite their twisted nature. With a heave, he pushed himself upright and dragged his legs beneath, his body trembling with the effort to stand. His body bent to one side, his head leant towards the other. In a matter of moments, he'd lost six inches in height, and in places his skin sagged, whilst in others it stretched tight leaving unsightly marks. She lowered her head as his glaring eyes sought out her own. 'I am not what you'd hoped for.' It was not a question.

'You are still beautiful, my Lord,' she knew the words to be a lie the moment they escaped. She sensed Ahriman also knew.

'This is the price I pay for trusting you,' he said, his voice a whisper. She cringed as his shoulder twitched, which in turn caused his head to jerk violently. Further spasms continued to rake his body.

'I am sorry, my Lord,' she trembled as tears began to roll down her cheeks.

'This man is not Arkos' successor, Avra Creswick,' he pointed a crooked finger towards Lucius' corpse, 'and "sorry" hardly constitutes an apology for your serious lack of foresight.' The faint glow from her small lantern was suddenly extinguished, leaving the cellar unnaturally dark. When she next heard Ahriman's voice, it sounded distant, as if from a place far away, his words laden with cruel intent. 'Prepare yourself, witch,' he snarled, 'to be punished by a god!'

CHAPTER TWENTY-FIVE

Neema let out a heavy sigh as she completed the last of her protective wards.

She sat inside the Forever Chamber, young Jarred by her side, alert and apparently in control of his own faculties. There had been much discussion concerning Ruvin's charge, but the lad appeared better placed than previously thought. For the last hour, he'd hounded her every movement, curious as she went about her task sealing the chamber with mystical wards: wards strong enough to repel Avra should she seek entrance once more.

She shifted her gaze towards him, looked down at his innocent face framed with long blonde hair. It was the face of youth except for his eyes. The eyes were old and full of knowledge, somehow the keepers of wisdom long forgotten.

'How do you feel, Jarred?' she asked softly.

Jarred scratched above one eye, then stretched his neck to either side. 'I feel well, Neema.'

'Are you tired, still?'

'Not as much as previously. The voices inside my head have abated somewhat. I feel in control for the time being.'

Neema nodded with understanding. She'd dealt with possession before, knew how dangerous it could be. Even though Jarred's possession appeared to be helpful, the ties between his soul and those newly arrived could easily sever his grip on reality. If the entities currently housed within the young man were truly here to offer guidance, they would allow him some respite. Too much information too soon could very well see him lose all sense of purpose.

'Do you remember what you spoke of earlier?' she prodded.

'I do,' he replied, 'although there are clusters that remain unclear.'

'What of the Portal to the Gods? Do you recall its significance?'

She watched him spin about to peer at the golden sphere. Recognition flared in his eyes and a smile twitched the corner of his mouth. 'I do, Neema.'

'Can you tell me?'

He spun back to face her, settling himself until he was comfortable. They both sat inside the Forever Chamber, just a few feet past the metal doors and the handful of Sword Brothers who stood guard. Since she'd discovered Avra's presence, the guards both within and without the pyramid had doubled. It did little to make her feel at ease.

'The words I use are not always correct,' he began. 'The . . . friends who speak for me are not entirely familiar with the kingdom tongue. They are still learning, although they are quick to grasp what they hear and see.'

'What of the portal?' Neema lifted her eyes towards the golden sphere as it continued to shine like the midday sun it represented.

'It is the *Kardiversum*: the Heart of the Universe, the Portal to the Gods,' his eyes glazed momentarily. 'When I say it is a portal to the gods, the gods I refer to are nothing more than what you have here.'

'You mean our eight gods . . . the gods of Dervae?'

'No, I mean the world you live upon and everything it is comprised of. Through the portal you will find creation. Creation is life. It is the essence of the Universe. It is God.'

Neema sat back, resting her heavy frame against a black wall. It was all beginning to make sense in a strange fashion. At the pyramid's core sat a portal capable of sending a person to another world; twelve worlds, to be exact. 'Can we cross the portal to these other worlds in safety?' she asked, wondering if the Nepharii built the pyramid to escape a ravaging god.

'We can cross to other worlds in safety,' he said with a frown, 'but safety, once we are there, cannot be guaranteed. Man is not the only sentient creature to exist throughout the Universe. There are others, some very dangerous. You must choose your destination wisely, this much I know. Not every world you travel too will provide a haven.'

The news, therefore, was bitter-sweet. They were offered a chance to escape a fallen city, but the guarentee of safety remained elusive. She thought of the Seeker, Ruvin Ciricello, and wondered what he saw once he stepped across the plaque depicting Tyrranus. Hours had passed, and he hadn't returned. Even now Cappitus paced before the golden sphere hunched with worry. She knew Jarred's presence by her side was his means of keeping occupied. From what little she knew of Ruvin, he'd been Jarred's master for several years. The boy must certainly be concerned.

A sudden shout sounded from the entrance to the chamber, startling her from her thoughts. Raised voices could be heard, so she rose to her feet and stepped between the double doors to peer down the corridor's length. It was difficult, for the jostling figures were many and even the lit braziers did little to reveal the newcomers. As they crept closer she could see a tall lady with dark hair and a young boy, three or four years younger than Jarred with scruffy blonde locks. Their presence was trivial, though, when compared to the slight frame of Ruvin Ciricello, Seeker of the Brotherhood.

'By all that is holy,' she clapped her hands together. 'Ruvin has returned!'

She felt Jarred step close to her side and grab her arm. He stood on the tips of his toes, eager to see his master and friend. There was much to love about the old man and Neema knew there were many amongst the Brotherhood who shared their feelings. Since he'd stepped into the light, it felt as though the Brotherhood had collectively held their breath.

'Who are the others,' Jarred asked, 'the lady and the boy?'

Neema was about to respond when voices erupted behind them, followed quickly by a half-hearted cheer. Within moments a crowd of elders surrounded Ruvin and his companions, a hundred questions voiced at once.

'You've returned, Ruvin,' Neema grabbed his wrist and dragged him free of the press. Ruvin reached out his other hand to beckon the lady and boy, then followed as Neema walked across the spanning bridge to reach Cappitus.

'Brother,' Neema saw Cappitus smile as he stepped forward to embrace his friend. He then pushed the smaller man back at arm's length for an appraisal. Tears rimmed his eyes, but he held them back and swallowed once to regain his composure. 'I thought you were lost,' he finally said, his voice subdued.

'For a time, I thought I was,' Ruvin answered. He spun to his left and ushered the lady and boy to his side. 'Allow me to introduce Kayla Tolsten, daughter of Lord Derrick Tolsten, and her companion, young Donal.'

Elder Cappitus nodded once in greeting, his eyebrows arched to provide a quizzical look. 'Your father's work is of immense importance to us, Kayla,' he offered.

'My father,' Kayla settled herself with a deep breath, 'is dead.'

Kayla's words silenced any further questions as abruptly as they began. Neema knew Derrick Tolsten was not only an established leader of the Brotherhood; he'd also been an advisor to King Arkos. His loss, amongst all the confusion and terror of the past days, would only compound their dire predicament.

'You bring grave news, Kayla Tolsten,' Cappitus bowed his head.

'There is worse to come, I'm afraid,' said Ruvin with a sigh. 'King Arkos never left Highcastle. He remains within, no more than a corpse.'

Whatever profound wisdom those gathered shared, it was seriously being tested. Arkos' loss would be deeply felt. Neema saw the look plastered across Ruvin's face; she understood how demoralizing his information was. He may have returned from another world, a feat worthy of praise and celebration, but it was quite the opposite. The pyramid, Aston's Tear, once touted as being their panacea, now looked likely to be their doom.

'There is something else you should be aware of,' Ruvin continued. 'The world I visited . . .'

Neema could see him struggle with his words. He was exhausted, dark patches pooling beneath his eyes exacerbating his lack of rest.

'What did you see?' Cappitus frowned, an action suggesting he was wary of Ruvin's response.

'A hot world ruled by a red sun, and as far as I can tell, governed by dragon-men.'

Neema heard the collective gasp of a dozen men and women at Ruvin's news, but many simply lowered their heads in reflection. The glyphs upon the inner ring suggested such a possibility, the Seeker now confirmed it. It also created new waves of thought concerning the remaining plaques. There were eleven other humanoid figures circling the sphere.

'You've given us much to ponder,' Cappitus stroked his wispy white beard.

'I fear the time for rumination is over,' Neema heard Ruvin say. 'The dragon-men are here, and they are ferocious. They have stepped through the portal; harried us all the way back to the surface. Lord Derrick Tolsten has already sacrificed his life to halt their mad rush. I suggest we not waste it. And I'm afraid there are other issues to deal with, Cappitus. Tarsin Va and the remnants of the Unseen seek Avra even as we speak. There is a possibility they may find her.'

'Are you certain of this?' the elder asked.

'Absolutely.'

Neema shook her head then looked towards Cappitus. Such a course would be fraught with peril, especially if Ahriman was near. No matter how strong Tarsin was, or how skilful he was with a blade, he was no match for the shade of a god.

'How many are with him?' she asked, wondering if it really mattered.

'Three others of the Unseen, but I believe they'll gather what remains of my mercenary company before they confront her. If the mercenaries haven't fled, they may increase their numbers to beyond twenty, possibly thirty.' She saw him rest a hand near his belt, close to the pommel of a sword. Another sword rested on his other hip.

'Are they not the king's swords?' Neema pointed a finger.

Ruvin looked down. 'They are. Tarsin asked me to keep an eye on Kayla and Donal before we left and entrusted me with these twin blades.'

Neema watched Ruvin draw one forth. They were of practical use, neither fashioned with elaborate ornamentation or excessive flare. The silver pommels carved into the likeness of a jaguar's head their only discerning element. With due care Ruvin held it up to catch the golden light of the portal.

'Those are the jaguar blades,' she said, admiring the sword in his hand, 'and yet with King Arkos dead, the last of the jaguars is no more.'

Elder Cappitus shrank an inch at the news. 'So, he is truly dead, the last of the jaguars,' he remained silent a moment before slowly lifting his eyes. 'We have all read the chronicles, we know where we stand. With the last of the jaguars dead, the city of Bastion will fall. It is inevitable. It has been ordained.'

'What shall we do?' Neema's voice quivered.

'We shall flee the city; evacuate what remains of the populace. The Dark God approaches and now demons from a hellish world crawl though our streets. There is nothing here for us now. Our time is up.'

'Nor desa nae!'

The sonorous voice sounded from beyond the platform. As a group, everyone spun to see who spoke, clamouring for position with necks craned high. Neema immediately saw Jarred squirm through the throng until he reached the front; his skinny frame easily slipping past the stooped brothers. The metal span lay before him, bridging the platform to the chamber's entrance. Upon it stood a single dark cloaked figure: tall and slender.

'Jarred!' Neema shouted, hoping to stall the boy. Only he didn't listen; he just kept walking towards the tall stranger. Before she or Cappitus could even begin to think of a plan of action he'd crossed the last remaining steps to peer up at the cloaked figure.

Without a word Jarred raised his hand, palm out, and waited for the newcomer to do likewise. Seconds later their hands touched, their heads now bowed as they communed in some unfamiliar fashion.

'What is he doing?' Ruvin asked, his hand gripped tight about the hilt of his sword.

Neema placed a comforting hand across his. 'I do not know, Ruvin,' she replied, but she suddenly felt no fear. Whatever was transpiring here, she knew it to be beneficial.

A minute passed without a perceived movement from either two, but then the tall stranger lifted his head. Seconds later he pulled his cowl back to reveal a slender face with high cheek bones and a tapered jaw. Long black hair hung to his shoulders and his eyes, even from such distance, appeared to reflect the golden sphere in its entirety. He was handsome yet alien at the same time. He placed a delicate hand over Jarred's shoulder and together they stepped forward a pace.

'I am sorry,' he said with a lilt to his voice, 'your language was not mine to know. I could understand your words, but my conveyance was . . . imprecise. What I meant to say when I first entered this chamber was, "your time is not up".'

'I beg to differ, stranger,' Cappitus' gravelly voice boomed in return. 'Death surrounds us, poised to swallow us whole if we do not act with haste. We cannot see our way clear.'

'How can you not see a way clear when the way sits right before you, shining like the beacon it is?' His eyes drifted to the portal: to the *Kardiversum*.

'I have been through the portal,' shouted Ruvin, 'and the world I saw was far from hospitable.'

'Not where you travelled, perhaps, but there is a plaque soon to arrive that will harbour you and your people safely. There you can rest, recuperate, and return when you are organized.'

'How can we trust you? We don't even know who you are. You could be the Dark God himself?' asked Ruvin with fervour. Neema could see his eyes focused on the hand resting on Jarred's shoulder.

A chuckle escaped from the man's thin lips. 'I am no Dark God. Nor am I here to cause harm.'

'Then who are you?'

'I am Kian, gatekeeper and guardian of Vidae.'

A score of blank faces stared back at him.

'I am here to help, ladies and gentlemen,' he continued, 'I am Nepharii.'

*

A wan sun shone through wispy clouds as Ra'tor strode down the street. He grimaced at its sight; not due to the sun's brightness or heat, but due to its apparent lack. It made perfect sense to the ancient Deiosian, though, for he saw the people of this world as weak. Weak creatures governed by a weak sun. The few they had crossed paths with were small and fragile; nimble, yes, but also fearful. He shouldn't have been so surprised, for the evidence lay all around him. Never had he been witness to such elaborate constructs. Walls of brick and timber and stone were fashioned into square buildings to house the fearful creatures. It was a mystery to him as to why they would shun the elements. On his world, living under the light of Bhral: the Blood-god; was their birthright. Facing the elements in all their fury was testament to one's strength and courage. It appeared the creatures on this world had forsaken nature's gifts, shying away from their god by chosing to cower amongst their artificial shelters. For all their faults, though, when caught, they tasted sublime. He couldn't remember savouring anything so sweet before.

He shifted his gaze to the left as Rax't stepped alongside. The tall Deiosian flicked a pointed tongue from between glistening teeth. Droplets of blood splattered his nose and chin and his clawed hands were stained red. 'Have you any word from our runner?' Ra'tor asked, eager to learn if other broods had ventured through the portal behind them.

'Serrax just arrived,' Ra'tor showed his teeth, glad the young Deiosian had returned. 'Zaxa and Terrak both made it through, along with their broods. There is something else you should be aware of, though.'

'And that is . . .?'

'The door-between-worlds has closed,' Rax't clicked his teeth shut.

'Closed! What do you mean?'

'It is no more. We cannot return; no more can step through. We are alone on this world, in this . . . dwelling place.'

Ra'tor mulled over the information. Thoughts of failure assaulted him. What if he'd made a mistake by dragging his brood through the gateway? What if he was held accountable by Zaxa and Terrak? Both were formidable, strong and in their prime. He could ill afford a challenge by either of the two. But he sensed this was his calling. Bhral showed him the light and paved the way. Surely the Blood-god knew his purpose. He must retain his faith.

'The door-between-worlds will reopen in time,' he said, believing his words despite his lack of knowledge. 'And we are meant to be here, Rax't, for the bounty speaks for itself. Bhral would be pleased.'

'It is as you say, Ra'tor.'

He snorted and spat, then turned his attention back to more pressing matters. 'Zaxa and Terrak; how many do they bring?'

'Terrak runs with six score; Zaxa runs with twice as many.'

The numbers were good. His brood alone counted for one hundred and fifty. It meant Zaxa would have weight of number, and by right, command of their combined forces. He could see Rax't coming to the same conclusion. 'We'll move on, I'll not wait for them.' It was the most logical option. So long as he kept his brood separate, he would retain control. By his reckoning, there were enough pale skins to satisfy each brood. 'Besides,' Ra'tor sniffed the air, sensing more blood spilt, 'there are wonders here beyond our knowledge. I would be first to lay eyes on them.'

'What of the hunt?' asked Rax't.

'It will continue.' Ra'tor's tongue raced over his teeth as he thought of the supple flesh still to be found. Apart from the first body discovered, wounded and reeking of poison, every other had proven to be cause for excitement. Even as he remembered a scream cut through the air to alert him to another victim caught in the labyrinth of rock and wood. Two of his brood exited a building, a pale skin dangling between them, held upside down by its legs as it flayed futilely in a vain effort to escape. Deep chortles sounded as the surrounding brood watched in amusement. Ra'tor smiled, knowing what was to come. The pale skin's cry of despair suddenly reached a crescendo as the two Deios tore the creature in two, splitting it down the middle. Hot blood spewed forth to drench the two hunters in gore, whilst slippery handfuls of pink flesh: worm-like entrails speckled red, looped wetly onto the cobblestoned street.

'With so much meat on offer,' said Rax't, 'we should send for the breed-partners.'

Ra'tor nodded in agreement. He'd already sent a bloodling back with the call. Provided the gateway reopened, their breed-partners would be through within days. Now all that remained was for them to hunt down the pale skin with the lightning sword. Find him, and they could exact their revenge. He was adamant the creatures of this world were weak, like their sun, but that one . . . he was different. When he found him, he intended to confront him as a warrior, Deiosian against . . . whatever it was they were.

Then with blood satisfied, they could explore this strange world with their implacable hunger.

*

Avra squinted as she peered about the cellar. Dust motes hovered in the stale air as a shaft of light pierced the gloom. Her heavy sigh was followed by a wince as air expanded her tortured chest. She was on her hands and knees, white hair now lank and trailing in a pool of blood. She couldn't tell if the blood was hers or the remnants from Lucius Vupello. He still lay at the bottom of the stairs, his chest ripped open, a chalk circle surrounding him. His golden crown still sat atop his head.

'Rise, Avra,' the words were deep and powerful, emanating from the rear of the cellar, somewhere in the dark.

She shivered, her wretched body weak and exhausted. Ahriman had punished her, as promised, and it took all her effort to crawl towards the light where Lucius' corpse still lay. She'd persisted, though, because in the darkness lay terror the likes of which she'd never imagined.

'I said, "RISE!"' the shout caused the walls to shake and the air to tremble. A wave of pure hatred assaulted her, forcing her to comply, to act without thought. She placed a knobbly knee beneath her, rising several inches in height. 'Now look at me, witch,' the words dripped venom.

Avra did as bid, twisting her head about and raising blood-shot eyes to look upon her lord. A soft radiance permeated the rear of the cellar, lending light to the darkness. Ahriman stood there, naked; his heavily muscled arms all bent and twisted and his hips clearly out of alignment.

'This is your doing, witch,' he spoke the words softly. 'I trusted you.'

'I am truly sorry, my lord,' her whimper was barely audible. To compound matters further, her Dark Lord's skin was beginning to produce blood-coloured welts, blistering like a peasant with scrofula.

'It will take thousands of souls to empower me enough to alter my form and heal my wounds, witch. I was not expecting to embark upon such a journey so soon.'

Avra lifted an eyebrow. 'You can change your form, my lord?'

'Given time, and with enough souls gathered, yes, it can be done.'

A minute spark simmered in her eyes as she heard the words of her lord. All was not lost, not yet. Ahriman maybe crippled, but he was still a force to be reckoned with. If he needed souls, he need only step out into the light. Tens-of-thousands had perished when the earthquake struck, and thousands more would succumb. She thought quickly. 'I can lead you to the souls you require, my lord, if you wish?'

Ahriman lurched forward, his face contorting with the effort. 'I do not need your spells, witch, nor do I need your rituals. Now I am flesh, I can see the souls of the living and those who have recently departed. I can draw them in myself; suck them in until they cannot escape. I am the Apocalypse, Avra, a maelstrom of dark energy seeking to engulf all humanity. Right now, I believe, I'll start with you. I'll take your twisted, pitiful soul, even though it will be of little value.'

She watched as Ahriman took a jarring step closer, his gait ungainly but his eyes urgent. Pain flared in her skull, pain like she'd already experienced when in her Dark Lord's clutches. He was inside her head, lashing her mind with whips of flame, spinning her thoughts in wild arcs until she heaved and coughed and vomited what little bile remained in her stomach. Another foot slid closer, the scrape across the floorboards loud, the creak of his tortured bones horrifying. She'd done this to him. Whatever torment she suffered now, her Dark Lord endured worse. She deserved to die for her failure. She yearned to die for her failure.

'Stop!' Avra cried, the pain in her mind tearing out the word. 'Stop, my lord,' tears streamed down her cheeks, stinging as they crossed deep scratches she'd given herself when in her Dark Lord's embrace. She'd gouged three lines to either cheek, appeared to be crying tears of blood. 'I can help,' she sobbed, 'I can still be of use.'

'How?' the walls shook at the sound of his voice.

'I can offer you more souls, my lord. More than you can possibly imagine.'

Ahrmian halted his advance and Avra slumped to her knees, the pain fleeing as quickly as it arrived. 'There are millions of souls on this world, Avra, eventually I shall claim them all. How can you possibly offer more?'

With considerable effort Avra regained her feet and placed a trembling hand out to lean against the wall. To her left lay the staircase, rising to a short hallway before a door led onto the street. She needed to feel the sun on her face, to feel the wind's gentle caress. Lucius' dead body stank, as did she. She couldn't remember having felt so filthy before. 'There is a temple, a pyramid in the centre of Bastion,' she began, 'and within rests a portal fashioned by ancient hands. I do not know the intricacies concerning its operation, my lord, but I believe it leads to other worlds.'

She felt Ahriman's brooding visage regard her intently. 'How many worlds?'

'Twelve, my lord,' she said with a grimace, 'twelve new worlds teeming with life.'

'Where is this temple, this pyramid of wonder?'

Avra tilted her head to peer up the staircase. 'Out there, my lord. Come, I'll show you where the portal resides.'

*

The journey into the light was painful for Ahriman, the staircase difficult to climb with his tortured body. Once he reached the hallway he found Avra standing there waiting, a pair of trousers and a cloak lying across her arms. She helped him dress, a task even more arduous than traversing the stairs.

'This way, my lord,' she beckoned with her gnarled hand.

He obliged, limping heavily on one leg as the other scraped behind. He made it out the door and onto the street where he smelt and tasted air for the first time as a god made flesh.

'There is ash in the air, my lord, and the breeze finds it difficult to sweep it away when deep in the city's heart. Beyond the wall,' she pointed down one street, showing him towards the east, 'the air is cleaner, the wind more prevalent.'

'What of the sun?' he asked, lifting the hood of his cloak to cover his eyes.

Avra scanned the horizon. 'It will shine brighter come midday, and brighter still if the clouds disperse.'

Ahriman kept his head low at her words, already aware of the sting in his eyes from the sun's gentle glow. He never believed he would suffer pain from something as trivial as light. The flesh of man was not as strong as he once thought.

'Come, my lord,' she held out a hand to steady his walk, 'the pyramid is but a short way.'

He leant on the frail witch, careful not to burden her with too much of his weight. She was slight, mostly skin and bones and her ordeal in the dark cellar had decimated her constitution. Like Ahrmian, she had covered her face with the cowl of her robe, masking the bloodied lines across her cheeks and her deeply sunken eyes. He was thankful for such modesty for she was a frightful specimen. When he came into his full power he would consider changing her appearance. He'd promised her such when bargaining for her support. Such promises depended on how well she helped him now.

They moved slowly past an intersection, a half-crumbled building leaning precariously into the street. Several stone bricks cluttered their path, providing obstacles for the duo to overcome. Ahriman felt anger boil inside. He felt confined in his newly found flesh. He was a god, albeit newly formed, but a god nonetheless. Trivial matters such as bricks in the road should never have been an impediment. With narrowed eyes, he cast a baleful glare at the offending masonry, channelling his power before sending it forward in a blaze of hatred. The bricks were engulfed in a wave of searing heat, popping and then disintegrating into a thousand pieces.

Avra wiped the back of her hand across her forehead. 'Your powers are still considerable, my lord.'

'They are, Avra, but I feel drained. I need more souls if I am to be flexible with such displays.' He looked to his left, then his right, adjusting his vision by raising a hand to shade his eyes. The building to his right was mostly intact, but its door lay in the street, warped and splintered, yet the half-timbered walls were secure. Inside he could see the gentle glow of a golden soul, drifting in lazy circles over a recently expired body. With teeth clenched firm he beckoned the fey light, holding out a hand, his clawed fingers curling inwards.

The soul of the deceased, once beckoned, swept straight into his body.

A hiss escaped from his clenched teeth as the soul joined his, his back arching as the meld was completed.

'Are you alright, my lord?' he could see concern on Avra's withered face.

'Better, actually,' he replied. 'A soul has joined with me,' he looked about the intersection, peering in every direction. He almost swooned as his vision encompassed hundreds of souls drifting close by. Beyond, faintly out of reach for now, he could sense thousands more. He sent out a pulse of energy, summoning the souls to his own, creating the first semblance of a dark maelstrom to surround him. In time they would come, but for now, they would circle, tightening ever closer as time passed. As he walked, more would be enticed to merge with his own private storm cell.

He remembered well his act of rage, his shaking of Bastion's foundations. He was thankful his summoning hadn't been delayed too long. Many of the souls were from the newly deceased, but there were thousands belonging to those who died when the earthquake first struck. They were high in the sky now, ready to depart on the next phase of their journey. Even Ahriman's maelstrom could not entice all of those in attendance. Some would slip through his clawed fingers to drift onwards and upwards to the *other* that was not he.

'Ahriman, my lord,' he could sense fear in Avra's voice.

'What is it?' the words were out of his mouth before he laid eyes on the beast walking towards them. It was extraordinary: tall and broad, red-scaled with a slightly elongated snout. Sharp teeth lined a maw that he pictured opening wide, and clawed hands gripped a cleaver of steel three feet in length. A short leather kilt draped its muscled thighs, but otherwise it wore few accoutrements.

'I've never seen anything like it,' Avra whispered back.

The beast halted several feet away and sniffed the air. Ahriman watched as sharp teeth clashed together before a collection of words were spoken in an alien tongue. It waited seconds for a reply, or perhaps for the two of them to turn and flee. When neither event occurred it casually lifted its cleaver and charged.

Heavy, clawed feet stomped the ground in quick fashion, the beast's long strides eating up the distance in a heartbeat. As it came within striking distance Ahriman lifted his own twisted hand and uttered a command. The beast stopped in its tracks as if struck by an invisible wall. Confusion caused its yellow eyes to narrow, its tongue to taste the air. Huge shoulders flexed as it lifted its cleaver high over a shoulder, ready to strike.

A softly spoken word by Ahriman caused the beast to erupt in a pillar of flame.

Ahriman grinned as flames soared over the beast, enveloping every scale, sliding over every inch of its body. A terrible cry issued forth from its open maw, only for the flames to swarm down its throat. Scales blistered and popped, claws shrivelled, and teeth blackened. A minute later there was little more than a pile of ash and bone.

'How do you feel, my lord,' Avra looked shaken but relieved all the same.

'Well, Avra,' he shared a crooked grin as he smelt the charred flesh. It was intoxicating, had his tongue licking dry lips. He then turned his sight back to what remained of the beast. He adjusted his vision as he sought the soul of the creature. He found it moments later, a minute ball of red light that shone with molten radiance. He beckoned, and a second later felt the soul merge with his own.

With the merging of the soul came the knowledge of the Deios. Ryv'k he was named, a Deiosian running with a brood under the leadership of one called Ra'tor. Myriad images flashed before his eyes as he gazed upon the life of Ryv'k. With such recollection, he could envisage their lifestyle and understand their culture. He now knew their language, was privy to their hopes and desires. He felt the urge of the hunt and smelt the sweet scent of blood. He knew of the Blood-god, Bhral, and the sacrifices made to appease Him.

Most importantly, though, he knew how to reach their world.

CHAPTER TWENTY-SIX

Tarsin peered across the yard to where his men sat, perched atop segments of cut wood for the Oakwood and Stout's large hearth. Alongside lay the remains of the tavern's stables, now a shamble of splintered beams and loose planks. The men had remained at the tavern despite the upheaval, although the owner had fled with his family the same day as the earthquake. Bevan, second in command of Ciricello's Swords, stood by Tarsin's side, his aged face grim. The two men had spoken at length since Tarsin's arrival, and both had just finished addressing the men.

'You paint a terrible picture,' Bevan said after a moment of reflection.

Tarsin nodded. 'Aye, but it is the truth. Even as we speak Griffith, Captain of the Sceptres, prepares for our defence. War is upon us, my friend.'

'Well,' replied Bevan, 'the men are restless. Six weeks at sea will see to that, especially to a crew such as these dogs,' he smiled, casting an eye over the armed men.

The mercenaries shifted nervously upon their seats, despite the forced smile. The prospect of battle was generally not a concern, only this time there would be little in the way of compensation. Tarsin knew they would fight, though, for it was in their nature to do so.

'Is it time?' Beven fastened his sword belt tight.

'Aye,' Tarsin replied, remembering their nerve-racking race to the Oakwood and Stout, Jaegar and Vittorio constantly on the lookout for any dragon-headed beasts as they traversed the streets of Bastion. He'd fleetingly considered keeping Griffith with him for the run to the tavern, knowing his heavy hammer would be an asset once they confronted Avra, but the large man was close to exhaustion, the armour he wore weighing heavy on his frame. Besides, he thought it prudent to have a force of men prepared once they returned; if they returned.

He spun to his left to talk to Jaegar and Vittorio, the two men quiet as they gathered their strength. They knew what was to come. 'I'll gather the men, you lead the way.'

Jaegar nodded, gripping his axe tight as he did so. The distance between the tavern and Avra's villa was minimal. It would take the group no more than a handful of minutes to reach the house.

'What of your shoulder?' Tarsin pointed to Vittorio's bandaged arm.

'It smarts, but I'll live,' he replied. 'I can still fight, if that is your query?'

Tarsin could see his pale skin and knew the swordsman was struggling. Lucius' sword cut deep, the blade razor sharp. He already harboured grave concerns for his friend's survival. Running about the streets wasn't doing his health any favours, but he'd insisted. In the end, Tarsin knew he needed every sword he could muster.

'Then let's move out,' he spoke so everyone could hear. The gathered mercenaries stood as one, picking up their swords and strapping them to their waist. Thirty seasoned men: hard men, eager to protect their Master of Swords; eager to defend their city. With muttered oaths to Terros: god of war, and Frey: goddess of Fate, they readied themselves as best as able.

Tarsin fell in alongside Jaegar and Vittorio as they walked through a side gate and onto the street. Bevan followed close behind, the mercenaries forming into lines behind him. For several minutes they walked with purpose, Jaegar leading the way, before they crossed the broad expanse of the Avenue of Kings and moved into another side street, this one called Peddler's Way.

'We are not far,' the Herkosian said over his shoulder.

Tarsin turned to Bevan, motioning for him and his men to draw their swords as quietly as possible. A faint scrape was the only response as silver blades snaked free. They pushed on; Jaegar's pace slowing as they crept closer to Avra's abode. Even now, with the morning sun fast reaching its zenith, the shadows along Peddler's way were numerous, their reach long. Tarsin could see more than one mercenary experience a shiver as they rounded on a shoddy building with a green door streaked with blood.

'This is the one,' Jaegar motioned with his axe. The door was slightly ajar and swung inward with a gentle push. Beyond was a corridor with two dark doorways leading to private chambers, a set of stairs at the rear leading down to a cellar. 'If she is here,' he said, pointing his finger, 'she'll be down there.'

Tarsin gripped his blade tight and slid past Jaegar. 'Follow, and be vigilant,' he whispered, moving silently down the corridor. With utmost care the men stepped over the bloodstained floor and made for the staircase. 'Torch,' Tarsin offered his hand and waited whilst one of his men lit an oil-soaked cloth and wrapped it about a piece of wood. The flaming brand was then passed to him before he held it high to aid his descent. He reached the penultimate step and stopped, looking down on a scene of horror.

'Gods above,' he heard Jaegar's whispered curse as the tall man looked over his shoulder.

'Aye, it's a gruesome sight.' The remains of a body lay splayed on the cobblestoned floor; its chest ripped open, black gore everywhere. The steady drone of buzzing flies made their silent approach obsolete. Careful to avoid the corpse, Tarsin lifted a foot and stepped further into the cellar, holding his torch aloft so he could peer into its dark recesses, searching for any sign of the witch.

She wasn't here, he knew. The moment he saw the corpse he knew she'd be gone. All that remained now was a cellar masquerading as a charnel house.

'Tarsin!' it was Vittorio's voice that cut like a knife. 'I think you need to see this.'

He moved back to where Vittorio and Bevan stooped over the corpse, studying it intently. As he reached their side and lifted his torch he caught a glimpse of what drew their attention. 'Anok and Eli!' he shook his head. 'It's Lucius Vupello!'

Vittorio placed the tip of his sword under the golden crown still lying atop Lucius' head and gave it a flick. The crown fell away and rolled towards his booted feet where it fell with a clank.

Tarsin passed his burning brand to Vittorio and bent to retrieve the golden circlet, running his gloved thumb across the jade stone at its centre.

'How did he arrive here?' asked Jaegar. 'I thought you killed him, Vittorio.'

'Obviously not. Perhaps he was stronger than I gave him credit for, or maybe someone picked him up and carried him here.'

'Either way,' Tarsin pointed to the chalk circle surrounding the corpse with its elaborate symbols, 'he was sacrificed like so many others. Only this time, the sacrifice wore a kingly crown.'

'What does that mean?' It was Bevan who spoke.

'It means Avra's pet may now be flesh.'

'And that is bad because . . .?'

'. . . Ahriman, the Dark Lord of Chaos, is here for one thing. He is here to destroy the world.'

'What we can do to stop him?' Jaegar slapped his axe head hard against a palm.

'I do not know,' Tarsin moved to the bottom of the stairs, 'but I'll not stand idle. I cannot ask any of you to follow me, but if you do, know this; I go now to confront a god and his wretched witch.'

'Can they be killed?' Bevan smiled, his eyes gleaming with a hint of madness.

'I guess there's only one way to find out,' Tarsin returned the mad grin. 'Come, we make for Aston's Tear. I've an inkling that's where they're headed.'

The men stepped aside as he raced up the stairs before quickly following him onto Peddler's Way. Moments later they stood on the Avenue of Kings, the light from Aston's Tear a beacon few could resist.

'We keep close formation,' Tarsin shouted to the assembled men. Not one failed to step forward for the potentially fatal confrontation. But then he knew they would follow; for they were Ciricello's Swords: men of blood and steel, men of courage. Now they were ready to fight against a mad god and his crazed witch, ready to defend their lives.

Vittorio threw the flaming brand to the side as he stepped to Tarsin's left. Jaegar stepped to his right. With a single motion Tarsin lifted a hand high, then bought it down, pointing in the direction of the pyramid.

Every member of Ciricello's Swords moved on, naked steel in their hands, faith coupled with hope in their hearts.

*

Reefe O'Bannon stumbled in his mad rush and fell. He hit the ground hard, hands out, and slid across sand and dust. A cry of anguish burst from his lungs, a sob raked his body. He'd run for longer than he cared to remember, but his hopes of making it to the pyramid were fading by the minute.

He looked over his shoulder as he regained his feet. The shattered street was empty, but he knew the beasts were coming.

He whimpered and pressed on, putting one foot in front of the other as he lifted tired legs to stomp over uneven ground. He still couldn't believe he'd escaped the dark confines of Undercity; pinched himself every time he looked up to see the dismal sun. He'd gathered the Shadow Brethren as the Underlord asked, returned only to see him die, his head crunched by an enormous beast with fangs like daggers. The remaining knights charged, swords held high as they sought to engage, whilst Reefe backed away as fear gripped his soul.

He'd been running ever since.

Now he raced towards the pyramid, its shining light a summons to a man bereft of reason. He'd lost his sword at some point, remembered hearing it clang against stone as it fell from his weakened grip. He hadn't even looked back to see where it lay, just pressed on as he sought to put as much distance between he and those who pursued. He still had his jewelled dagger, the one he'd taken from the king's own study. It was little comfort, but if he could reach the pyramid, there would be soldiers standing guard. If he could reach the pyramid he'd be safe.

The street he followed ended abruptly, spilling onto a major thoroughfare of well-worn cobblestones. Deep wheel ruts lined each side, most lined with debris from the countless fallen homes. He stopped to catch his breath, looked to his right in the direction of Aston's Tear. A second passed before a guttural roar sounded in the distance.

Once again, he continued to run.

'Reefe!' the voice came from behind him, loud and clear. He stopped his flight, his mind telling him to turn, to see who called his name. 'Reefe O'Bannon?'

He spun to see what nightmare sought to present itself, fearing some demonic atrocity had materialized to cut him down. Instead he saw Tarsin Va and Enrico Vittorio standing in the street, a contingent of armed men in tow. All were carrying swords, except for a seven-foot-tall Herkosian wielding a vicious looking axe.

'Tarsin,' the relief in his voice was obvious, a fact he inwardly acknowledged as he strode towards Tarsin and his men. As he approached, he puffed out his chest and held his head high, a vain attempt to retrieve some of his pride and dignity.

'I see you made it out of Undercity,' Tarsin gave him a cursory look, noting his missing sword before lingering on his face where a large graze still stung and cracked lips bled.

'I did,' Reefe replied, 'but not without escaping the conflict. The dead below are many and I barely made it out alive.'

'Join us, then, as we head for Aston's Tear. I cannot guarantee your safety, though, for even now we march towards death.'

Reefe was about to comply when an almighty screech rent the air. Several large shapes sprang from between the buildings, drifting out of laneways. He looked beyond the gathered men; saw a dozen or so beasts step onto the street. A collective shout erupted from the swordsmen as they fell back to surround Tarsin.

'What are your orders?' Reefe heard one of the men raise his voice over the din.

Tarsin lifted his eyes towards the Herkosian and listened as the axe-man detailed what he saw. 'They've sent two for reinforcements,' the barbarian said, his eyes shifting as he counted their adversaries, 'a dozen remain.'

'We're thirty-three, not including Reefe O'Bannon,' Tarsin said as he spun his gaze towards him. 'Go,' he flung a hand towards the pyramid, 'make for Aston's Tear and call for aid. Griffith should be there with his Sceptres. Find him. Send him!'

'You cannot stay here, they'll slaughter you!' Reefe yelled back.

'I can, and I will. Now go!' Tarsin's voice was commanding. 'Once you've found Griffith,' he continued, 'head inside the pyramid. Kayla and Donal are there, they'll need your support. Tell them I'm coming. Tell them I'll be there soon.'

Reefe nodded his head in understanding. He was about to say something, anything before he parted ways, but another roar sounded as the beasts prepared to charge.

The former thief spun about and headed for Aston's Tear.

*

The constant chatter amongst learned men and women was becoming too much for Kayla to bear. Talk of portals, other worlds and alignments in the night sky were far from her grasp and did nought but make her giddy. Even when the stranger, Kian, spoke of the Deios, those she called the dragon-men, she failed to comprehend most of what he claimed. It was only as the talk shifted towards the last of the jaguars that her interest was finally piqued. Cappitus related all he knew concerning the portents he was familiar with, explaining to Kian, the Nepharii, what he considered to be Bastion's final days.

'When the last of the jaguars falls, so too does the city of Bastion. They are one, the city and the Vantos family. They share a symbiotic relationship. When one ceases to be, so too does the other.'

'It is more than that, Cappitus,' Neema shuffled forward to engage in the conversation. 'Bastion has long been the centre of civilization. Destroy Bastion, and the kingdom of Dervae will follow. The rest of the world will suffer in turn. Ahriman will see to it.'

'Aye, and with Arkos dead, the Vantos name is no more,' Cappitus appeared crestfallen.

'Is there nothing we can do to halt this madness?' Ruvin Ciricello spread his hands wide. Like many who crowded within the chamber, he too felt a need to be heard. Talk of leaving Bastion had met with strong resistance. Many felt obliged to stay and fight in some capacity, whilst others feared crossing into the unknown. Despite Kian promising a haven, few dared trust the word of a stranger, even one who claimed to help.

'I can help you evacuate to another world, one I know to be safe,' Kian remarked. 'There you can escape the Dark God you fear approaches, at least for a time. Then when you are ready, you can plan your assault and return.'

'What is to stop Ahriman from stepping through the portal and onto the new world?' Cappitus solemnly asked.

'Me,' Kian said.

'You,' the elder's eyes grew large. 'You've power enough to stop a god?'

'No, but I am guardian of the portal, and if I so choose, I can prevent its operation from the other side. It will not be possible for anyone to pass if it is misaligned.'

'You can do this?'

'I can,' Kian bowed before lifting his head, 'and I shall. On my word, you shall be safe for as long as need be.'

Kayla listened as the noise escalated once again, men and women raising their voices to offer all manner of advice. She didn't know how long the brothers and sisters would bicker for. They certainly didn't have long. The Deios, if that was their name, would arrive soon, she could sense it.

'Elder Cappitus,' a voice rose above the din. The crowd parted to better see who called. As they did Kayla saw two Swords of the Brotherhood striding into the chamber, Reefe O'Bannon held tight between them. He appeared to be exhausted; his eyes wild. There was blood smeared across his face.

'This one claims to know Kayla Tolsten,' one of the Sword Brothers began, 'and asked if he could speak to her. He says he comes bearing news of Tarsin Va.'

Elder Cappitus nodded, then made for the spanning bridge, whilst Ruvin and Jarred escorted Kayla to where Reefe was being held.

'Reefe,' she said as she reached his side. His head hung low, his body barely able to stand. Whatever torment he'd endured, it had taken its toll. 'Are you alright?'

The former thief raised weary eyes and she could see blood from a grazed cheek seeping towards his trident beard and bloodied lips. Scrapes and cuts lined his hands and knees and his clothes were sweat-stained and covered with dust. He still managed to smile at the sound of her voice, though. 'I'll be fine, Kayla,' he replied with a hoarse voice. 'I bear a few scratches and bumps, 'tis all.'

'What news do you bring of Tarsin?' Kayla almost begged.

The smile on Reefe's face faded to be replaced by a worrisome visage. His skin seemed to sag; the near-purple pools of darkness under his eyes prominent. He cleared his throat, so he could better convey his news, but looked troubled with what he had to say.

'Out with it, man,' Ruvin snapped. Like Kayla, Ruvin felt an urge to know where Tarsin was.

Reefe propped himself up and looked Kayla in the eye. 'I fear I'm the bearer of grave tidings, Kayla Tolsten,' he began. 'As I climbed the red steps before the pyramid, I chanced a look back along the Avenue of Kings. I saw Tarsin and his men, they were surrounded by dragon-beasts. Like your father did in the Undercity, I'm afraid he's chosen his last stand.'

*

Reefe watched the light in Kayla's eyes falter as he told her his news. He grimaced at seeing her so pained but knew in time such pain would fade. With Tarsin soon forgotten, he would fill the void, as he always vowed he would.

Old hands patted him on the back as they assessed his revelations. Reefe almost flinched at their touch. He cared nothing for the Brotherhood, and he certainly cared nothing for the city. He cared only for Kayla; his sweet Kayla. Having climbed the steps to stand before Aston's Tear, it was easy for him to avoid Griffith and his yellow and black garbed Sceptres. He'd feigned ignorance before, on countless occasions when the need arose, and he did so now. Tarsin's request for aid was easily forgotten, a thing of the past, irrelevant. What did he care if the swordsman died? He hoped he would. It wasn't natural for a man like Reefe to defy his longing for another; nor to endure such an interminable separation. Kayla was his; she simply didn't know it yet.

In time, she would come to understand, for he would be there to pick up the pieces.

'Are you certain, Reefe?' he heard a longing in Kayla's voice. 'Is there nothing we can do?'

'I'm afraid it may already be too late,' Reefe said with apparent conviction. Talk of dragon-headed beasts would stall even the foolhardiest. He knew few would dare face such hellish creatures by choice.

Kayla glanced wildly about those assembled, her emerald eyes wide, pleading to be heard. 'There is something you should all know,' she raised her voice, straightening her back.

A tall man with long dark hair stepped to her side. His skin was pale, his features unusual. Reefe had never seen his like before.

'What do you have to say, Kayla?' he asked with a foreign accent.

'It concerns Tarsin Va,' she began, locking eyes with elders and matrons alike. 'You claim the last of the jaguars is dead, and that all hope for Bastion is lost. But you are wrong. Tarsin Va is the last of the jaguars. His blood comes from the Vantos family.'

'How can this be?' Reefe heard the same question repeated several times in quick fashion.

'He is a bastard,' Kayla continued, 'but he's bastard to the king.'

'How can you know such . . . secrets?' Reefe heard himself ask, betraying his thoughts.

'He told me he spoke to Arkos when we searched for him in Highcastle. Here,' she reached over to Donal who held a hessian sack and pulled out the mahogany box, 'there are scrolls inside penned by the king himself that detail his claim.' Kayla flicked a latch, pulled out a scroll bound with cord and waxed with the king's seal. Elder Cappitus reached for it and ran his thumb against the wax until it cracked, then he untied the cord to allow the parchment to unravel.

'It is true,' Cappitus said as his eyes flickered over the script before him. 'This is the king's hand and here lies his mark,' he pointed to the signature at its conclusion.

'Arkos was dead when we found him,' Reefe said. 'You saw his body.'

'The fact remains, Reefe, I swear it. Tarsin is the king's only living son. He is heir to the throne of Dervae.' She reached out to the onlookers, and there were many. 'If you would see Bastion survive this invasion, if you would see a king newly crowned, then I suggest we send aid.'

Reefe couldn't believe the words he was hearing. Not only did Tarsin have a complete hold on Kayla, he'd even concocted some outrageous tale claiming he shared the same blood as the king. The kingdom lay poised on the brink of destruction and the man still found time to seek the throne. The entire premise was preposterous.

Yet the elders were being swayed into believing the same lies Kayla had been served.

'Brothers two, so young and free, now lie at peace, no longer three.' Cappitus said the words as if in a trance, yet many were the eyes that swivelled to gaze upon the old man. 'It was there all along; *"Brothers two, no longer three"*. It was not Arkos and the Princes Atillus and Theos mentioned in the verse, it was Arkos' three sons.'

'I'll leave at once,' the tall foreign man said. Long strides took him to the chambers entrance, where he paused to speak to the Sword Brothers who walked Reefe into the pyramid's confines. Reefe heard his strange voice call out. 'Find as many of your men as possible, raise the alarm. The time has come, ladies and gentlemen,' he peered back towards the gathering, his gaze sweeping each and everyone, 'war has come to Bastion. You have a choice, people. You either fight, or you flee!'

Then he was gone.

Reefe snorted at the man's departure and shook his head. 'Who was that crazy fool?' he asked, seeking someone who shared a similar sentiment.

Only no-one was listening.

*

Pain flared in Tarsin's hip as he ducked a viscous swipe. He grimaced, aware of blood seeping down his leg from an earlier slice but forgot the pain just as quickly as he thrust his sword into scaled flesh. A heavy grunt followed, and he almost fell to his left as the beast returned a backhanded blow. He crouched forward, thrusting his sword up once more until he felt hot sticky gore splash across his face.

The beast fell to the ground, its breathing ragged, its tongue lolling between huge fangs.

'Tarsin!' the deep voice belonged to Jaegar. Tarsin looked to his left; saw the mad Herkosian swinging his twin-bladed axe with deadly intent. The Northman stood as tall as many of the beasts, his long reach and ferocious axe taking their toll. But scarlet strips marred his leather armour, the axeman bleeding from numerous cuts. From where he stood, he could see his sweeping axe was beginning to slow.

Tarsin moved past the dying beast to reach Jaegar's side, playing the skirmish through his mind in the process. He remembered barking an order to his mercenaries as the beasts charged towards them, signalling for a line to be formed across the Avenue of Kings fifteen across and two deep. He and Bevan positioned themselves at the centre, whilst Vittorio and Jaegar took the flanks. When the demons arrived they charged and leaped with heavy blades and long claws, snarling and snapping as they closed, their multi-coloured scales glistening in the sun. Tarsin brought his hand down and fifteen blades rose to form a wall of cold, hard steel. The impact was thunderous.

Yet remarkably, amongst all the chaos of swinging swords and flaying arms, the wall held. Only he knew then as he did now; it was only a matter of time before the demons broke through.

The first to fall was Reinhart, a solid lad with round shoulders and a heavy swing. An overextended thrust was parried wide before a beast took his arm off at the elbow with a vicious chop. His howl of pain was cut short by a clawed hand ripping his face off before a mercenary in the second rank stepped forward with a two-handed strike and sunk his sword into the beast's muscled neck. Blood splattered across the street, its scent rousing the beasts into a further frenzy. Within seconds three more men were down and the carnage truly began.

Tarsin slipped in behind seven feet of blue scales and hammered his broadsword deep into a thigh. The beast fell forward in pain, its elongated head twisting to seek its quarry, but a sword chopped into its neck, once, twice, before severing its head. Tarsin moved on, barely stopping as he made his way to Jaegar. The Herkosian was fighting alone, battling furiously at the end of the line. Whatever advantage the mercenaries enjoyed in outnumbering their foe had been quickly eroded. Now they fought two against one, but it wouldn't last long. If Reefe didn't return with reinforcements soon, the battle would be lost. He prayed Griffith received the summons. They could do with his help.

He raced over several corpses, man and beast alike, and slid low as a blade whistled through the air where his head had been a second earlier. His calves strained as he pushed up, leaping and spinning as his sword sang in return. It sliced deep, cutting heavy golden scales with ease, and then sliced again. He landed cat-like, poised, alert, and within moments his sword had traced a pattern of death across a scaled torso. It fell, blood bubbling from numerous wounds; twitching, clawed fingers releasing its heavy cleaver.

Then he was by Jaegar's side.

The tall Herkosian was hemmed in close to a broken wall, his huge axe ill-suited for such confined combat. He required room to flex his shoulders, to spread his arms wide. For over a minute now he'd been forced to defend for his life, swinging his axe in small arcs to deflect the blows from his two adversaries.

Tarsin never even slowed as he waded in, his sword leading. The clash of steel rang loud as his first attack was blocked, but his second and third arrived so fast the beast could barely keep up. Crimson streaks criss-crossed its chest as it sought to retaliate, but its momentum was lost, along with its sense of victory. He could see the realization in its yellow eyes. He pressed in close, battering four blows high, forcing the beast back before slamming his razor-sharp blade deep into its throat. He turned to see how Jaegar fared, only to flick his head to the side as blood sprayed from a split skull, Jaegar's axe buried deep. The beast slid to the ground with a thud, steel grinding against bone as the Northman kicked the beast in the chest and ripped his axe free.

Tarsin took a deep breath, taking time to survey the battle from where he now stood, before wiping a hand across his brow. It came away wet with blood, but he barely noticed as he sought the line he and his mercenaries formed, only to find it had vanished. Bevan still fought at its centre, three mercenaries with him, but the rest of the line was broken, his mercenaries sorely pressed. Amongst all the chaos he feared fewer than a dozen survived.

'Where is Vittorio?' Tarsin heard Jaegar ask as he moved alongside.

Tarsin sought out his comrade, looking for his slight frame and his long dark curls. He gasped when he found him; saw him held high with a scaled fist wrapped about his throat. His feet dangled two feet from the ground, his bandaged arm streaming blood. There was no sign of his sword.

Tarsin ran, his mind brimming with anger as he watched the beast raise a pointed dagger to press against Vittorio's belly. With slow precision, it began to push the blade deep, holding his comrade still as blood began to stain his shirt.

'No!' Tarsin yelled, leaping past a duelling beast, his sword slashing across its eyes. 'Vittorio, I'm coming!'

Vittorio heard his words and fixed him with sad eyes.

A cleaver hammered close, Tarsin's sword blocking its descent at the last instant. He pushed past the attack and continued to run. He was twenty feet away; he'd be there in a second.

The beast plunged the dagger further, under the ribcage, deep into Vittorio's chest.

Tarsin didn't utter a sound, he just fell atop the beast like a whirlwind, his sword slashing and cutting and stabbing, his eyes red with rage, his strength primal. When Jaegar finally caught up to him, the beast was a ruined pile of scale and flesh.

'Tarsin!' Jaegar yelled, trying to reach his Captain, 'Tarsin!'

The red mist waivered then was gone. Tarsin saw the dead beast lying next to the crumpled form of Vittorio. He knelt and placed fingers at the swordsman's throat, feeling for a pulse.

'I'm here,' Vittorio's eyes flickered open.

'Lay still, my friend,' Tarsin said as he placed his hands over the wound. Blood seeped from between his fingers, running freely despite the pressure he applied.

'It's over, Tarsin,' Vittorio offered a half-smile. 'I go now, knowing my brother was avenged. I go now to meet him once again. I have wished for this. From the moment he died.' His eyes closed briefly. 'I would be by his side. I need to tell him how sorry I am. I need to ask for his forgiveness.'

'There is nothing to forgive, my friend,' Tarsin scanned the street, but then he remembered Vincent Vittorio's headless body falling into the muck. The image shook him, and he wondered how Enrico fared the past years, knowing it was he who pulled Vincent out of the mirror. Tarsin lifted tired eyes, then leant close and whispered in his friend's ear. 'Find your brother and know peace, Enrico Vittorio.' There was no response. Enrico Vittorio, like his brother, was dead.

'We need to move,' Jaegar snarled, the big man standing guard over his kneeling frame.

Tarsin closed Vittorio's eyes and stood, knowing now was not the time to grieve. He spun to appraise the situation, saw death and mayhem in return. His men, his thirty men, had dwindled to half-a-dozen. A handful of beasts still pressed the attack.

'More are coming,' Jaegar motioned with the end of his axe down the street. He followed the gesture, then spat to the side as he gripped his hilt tight. A score more raced towards them. He knew this was not a fight they could win. 'Do we take Vittorio with us?' Jaeger looked at his fallen comrade.

'No, he is dead; there is nothing we can do. If there's time later, we'll come back for him.'

'What of the dragon men? What if they eat him?'

Tarsin shrugged, 'Then I hope they choke. Come, let us go.'

Tarsin spun towards Bevan and his remaining men, only to see a tall, slender figure in dark robes plunge into the fight. Long black hair fell across his shoulders, framing a face cast from a different mould. High cheekbones sat beneath almond shaped eyes, his chin narrowed almost to a point. He wielded twin blades, grey in colour, their length like that of a hunting knife.

And he could fight.

The stranger spun into the fray, twirling and slicing as he went, swaying to the side to avoid the beasts return attacks, before stepping in quick to plunge his blades deep. Within seconds the beasts surrounding Bevan were down, and apart from the score charging down the street, their immediate foe was vanquished.

'I'm here looking for a man named Tarsin Va,' the stranger yelled as he met their gaze.

'You've found him,' Tarsin stepped forward. Before he could say another word a tide of black and yellow swept past him: two score of Bastion's Sceptres with ten-foot pikes held at arm's length, pointing towards the enemy. They positioned themselves twenty feet in front of where Tarsin stood; creating a wall of steel greater than Ciricello's Swords could muster. The familiar face of Cale Griffith reached his side a moment later, armoured still and holding his heavy hammer. He took one look at the fallen

Vittorio and bowed his head. 'I couldn't save him, Griffith,' Tarsin said.

Griffith nodded once then looked to his Sceptres, scanning their ranks before issuing an order for his men to stand strong.

'Tarsin Va, I am Kian,' the stranger strode to stand before him, his eyes taking in his blood smeared face, 'and it has come to light that you may be the last of the jaguars,' he was taller than Tarsin first thought, about the same height as Griffith.

Tarsin searched his golden eyes. 'How have you come across such knowledge?'

'It matters not, Tarsin,' he replied. 'What does matter is your immediate safety. The survivors of Bastion need you, as does the city itself. You are now their only hope.'

'What's he talking about?' Griffith moved close to his friend and placed a gauntleted hand on his shoulder.

Tarsin called Bevan over and asked him to turn about so he could retrieve the crown he'd placed in the older man's pack. He pulled it forth, the golden circlet with the Eye of the Jaguar. The jade stone sparkled brightly in the sun as he held it up for all to see. There was power in the crown, but it also came with responsibility. Tarsin could feel the weight of a kingdom residing within.

A clash of heavy bodies sounded as the beasts threw themselves hard against the piked wall. Shouts of encouragement could be heard amongst the defenders, officers yelling for the men to stand firm. Screams of pain erupted seconds later as claws found their mark and snapping jaws tore at flesh.

'We need you to retreat, Tarsin,' Kian spoke quickly, 'and to rally whatever forces you can find about the pyramid. If you would see your people survive, you must act now. You are their rightful leader.'

Tarsin met the stares of his men. He'd never asked for this, never asked for such responsibility. He certainly never expected it. All he ever dreamt for was recognition from a father to show that he cared. Now here he was, without a father once again, fighting a battle for a city now rightfully his. 'I do not know you,

Kian, but you speak the truth,' he bowed his head as he gathered his thoughts. Clarity was what he sought; clarity and a clear conscience. So, with a sigh he looked to the sky, hoping the sun would warm his skin and possibly ease his sudden fears. A small part of his conscience searched in vain for divine intervention. Only he rarely called upon the gods and he doubted they'd heed his call now. Instead he asked what his father would do, thought about what he would say. He was a jaguar, after all. With hands of steel, he lifted the crown and placed it atop his head.

'I am Tarsin Va,' he said to those assembled, 'bastard son of the late Arkos Vantos. And I am king.'

CHAPTER TWENTY-SEVEN

Ahriman smiled as another shining soul swooped towards him. It plunged deep into his chest, merging with his own dark, twisted life force. Despite their obvious differences, the souls of the recently dead could not resist his magnetic pull. With every tortured step he took with his crippled body, he became stronger and more alert. He'd felt disconcerted for a time when he first stepped into the light of day, for the restrictions he harboured now he was flesh tore like a serrated knife in his guts. As a shadow his influence was legendary, but confined to the material plane, confined to flesh stretched awkwardly across an ill-designed frame, his power was grossly limited. Step within his field of influence and hellish flames could devour a foe in an instant. Outside his influence, like any mortal, he would need to rely on cunning alone.

As the souls of the departed converged, though, he suddenly found his area of influence expanding.

He continued to place one heavy foot in front of the other, slowly making his way towards the glowing pyramid, the one Avra called Aston's Tear. He smiled inwardly, knew Aston to be nothing more than a fabrication, an entity founded to appease the masses in times of stress and despair. Aston was the embodiment of the sun, the life-giver. But unlike Ahriman, he was false, for he could never walk as a man upon the soil of this world.

Yet the temple built in his honour was real. The longer Ahriman studied its glowing walls of blue, the more he realized the ancient structure was never fashioned by the hands of man; at least not these men. The lines were too perfect, the symmetry otherworldly. Whoever erected the pyramid did so with power well beyond the ken of mortal man. Besides, Avra suggested within lay portals to other worlds, a feat even he could not fathom at present. No, whoever was responsible for the glowing pyramid was powerful, but if what the witch said was true, they'd provided a means for him to become the Supreme Being he'd always dreamed. No longer were his sights fixed solely on this world of man; now he was tantalized by thoughts of becoming the Blood-god, Bhral, on the world of the Deios.

With such possibilities open to him, his power would rise faster than expected. His desire to fashion a world in his own image was now a mere formality.

Until an unseen jolt of energy hit him like a thunderbolt.

Avra reached out for him as he fell, her withered, frail hands grasping at his cloak. The cloth tore in her feeble grasp as he hit the ground hard to roll in the dust. Vertigo swamped him, along with a keen buzzing in his mind, until he eventually found himself half perched on the side of the road.

'Are you alright, my lord?' Avra practically squawked as she knelt by his side.

He slapped her fawning hands clear and slowly stood as a wave of nausea swept his body, causing lights to sparkle before his eyes.

'What ails you?' Avra's voice was becoming high pitched.

He breathed deep to steady himself, seeking to keep a twisted arm out-stretched for balance, but lights continued to flare before his eyes. The wave of nausea returned, this time with greater force and he doubled over so he could vomit black wads of bile onto the ground. As the violent spasms passed, he wiped the back of his hand across his mouth and raised a weary head skyward. He thought to call the souls swirling nearby, seeking to assimilate their power for he felt a sudden weakness. Only when he searched for their tell-tale golden glow, he saw nought but a dusty sky.

'My lord?' Avra placed a hand on his shoulder.

'Do not touch me, witch!' Ahriman screamed, his face contorted with rage. He could feel the blisters around his mouth split open, could feel pus and blood seeping down his chin.

He almost grinned as the witch withdrew her hand as if scorched by the very fires of Hell. 'I seek only to help,' Avra pressed, undeterred by his outburst. 'You are a god, you should not suffer so.'

A calming breath settled his nerves. Avra was right, he was a god, but he felt weak and drawn. The souls he'd claimed in their short walk still resided within, but the thousands circling were no more. Tens of thousands of them; vanished. He shook his head, hoping the nausea affecting his vision was alone responsible for the absence of golden globes, but as he scanned the streets and the sky above he knew they were gone.

'The souls have vanished,' Ahriman finally said, more to placate Avra's growing concern than to engage in conversation. 'I shall not increase my strength without them.'

'Where did they go?' she asked, also looking to the sky. He knew she could not see the golden globes, but she searched regardless.

'I do not know,' he replied, wincing at the glaring sun. 'They have simply disappeared.'

'Well, they cannot have gone far,' Avra spoke as one vested with wisdom.

He shook his head once more, clearing the last vestiges of nausea. 'Come, witch,' he beckoned with a gnarled hand, 'I would see this glowing temple and its portals you speak of. There is power there, frightfully strong. I would taste it, if I could.'

He heard her sigh and instinctively knew the walk would take its toll. 'We will be there soon, my lord,' Avra said as she helped him regain his feet. His pain remained, acute spasms flickering beneath his skin, his bones jarring with every step. Despite the discomfit he needed to believe in Avra's counsel concerning the pyramid. With or without the souls of the dead, he would be there soon, and the power contained within would be his.

*

Men of the Brotherhood raced madly about the chamber.

Kayla watched, fascinated as they bustled every which way. Kian, foreigner from another world, claimed war had arrived. She knew he was right, for she'd seen the enemy. She felt safe as she looked about the chamber, but only whilst the demons were kept at bay. If they should fight their way inside the pyramid, all would be lost.

A shout heralded the arrival of a contingent of Swords of the Brotherhood. A dozen armed men, old and stout with swooping moustaches and greying hair, stomped in unison as they entered the chamber and took up position along the curved wall. Black tabards covered steel mail, and the Sword Brothers' customary long sword could be seen belted at their waist. They were to be the last line of defence. Despite their war-like stance and air of authority, Kayla feared they would not be enough. Not against the tide of slashing claws and ripping teeth she knew was coming.

'What are we going to do?' Jarred asked the obvious question. The lad sat next to Donal, a comforting arm around the younger boy's shoulders.

Beside Kayla stood Ruvin Ciricello, with Reefe O'Bannon seated on the floor next to the boys. Neema paced several feet away. 'We wait,' Ruvin replied, his manner somewhat surly. Ever since news of Tarsin Va reached him, he'd contemplated leaving the chamber and searching for his friend. Several times Kayla had spied the older man mouthing the words "I owe him my life", and his torment was beginning to show. A second later he would calm himself down, reminding himself of Tarsin's prowess with the blade.

A chuckle sounded from Reefe as he sat upon the floor. Kayla saw him look up at Ruvin with tired eyes. 'The beasts are out there, old man, and they'll have our heads. You cannot stop them, nor can Tarsin. Not all of them.'

'What then, do you suggest?' Ruvin asked, although Kayla could see from his narrowed eyes he thought little of Reefe's opinion.

'Flee, as the foreigner said. We cannot fight the beasts and hope to live, not if they come in number. We should do as he suggested and step through the portal. At least there we'll be safe.'

'What of those fighting the creatures? How will they make it through the portal alive?'

Reefe shrugged. 'Some will, others won't, we can't save everybody. Sacrifices have to be made, old man.' Reefe stretched out his arms, cracking his joints in the process. Kayla then watched as he turned to her and offered half a smile. 'Lord Tolsten stood his ground so others could flee,' he said, 'perhaps Tarsin has done the same.'

'Tarsin Va is not a man easily killed,' spat Ruvin.

'So you keep saying, old man,' Reefe returned. 'Perhaps he'll fare better if you go lend a hand.'

'Enough!' Kayla raised her voice, hoping to divert their attention. 'This endless bickering is not helping.'

'Then tell the old man to keep quiet,' Reefe gritted his teeth then winced in pain as his split lip re-opened.

'I'm scared, Kayla,' Donal lifted tired eyes, his comment timely. She wanted to say something to ease his fear, but the lad had seen the beasts. She was having a hard-enough time herself, and thoughts of Tarsin continued to swirl within her own mind. She knew he was Arkos' bastard son. She knew the line of jaguars had not ended. Tarsin had cautioned her with his knowledge; told her she would know what to do with it. Now she felt ill just thinking about it, her head swimming and her heart racing. She wiped sweat from her brow and blinked as stars sparkled overhead, catching her eye. Then a tremendous jolt swept through her body and everything went black.

She woke to a calm voice, a soothing voice. Neema, robed in white, was kneeling over her prone form. Sturdy, strong fingers pressed against her temples, rubbing gently in small circles. 'How do you feel, Kayla?' she asked with a concerned smile.

'Disorientated,' she replied, and there was pain in her back causing her to squirm. Neema moved a hand and held it over her torso. She closed her eyes and kept it hovering in place for several seconds, then let her hand drift lower. When her eyes opened, she shared a brief glance with Cappitus, the tall elder having raced to her side. She couldn't tell from where she lay, but Kayla felt some communication pass between the two.

'You can sit up, now,' Neema helped with a strong hand on her back.

'Thank you,' Kayla replied as she lifted a hand to her head. 'What happened?'

'You passed out, young lady,' Cappitus intervened. 'Lack of water, I'd say. It's a warm day and you've travelled far.' He leant forward and offered a wooden cup filled with water. She drank the cool liquid and closed her eyes, aware of a dull ache at the base of her skull. Donal's small hand wormed into her own, a brief comfort as she squeezed it tight.

'Rest, Kayla, and do not worry about what is to pass,' Cappitus offered a thin smile, obviously his method of calming everyone's nerves. 'If what you say is true, about Tarsin Va, that is, then hope still remains. The noose may be tightening, but we are not finished yet.'

'No,' said Neema, 'but the thief has the right of it.' She looked towards Reefe and held his gaze with an icy stare.

'Me?'

'Yes, you,' Kayla watched as Neema stabbed a thick finger into his chest. 'We need to flee, as Kian suggested. We need to flee now.'

'Why?' several voices asked at once.

Neema turned her head, offering a quick glance in Cappitus' direction. 'Because there are allies to be found on this other world; allies who could help sway the battle against the Dark God. Right now, we are sorely pressed.'

'What of Tarsin?' Kayla asked. 'I'll not leave him behind.'

Neema moved away from Reefe and placed a hand on her shoulder, looking deep into her emerald eyes. 'If what you say is true and Tarsin is last of the jaguars, then he can take care of himself. Trust me when I say this, for he is marked for greatness.'

'But . . . I shan't leave him. I can't.'

'Kayla, my dear Kayla,' Neema shut her eyes, allowing a single tear to slip down her cheek. When she opened them again, there was a steely glint that spoke of grim determination, of hardship coupled with longing. 'My dear,' Neema continued, 'with the situation we've been dealt, I'm afraid you do not have a choice.'

*

Tarsin heard the splatter as one of his men doubled over to heave, vomit striking the cobblestoned street. It was Conall, one of the youngest of Ciricello's Swords, a man in his early twenties. Tarsin reached forward and lifted him by the collar of his leather vest. His wan complexion seemed out of place in the midday sun.

'Are you alright?' he could see fear in Conall's eyes, strands of bile on his chin. A nasty cut above one eye still seeped blood, but otherwise, the red-haired youngster seemed unharmed.

'I'll live,' he spat to the side, 'at least for now, your majesty.'

Tarsin raised a hand to touch the crown. He still couldn't believe he'd done such a foolish thing, but his men accepted his transition from captain to king without a word. He knew they would, though, for they were *his* men. It was the rest of Bastion's population he feared to address. How would they respond to a man they didn't know?

Kian, the tall man with the almond shaped eyes moved close to his side. 'We need to act quickly, King Tarsin,' he said as they raced along King's Avenue towards the pyramid. 'The people are distressed, they need a leader. You are that man.'

'I never asked for this.'

'It is yours regardless.'

Tarsin nodded and flicked a glance behind, appraising the retreat he'd ordered. Griffith and his Sceptres were spread across the avenue, their pikes still held firm as they stomped a steady beat backwards. Tarsin, Jaegar and Kian raced ahead, along with Bevan and Conall and the three remaining mercenaries who survived the clash. The Deios, as Kian called them, were beyond. After the initial charge, they'd fallen back to await reinforcements. Tarsin couldn't be certain, but it appeared their number was rapidly increasing, lithe forms continuing to sift from between ruined buildings to crowd the avenue.

'We need to form a perimeter once we reach the pyramid,' Tarsin said, speaking his thoughts aloud. 'We'll stand atop the red granite and defend the steps. We should be able to hold long enough for the citizens to escape.' He knew such a stand was a considerable risk. There were four sets of steps leading from

Aston's Circuit to Aston's Tear, positioned at each of the cardinal points, and the granite base the pyramid sat upon was enormous. If the Deios fashioned a means to climb the thirty-foot walls, they would never hold. Their only defence lay in being decisive. They didn't have time to ruminate over tactics or reposition men, nor could his authority be questioned. If the people refused to listen, they would die. 'Jaegar,' Tarsin glanced towards the Herkosian, 'find what remains of the Palaceuard when we reach Aston's Tear and take command.'

'Aye, consider it done. Where would you like us?'

'On the eastern steps, where the fighting will be fiercest,' Tarsin replied. 'If we cannot hold there, then it's over before we begin. I'll leave Griffith and a large contingent of his Sceptres also. You gather your men as quickly as able and join them.'

'What of yourself?' Jaegar asked.

'I'll be there when I'm needed, but first I'll need to speak to elder Cappitus.' He spun his attention back to Kian. 'You mentioned the portal to your world would open soon,' he said, 'how long do we have?'

Kian glanced skyward and sought the sun's position. 'An hour, no more,' he replied, 'and it will remain open for two hours thereafter.'

'So, we have three hours,' Tarsin mused, knowing the battle to come would be vicious. But first he needed to persuade the people of Bastion to flee their city, to step into Aston's Tear and place their trust in never-before-seen magic. More troublesome still would be the fact they would hear the words from a man unknown to them, a man wearing their beloved king's crown.

The only solace Tarsin felt in the rising chaos was the likely reaction of the populace. Once they saw the Deios charging towards them, they would run. He hoped when they did, they would choose the right direction.

A shout was raised as the group arrived at the base of Aston's Tear, the thirty steps leading to its platform crowded with onlookers. Some were mildly curious; others fearful, for the guttural roars of the Deios were even now drifting on foul winds.

At the top of the steps a line of yellow and black liveried guards stood alert, their eyes focused on Cale Griffith's ordered retreat.

'Move, people!' Tarsin yelled as he took the steps two at a time. 'Move! War is upon us!'

It had the desired effect. Stragglers loitering about Aston's Circuit quickly made for the steps. Few knew of the danger creeping close, and those who did were already in position, blades and pikes held firm.

Tarsin and Jaegar took the steps side-by-side with Kian, the three reaching the top all bloodied and spent. They stopped to catch their breath, then looked back the way they had come. From here they could see straight down the Avenue of Kings, its broad thoroughfare cluttered with debris following the earthquake, its once straight lines now buckled and twisted. But it was the sight of a hundred scaled figures glittering in the sun that aroused sudden gasps amongst the crowd. If it wasn't for the sharp claws and glistening fangs, the sparkle of colour along their serpentine length could be construed as rather beautiful. It was certainly mesmerizing.

'Who are they?' someone asked from behind.

Kian raised his voice, 'They are Deios,' he said, 'from a world called Dei. They are hunters.'

'What do they seek here?'

Tarsin saw Kian tilt his head to the side in thought. 'They seek blood; your blood,' he finally said. 'Bastion is now their hunting ground, you are their prey.'

A guard of the Sceptres stepped forward, his hands wrapped tight around the shaft of his pike. A glimmer of recognition flashed in the man's eyes, only Tarsin couldn't recall having met the man before. He wore the yellow and black surcoat over chain mail, a sword belted at his waist.

The guard looked up at the crown, moistening dry lips with his tongue. 'Am I right in saying well met, King Tarsin?'

'You are,' Tarsin offered a nod, his jaw clenched firm. He still couldn't recall having met the guard before, but somehow, he knew his name.

Tarsin watched the guard as he offered a slight bow. 'I am Setorious,' he said, 'Lieutenant Setorious of the Sceptres. Cale Griffith asked me to keep an eye on you when you first arrived in Bastion.'

Tarsin looked him in the eye as a flash of understanding swept over him. A wave of anger was suddenly suppressed by a notion of guilt. If he'd been the man he was supposed to be, he would have never been placed under such observation. He shook his head to clear it of unnecessary thoughts and appraised the lieutenant. This was his first real test of acceptance. Fail this, and the people of Bastion would disclaim him, possibly even tear him down. 'Walk with me, Setorious,' he motioned with a hand towards the pyramid and the increasing crowd surrounding it.

'As you wish, your majesty,' Setorious offered a bow before signalling two of his men to fall in behind. Jaegar took his leave and set out to find the remnants of the Palaceguard.

'Kian,' Tarsin yelled over the escalating din, 'inform Griffith to stand firm until I return.'

The tall man nodded and set about lining men of the Sceptre along the perimeter. Cale Griffith and his retreating men were almost at the steps, still ushering stragglers before them as they sought to reach perceived safety.

Beyond stood the Deios; silent now as they watched men flee.

Tarsin pushed ahead, realising how fragile their situation was. Kian had discussed with him the possibility of escaping through the portal and retreating to a world he was familiar with. Tarsin harboured doubts as to how safe the world might be. He'd seen the world of the Deios with its bloated red sun and unfathomable heat. It was nightmare incarnate. The prospect of informing the general population of his decision to flee was not one to relish, either. Here he was, an unknown quantity, reaching out to survivors who'd been through Hell, and all he could offer was flight.

He felt his teeth clench hard together, aware his choices were now limited. He was the last of the jaguars, so hope remained so long as he lived. At least elder Cappitus believed such nonsense.

He vowed to remain alive, though, even if it meant fleeing to another world.

The rest of the population could either adhere to his decision or become food for the Deios. That or die at the hands of the Dark God.

A shout flew ahead as Setorious raised his voice, clearing a path to the pyramid entrance. Tarsin could see a dozen heavily armoured Swords of the Brotherhood standing guard, grim faces doing their best to keep the curious and fearful at bay. A handful of elders spoke to the agitated crowd, seeking to calm nerves and offer advice on the situation at hand. It appeared to be having some effect, although he sensed it would be fleeting. For a moment, he pondered how to approach the converging mass of people before he saw the tall frame of elder Cappitus stride out to meet him, relief evident on his tired face.

Tarsin held up a hand as the elder reached his side, 'Although I do not wish it, elder Cappitus,' he said, 'I have claimed the crown and with it the title of king. It is my right to do so, for Arkos was my father.' Several onlookers whispered behind raised hands. He ignored them and pressed on, 'I have no political prowess, but I do understand the lay of the land. I can also fight, elder, better than any man I know. I will fight for you, give you time to escape, for I fear that is all that is left to us now.'

'This turn of events is unprecedented, my king,' Cappitus offered a bow, his eyes alight with renewed hope, 'and I find it remarakable Arkos could keep your birthright a secret for so long, although your father was a canny tactician with an astute mind. I shouldn't be so surprised. To have a jaguar return is a blessed relief, I might add.'

'Not if we can't survive it isn't. The Deios . . . the dragon-men, have greater numbers than I imagined. I doubt we can hold for long. Not with so few soldiers on hand. If I could send word to Admiral Rhys I would be glad, for he has a thousand men and more aboard the *Leviathan*. Given time we could summon those who are south fighting against Al-Za'im,' Tarsin wiped blood from his hand on a sleeve. 'Only we don't have time on our side, do we Cappitus?'

'No,' replied the elder, 'we find ourselves in a deep pit, deeper than most would imagine. Still, I sense a sliver of light remains.'

'Aye, but it is dim,' Tarsin leant forward so that he and Cappitus could converse in private. 'What of the Dark God, elder,' he asked, 'where is he in all of this?'

'We do not know, your majesty, but he is close,' Cappitus steepled his fingers together as if in prayer. 'Whatever power he has at his disposal, I believe it will be greater than our own. I do not think we can best him. Not here, not now. We are too depleted and disorganized.'

'Do you trust Kian?' Tarsin asked.

'I believe I do.'

'Then you agree we should leave through the portal?'

The elder breathed deeply through his nose as he contemplated the question, his chest expanding. When he released the air from his lungs, an accompanying sigh ensued. 'I agree, sire. We should flee, but only to consolidate our forces. Then we return.'

'When we do, we send word at once. I would have our forces here in number,' Tarsin paused as a thought crossed his mind. 'When we return, we'll not arrive via the portal inside the pyramid, but some underground portal buried beneath the city.'

'Aye, so I've been informed by Ruvin.'

Tarsin pressed his lips together as he looked towards Aston's Tear. 'What of young Donal,' he asked, 'did he accompany Kayla inside?'

'The young lad with the blonde hair, yes,' Cappitus nodded.

'Find him. The lad is a mastermind, can remember everywhere he's been. He has maps, maps taken from Arkos' study,' He tapped a finger against his chin. 'He can show you where the Deios portal lies; possibly show you where others may be. If we can return and know the location beforehand, we can escape the city.'

'What of the Deios who remain?' asked Cappitus.'

Tarsin pushed his shoulders back and placed a hand on the pommel of his Rykedian broadsword. The armour he wore, claimed from Highcastle, was already blood-stained and marked. He chanced a look at the blue steel, knew it was fashioned for a king. He also knew it was strong. 'Leave them to me,' he answered, a gloved finger tracing the jaguar embossed on his breastplate. 'It's about time we took the fight to those overgrown lizards.'

*

With so much blood on the streets, Ra'tor was finding it increasingly difficult to remain alert. Several times he found himself salivating at the smell, his tongue snaking forth to taste the air, his blood coursing through veins bulging with suppressed fury. Yet he controlled his urges to stave off his hunger. He would feast when the time was right.

Now was not such a time.

He walked past several of his slain brood, their scaled bodies lying bloodied on the ground. Gaping wounds still oozed as he shifted one with his clawed foot, whilst others lay with punctured torsos, some with caved in heads. A great many suffered long, vicious slices, reminiscent of the wounds Shyxt wore when he died in front of the golden ellipsoid. Ra'tor wondered if they were killed by the same creature, but then saw a heavy blade embedded in the skull of a bloodling and knew it couldn't have been the one with the lightning sword alone.

'Tysta is now before Bhral, offering his blood,' Rax't appeared at his side, his voice heavy.

Ra'tor pulled the axe out of the bloodling's skull, examined it, then threw it high and far. It crashed with a ping seconds later. Like Shyxt, Tysta had been far too eager for a kill. Young and brash, now both had died unnecessarily.

'It is this world,' Rax't kicked at a pale corpse dressed in leather, black cloth covering its torso. 'These weaklings fire the blood, make us reckless. Then they turn on us with blades of steel and fight.'

'It is unusual,' Ra'tor sighed. More than a score of his brood had died since they crossed over. Never had he lost so many in a single day. On their world, it was rare to lose more than one per hunt. Here, the odds had changed.

'Do we continue?' Rax't lifted his large scaled head.

'We continue,' Ra'tor spoke without hesitation. He knew they were here for a reason. The Blood-god had shown him the way. 'Only we move with caution. The weaklings fight back, unlike the *breviks* back home.' The thought of hunting the large, cumbersome beasts caused doubts to surface. Hunting the four-legged beast was relatively risk free, and one beast alone could feed fifty with ease. But the red-skinned beast with its prodigious girth tasted foul in comparison to these weaklings. 'Despite their lack of size, the flesh here is quality.'

'The price is high,' Rax't reminded him.

'Then we shall be more careful. We'll wait for Zaxa and Terrak to bring their broods forward and let them lead the hunt. I doubt we'll have to convince them, especially Zaxa.'

'No, he'll relish the task.'

'And if he should fall, I'll be there to pick up the pieces,' Ra'tor smiled, an unusual grin revealing numerous ivory fangs. He knew Zaxa better than Zaxa knew himself. The Deiosian wouldn't be able to resist the call of blood, and when he tasted his first, his blood-rage would take hold. How the pale skinned weaklings would deal with Zaxa's seven-and-a-half-foot frame he had no idea, but it would be worth the wait to find out. Maybe if Bhral deemed it fitting, the towering Deiosian with the bronze scales tinged gold would falter.

Ra'tor would be close when he did, all purposeful and proper with fangs bared and a twinkle in his eye.

The sound of clawed feet striking stone approached from ahead and he fixed his gaze on two runners, watching as indigo scales shimmered in the afternoon light.

'How goes the hunt,' Rax't asked as he stepped forward to address the bloodlings.

'The pale skins flee to the temple of blue light, my lord,' the bloodling, Vrax by name, spoke with eyes downcast. 'We followed, but there are many gathered; more than we could count.'

'There are some wearing cloth of yellow and black who bar our way,' offered Kree, the second of the two. 'They stand atop a blood-stained block, with poles of silver in their hands.'

Ra'tor flared his nostrils and breathed deep. He'd spied the temple of blue light when they first stepped above ground, its shining peak a beacon in this fragile world. Whatever it represented, he'd felt an urge to see it in its entirety. He would do so now, especially now.

For the temple sat atop a blood-stained block.

Ra'tor knew he'd been summoned to do the Blood-god's work. Now he had proof. Bhral was here, bound in this temple of light, waiting to be freed. Why else would the rock be blood-stained? Somehow the pale skins had captured him, entombed him, and sought to keep the Deios from finding him.

Ra'tor had been given a sign, now he was here.

Whatever else happened this day, one thing was certain. Bhral would be freed, even if he had to shed the blood of every pale skin standing in his way. It was his destiny. When this day was done, the blood-stained rock would become a darker shade of red.

With a wave Ra'tor beckoned the two bloodlings to join him and Rax't as they began to walk towards the temple. They crossed a junction, moved past a fallen building and walked onwards, their clawed feet clicking against stone until they finally looked ahead to see almost a hundred of Ra'tor's brood crouched upon the path. Beyond sat the temple in all its glory, its walls a magnificent, vibrant blue. It was as Kree said, and a thin line of weaklings stood guard about its perimeter.

Deios faces spun to see their leader, lust sparkling in their yellow eyes.

'Do we hunt?' asked Kree.

'No, we wait,' Ra'tor answered. 'We wait for Zaxa and Terrak to arrive. Bhral is confined in the temple beyond; his blood stains the rock below. To free him, we'll need greater numbers.'

'When they arrive, then shall we hunt?'

Ra'tor scanned the pale skins standing atop the red granite wall. He searched for the one with the lightning blade, looking for his close-cropped black hair and broad shoulders. He desperately hoped he would be there; prayed he would be there.

He wasn't, at least not yet. When he did show, Ra'tor knew he would seek him out.

He breathed deeply; calming himself. He knew to cede all control to the blood-lust now would be detrimental to their goal. He must be patient, as Bhral would expect. This was his test, his rite of passage. He couldn't let emotion blur his path, yet at the same it was raw emotion fuelling his body. He knew a balance between the two was necessary. So, with a wry grin Ra'tor appraised his brood, waiting for the yellow eyes to lock onto his own. When they did he slowly raised a heavy arm to shake a mighty clawed fist in acknowledgement. 'When Zaxa and Terrak arrive,' he roared, fury barely restrained, his muscles stretched tight, 'then we shall hunt!'

A roar sounded in return as his brood raised fists and swords and cleavers of steel.

For an instant, it felt as if the very ground shook.

CHAPTER TWENTY-EIGHT

A blazing sun beat down on Bastion, tempered only by a southern sea breeze tinged with salt. Tarsin could smell the brine, a welcome respite when compared to ash. He thought of Admiral John Rhys and his thousand men aboard the *Leviathan*. If they were here, he could sweep the Deios from the streets. Without them, he wondered if they could hold at all.

He made his way to the top of the eastern steps, where Kian and Griffith stood, men of the Sceptre spread to either side. The steps were thirty feet wide, carved into the granite an age long past and worn at the centre by the passage of countless feet. The steps north, south and west were likewise manned, fifty of Griffith's men positioned at each, accompanied by a handful of the Palaceguard. Tarsin knew they were not enough should the Deios seek to out flank them, but for now the beasts remained before the eastern steps. Opposing them stood more than a hundred men of the Sceptre accompanied by Jaegar and forty seasoned knights of the Palaceguard. To bolster their number, he'd recruited an assortment of fighters and thugs found loitering amongst the crowd, along with a handful of survivors from either the southern barracks or guardsmen from the north gate. Behind the first line of defence he then organized another row of men, mercenaries mostly, including his own survivors from Ciricello's Swords. Bevan stood at their centre, ready to command once again.

'Their ranks have grown,' Griffith huffed as he fell in beside him.

Tarsin scanned the Avenue of King's, adjusting his estimates as he assimilated their size and number. He fumed quietly, briefly toyed with the idea of calling the Swords of the Brotherhood to stand with them. They numbered close to eighty, seasoned men strong of arm and stoic to the last. Their presence would help fortify the spirits of those standing on the brink, but they also served another purpose.

'Kian,' Tarsin said as he reached the tall man's side, 'I need you back at the pyramid with elder Cappitus. As soon as the portal shifts, you need to lead the way. The evacuation will not proceed unless you are there to convince them otherwise.'

Kian held a hand over his eyes as he peered towards the pyramid's shining blue walls. A shadow crept up its eastern face. 'The time is almost upon us,' he said, 'I'll do as you say, King Tarsin.'

Tarsin nodded consent, then grabbed the man's arm as he passed. 'I've placed a great deal of trust in you, Kian,' he said with baited breath, 'do not fail me.'

'Have no fear on that count, King Tarsin, for Bastion was once my home also. Although back then she was called Aos: the first wonder of the world. I would see her reclaim such a title.'

Tarsin offered a nod, 'Then do as we suggested and lead the people through.'

'It shall be as you command,' he returned. 'Remember, King Tarsin, to look for the plaque with the glyph of the deer. If all goes well, I'll see you on the other side.'

The tall stranger raced away with long strides and merged with the crowd of onlookers. Tarsin spun back to find Griffith and Jaegar standing with grim looks. Like many, they feared this was their last stand. There was no escape out here, nowhere to run. All they could do was stand their ground.

'So, this is it,' Griffith swung his hammer over his shoulder.

Tarsin shrugged, then stepped past the man to stand on the top step. Two hours they needed to hold for. Two hours standing atop a set of thirty steps. He harboured no illusions regarding the feasibility of their resistance. They simply weren't strong enough to hold against beasts of greater height and weight, and from his latest assessment their numbers mimicked their own. If they charged en masse, it would be difficult to halt their rush. Right now, he needed to make a statement, cause chaos to blossom in their ranks, not his.

Right now, he needed to be unpredictable.

'Gentlemen,' Tarsin yelled, turning to address the armed men. 'Very few of you know me, most will have never heard of me. I am Tarsin Va, bastard son to the late King Arkos. Through events beyond my control I am now the rightful King of Dervae.' He moistened lips suddenly dry. 'I am the last of the jaguars, the last in a line who have called Bastion home for a thousand years. This is your home also, a wondrous city, the capital of the world. It is rightfully ours. It belongs to us!' He swept a hand towards the Deios crowding below as they inched closer by the second. They could hear the words above, even if they could not understand them. Tarsin knew they sensed battle was near. 'They come with conquest in mind, at a time when we have suffered. Bastion has toppled to become a crippled shell and they crawl from her depths to take what is mine and to take what is yours.' He paused for a moment, taking a chance to look down on their antagonists. A handful of beasts pushed their way to the front, their height over seven feet, their shoulders broad and heavily muscled. Tongues snaked forth to taste the air and Tarsin wondered if they could taste fear from the men above. He turned back to his men and yelled, 'I say they are cowards!' The men began to stir, anger in their eyes. The clinking of chain mail and the scrape of swords being drawn was music to his ears. 'Now they'll confront true men, strong men, men with steel in their hands and steel in their hearts. I say let them come, let them climb our red steps. Because we'll be waiting. And when they ascend, we'll send them straight back to Hell!'

Tarsin raised his arm high, his fist clenched tight.

More than a hundred swords and pikes rose to join him, naked steel flaring in the afternoon sun as furious voices yelled their displeasure. Tarsin waited for the noise to subside then lowered his arm. 'Men of Bastion,' he yelled, 'step back!' They did so haltingly, confusion on many faces. 'Archers, step forward!'

Twenty-six men lead by Bevan stepped between the retreating Sceptres, all equipped with salvaged long bows, arrows nocked. Without a word, they took aim at the Deios below, feathers brushing ears as bows creaked, awaiting their king's order.

Silence descended between the two forces, broken only by the wind's gentle sigh.

'Loose!' Tarsin ordered as his hand cut through the air to point directly at the Deios.

Twenty-six bows twanged in unison, arrows streaking towards scaled hides glittering in the sun. By the time they struck, twenty-six more were nocked.

'Loose!' the second call sounded.

Screams rent the air as death fell from the sky.

'Loose!' he called a third time, arrows flying straight and true.

Below was pandemonium as Deios swatted and ducked to avoid the carnage streaking from above. Arrows jutted from protected hides, piercing scale and flesh with consummate ease at such close range. Dozens were down, ripping shafts from shoulders and chests, arms and legs. Others fell never to rise again, arrows finding their mark and striking throat or heart. The twang of loosed arrows persisted as the mercenaries blurred the sky with wooden shafts, continuing until their quivers emptied.

'Archers, fall back,' Tarsin barked the order, although he wished he'd found more marksmen within the crowd, wished he had another score of bows. He lifted his hand high once again. 'Men of the Sceptre, step forward.' A single line of yellow and black appeared at the forefront, silver pikes lowered towards the gathering beasts, Liuetneant Setorious at their centre. Tarsin bade them advance four steps, coercing them to walk down towards their foe. They did so, but were then stopped, enabling them to brace their long-shafted pikes against the step behind them. Fifteen men crowded close together, another fifteen directly behind. The pikes' steel blades were held steady, creating a wall of pain for any who cared to advance. 'Hold your line,' Tarsin kept his hand aloft, 'and wait for the charge.'

It was not long in coming.

The Deios could offer little in retaliation to the archer's assault, but when the shafts ceased, the beasts rose off the ground and spat and cursed and hissed. Clawed hands reached for heavy cleavers and slowly, inexplicably, they began to climb. The men of the Sceptre held firm, despite the grim visage, listening as the scrape of heavy footfalls preceded their advance.

'Hold!' Tarsin yelled, seeking to steady his men. They obeyed, huddling together, awaiting the inevitable.

The leading beasts, already half way up, began to leap forward, taking steps three at a time.

'Brace yourselves!' Tarsin screamed as the charge struck. Pikes lowered, plunging deep as the Deios threw themselves wildly upon those defending the steps. Guttural screams sounded in unison with grunts of exertion and wild cries of pain. The front row of beasts fell almost as one, impaled beyond redemption, their torsos splashed scarlet. Those climbing behind reached with long, vicious arms and pulled and twisted, clawing their way forward to grasp at the defending men. Heads were snapped with meaty hands and steel thudded into flesh. Within minutes the line of pikemen was scattered, swords and daggers now flaying from side-to-side in a desperate attempt to keep the foe at bay, whilst the second line of pikemen thrust their weapons between gaps in the fighting, seeking to strike a killer blow.

Tarsin strode amongst his men, his eyes maddeningly bright as his sword sang a song of clarity in a battle of chaos. The Rykedian broadsword was a blur of motion, a blazon of silver tinged red as it bloodied one foe after another. He never stood still, his body swaying and twirling, always tantalising out of reach.

A second later and Tarsin was away once more, stepping nimbly across the steps as he avoided fallen bodies. Jaegar and Griffith joined him, swinging their mighty weapons two-handed as they pulverised heads and crushed chests. The beasts fell back, tumbling down, slipping on the blood of their own.

Tarsin took a breath, halting his mad rush before climbing back to the top step to survey the carnage. The Deios had ceased their attack and now milled at the bottom, their fury evident. More than a score of the beasts lay dead after the assault, bodies broken and bloodied, dozens of men wearing the yellow and black lying amongst them.

'Their path to us is more difficult with dead lining the steps,' Griffith pointed his hammer towards the fallen.

'Aye,' Tarsin looked beyond and scanned their line, seeking to read their thoughts. The charge was light, a tentative measure to judge the strength of their defence and nothing more. Next time, they would charge as one until they powered over their thin line. How he wished for a regiment of archers to line their flanks, or the king's cavalry to come thundering down the avenue. Either would help sway the battle in their favour.

Such dreams were akin to lost hope, and whilst Tarsin still lived, he'd harbour no such illusions. Instead he cleared his mind as he began to walk before his men. His sword dripped gore at his feet, glossy, sticky strands that fell without a sound. He barely noticed for his eyes were fixed, his steel gaze and firmly set jaw speaking more than words. Fury swam through his veins and his eyes were alight with an unquenchable fire. Tarsin knew he was the spark; his men the kindling. Somehow, he needed to ignite them into bloody, fearless action.

'Here they come!' Griffith screamed loud and clear, swinging his arms wide as he prepared to stand his ground. Pikemen stepped forward to present a bristling wall of steel, whilst mercenaries fell in behind, ready to cleave their foe.

Tarsin reached out with a hand and grabbed a liveried guard, pulling him close. 'Go,' he said, 'and call those guarding the steps north, south and west. Tell them the battle lies here and they're desperately needed. Go!'

The man raced away, his feet slapping the granite hard as he put his head down and swung his arms. Tarsin watched for no more than a few seconds, watched him veer to the left to avoid the mass of men, women and children still clustering about the pyramid's entrance. Hell, he didn't even know whether Kian's portal had even opened yet. It was entirely possible not a single citizen was safe.

Curses uttered by frightened men swung his attention back to the leaping beasts. They came silently, with deadly intent, bounding over their fallen brethren. Tarsin narrowed his eyes to see shiny hatchets held firm. Then, as one, the beasts threw back their arms and let fly, throwing their hatchets at close range with aggressive force. Tarsin ducked a streak of silver only to hear a thud from behind as a guard's chest exploded. Grunts of shock and screams of pain escalated as the hatchets found their mark, men dropping one after another down the line. Those few who avoided the deadly missiles suddenly found themselves standing before a tide of burnished scales and glistening fangs, claws and cleavers screaming for their heads.

Tarsin moved, sliding forward to meet the first to reach his position. His Rykedian broadsword swung through the air, bit into a thick neck. Blood spurted from a severed jugular, adding its own unique squelch to the melody of death. The beast fell to be replaced by another and Tarsin swung his sword again, slicing the tip of his blade across yellow eyes. The ululating beast raised clawed hands to cover its face, allowing him to step in and thrust his broadsword deep into its belly and under its ribcage, seeking its heart.

It fell like the first . . . to be replaced by another.

Tarsin never faltered, never slowed. He continued to dance across the steps, his footing sure, his poise legendary. Deios climbed and leaped and bounded towards him, snarling and hissing, roaring in anger. But he remained a blur of motion; an elusive shadow. Then he would strike, and blood would flow. How long he fought he could not say, but when he finally felt his arms tighten with cramp, Griffith and Jaegar were by his side, their heavy blows clearing the steps one sweep at a time. Behind them crowded their reinforcements: one hundred and fifty extra men and a score of knights from the Palaceguard. Tarsin's moment to ignite his men with words had passed, but his actions now paved a way forward, and those crowding behind began to push, using pikes and swords, the Palaceguard their shields, as one step at a time the men of Bastion held their ground, then took it back.

Tarsin sank to his knees, his body bruised and bloodied as the fighting eased. 'Up, sire,' Jaegar placed a hand under his arm and hoisted him back to his feet. 'The men need to see you strong and unfatigued.'

'I can barely stand, Jaegar,' Tarsin panted as he sought to catch his breath.

The newly crowned king felt the Herkosian wipe a finger across his forehead, smudging blood from a slice along his hairline, just under his crown. It wasn't deep, but Tarsin knew it bled profusely. 'I need some water for the king,' Jaegar shouted behind him. Men raced to do as bid, glad for the respite in the fighting, and glad to be away from the carnage. Even now flies began to buzz in the hot afternoon sun and the caw of carrion birds on the wing drifted with the breeze.

Tarsin exhaled and looked about him; only to find himself half way down the steps, surrounded by the dead and the dying. Two score of his men were with him, spread behind, but not in front, and the only Deios were those lying dead at their feet. Those still alive huddled at the base of the steps, agitated, by all appearances. 'Come,' Tarsin motioned to his men to move back to the top, deliberately turning his back on their foe. As they reached the height of the red granite, a water skin was passed. He tilted his head back and drank willingly, his throat parched. As he finished, a shout went up from the gathered men, their voices rising as one in recognition of their king's heroics.

'What are they yelling for?' Tarsin asked as he looked from Griffith to Jaegar.

'They are not yelling, sire,' Griffith smiled, showing bloodied teeth, 'they are cheering. They cheer for their king.'

Tarsin nodded his approval and offered a slight smile, then turned to appraise the enemy once more. Despite all his efforts, they outnumbered them still, and the citizens of Bastion were still crowded about the pyramid and its entrance. Further, he had no recollection of time passed, nor did he know how many were safe. All he could do was protect the steps; give Cappitus and his Brotherhood time to usher people through. Despite their apparent victory, the number of men lying broken on the steps was considerably more than he cared for.

He took another swallow of cool liquid and passed the skin to Griffith. After wiping his mouth with the back of his hand he said, 'They're preparing to attack once again. Jaegar, order the knights with shields into position. Griffith, assemble your men behind. This time we'll hold firm at the top, make them climb the entire height of the steps before they reach us.'

Tarsin felt old Bevan slap him on the back as he joined him. He was exhausted, cut and bruised like the rest of them. In one fist, he gripped a sword; in the other he held a salvaged hatchet. 'When they reach the top, sire,' Bevan asked with a smirk, 'what then?'

Tarsin smiled back, holding his sword up so light could reflect off its silver-blue blade. 'Then we smite them with cold steel, my friend,' he said, 'and send them back to whatever Hell spawned them!'

*

A groan of exertion slipped past Ahriman's lips as he reached the last step. Avra still held his arm, seeking to help in her own way, although in truth her frailness was becoming a burden. Not only was her presence a frustration, it was also a reminder of her failed offering. Even now, perched atop the red granite block and standing before the remarkable shining blue pyramid, Ahriman still felt an urge to rip her bony head from her shoulders and hoist it high and far across city streets.

Only he refrained from such an act. Not because he felt sympathy for the crone, but because he knew she could still be of use. Here, for the first time, he was close to the people of Bastion. He could see them crowded about the entrance to the pyramid, he could hear their cries of anguish and fear, hear their wails of grief.

He could also sense their souls; minute baubles of gold flickering within their chests. Souls, he thought, that would soon be his; souls that would once again make him strong and powerful.

He shuffled forward, making his way towards the crowd, eager to see what lay inside the pyramid. Avra had already outlined its interior, telling him what to expect. They would have to wait at the rear of the gathering, though, for their pace was slow. It was a predicament he chafed at until he smelt blood on the wind and heard the shouts of battle and the cries of fallen warriors to the east. He'd climbed the northern steps with the witch and they were only now seeing with their own eyes the ferocious fighting. Ahrmian grinned wickedly; his impatience no longer a concern, for the tell-tale glow of souls rising from the dead had his tongue sliding out of his mouth. Golden balls drifted with those of a molten red hue, popping above the deceased with a regularity that had his mood brighten considerably.

He dragged his heavy frame towards the fighting, ignoring the mass of people fleeing into the pyramid. He could see the souls of the deceased, and sent out a call they could not refuse, a mental command demanding they stream towards him. One-by-one they sailed towards his crippled form, caught in a black-hearted maelstrom of pure energy they could not escape. By the time he'd reached the outskirts of those crowded about the pyramid's entrance, more than a hundred souls had merged with his, energizing his body as souls of light were consumed by the darkness within.

He quickened his pace, excited and alert. 'Come, Avra,' he said, 'I would see this battle being fought on bloodied steps.'

She lifted tired legs to keep up, her face drawn and tired. Ahriman could see she was near the end. The punishment he dealt her in the cellar sapped her mental strength, it was true, but she also suffered physically. Right now, she appeared more crippled than he.

'Here,' he laid a gnarled hand upon her shoulder, pressing hard. Her legs almost buckled under his grip, but then a flow of energy passed into her frame, dark, coiled strands of hatred and malice. For any other mortal, such a transfusion would herald death, but for Avra and her vengeful soul, it was life.

'Thank you, my lord,' she wheezed, sucking in air with eyes wide open.

'Consider it a small repayment for your efforts to bind me in flesh. You erred in your judgement, witch, but not by much.'

He saw Avra breathe deeply, her face now rounded and not so gaunt, her scratches less prominent. Even her lank white hair shone with a radiance not seen for a decade.

Without a word they pressed forward, skirting behind the crowd whilst listening to the drone of constant bickering and shouting as men and women sought to jostle for a more favourable position. As they moved past their ranks, a deathly silence began to permeate the air, and the jostling was now centred on keeping a respectable distance from the new arrivals.

'What did you do?' Avra whispered.

Ahriman pulled the cowl of his hood over his eyes. 'They sense who I am, witch,' he said. 'They do not know the reason for their sudden fear, but their souls feel the pull. I cannot claim a soul from the living, but they feel death so very closc. Right now, they fear dying like never before.'

'Will you kill them, my lord, and take their souls?'

'I will,' Ariman replied, 'but not at once, not here. I will bide my time, take souls quietly and in secrecy. It would not do to have those I crave oppose me. United they are strong. There are even some amongst them with power of their own.' He tilted his head to the side, feeling his bones crack. 'But soon I shall have multiple worlds at my disposal, and my strength will rapidly increase. Then, and only then, shall I unleash my devastating power.'

'Will there be a place for me by your side, my lord?'

He took in her appearance. She was a terrible sight, even with the added benefit of his dark energy. 'Perhaps,' he mused, 'for your shrivelled, black soul is of no use to me. It is a tiny, cancerous bulge of corruption, a stain on the world. It harbours no energy for me to utilise, no fuel to fan my ravenous flames.'

'I can be of help, my lord, if you enhance my vitality. I can provide an extra set of eyes and ears. I can gather souls for you, if you so choose.'

'I know, Avra,' he said, salivating at the sight of the crowd. There were hundreds, perhaps thousands of souls standing before him. If what Avra said was true about the pyramid and the portal within, there would be hundreds of thousands more. Enough to fuel his hunger in any case, despite the thousands that went missing earlier. 'For now,' he said, looking at the witch with her blood-streaked face, 'you can stay by my side. But if you disappoint me, crone, I shall flay the flesh from your body and hang you by your entrails.' He kept walking, his gait still laboured, his legs disjointed. He kept his eyes fixed on the battle between the men of Bastion and the imposing Deios. Out of the corner of his eye he saw Avra appraise him, knew she was about to ask another question. He held up a crooked hand. 'Be quiet, witch, so I can savour this moment.' He paused, feeling the souls of the dead as they continued to flow into his crippled form. Then he spoke once more, his tone threatening, his words bleak. 'The history of this world is about to change, Avra.

'After centuries of banishment, I have finally arrived!'

*

'There he is,' Rax't pointed a clawed finger towards the top of the steps. 'He is the one with the golden circlet about his head.'

Ra'tor nodded, holding an arm above his eyes to shield it from the sun. He could see him now, the one with the silver sword. He was the one who killed Shyxt on their world, the one who'd killed so many of his brood since. 'Whoever they are, Rax't, I do not believe they are weaklings anymore. They have shown great courage and strength.'

'They are not all pale skins, either. I have seen dark skins amongst them,' Rax't sniffed the air, the scent of blood still strong. 'I wonder what they are called.'

'I care not,' Ra'tor snarled, 'they are meat, nothing more.' He flicked his heavy blade with a sharp claw. Inwardly he was fuming at Zaxa and Terrak's attempts to storm the steps. On three occasions, he'd watched as they raced upward only to be repulsed: once by cunning, the other two by sheer will power. Whoever these creatures were, they were resourceful. He'd never seen such an array of weapons made from so many materials. On his world, wood was scarce and served only as fuel for the fires of Bhral, but here, they'd fashioned instruments capable of releasing shafts that struck like bolts of lightning.

'What are you thinking?' Rax't asked.

'I'm thinking I shall challenge their leader, one-on-one, as we should have done to begin with.'

'Is that wise? He is incredibly fast and highly skilled.'

'He is small. One strike and he shall fall,' Ra'tor growled as Zaxa stomped towards him. The Deiosian was huge, half a foot taller than himself and blessed by Bhral with corded muscles the envy of all. He was a tower of strength, and his bronzed scales shone like the beacon he was.

'The weaklings can fight,' he said by way of greeting.

Ra'tor snorted in reply. He had little time for Zaxa. The Deiosian was a fool, driven by strength alone. The only reason his brood was currently more numerous was due to him defeating Chiax two moons past. The old hunter was past his prime, it was certain, but only a foolhardy youngster would dare challenge one so respected. That was Zaxa, forever seeking glory.

'Shall we charge again?' he heard Zaxa ask.

Ra'tor could see the eagerness in his eyes. He hadn't tasted blood yet. 'No,' he grinned, showing all his teeth, 'I will challenge their leader, the one with the golden circlet about his head. I'll kill him in single combat. His brood will then be mine, and so shall their temple.'

Shouts of encouragement could be heard from those gathered close. It was a bold suggestion, one granting the pale skins a respect well deserved.

'No!' Zaxa raised his voice as he cut a scaled hand through the air, 'I shall be the one to challenge, for I am strongest, my brood the largest. It is my right to vie for glory, not yours, Ra'tor.'

'But I found this world, Zaxa. If it were not for me, you would not even be here!'

'But I am strongest! Unless you wish to challenge me first, it is I who shall fight. I am younger, in my prime. If we are to succeed here, I am the logical choice.'

Keen eyes alighted on Ra'tor, awaiting the respected elder's decision. 'You are right, Zaxa,' Ra'tor said with a snarl as he bowed his head. 'You are the logical choice. The challenge is yours. May Bhral watch over you and give you strength.'

Zaxa curled his lips back to display his razor-sharp teeth. He then opened them wide and snapped them shut before departing, his final words thrown arrogantly over his shoulder. 'I don't need Bhral's blessing, Ra'tor, nor do I need his strength.' A cheer followed him, his brood raising fists into the air as they began to chant his name.

Ra'tor smiled.

'You do not appear to be as distraught as I imagined,' Rax't said as he looked sideways at his leader.

'I am not,' Ra'tor replied, 'for if I am not mistaken, Zaxa the fool will be dead very soon.'

'You believe the creature above will best Zaxa?'

Ra'tor moved a hand back to his cleaver, tapping his claws against the metal blade. The ring it made reminded him of the death knell performed by priests during a sacrificial rite. Smiling, he watched as the bloodlings followed Zaxa towards the dreaded steps, then grinned as they formed a half ring about their champion. The call was made, the challenge offered. Ra'tor continued to smile. He'd witnessed the one with the silver sword, believed he knew his capabilities.

'Ra'tor?' Rax't asked once again.

'Yes,' Ra'tor hissed, answering the tall Deiosian's question, 'I believe the creature above will best Zaxa.'

*

'How many?' Tarsin asked Bevan.

'At least sixty, possibly seventy,' the veteran answered, his eyes drifting over the fallen beasts as he continued to count.

'How many of our own lie with them?

Bevan shifted his feet before turning his dour expression towards his king. 'A few more, would be my guess. It is difficult to tell exactly. Not all of the fallen are in one piece.'

Tarsin nodded, for he knew the mass of flesh sprawled over the lower portion of the steps was a conglomeration of steel and scales and congealed blood blackening in the afternoon sun. The stench was already assaulting his nostrils; one of the reasons why he commanded his men to push the fallen to the bottom. The other was to form a barricade.

Griffith walked to his side, his armour battered, his hammer stained. 'Storm is coming,' he said, pointing towards the southern horizon.

Tarsin spied the broiling black clouds out to sea. Sheets of darkness trailed underneath their enormous expanse, punctuated by a steady flash of brilliance as a lightning spasm ignited their mass.

'Frey's Luck,' Griffith spat to the side, 'that looks ominous.'

'It's the last thing we need right now,' Tarsin offered, knowing a summer storm would wreak havoc on the city of Bastion and those few who remained. Several hands were already pointing towards the cloud bank amongst the crowd, fearful cries singing out.

'Fighting in such a storm will be difficult,' Griffith explained, 'and the steps are likely to become even more slippery than they already are.'

Tarsin heard Griffith's words, but his focus was on the semi-circular crowd of Deios forming below. Roars and hisses rose from those assembled, in conjunction with raised fists pumping the air. 'We may not have to,' he said with a sigh.

The men beside him spun to see what their king referred to. Two score of the scaled beasts formed a half-ring at the base of the steps, shouting and chanting as one of their own stepped into the vacant space. He was enormous: at least seven-and-a-half feet tall and broader than Jaegar. Ivory scales curled back behind his head and each hand held a heavy blade: a cross between an axe and a cleaver. A leather kilt was ringed with steel buckles, his forearms clad with steel bracers. A hiss sounded as sharp teeth snapped closed before he raised his sight to the men standing above and flung a clawed hand towards Tarsin, beckoning the king to join him below.

Tarsin, watching the display, suddenly knew what the gesture called for. Why he would challenge him he did not know. The Deios had hit hard and quickly, giving the men of Bastion precious little time to prepare for another onslaught. Now, for some unknown reason, they stalled, and he believed they sought to single him out for a duel to the death.

'You cannot accept the challenge,' Griffith and Bevan both said at once.

Tarsin stretched his arms high. He knew what he had to do. They stood here to protect the mass of people behind them, hoping they could provide enough time for their escape through the portal. He could give them that time; prevent the beasts from surging over their dwindling ranks. He looked to Jaegar, the Herkosian with the bald head and twin braided beard nodded once. He understood what was at stake, knew what the consequences were if he should fail. He also knew he would accept.

'I told you once, Griffith, that I'd lost purpose with my life, that I didn't know who I was anymore. Now I know. Now I know what I'm supposed to do.' He shared a look with his men, watching as one after the other met his gaze. 'I'm here for my people. I'm here to protect them.'

'You can't do this and think to save us all,' Griffith raised his voice to have his words heard over the sudden commotion.

Tarsin returned his mad look. 'Has it occurred to you I might be doing this to save myself.'

Griffith shook his red mane. 'You are our king, granted, but you cannot do this. Let me challenge the lizard.' He lifted his hammer, *Bloodstain*, his gauntleted hand gripping it tight. 'I'm a member of the Unseen, my king. It's my duty to protect *you!*'

'No, this is my fight,' Tarsin replied, his voice sombre, his tone hinting the conversation was at an end.

'What if you die down there? The Deios will swarm the steps the minute you fall. You know this.'

'Then I will not fall,' Tarsin swept his Rykedian broadsword through the air, holding it firm so the sun, fast disappearing behind growing storm clouds, could shine its last rays upon the silver-blue blade.

'Frey's Luck then, my king,' said Jaegar, the Herkosian calling on the goddess of Fate.

'This is madness!' Griffith snarled, determined not to give up.

Tarsin didn't reply. Instead he put one foot forward and slowly began to descend the steps, avoiding the bodies and blood strewn across their breadth, shutting out the calls of encouragement from above. He was king of a fallen city, his people dead, scattered or fleeing into unknown territory. Beasts challenged his claim to rule and a witch and her Dark God hid in the shadows; and on the horizon brewed a thunderstorm, creeping closer by the second.

But he was Tarsin Va, the last of the jaguars.

And he would not fall.

CHAPTER TWENTY-NINE

Kian reached the crowd of heaving flesh and paused. Men, women and children squirmed as they sought to push closer to the pyramid's entrance, their high-pitched cries falling on deaf ears. Kian held back and watched the press of bodies. He could hear their voices calling out, shouting questions to those Brothers standing guard. Word of the assault had already caused panic to stir and the threat behind them was escalating. Now the survivors of Bastion sought solace in the temple of light, its shadowed depths assumed to be a place of sanctuary.

Only the sanctuary they craved was neither confined to the temple nor of this world.

Kian cast his bright eyes across the pyramid's eastern flank; saw the shadow continuing its upward creep. The time for the portal to shift was close. Almost twenty-four hours had passed since he stepped back into what he thought would be the city of Aos. He'd been gravely mistaken. The golden ellipsoid he stepped from was deep underground, surrounded by shattered walls submerged in ankle deep water. He'd taken a moment to let his eyes adjust to the dim illumination then worked his way around the circular dais. From there he walked timid steps to a tumbled wall. Stepping over a mass of toppled bricks he found a passageway that smelt of sewage. He followed its twisting turns for several hours before he finally found a path that led to the surface, only to find night had fallen.

It bothered him not at all. He let his eyes adjust to the gloom and found a perch, then sat in silence whilst he looked over a shattered city. He was confused, unsure of his surroundings. But then he spied the silver-blue pyramid: Ao. She was there, as she'd always been. A sliver of light embedded in the hard rock of eternity. It was a rewarding sight, comforting. Kian remembered the day of its completion, remembered like it was yesterday. Ao: House of God; raised with a single clear thought from the combined will of ten thousand Nepharii.

Now he knew thousands of years had since passed.

He let his sight drift over the ruins for a time, then rose and began to walk the deserted streets. He could smell the dead in their thousands, knew a great catastrophe had fallen. With every step, he felt the groans of a dying city shift beneath his feet. What concerned him most of all was the apparent lack of Nepharii. He could not sense his brethren nearby, could not feel their thoughts. It appeared they were neither here in any capacity nor buried under its mass. For one lost to his brethren for thousands of years it was unsettling. He'd hoped to find answers to why his portal was dysfunctional for so long. Only it appeared there was no-one to ask.

He kept moving, scouting the streets for survivors, sensing their tired bodies trapped under masonry. He released those he could, passed others too far gone. Then as the sun rose in the east he watched and listened to the people he rescued, hiding in the shadows whilst he learnt their manner and speech. He knew man dwelt here, had recorded their movements for decades before he was assigned as gatekeeper and guardian of Vidae all those centuries ago.

Kian also knew what they were capable of, had seen firsthand how destructive the early tribes could be.

He noted they had grown considerably during his absence.

Now they'd built a city atop his ancient Aos: a sprawling network of roads and paths entwined about elaborate towers and buildings of magnificent size. They'd claimed it as their own, which had Kian once again wondering where his brethren had gone and how long they'd been absent.

Finally, he spent an hour in contemplation, concealed behind the cowl of his black cloak, his form merging easily within the darkened streets. Those poor souls he spied traversing the ruined city failed to sense his presence. He saw no need to alert them to his arrival. They had more important matters to attend, matters he was fast becoming aware of.

A sudden shift in the air had his mind tuned to the harmony of the city. She was broken, no doubt, but she was far from finished. Kian knew he was testament to her ongoing revival. The portals had finally reopened after lying dormant for thousands of years. He knew what such a fact would entail; knew with certainty he wouldn't be the only one to step into the ancient city in the days ahead.

When he saw the Deios sift from between the shattered ruins even he gasped at their regalia, though. They were tall and strong, it was obvious, but it was their manner that caught his eye. There was no sense of society or camaradarie amongst those who skulked through the streets. They were mere representations of primal thought; little more than beasts hunting weaker prey. But they were large beasts, and their clawed hands were accompanied by heavy steel blades. Kian knew then that the citizens, whoever they were, were unlikely to stand against such a foe. From what he'd seen in the wee hours of morning they were inferior in almost every aspect.

Such an insight had been hours ago. Now he'd seen them fight, had watched their king, Tarsin Va, summon his men and stand his ground. Considering their lack of size when ranged against the Deios, they certainly didn't lack for courage. Whereas the Deios were frightfully savage, the men of Bastion were cunning and resourceful.

Reminding himself to keep his focus on the present, Kian slipped past several men and women who stood before him. They let him pass, cloaked as he was, believing him one of the Brotherhood. Right now, he needed to be inside the temple, within its dark confines to help lead the way. Elder Cappitus would have need of his guidance. And he knew the young boy, Jarred, would have need of his counsel before long. The lad was privy to information best left to the Nepharii, information that could potentially cripple the young boy's mind. He also knew those who dwelt within were here for a reason. When construction began upon the temple called Ao, a handful of Nepharii had poured their heart and soul into its fabrication. It appeared their memories had remained through the ages, entwined within but enticed with a gentle stroke of a hand. Kian was thankful, for without their timely intervention he feared he'd never have grasped the kingdom tongue in time. Joining his mind with Jarred had taken but a moment, but it was a moment well spent.

He reached the entrance and lifted the cowl of his hood, allowing the Sword Brothers to see his face. They let him pass with a nod, the light in their eyes already dim. They'd been given word of the horde of scaled flesh creeping along King's Avenue. He knew they feared what was to come.

Kian didn't stop to offer words of wisdom. He didn't have time. The plaque for the world named Vidae was fast approaching; it would slide into place within minutes. When it did, he'd have to convince the Brotherhood and those priests still in attendance of its validity as a place of refuge. Neema, he knew, would believe, for she could see the pattern between worlds. Amongst the others, he feared, much bickering would ensue. He could only hope that when the plaque slid into place and the symbol of Panos: the deer, lay before them, any conflicting doubts as to the denizens of the world of Vidae would vanish. If they didn't, then he could not help them further. He needed to rely on their trustworthiness. In the end, it would be their choice and theirs alone.

His booted feet crossed the spanning bridge without a sound and halted before the *Kardiversum*. Elder Cappitus raised tired eyes at his appearance, worry etched firmly into his aged skin. 'You've returned,' he said.

'Aye, elder, I have returned.'

'What of Tarsin Va?'

Kian stepped close and took a deep breath. 'He lives and is well for the time being. I should tell you his thoughts are my thoughts concerning the welfare of Bastion's citizens, though. The enemy is too powerful and too numerous. Your only chance at redemption lies beyond,' he lifted his chin towards the glowing *Kardiversum*.

'There is nothing else we can do?' Cappitus voice was barely a whisper.

'We are out of options, elder,' he met his gaze. A loud bang suddenly peeled throughout the Forever Chamber, heralding the arrival of a new plaque, the one whose zodiac symbol resembled a deer, named Panos by the Nepharii. Kian offered a sympathetic nod before he uttered words he knew Cappitus feared to hear. 'I'm afraid it is time. You need to make a choice, elder. I'll lead the way . . . I hope you'll follow.'

*

Tarsin descended another step. His booted feet were sore, his legs tired. Behind him he could hear Griffith and Jaeger do the same, a dozen others by their side. They may not have agreed to his dangerous plan, but neither would they desert him. He was their king, had formerly been their captain. If they could, they'd die for him.

Only he'd chosen his path.

He remembered Lord Derrick Tolsten's face as he prepared to stand his ground against the Deios. It had been unyielding, as if chiselled from stone. The old man knew what was to come. "Hard decisions made by hard men", he'd said. Tarsin knew what he meant, had understood the sacrifice. But there was a time when sacrifice was a dagger twisting in his heart. He'd lost nineteen of his men on the outskirts of Benwith, saw their demise as an unnecessary sacrifice at the time. Every night since that day he closed his eyes and wondered if there was anything he could have done differently to save them. No matter how often he played the scenario through his mind he couldn't find an answer. All he remembered was the red rage surfacing as he helped those four he rescued out of the pit. They'd climbed back into the barn, drenched in blood and bereft of reason. Jaeger alone could stand unaided. John Rhys kept heaving bile, Cale Griffith was mad with panic and then there was Enrico Vittorio.

Tarsin shuddered at the memory. What could you say to a man who'd inadvertently killed his younger brother; one he'd sworn to protect with his life? Gods above, he'd severed the young man's head.

454

Tarsin didn't know then and he couldn't offer any condolences now. All he knew was a red rage had sparked inside, fanned by the flames of supposed betrayal. He cursed and spat as his men gathered their weapons, but their minds and bodies were not fit to fight. So he left them in the barn and walked alone towards the keep, a white-knuckled hand gripped firmly about the hilt of his Rykedian broadsword.

With a booted foot, he kicked open the door.

Moments later the carnage began.

He was mad beyond reason, fuelled with a desire to see every living soul skewered on the end of his sword. Witch or not, they all fell foul as he searched the chambers within. When he left the keep with its walls splashed red, he summoned his men and made for the tavern where he'd first suffered the effects of the Benwith coven. They reached the establishment as dusk fell across the land.

And not a soul survived his rage to see a new dawn arrive.

'Tarsin!'

The sound of his name pierced the gloom threatening to engulf him. He looked behind him; saw Griffith standing with *Bloodstain* in a gauntleted fist. The hammer was plastered with gore, blending eerily against the blood-red steel. He saw the wild man's eyes and knew what he was offering. With sheer will he turned his back on him and took one last step, placing his feet upon the paved stone.

Before him stood the tallest Deiosian he'd ever seen.

As he surmised earlier he was seven-and-a-half feet tall and broader of shoulder than Jaeger. Bronzed scales turning gold made the colossus appear like some ancient demon-god, his chopping blades twirling before him. He noted the strength in its arms and chest, saw bunched muscles waiting to explode. A metal ring was clasped about its throat to resemble an ill-fashioned gorget, its purpose purely protection, whilst thick bands of steel clamped about its forearms. Like every other he'd fought against, it wore a leather kilt embossed with steel. The sheer size difference between the two was only now becoming evident. Considering the breadth of its shoulders and its thick upper legs, it was possible the Deiosian weighed twice as much as he, even with his armour on.

'Here,' Griffith tapped him on the shoulder and passed him one of the daggers he'd claimed from King Arkos' study. Tarsin took the proffered blade and held it firm. 'You know this is folly of the grandest scale, my king?'

'I know what it is,' Tarsin replied through clenched teeth. 'Look around you, Griffith. Tell me what you see that makes any sense? All I know is that a challenge has been made. Their very nature is alien to us, including whatever code of conduct they adhere to. Whatever it is they strive towards, I know it will be detrimental to our cause. Our purpose here is to stall so our people can escape. I may be mad, my friend, but I'll take the chance.'

Griffith accepted the fact, but his eyes betrayed his thoughts. 'I can do this for you, you know.'

Tarsin shook his head and stepped away from his friend, walking several steps into the ring formed of Deios and men. Now it was simply he and the beast.

He inched forward, sweat beading on his forehead as he levelled his sword at his adversary. His muscles ached, his arm threatening to shake from exhaustion. He felt as though he'd fought for days, not hours, and yet the precious minutes he'd taken to descend allowed his mind to clear itself of doubt and confusion. He was here because he was king. It was his right and his duty. He would sacrifice himself for the people of Bastion.

Tarsin met the golden eyes of the beast only to see pain and suffering residing within. His pain and suffering.

Seconds later heavy blades came screaming for his head.

Tarsin ducked as a blade sang past, whistling from his left to pass a mere inch above his skull. The sheer ferocity of the attack took him by surprise. There had been no warning, no sound. The demon simply charged; the speed of its heavily muscled body frightening. With one quick flourish, it had slapped his sword to the side with consummate ease and powered a blow towards his head capable of cleaving him in two. Tarsin swerved to the right at the last instant to find himself in close; where he could smell oiled leather and spice. He brought his sword back, swinging it in front as he sought composure, but felt air blast from his lungs as a scaled knee rose and caught him in the chest.

He gasped as he sailed ten feet through the air only to land hard on dusty cobblestones. Then he slid to a stop at the edge of the ring. He looked up, saw a smaller version of the demon he fought, bared fangs grinning down at him. Tarsin thought he would die then, beaten and bloodied in less than a dozen heart beats. But he sucked in a lungful of air and rolled to his left, then leapt to his feet as the giant roared towards him. He needed to find his balance, gauge his foe's strength and weakness.

He ducked another swipe and flicked his broadsword towards the demon's abdomen. It clanged as it struck the metal plate of its flared belt, ricocheted up to leave a slice three inches long across its torso. The beast offered a snort and stood back a pace, looking down at the blood seeping from its wound. Tarsin could see it was shallow, but at least it halted the demon's mad rush.

He took a moment to catch his breath. The onslaught had been ferocious, his heart beating rapidly as adrenaline pounded through his veins. This was as visceral as anything he'd experienced. Standing here, now, was like coming face to face with every inner demon he cared to harbour.

He thought back to his moment of lucidity as he descended the steps, recalling the feeling of anger as he thought of Enrico Vittorio's pain. He'd carried that same anger and frustration. He'd let the witches of Benwith feel his wrath, had given them a taste of his blade because of their meddling. He'd suppressed the anger shortly after, though, keeping it hidden deep inside. There was cause for him to gather his men, the few who survived, and bring them home to Bastion. He couldn't afford to let himself loose.

Only the red rage was never far from his thoughts. He lifted his blade to point its tip at the demon and searched out its eyes. Then Tarsin felt for the anger he knew was chained deep within.

As the demon began to circle, Tarsin released the chains.

He shifted his feet to regain his balance and brought his dagger out in front to lie horizontally next to his sword. The demon snorted once more whilst a thick tongue flicked between vicious fangs. Tarsin barely noticed. His mind was focused solely on destruction. Unlike a battle where he needed to keep his mind alert to those around him, here and now he had only one adversary. Every fibre of his being was now taut with the promise of retaliation: retaliation for all the hurt he'd felt; retaliation for the suffering of his men.

Consumed once more with hatred bordering on suicide, Tarsin forgot about his intention to stall for time.

He took three quick steps forward, planting his foot down sharply as he plunged his broadsword towards the demon's chest. Before the beast could swipe a blade in defence, he pivoted on one heel and sprang to the side, bringing his blade out and then back in with a heavy slice. The beast deflected the blow with a well-timed parry, but the tone was now set. No longer would Tarsin stand and defend against the beast in a vain attempt to survive. Now he'd take the fight to the beast and let his rage and frustration fuel his desire to kill.

For several minutes, the two combatants traded blows, the clash of their blades singing as man and beast watched intently to the side. Tarsin was oblivious to their shouts of encouragement and gasps of fear. All he could see was a snarling Deiosian, huge and powerful, standing in his way. Kill the beast and he could end his torment. Kill the beast and he could end his pain.

Vicious chops of the heavier blades slammed from overhead. Tarsin defended as best he could, shifting his weight to soften the blows. He felt weak compared to the beast, knew the strength in its arms was considerable. He also knew he couldn't stand toe-to-toe for much longer. He slid one foot behind the other, shifting his stance so that he was facing squarely against the beast. His dagger was raised defensively, but his sword hovered low, enticing another overhead chop. The blow came quicker than anticipated and pain flared in his arm as he brought his dagger up for a block. With a grimace of pain, he then swung his sword, not for the chest of the beast, but for his leading arm.

His Rykedian broadsword struck scales then flesh, biting deep into an upperarm before being smashed aside by the other cleaver. Tarsin twirled away with the blow and felt a crunching blow to the shoulder as he spun. He fell forward, rolling with his momentum before springing back to his feet. Blood fell across his eyes and splashed to the ground and his shoulder felt aflame. He grimaced once more and lifted his eyes to find the beast, seeing a mass of scales hurtling towards him in a rush. He braced himself for the onslaught, then dived to his right. Once again, he found his feet.

This time they circled, respect for each other evident in their approach. Both were bloodied, their breathing ragged. Beyond their deathly dance lay a vociferous circle of raised fists and swords, shouts and screams offering the illusion of strength and encouragement. Neither combatant paid them any heed, for they knew their focus could not waiver. One false slip and death would take them, it was inevitable.

Tarsin raised his broadsword, parrying a blow aimed for his neck, then sent a slashing riposte to mark the beast in the bicep. It landed true, leaving a line of crimson. The beast struck again, twice in succession, its blows raining from on high with a blood-curdling roar designed to overpower. Tarsin swivelled and slapped at the blades, retaliating with three thrusts of his own that sent the beast scampering backwards in haste. He could see it tiring, its bronzed-scaled arms now stained red, its eyes flicking nervously from side-to-side. He couldn't strike close enough to cause it grievous bodily harm, but he could hack away at its arms with apparent will. His sword was faster, his moves well timed. The beast, for all its size and strength, couldn't keep his keen blade at bay. As he spun once more out of harm's way, a wicked smile touched Tarsin's dry lips.

A moment later he moved in for the kill.

*

Ahriman scraped his foot across the ground one last time. He stood at the edge of the red granite base, Avra cowering beside him. Below lay a force of Deios, their numbers close to three hundred. Above them, standing guard over the steps were men of Bastion, their number only marginally less than that of the beasts. They were exhausted, their minds and bodies battered, their loved ones fleeing even as they stood their ground. It would take no more than two or three charges from the Deios to decimate their ranks, but for some unknown reason they'd offered a challenge instead. Ahriman shook his head. He'd been grateful for the carnage on the steps. A steady stream of souls kept sweeping into his body as man and beast fought. It had been intoxicating to the newly formed god, left him craving more once the skirmish ceased.

Now fury contorted his already malformed features. The souls of man and beast fuelled him with power, but they also revealed to him their inner-most secrets, spoke of their life experiences. It was difficult to listen to the voices as they joined him, and to delve into their memories was more complex than he bargained for. But as he stood with hip askew and watched the two warriors below trade swift blows, their names, in time, became apparent to him. The Deiosian, he learnt, was named Zaxa. He was formidable, his strength and courage unquestioned. His standing amongst the Deios had been brisk, his exploits brutal and his apparent lack of fear infectious. There were many hunters amongst the Deios who believed him destined to wear the Crown of Blood.

Yet it was the man he fought who caused Ahriman to fume and splutter with vexation. For he wore a kingly crown: the very crown he left lying atop the fool Lucius Vupello. The memories of the men that swirled within spoke his name with adoration. Tarsin Va, he was called, bastard son of King Arkos Vantos.

Ahriman raised a hand, allowing it to hover over the witch before bringing it down with godly force. The sound of his fist striking flesh was brutal, causing the crone to fall and smack her weathered face against the granite.

A faint whimper was her only response, but Ahriman cared not at all. He could sense she was still alive.

He raised his hand again, this time to shield his eyes from the afternoon sun before black clouds swallowed it whole. The duel below was intriguing, the twirling blades striking with deadly finesse, the sound of their contact piercing even from where he stood. Still, he cursed the man who carried Arkos Vantos' blood. Cursed him with every breath he took. If only he had fallen under Avra's sacrificial knife, then his plan to conquer would not have been stymied so. More importantly, his body would not have endured such a torturous transformation.

The cries of men and beast began to escalate, the fight to the death nearing its climax. They'd duelled for some time, their strikes interspersed with bouts of circling as they gauged each other's strengths. It had been a furiously fought contest, an exhibition of some of the finest blade-work and deft footwork ever seen. Yet Ahriman could see the beast was spent, its arms criss-crossed with blood. Now he watched the finale with a smile, watched Tarsin Va slice his sword once more at the leading arm of Zaxa. The beast pulled back at the last instant and sent a vicious left chop towards Tarsin. The newly crowned king saw the blow arching for his head and ducked, but instead of retreating he stepped beneath Zaxa's arms and towards his torso. His right hand, gripped about his sword, hammered into the raised thigh of Zaxa, then Tarsin spun in a tight circle, his dagger slicing just below Zaxa's ribs before he finished his rotation. As he did so Tarsin's sword slammed into the beast's bleeding belly all the way to the hilt. It travelled upwards, through Zaxa's chest and into his throat, the tip of the broadsword exiting high on his neck, above the steel gorget.

Blood spewed forth from Zaxa's mouth as Tarsin put his foot to his stomach and yanked free his sword. The beast toppled to silence.

Ahriman waited, his eyes straining to see the molten ball as it began to rise from the still warm corpse. He sent out a mental command, summoning Zaxa's soul to join with his own. It did so, and he focused his thoughts internally, awaiting the rush of memories he knew would come. As he did the Deios below bent the knee as one and bowed their heads. Ahriman watched as Tarsin backed away, his energy all but spent. Two tall men reached for him and together they retreated up the steps.

Moments later the surge of knowledge from Zaxa's soul merged with his own. In quick fashion Ahriman learnt of their duels, knew Tarsin, by right, now had command of Zaxa's brood. The knowledge was trivial. Tarsin knew nothing of Deios rituals, nor would he acknowledge the claim. But he also learnt the Deios would now refuse to fight the men on the steps so long as Tarsin led. Ahriman frowned, for such was not to his liking. He'd savoured the fresh souls of the dead, still yearned for more of the same. So long as the races were here and opposed, he'd see them fight. A stalemate would never suffice.

With a deft thought Ahriman placed a hand around Avra's scrawny neck and lifted her to her feet. He then sent a pulse of energy into her frail frame, giving her a semblance of life. She stirred, then opened blackened eyes rimmed with tears of blood.

'I have a duty for you to perform, witch,' the hint of a smile cracked his thin lips as she convulsed in fear.

'What do you require, my lord?' she croaked.

He pointed a disjointed finger towards the mass of men and women crowding the pyramid. 'Find me a man,' he said, 'who is strong of arm. Use your skills and bring him before me.'

Avra left of her own volition, wobbling over to the crowd to seek a man of suitable pedigree. She found him in quick fashion and used her hypnotic talents to sway him to her side. Then they approached, both under duress, it appeared.

Ahriman smiled as they stood before him. The man was six-foot-tall and round of shoulder, his arms thick. A black beard covered half his face and his eyes were a dull grey. 'Give me a blade, Avra,' Ahriman held out a hand. She reached into an inner pocket, then pulled out a six-inch dagger. He held it briefly, admiring its thin edge. He then passed it back to the crone. 'Pass it to your friend.'

Avra did so, placing it into the man's outstretched hand.

'Good,' Ahriman reached out, grabbing the man's homespun shirt with twisted fingers and pulled him close. 'I need you to complete a task for me.' The man nodded once, his eyes vacant even as they took in his pus-covered sores. He leant close and whispered in his ear.

A moment later the man strode to the edge of the granite base and jumped thirty feet to the ground below.

*

Ra'tor lifted his eyes and watched the creature with the golden crown as he climbed back up the steps. The plan had worked, to a degree. Zaxa was gone, his body no more than a pile of meat. More importantly Zaxa's brood would now be his. He doubted the creature with the lightning sword would understand their culture. In fact, he'd relied on his not knowing. It had been a gamble, certainly, but one he felt comfortable in orchestrating. The only hitch would be the ongoing attack. Those who called Zaxa their master would refuse to fight any further, and right now Ra'tor couldn't see a way past such a quandary.

A sudden flurry amongst the Deios piqued his interest a moment later. He searched for the source of the commotion and found one of their adversaries had jumped from the red wall to land awkwardly. The creature then rose to his feet in some discomfit and hobbled towards them, his gait unruly but a shiny piece of steel held firmly in one hand. Ra'tor watched with curious eyes, bemused, before the creature finally stumbled to within striking distance. He showed no fear as he stood before one of Zaxa's bloodlings, then without warning he plunged his dagger deep into a bloodling's chest.

A roar rent the air as Deios fell upon the creature and within seconds limbs had been torn from his body and thrown to the wind. Why he would do such a thing was beyond Ra'tor, but as he stood and listened he knew Bhral had provided a sign. The Blood-god was still held within, his prison the silver-blue construct sitting atop the blood-red walls. No matter the circumstances, Bhral craved release. Ra'tor could sense it and knew their path here was no mere coincidence. The Deios had been summoned. They couldn't waiver, nor should they stall. And now, with the cowardly assault, Zaxa's brood were in a frenzy and eager for redemption. No longer would they sit out the coming battle. Not after such a dishonourable attack.

Ra'tor grinned as Rax't stepped to his side. 'Zaxa was a fool to fight the creature, as you said.'

'He was.'

'Now you have control of his brood,' Rax't shared his grin.

'I do. Bhral has seen to it, he has provided the spark that will lead to his freedom.'

'You still believe he is trapped within the red stone?'

Ra'tor met his questing eyes. 'Yes,' he hissed, 'either that or the shard of light that sits above. I have long thought Bhral to be absent from our world. The Patriarchs believe it also. Too many signs in the night sky spoke of evil portents to come. Now we are here, walking across stone placed by the hand of creatures we know nothing about.'

'We know they can fight.'

Another hiss escaped his lips. 'They can, which lends credence to the fact they have entrapped our god. What sorcery they have at their disposal is still unclear, but we must remain vigilant. If it is they who fashioned the door-between-worlds, then I fear our fight to release Bhral may be long and protracted. There is power in this dwelling place. If we can claim some of it for ourselves, our fight may be less arduous than first imagined.'

'What would you have us do now?'

Ra'tor shared a look with Rax't then beckoned him follow. He walked to stand before the Deios and raised a clawed fist to attract their attention. When the growls of discontent subsided, Ra'tor took a step towards the mangled corpse of the creature who had fallen from the red wall. He peered down at it, seeing the torso ripped open and its splayed shards of bone, noticed the absence of limbs. Then he spat atop the carcass before addressing his brood. He knew he didn't have to say much to fire their blood.

'The hunt continues!' Ra'tor yelled, aware rolling black clouds were creeping across the sky, a storm imminent. The brood yelled back, their voices rising as one. It sounded like thunder.

Ra'tor bared his fangs and looked to the red wall, then back to his brood. He knew the storm had already arrived. He then swept his clawed fist with a flourish towards those creatures standing at the top of the steps.

Maddened beyond reason, the Deios charged as one.

CHAPTER THIRTY

The procession, hesitant at first, at times even disjointed, now found a rhythm of speed that underlaid the people's need to survive. Kayla watched, noting heads bowed and tears lining troubled faces. Most moved in a dazed fashion, vacant eyes lost to the wonder of the Forever Chamber. She could hardly blame them. Wounded and weary, they followed the line, crossing the spanning bridge of steel to walk with trepidation into the golden sphere of light. They did so because elders of the Brotherhood proclaimed such a venture to be their only solace. Death stalked the broken streets of Bastion. Death whispered veiled promises in the ears of those who remained.

And Death no longer skulked alone, for a horde of Hellish demons strode with him.

Kayla wiped her brow, worried and exhausted. She'd blatantly refused to step into the portal, even at Kian's request until she knew Tarsin's fate. Yet word of the fighting was scarce, for the pyramid was crowded and becoming more so. Even Declan and his fellow Sword Brothers were now out of sight, lost amongst the mass of flesh as they stood guard at the chamber's entrance. Word from outside was never going to reach her here standing beside the portal. Not now, but she still refused to pass through.

'We cannot leave it much longer, dear,' Neema brushed a lock of Kayla's long black hair behind an ear. 'It's imperative we pass over to the new world, away from this place. Bastion is no longer safe . . . for any of us.'

Kayla offered a desultory nod. Events were unfolding too rapidly for her to fully comprehend. She felt sick merely thinking about Bastion's fall, felt grief-stricken at the loss of her father. As the line of destitute survivors filed past, she could feel the threads of hopelessness worming sinuously into their shattered minds, could feel cold threads of despair begin to flow in her own.

'Listen to the lady,' Reefe raised a tired hand in a desperate bid to sway her mind. 'Bastion is lost, it's time to flee. There is nothing here for us now.'

'The city is not lost,' she replied, an edge to her voice, 'not while Tarsin still fights. Whatever sanctuary Kian has planned is only temporary. Our flight through the portal is for survival; we'll return for retribution!'

'With what?' Kayla saw him shake his head. 'Look at these people. They're beaten and downtrodden.'

'Not all of them!'

'Easy, Kayla,' Ruvin, standing near the portal with members of the Brotherhood moved to offer calm. His dark-ringed eyes revealed his lack of sleep, but his back remained rigid, so too his demeanour.

'Sorry, Ruvin,' Kayla sighed heavily and placed hands on her hips, dimly aware of an ache at the back of her neck still causing discomfit. Sweat continued to bead on her forehead.

Neema placed an arm about her shoulders. 'You need to sit, Kayla, rest,' she spoke softly, her voice soporific. 'Your body has endured much, your mind more so. Such traumatic experiences require recuperation.'

Kayla knew Neema's words were spoken with wisdom, knew she should listen to her counsel and that of her friends. The path was right before them, golden and enticing. On the other side lay another world: vibrant and safe.

At least Kian said so.

Kayla thought of questioning the Nepharii guardian when he first proclaimed they step through, but there was an aura surrounding him, invisible yet strangely tangible that evoked trust and compassion. Few openly doubted his words, and the Brotherhood of One to a man trusted him implicitly. Even now elder Cappitus stood near the sphere, scribes of the order at his side marking parchment as they counted those who walked through. An hour glass sat on the lectern, the sands sifting gently to mark the time. When it finished, old Fratelli would turn it once, granting one more hour. When that hour was up, the portal to Kian's world would close as another plaque slid into place.

From where Kayla stood, she could see the first hour was almost complete.

Kayla turned to look at Neema and offered half a smile. Young Donal and Jarred still sat behind her, leaning against each other for support. Seeing the two boys was enough to resolve her doubt and fears. They, like everyone else, needed to feel safe. Remaining here with danger so very close was akin to torture. Yet despite her selfishness, they remained, even when Kian spoke to Jarred as he passed and offered him his hand. She couldn't tell why he remained with the group, although she believed it was Ruvin's presence alone that held him back. The others, so she thought, did so because she was Lord Derrick Tolsten's daughter. Either that or they feared to travel alone.

'Alright,' Kayla finally said, looking to the artificial heavens twinkling above, 'let's do this. Reefe, on your feet, help me with the boys.' He obliged much to her surprise, mustering the strength to stand after a dirty finger scraped dried blood from around his trident beard. 'What of you, Neema,' she asked, 'are you coming with us?'

Neema met her gaze. 'Of course, Kayla,' she said, 'you'll need me by your side in the days to come.'

Kayla paused, attempting to read the old woman's thoughts, but found her stare somewhat perplexing. She was about to ask for clarification when Ruvin stepped to her side.

'I'll come with you also,' he said. 'Tarsin asked me to protect you and I shall do so. Besides, where Jarred goes, so do I.'

'You'll not wait for Tarsin either?'

A flash of pain caused Ruvin's weathered face to crease. 'No, he can take care of himself. He is a swordsman first and foremost, my dear. I have never seen his equal. He'll make it. He'll come for us.'

Donal and Jarred stood, rubbing tired eyes. She could see they needed a good night's sleep. Whatever lay on the other side of the portal, she prayed they could find a place to lie down and rest.

'Shall we go?' Neema asked, pointing towards the line of people filing past elder Cappitus and his scribes.

'Yes,' Kayla sighed, her hand grasping the rucksack containing the treasures they'd found in Arkos' study. She reached inside to pull out a necklace of silver with copper beads and several petite feathers coloured like a rainbow. Ruvin likewise stood, his hands securing the twin swords about his belt. Kayla waited for him to finish, then fastened the necklace about her neck on a whim. 'Let's do this.'

Together they stepped into line, joining the procession as it made for the golden sphere. Several steps took them across the bridge before they reached the *Kardiversum*, as Jarred called it. There was no heat as they stepped within its radiance, nor trembling of fear. There was only hope and the promise of salvation, accompanied by a flash of white light to herald their departure.

Seconds later Fratelli, standing watch over the *Nepharii Urnaometria* as it spun within the lectern, reached over and flipped the hourglass. His focus was resolute, oblivious to the people stepping through. His eyes never left the spinning relic.

And the shifting sands of the hourglass counted down the second hour.

*

Declan wiped blood from his face.

He breathed deeply as he looked back down the corridor. A mass of slashing forms still fought at the entrance to the pyramid, Tarsin amongst them. Only the Deios were pressing hard, their greater height and strength telling in the past half-an-hour. The attack had been fierce, the carnage great. Even with the Brotherhood's help the tide could not be broken. They were crazed, ferocious like nothing he'd ever seen. Never had he bore witness to such brutal force, nor such macabre sights. Twice he'd vomited: once at the beheading of a brother, the other when a guard's arm had been ripped from its socket. Now he had nothing left in his stomach to heave forth, but he felt ill all the same.

He blinked, then sighed as the last stragglers scampered past on their way to the Forever Chamber. They were as frightened as he, their eyes wide, faces pale. Declan said nothing, he could only nod. A vicious cut along his hip still bled profusely and he knew several ribs were broken. He couldn't even manage to hold his long sword any longer, had left it lying somewhere back where the fighting was thickest. All he could hope to accomplish now was to evacuate the last of Bastion's citizens. That and pray the portal remained open long enough for Tarsin and his men to cross over. He knew their time was almost up. This last, desperate counter was to be their final act.

With feet made of lead he walked to the Forever Chamber's entrance. He could see the tall figure of elder Cappitus, a dark silhouette against the golden sphere within. A few men and women still loitered before the portal, the last to cross the spanning bridge, now waiting their turn to escape certain death. The dying screams of men drifted down the corridor, accompanied by beastly growls and the thud of cleavers hitting flesh. For a moment, he wondered if any of those fighting would survive, wondered if he would be the last.

He spun for one last look and saw a flicker of movement at the pyramid's entrance. The light of day was masked by so many combatants, but three braziers lit the corridor's length, offering light and hope to those who'd previously passed. As he strained tired eyes to peer down its length the furthest brazier was suddenly extinguished. A dark cloud grew to encompass the corridor from floor to ceiling, blocking all light from outside, even muffling the horrendous screams of dying men. Declan squinted, seeking to spy the source of the strange manifestation only to hear a faint pop as the second brazier was in turn extinguished. The intrusive dark cloud continued to billow forth, quickly now, reaching with claw-like tendrils towards the final brazier. He watched in abject horror, no more than ten feet in front of where the light source flickered, then witnessed Neema's protective wards fizz out of existence before they could even manifest. He felt numb, found it difficult to breath. A loud buzzing permeated his thoughts. At the last instant, he thought to turn and warn Cappitus, but his eyes were drawn to a cloaked man as he stepped out of darkness.

Power emanated from the figure in waves of hatred, buffeting then drowning him in fear and loathing all at once. He knew who stood before him, could feel his presence and sense his evil. His mouth became dry, he found it difficult to breathe. Then the withered form of an old hag appeared to his right. She was a sorry sight, looked to have been beaten with bloody hands. Declan wished for courage then, courage to stride one last step and strangle the witch, for he could only assume it was Avra before him. Only he couldn't move a muscle, couldn't even turn and run. He certainly didn't have the stomach to fight. He was spent, his faith lost. All he could do was watch as a large, crippled hand rose to point in his direction. He heard a faint word spoken in a foreign tongue.

Then Declan, Sword of the Brotherhood, erupted in a pillar of flame.

*

Elder Cappitus watched as the last remaining men passed through the portal. A scribe scribbled his final number onto a piece of parchment at his side, then followed, his passing marked by a white flash. Fratelli kept vigil over the hour glass, watching the sand rapidly shrink.

'Less than five minutes, elder Cappitus,' the brother's voice was nervous, sweat beading on his brow.

Cappitus placed a hand on the old man's shoulder. 'It is almost time, brother,' he offered a tired smile, knowing he would wait for Tarsin and his men till the last. It was important that he do so, for their sacrifice provided salvation for many.

He also waited because Tarsin was now king and the last of the jaguars. He was their hope in this period of darkness.

He turned away from the portal to peer back over the spanning bridge. Two shapes hustled along its length, an elderly lady and her crippled son by the look of things. They would make it, he mused, by the barest of margins.

They ambled closer, the cripple scraping one deformed foot along the path, a hand outstretched in desperation, fearful of being left behind. Cappitus took a step forward, preparing to cross the short distance to lend a hand when a gurgle followed by the crackle of flame sounded from behind. He spun; eyes narrowed, only to see Fratelli bathed with fire, his skin melting from face and hands. He fell seconds later, the hour glass falling to smash upon the floor. Cappitus raised an arm to shield him from the heat, then turned slowly as Ahriman and Avra stepped close behind.

'Greetings, elder Cappitus,' Ahriman practically drooled, his hunched form coming to a rest.

Cappitus felt a wave of fear wash over him, felt blackened tendrils snake beneath his skin, seeking to pull him down into a pit of pain where scarlet flames danced above a bubbling miasma. With a muffled grunt Cappitus shook his head and sought composure. He slid his eyes towards Avra, noting her dishevelled appearance. She'd aged since he last saw her, considerably. In fact, she looked like she was already dead.

'I must say I have anticipated this meeting for some time,' Ahriman continued, 'Avra has told me so much concerning your history.'

'She knows nothing,' Cappitus couldn't help himself, cursed inwardly at his lack of discipline.

'Ah, but she knows you, Cappitus, knows your type. Long have you sought to undermine her achievements.'

'What has she achieved, Ahriman, other than summon you?'

'Nothing,' the Dark Lord sneered. 'But then she only had one goal. Try as you might, brother, you could not stop her.'

Cappitus tore his gaze to the side to see the broken hour glass. He knew only minutes remained. If he could stall Ahriman and Avra here, prevent them from crossing to the new world, the world of Vidae, as Kian called it, he would be satisfied. Whatever hope he'd pinned to Tarsin was now forfeited. He couldn't see a way out for the newly crowned king. Bastion was lost, the kingdom was lost. Even if he did flee the beasts, the father of all their torment stood before him and their salvation.

Then a sobering thought crossed his mind. Perhaps Tarsin was already dead?

For Ahriman, Lord of Chaos and Stealer of Souls, was here in the flesh.

'Your time is up, Cappitus,' Avra finally spoke, her voice a pitiful croak. Perhaps she was dead? Who knew what powers the Dark Lord could utilize?

'Yes, Cappitus,' Ahriman raised a hand, the fingers bent and misshapen, dark scabs marking his skin. 'It is time for your soul to join with mine.'

'Never,' Cappitus gritted his teeth and straightened his back. 'You can kill me, Ahriman, but you shall not have my soul!'

'You cannot stop me, fool. In death, you have no power.'

Cappitus shared a smile with the Dark Lord, his eyes bright. 'It is you who is wrong, Ahriman, for in death, I *am* power.' He flung his arms out wide and threw his head back. He was certain there remained only seconds before the disc spun. He hoped Ahriman would spend those seconds looking for his soul.

Then fires fiercer than those in Hell engulfed his body and Cappitus, elder of the Brotherhood of One . . . died.

But his soul fled.

*

Ahriman prodded the charred corpse with his foot. There was nothing there, no golden flicker, no orb of light. Somehow the old fool played the last hand, deceiving him with trickery.

'Have you taken his soul?' Avra peered down at the remains.

He considered her words, knew now was not the time to appear weak or confused. 'Yes,' he replied, 'his soul is mine. The old fool was bereft of options, desperate.' He lifted his eyes to peer at the golden sphere. 'This is the portal, then?'

'It is,' Avra moved to stand before the inner ring to look down on the plaque. 'This is the world the people of Bastion have crossed over to.'

Ahriman saw the human-like figures in the corner, saw the constellation embossed in the night sky. With the knowledge garnered from the brother's soul at the entrance, he could now understand its function and divine its purpose. There was wealth here, knowledge beyond compare.

'Come,' he grabbed Avra's frail arm and dragged her towards the portal, 'there are souls on this world that belong to me and others I wish to steal.' Thoughts swirled through his mind as he made for the golden bridge, thoughts belonging to a Brother named Declan. He gazed at the zodiac symbol and knew it to be Panos. Unlike the Deios who favoured dragons in all their savagery, he expected the men and women on this world to be meek in comparison. 'My power grows rapidly, Avra, but I believe there is room for improvement.'

He placed a foot on the bridge of golden energy, testing its solidity, then stepped into the golden light. Avra followed, her foot disappearing into the sphere a second before the inner ring spun.

As it did, the portals destination changed from Panos: the deer, to that of Sable: the panther.

*

Tarsin spat blood as he gripped his side. For too long now he'd sought to hold the line against the Deios. Now he fell back, Griffith and Jaegar with him bloodied and spent.

'I cannot see where I'm going,' Jaegar grunted as his knee smashed into metal and sent an object flying. They were traversing the corridor inside the pyramid, attempting to run its length until they reached the Forever Chamber. Tarsin recalled all Ruvin had said about its location and appearance, but the braziers he mentioned lining the way were gone, for some reason extinguished.

'Put your hand out until you touch the wall,' Tarsin called out, loud enough for everyone to hear. He couldn't tell how many of his men followed, but he knew they were few. He just prayed the Deios weren't close on their heels.

The men did as bid whilst he also found the wall, an act that helped balance his tottering form. He was beyond exhaustion, suffered several wounds and could barely stand. Blood covered his face and arms, splattered his breast plate with its embossed visage of a snarling jaguar. And he was still coming to grips with the final Deios charge.

Mayhem was all he could envisage. The beasts had rallied as the summer storm struck, drawn to the strident commands of a large Deios waving heavy blades high. Tarsin offered his men a similar tactic, encouraging them to stand strong and proud as he searched for a means to fire their blood. The men and women of Bastion were almost through, their number surrounding the pyramid dwindling by the minute.

The Deios charged, a mass of blood-thirsty savages hurling hatchets and screeching in anger. They bounded with vitality and intent; ripping heads clean off with swipes of their massive blades. The city guards crumbled at the onslaught, butchered in quick succession, falling on the very steps they vowed to protect.

Tarsin could see the disaster unfolding, could sense the loss before it occurred. He called for a steady retreat, ordered what remained of the Palaceguard to lock shields and bar the way.

They held for several minutes, allowing Tarsin and his remaining men time to compose themselves and summon the Swords of the Brotherhood: eighty men sworn to arms and defiant in the face of fear. They bolstered their forces, boosted their morale. As he formed their line, he saw the Palaceguard being pummelled into the red granite. They died to a man.

Once the top of the steps was secured, the Deios paused to assess their options. They could see the shining pyramid behind the forces of men, but Tarsin doubted if they knew its true purpose. As one they hesitated, then conferred with their leaders. It was a welcome respite for the defenders of Bastion, but he knew it wouldn't last. Now they literally had their backs to the wall, engaged with an enemy until their people were safely away.

Somehow, when the second attack came, the men held their own. Fuelled by the presence of eighty Sword Brothers, the men found the adrenalin to lift tired arms and smash swords and spears into their foes. The fighting was brutal, primal, a mass of clutching, tearing hands as men stabbed eyes out of sockets and thrust blades into soft throats. The Deios eventually fell back, scores of the demons lying dead at their feet. A feeble cheer sounded from the men.

The Deios charged again.

Time lost all meaning as the men of Bastion fought the beasts. They rolled with the advances, pushing back when they could. Griffith and Jaegar fought tirelessly, their weapons smashing skulls, their cries of vengeance rallying the disheartened. All the while Tarsin stood like a rock, his sword a blur of motion as it sliced scales and pierced chests. The beasts were incapable of dislodging his stance, their efforts rebuffed time and time again. Once again, the dead at Tarsin's feet continued to grow.

At some point a hand pulled at his shoulder during a lull in the fighting. Bevan, his face a mask of gore, pointed towards the pyramid's entrance. Tarsin followed his outstretched arm, saw the vacant space. He knew the last of Bastion's citizens had finally escaped.

Now they traversed a corridor in the dark, seeking a chamber described by Ruvin as a wonder to mankind.

Only it was the stench of charred flesh he found first.

Impressive double doors invited the men inside the chamber, but a smouldering body barred their way. Tarsin bent close, holding a hand to his mouth. A faint golden emanation from within the chamber itself was enough to see by.

'What is it?' Griffith peered over his shoulder.

'A body,' Tarsin stood to his feet, 'burnt beyond recognition.' He stepped through the open doorway and signalled his men to follow. He ran a hand over his short-cropped hair, feeling the metal of his crown. It remained still, despite the brutal fighting. He wondered then if he truly deserved to wear such a piece, wondered if his father, Arkos Vantos, would approve of his tactics. He flexed his sword arm, comforted by the weight of the blade, and knew there was little else he could have done.

Whatever his doubts, they were now a thing of the past. He now had purpose. He knew what he was capable of. 'Keep your eyes peeled,' he said as the last of his men crowded within the chamber, 'we may not be alone in here.'

The company of men grunted in unison, and those who'd sheathed swords quickly drew them forth again. As one they stepped into the Forever Chamber, hoping word of its wonder wouldn't disappoint.

It didn't, and a sense of calm pervaded their thoughts.

With tired legs Tarsin moved ahead, his pace set as he made for the spanning bridge. There was illumination here, enough to comfortably see by. Clusters of light resembling minute stars shone down upon the men as they peered wistfully about the chamber. Ruvin's brief description of what lay within the pyramid failed to convey the magnificence he now witnessed. Tarsin's breathing quickened as he crossed the narrow bridge spanning the room, leading directly to a large golden sphere swirling at its centre. He felt a surge of adrenalin suffice his body, lending strength and energy to his exhausted frame.

Then he reached a silver lectern. The familiar sight of the *Nefarii Uranometria* sitting entrenched within caught his eye, but it was the two charred bodies at its base that caused him to gasp, smoke drifting lazily from their scorched remains. Amongst the cadavers he could see shattered glass and sand strewn haphazardly across the floor. The stench was overpowering.

Jaegar prodded a corpse with a boot and watched as ash sifted from ivory bones. 'What devilry is this?' he asked as a curse rolled from his tongue.

Tarsin sighed, sensing a black cloud forming in the pit of his stomach. He knew witchcraft when he saw it, but this was a power far greater than anything Avra could hope to fashion. 'It is the work of Ahriman,' he spoke softly; afraid mentioning the Dark Lord's name might summon him in a burst of flame. 'He was here.'

'Where is he now?' Griffith looked back over his shoulder as he sought movement in the shadows.

'He has passed through,' Tarsin pointed towards the glowing sphere. 'He has crossed into the new world.' He held a hand high, stalling Griffith's next question. 'I don't know why, my friend.'

Griffith nodded understanding. 'This is it, then.' Like nearly every man here he was blood-stained and tired, dents and scratches covered his armour, his great hammer still plastered with gore. But he stood tall, his tired eyes managing to widen as he marvelled at the enormous sphere with its molten flashes and gentle hum.

'This is it,' Tarsin repeated. 'Ruvin described it to me, said we simply step over the golden bridge and pass into the light.' He looked at the plaque. Where he'd hoped for the symbol of a deer he saw nought but a panther, the visage eerily like that embossed on his breastplate, reminiscent of the rampant jaguar of the Vantos family. He wondered if it was a lucky omen as he took a moment to count his men. Including himself, there were seventeen.

'Do we go,' Griffith asked, 'or do we stay and fight?'

Tarsin shook his head. 'No, we pass through. We need only reach the other side, then once we're all accounted for, we'll step straight back through. If Ruvin and I are correct, we'll find ourselves exiting a portal like the one in Undercity, deep below ground, but far from where we now stand. Then we'll climb to the surface and leave Bastion, send word to John Rhys and call back our southern army.' A few of the men nodded their approval, their eyes steeled for a future engagement. 'Then we take Bastion back, my friends,' Tarsin proclaimed. 'Then we exact our revenge.'

A guttural cry echoed throughout the chamber as a single Deiosian appeared at the entrance. He was tall and broad, his scales no longer vibrant, but an air of authority surrounded him. Tarsin met his gaze, instantly knew he'd seen him before, back on the world with the red sun and stifling heat. The sound of clawed feet clicking against stone heralded the arrival of his hunters. They paused, sweeping their gaze to the artificial heavens; their fanged maws open in wonder.

Tarsin had no energy to re-engage. He knew his men were out on their feet. 'Come,' he commanded as he pushed his men towards the portal. 'It's time to move.' The men filed past, stepping into the sphere with a flash. The last to pass were Griffith and Jaegar. 'Let us hope,' Tarsin said, his voice low, 'that our friends here do not follow. It could become rather complicated if they do.'

'If they do,' Griffith said, looking across at Jaegar, 'we'll hold whilst you escape. We can give you the time.'

Tarsin nodded, knowing nothing he could say would sway either of his men. One after the other they crossed the golden bridge . . . and stepped into the light.

*

Ra'tor stomped a heavy foot onto the metal floor to accompany his roar.

He was before a golden bridge that hovered about the equator of a golden sphere. Rax't stood beside him, a clawed hand scratching his scaled chin. The creatures they'd fought had passed into the light to escape their wrath, but it was not their passing that frustrated him so. It was the realization Bhral, their Blood-god, was nowhere to be found.

His roar subsided, but his eyes simmered still. He took another look at the broad plaque at their feet. The glyph was unfamiliar to him, so too the chamber itself. It was not what he expected.

'Do we follow?' Rax't turned back to appraise the Deios crowding the entrance.

Ra'tor shook his head. He was confused, perhaps even disorientated. He'd charged in hoping to see Bhral's huge form chained to the floor, his blood seeping from a thousand cuts to stain the rock below. Such had been the stories he heard as a bloodling. Stories of myth, it was true, but the underlying tone was Bhral had sacrificed much so that his Deios could prosper under the heat of the sun. Only Bhral wasn't here in any shape or form. There wasn't even a sense of him ever being held captive.

For all the signs he thought he'd been given, Ra'tor suddenly felt a fool.

'Bhral was never here,' he said as he spun to join Rax't. 'But there is purpose to our arrival. Greater hands than ours shape the events to come. We need to be here, not hunting strays in the wild.'

He watched Rax't nod his head in agreement. He was canny, Rax't was. Ra'tor could see it clearly. For too long now he'd been by his side, agreeing with his every decision. He knew Rax't would come for him one day, possibly soon. He was certainly strong enough.

Ra'tor clapped heavy hands together and walked away from the golden sphere. 'Come, I need to feel the sun on my face, even one that is weak. It is too cold in here.'

Together they walked back across the spanning bridge to stand before the mingling Deios. Ra'tor hissed an order for those Deios formerly under Zaxa's command to guard the chamber, then he and Rax't made for the open air. He inhaled deeply, smelling the sweet scent of blood tinged with ash and dust. With Terrak and Zaxa both dead, almost two hundred of his new brood waited for him, many squatting amongst the carcasses to feast on the slain. Only a handful looked to have forgone the pleasure, but their eyes betrayed their desire. Ra'tor waved a hand, then watched as they fell in amongst those already bloated.

'What are your plans now?' Rax't licked his lips and flared his nostrils.

Ra'tor walked past the carnage and headed for the edge of the granite base. Rax't followed him, as always, quiet and purposeful. 'We wait here in number; send a handful back to where we first stepped into this world. If the door-between-worlds reopens, we'll summon our breed partners and whatever other broods dwell close by.' He shaded his eyes from the weak sun and scanned the ruins. An enormous structure stood to his right, its elaborate columns now cracked and splintered, but its arches and towering peaks were incredibly detailed. Irregular slabs of white stone lay at its entrance, fallen blocks too large for any Deiosian to shift. How the creatures of this world could build such monstrosities, he would never know. They were clever, possibly too clever. Yet despite their achievements they were now meat for his brood.

He peered between two columns and saw what looked to be a statue of some beast standing upright and tall, shadowed from the sun. Its head was lupine, its shoulders hunched. It looked to be cloaked in fur, large clawed hands hanging slack at its side. Ra'tor found it impressive, a powerful representation of some wolf-like creature. He wondered whether it was a god to the creatures who lived here. It was incredibly fearsome looking. Once again, he wondered why the creatures here spent so much time sculpting and building, wondered where they found the time. On his world, the males hunted to keep the brood alive, whilst the breed partners, the females, cared for the young. There was no time for trivial matters, not if you wished to live. Bhral frowned upon those too slack to fend for themselves. Sitting idle was not a path one would choose to become tall and strong. Shaking his head, he shared a look with Rax't, catching his eye as he too scanned the ruins. 'We are meant to be here,' Ra'tor said, 'Bhral has a plan for us. I know it.'

He watched the familiar nod and wondered how much longer Rax't would care to listen to his words. A flicker of movement caught his eye, a dark smudge amongst shadows. Ra'tor peered back towards the ruin, seeking out the wolf-like statue.

But it was gone.

LATER

Ahriman stepped from the portal, Avra shambling by his side. He'd contemplated waiting for the remnants of Bastion to reach him as he stood before the portal, especially if Tarsin Va was still alive. Despite the ritual being complete, his soul would add favourably to those he already harboured. Only he craved the soul of Cappitus more. The elder was a Seer of the Brotherhood of One, his powers unknown but rumoured to be great. Tarsin was a mere swordsman, nothing more. Although he was king, he was a bastard king. Besides, there would be time later to find the man and take his soul. Cappitus was a different matter. As it stood, he had no idea how the elder's soul fled, or where exactly it had fled too.

He blinked as he and Avra stepped beneath blue sky speckled with white cloud. A gentle breeze offered a respite from the oppressive heat felt in Bastion whilst in the distance green foliage spread as far as the eye could see. It was a veritable ocean of trees covering an incredibly large expanse. He turned once to see the portal: an ellipsoid of jade and shimmering emerald that shone with a healthy radiance before it suddenly winked out of existence. He screwed his eyes shut at its disappearance, then looked to the frail witch for guidance. She appeared nonplussed, her thoughts fragmented. For a moment, he thought to chastise her, but then he realised such a display was unnecessary. He'd tormented her beyond reason for a mere mortal already.

With a sigh he ran his gaze over the brightly patterned tiles at his feet, noticing they circled outwards in hues of scarlet and magenta, citrus and lime, before branching into four separate pathways. Each disappeared into the forest at what Ahriman assumed to be the cardinal points on this world.

He breathed deeply, savouring the crisp air and relishing the sensation of thousands of souls crowded in confusion close by. He could sense their fear, could almost taste it. They were frightened, lost, castaways on a world and all alone. From below the cowl of his hood he began to mark their souls, eager to see if he could place that of elder Cappitus. He squinted as his sight passed over some that shimmered, realising their energy was spent, almost at an end. They belonged to the elderly and weak and at best were trivial to his purposes. Others shone bright and innocent, especially those belonging to the children. Even now they rallied in the face of adversity, their young eyes wide with wonder, their small voices even now asking questions of their parents. Some of the younger children even giggled and laughed; the horrors of their flight already forgotten.

He continued to sweep his gaze over the masses, a wicked smile creasing his face, until a blinding flare caused his eyes to squeeze shut and a cry of pain to escape his lips.

'My Lord,' Avra looked up at his face, but he bit his lip and did his best to stifle the discomfit he experienced. He noticed she failed to offer any assistance, failed to remark on his apparent turmoil. He cursed inwardly for his lack of composure, vowed to see her suffer once more in the future. 'Is there something wrong?' she finally asked.

With an effort, he pointed a gnarled finger, 'There is a raven-haired woman, tall and slender,' he said between clenched teeth. 'Who is she?'

Avra's brow knotted as she sought out the woman. 'She is nobody, my lord. I have not seen her before. Why do you ask?'

'Because the souls I lost in Bastion, those thousands of souls that were to be mine . . . now reside within her. She flares brighter than the midday sun.'

'How is such a thing possible? I sense no power emanating from her.'

Ahriman growled, rubbing the back of his hand against his eyes. 'I care not, witch. Just bring her to me. She shall be the first to feel my wrath. It will be her sacrifice that ignites the conflagration that shall mark my reign!'

He sensed the witch head towards the woman. Even with the pain of lancing light he felt elated. All those souls, thousands of them, thought to be lost. Now they were here, within easy reach, bundled together in a single host.

Ahriman felt a wicked smile crack his blistered lips.

*

Neema watched the portal like a hawk, waiting for elder Cappitus to march through after his aides, old Fratelli by his side. She knew their time was almost up. Even Kian paced close to the thrumming ellipsoid with nervous energy. He'd promised to misalign the portal once Cappitus and Tarsin stepped through, and like the rest of them he prayed for the swordsman's arrival. One thing the people of Bastion needed now above all others was a leader. Being the son of a jaguar, even a bastard son, would be enough to sway those who survived into following the swordsman.

A flicker of darkness caught her eye and Neema shifted her vision to encompass the emerald portal in its entirety. A hand appeared, as if from behind a curtain, pulling aside the fabric of energy to reveal a crippled man closely followed by his mother. A cold sensation rippled down her spine as she watched the two emerge, followed closely by a feeling of pure dread as the emerald portal vanished a second later.

Their time was up, it appeared, and there was no sign of Tarsin and his men, nor was there any sign of elder Cappitus and old Fratelli.

Worse still, Neema suddenly realized the old lady standing beside the crippled man was Avra, once an associate, now a sworn enemy. The connotations of her arrival were many, but none more so than the presence of the Dark Lord of Chaos hunched by her side.

'We have to flee,' Neema said with an air of despair, her lips curled back to reveal her teeth.

'Why,' asked Jarred, standing next to Donal as they watched children leap from one paved stone to another. 'Why should we flee?'

In a frenzy, she spun to grab Kayla, hauling her close, her eyes darting to find Kian. The tall Nepharii was racing towards them, fear in his eyes.

'We need to run,' Neema said as he reached their position.

'I know,' Kian looked pained, his skin sallow. 'I did not expect this.'

'Nobody did,' she returned, noting Ruvin and Reefe moving towards her position.

She sensed rather than felt Kayla as she pressed close. 'What is happening?' Kayla yelled, a wild look in her eyes. 'Where is Tarsin? Where is elder Cappitus?'

'They didn't make it,' Kian intervened, his voice calm despite his frenzied look.

'So why should we run? Why are you so fearful? You said this world was a place of harmony, a place we could find succour.'

Kian crowded the group closer and spoke in hushed tones. 'Because Ahriman is here,' he said. 'He has stepped through the portal, the witch by his side. We must flee.'

Ruvin nodded consent, then voiced the question on all their lips. 'What of our people, there must by thousands of men, women and children here?'

'Almost three thousand five hundred,' Kian replied, 'but there is little we can do at this moment. Some will flee and be safe, that is all we can hope for. Unfortunately, it is Kayla's safety that is paramount. It is she we must protect above all others.'

'Why?' Kayla looked confused. 'Why am I so important?'

Neema spun her around to peer into her eyes. 'Something has happened to you, Kayla, something incredibly profound. There is life inside you. Now, with Tarsin absent, the life you carry may be our only hope.'

*

Tarsin stepped through the portal to find himself amongst his men, huddled together about an ellipsoid offering a dim orange glow tinged with azure highlights. The illumination covered a ten-foot area, beyond was complete darkness. Even the sky above was masked, no twinkling stars shining through. If it wasn't for the cool breeze wafting over their forms and the sweet scent of lavender, he could have mistakenly believed they were indoors or underground.

He stepped alongside a bloody Jaegar and a bruised Griffith, the guard Setorious by his side. Next to him stood Bevan and young Conall, the only surviving members of Ciricello's Swords other than himself. Al-Za'im seemed so long ago.

'What do we do now?' Griffith spun in a circle as he looked for anything that might offer a clue to their whereabouts.

'Nothing,' Tarsin grabbed his shoulder with a bloody hand. 'We step straight back through like we said, find our way to the streets of Bastion and escape the city.'

'Aye,' Griffith nodded, 'I'm certain Lord Beaumont remains in Aspenvale with two hundred knights and twice as many men-at-arms. We could reach them in a day if we act fast. Then we'll send word to our forces in the south.'

Tarsin sheathed his sword, calmer now, but he knew they would have to be quick to return, just in case the Deios decided to follow. He faced the portal, his men behind him. He was about to step through when a whistle sounded from behind. He spun, knowing as he did so that he should have stepped forward instead, but he was wounded and close to exhaustion, his mind likewise spent. It took a second for his eyes to adjust to the gloom, but when they did, he saw tall shapes move from the darkness to encompass his men. They were cloaked in sable, hooded, like minions of Death come to take them away.

Tarsin's heart sank like a stone.

And clawed hands reached for them in the dark.